DEADLY REALITY TV SERIES: THE COMPLETE SERIES (BOOKS 1-4)

Sea Caummisar

CONTENTS

THE FIRST EPISODE

In the near distant future…

"Welcome ladies and gentlemen. I am your host Peter Conway. Welcome to the world premiere of 'Easy Money'. This reality game show is like no other that you have ever seen before. Do not try this at home. This is not a show of fake stunts. Everything that you will see tonight is real. Real and live in front of a live studio audience. We do have medical people on staff. I cannot stress this enough, do not try this at home. Now let's get on with the show."

The live audience roared with anticipation. Intro music played loudly, just like any other game show on television. Lights directed the viewers attention to 3 large glass cubes on the stage.

"As you can see, there are 3 glass cubes on the stage." Peter, the host, continued as he walked up to the first glass cube. "For safety reasons, tonight's challenges will be performed in glass cubes. Our audience safety is top priority. Now, let's meet our contestants."

There were 2 contestants standing behind podiums. The first podium read 'Amy', and the second podium read 'Stephen'.

"Hi. I'm Amy. A college student. As you can see I am no stranger to pain." Amy had an arm full of tattoos, and several facial piercings. She had 2 piercings in her nose, 1 in each eyebrow, and another piercing in her lip. Amy stuck out her tongue to show her tongue piercing.

"Hello. I'm Stephen. I'm currently unemployed. But I'm a tough guy. I think of myself as a badass." Stephen flexed his muscles to show off his bulging biceps and muscular physique.

"The rules are simple." Peter started explaining the game. "The game consists of 3 rounds. Each round gets harder. The 2 contestants make quick easy money by completing the tasks. The lowest bidder wins the privilege of attempting the task. Upon completion of the agreed upon task, they get paid. Simple as that. Now, let's begin."

The live audience roared wildly. Spotlights focused on the first glass cube on stage.

Peter pointed at the cube. Inside the windowed cube was a staple gun. "The first task is to shoot a staple into any part of your body with this staple gun. This is considered as 1 of our simpler tasks. The bidding will start at $1,000. The lowest bidder will then shoot themselves with the staple gun and get easy money! Contestants, you may now begin the bidding!"

Amy shouted as loud as she could. "I'll shoot myself for $1,000!"

Stephen shouted even louder. "I will shoot myself for $900!"

The bidding war had begun. The players were willing to hurt themselves for money. Damon Dahmer, executive producer of the show smiled from ear to ear. He could feel his heart pounding in his chest. It was the feeling of success. Damon was proud of himself.

Amy shot a glare at Stephen. "I'll shoot myself 8

times for $800!"

Stephen refused to be outdone. "I'll shoot myself 9 times for $800!"

Peter intervened. "No, we are supposed to bid lower..." Peter went quiet as he looked at Damon. Damon gave Peter a thumbs up symbol with a smile. "Okay, the bids are allowed. Keep bidding contestants!" Peter was a great host full of energy and vigor.

Amy showed her teeth to Stephen. "I'll shoot myself a dozen times for $800!"

Stephen went quiet as he studied the anger in Amy's face. "This chic is crazy. It's only $800. She can have it. I'll wait for the big money."

Peter grabbed Amy's hand and raised her arm in the air. "Congratulations Amy! All you have to do is shoot 12 staples into your body for the 'Easy Money' amount of $800!"

Peter escorted Amy across the stage to the glass cube and opened the door for her. Amy took a deep breath and stepped inside of the cube.

"I can do this. This is easy money." Amy did not look too sure of herself.

Peter shut the door behind Amy. The live audience went silent. "As you can see, Amy is inside the box. This is special unbreakable glass, to ensure that no audience member gets hit by a stray staple. Okay Amy. Anytime that you are ready, you may begin."

"Peter, I can shoot myself anywhere, right?" Amy didn't sound as confident as she felt earlier.

"As long as the staples enter your body, you can choose any part of your body." Peter looked to Damon for confirmation. Damon gave Peter a thumbs up. Peter flashed his pearly white smile at the audience.

Amy picked up the staple gun. She let out a low-pitched growl. Amy pulled her ear lobe away from her head with her free hand. "I need some new piercings!"

Amy put the staple gun to her lobe and squeezed.

Damon turned to watch the audience reaction. Some people flinched. A few people looked away. Damon looked at his monitor as a camera zoomed in on Amy's ear, which was. The staple was lodged in Amy's ear lobe, like a double piercing.

Amy smiled. "This is what I call easy money!" In one swift motion, Amy put 3 more staples in the same ear. She flinched each time.

Damon was amused by the audience who was now cheering. The crowd began chanting Amy's name. Amy was now piercing her other ear. When Amy recognized that the crowd was chanting her name, she paused and smiled. Both of her ears were blood-red, with a little bit of blood dripping out of the holes. Damon was shocked and disappointed that there wasn't more blood.

Peter who still had his television smile plastered on his face decided to comment on what was happening. "Great job Amy! Only 4 more staples to go. The crowd is loving you! How do you feel?"

"I feel alive. This doesn't hurt. It just feels like little bee stings." Amy took the staple gun and aimed it at her left shoulder. She quickly put 4 staples into her shoulder.

Damon watched as the crowd rose to their feet and cheered. Damon was very pleased with himself. He was giving the viewers what they wanted. He knew that he was in the peak of his career. He finally created a television show that he expected to be the most talked about television show of all time. Whether people loved it, or even if they hated it, people would talk about his show.

"Congratulations Amy! You just won $800 of easy money!" Peter opened the cube door for Amy, who took a bow. Amy walked back to her podium and noticed that Stephen didn't look very happy.

Stephen looked right through Amy. "Peter, can I do that too? I will staple myself more times for less money. I want to make some easy money."

Peter shook his head. "No, I'm sorry but round 1 is over. We still have 2 more rounds."

Peter walked to the second glass cube. "Inside of this cube we have a nail gun, loaded with 3-inch nails. As you can see, each round will get progressively harder. In return, the cash reward gets higher. Who is ready for the second round?"

The crowd and the contestants cheered. The people were loving it.

"The second round is worth $10,000. Imagine what you could do with $10,000. Contestants, are you ready? You may now start bidding!"

Stephen did not want to lose this round. He wanted to win some easy money. "I'll shoot myself with a nail gun for $10,000!"

Amy intervened super quick. "I'll shoot myself twice. I need some more money!"

Stephen puffed up his chest. "I will shoot myself 5 times. C'mon Amy! You already got some money. Why don't you wait until round 3?"

Amy rubbed her shoulder which still had 4 staples in it. Her shirt was stapled to her skin. "He can have this round, Peter. I'll wait until round 3. I can wait until there is some serious cash up for grabs."

Stephen clapped his hands. Peter opened the cube door, and Stephen entered. Stephen picked up the nail gun, and looked at the nails. His eyes got huge as he realized how long 3 inches really was when it came to terms of inserting 3 inches of metal into your body. The crowd laughed at Stephen's facial expression.

Damon looked at the audience. They were actually laughing. A man was preparing to literally shoot 5 metal nails into his soft flesh, and the crowd was laughing. Damon's audience was more warped than he had originally thought.

The camera zoomed in on the nail gun. "I think that I will take a page out of Amy's book. Thanks for the idea Amy." Stephen pulled his earlobe away from his head. Stephen took a deep breath as he squeezed the trigger. The gun shot out the nail at such a fast speed and with great force. The nail went completely through Stephen's earlobe. The force was so powerful that it tore his earlobe away from his head. The lower half of Stephen's ear was literally detached from his head. There was a clank as the nail hit the glass cube. Blood instantly poured down Stephen's neck. Stephen froze in shock as he held his hand to his ear. Stephen tried to wipe the blood away, but he just kept bleeding. Stephen held his bloody hand in front of his face and stared at all the blood.

Luckily, Peter was thinking fast. "Just so you know, this is why we have the unbreakable glass cubes. The cube stopped the nail, and it didn't even leave a scratch."

Damon watched the audience close. Most of them had their mouths open in disbelief. Some of them covered their mouths with their hands. Some people covered their eyes with their hands, but yet they were still peeking in between their fingers. Some audience members just turned their heads. The very few audience members who were still watching had a smile on their faces. Damon motioned for Peter to speak.

"Stephen, are you okay? Say something."

"Dude, this hurts really bad." Stephen was still trying to wipe the blood off his neck. His neck was leaking so much blood that his shirt was beginning to get saturated with the icky substance. Stephen could smell the iron from his blood.

"Just 4 more nails, Stephen. Just 4 more nails, then you win $10,000." Peter tried not to look at Stephen as he spoke to him.

"I can do this, just not in my ear again." Stephen began to look pale.

The entire studio was silent. Now people were watching and waiting to see what Stephen's strategy was now.

"Peter, I've seen many movies where people get shot in their shoulders with real bullets. And they live. I don't want holes in my hands or feet. I think I'm going for my left shoulder."

The crowd cheered once again. Stephen now had the encouragement that he needed to shoot himself again. Stephen removed his shirt, and looked at how much blood it had absorbed. He raised the nail gun to his shoulder. He squeezed the trigger and screamed like a small child. As he lowered the nail gun, the camera zoomed in to show the head of the nail embedded in his skin. His skin was red, but there was only a little bit of blood. Stephen screamed again and began to cry.

"I can't do it again. It hurts so bad." Stephen sobbed.

Peter looked at the crying man through the glass cube. "It takes 3 more nails to win the $10,000. You haven't won anything yet. Are you quitting?"

The crowd began to chant Stephen's name. Damon was very pleased with the audience. They were cheering for this guy. They didn't want this guy to stop putting nails into his body.

Stephen mustered up what little bit of strength that he had left. "Fast, like ripping off a bandage!" He raised the nail gun to his shoulder and pulled the trigger quickly, 3 times. As he dropped the nail gun, he screamed like a wounded animal. Stephen fell to the ground. The camera zoomed in to show the 4 nail heads embedded in his skin.

The crowd rose to their feet and erupted into the largest applause of the whole night.

Stephen eventually looked up at Peter. "Do I win?"

Peter flashed his television host smile. "Congratulations. You just won $10,000. Easy money! Now who is ready for the last round?"

Stephen stood up very slowly. "I hurt so bad. I need a doctor."

Peter opened the glass cube door. "We have doctors waiting to treat you after the show. We are live, Stephen. If you choose to see a doctor now, then you are forfeiting your chance to play in the last round."

"That's okay. Amy can have round 3."

A medic walked onto the stage, and escorted Stephen off camera.

"Amy, since you are the only participant left, you could win the full prize amount of $50,000." Peter smiled at Amy.

Amy jumped up and down. "I could really use $50,000. What do I have to do?"

Peter escorted Amy to the final glass cube. "There is a gun and a bullet in this cube. I do believe that it is a 22 caliber. Just shoot yourself. That's $50,000 of easy money."

Damon heard people in the audience gasp. He looked to see the faces in the crowd. They were looking at the stage in disbelief and whispering to each other.

Amy looked like a deer caught in headlights. "I just have to shoot myself once? Then I win $50,000?"

Peter shook his head. "Yes, Amy. You are correct. Or you could walk away now. You are not obliged to complete this challenge."

Amy looked like she was deep in thought. "I sure could use that cash. I guess that I don't need my left pinky finger. Can I just shoot my left pinky finger? I get medical treatment, right? I won't bleed to death or anything, will I?"

"A finger would be fine. And yes, you get medical treatment. Your contract assures you will receive treatment tonight. You probably won't bleed to death, but who am I to say? I am not a doctor. But I don't think that you will ever get another pinky though. Your contract does not cover any limb transplants. The only medical care that you get includes stopping the bleeding, disinfecting the wound, and short term pain management." Peter was smooth. The calmness in his voice was very comforting. "So, Amy? What are you going to do?"

Amy picked up the bullet and loaded the gun. "I am going to win some easy money!" Amy held her left palm in the air with her fingers spread. She held the gun in her other hand. She was shaking so bad that she couldn't hold the gun steady. Amy aimed the weapon at her pinky, and turned her head.

The crowd was still and quiet. The same time that they heard the bang of the gun being fired, they saw blood splatter on the windowed glass cube. Amy yelped a high pitch noise of pain and dropped to her knees. The audience jumped to their feet and cheered.

Peter was still in shock from what he had just seen. He brought himself out of his daze to do his job. "Congratulations Amy! You have won a total of $50,800 of easy money."

Amy raised her hand above her head as she stood up. A solid streak of blood was flowing like a river down her arm. She walked out of the cube crying. She lowered her left hand close to her gut. The camera zoomed in on the bloody stump of where her pinky used to be. A man dressed in scrubs walked onto the stage and escorted Amy behind the curtain.

Peter turned to the camera. "Do not try this at

home. What you have seen tonight is totally real. The challenges were not faked by smoke and mirrors. There was no costume makeup involved in any of this show tonight. Thank you for watching. And if you think that you have what it takes to win easy money, please check out our casting call on our website. Do not, I repeat, do not send us videos of you injuring yourself. We will not pick you as a contestant if you do. Until next time, I'm Peter Conway. Goodnight viewers." Peter waved bye to the cameras as the credits rolled.

A YEAR EARLIER

Damon Dahmer walked into his executive producer office. He had recently been promoted. Having worked with the same network for nearly a decade, his hard work had finally started to pay off. Damon was known as one of the best in his field that he worked in. He loved working exclusively with URN, Uptown Reality Network.

URN was the first premium channel devoted to all reality, all the time. The FCC regulated the normal over the air broadcast channels. However, being a paid premium channel, URN had a bit of freedom to include anything that they wanted into their programming.

Damon's reality dating show was the first show to include real life nudity. Viewers wanted sex and nudity. Damon's visions made that possible. The facts of life were that sex sells. Television had changed and evolved over time. Damon was always a producer with ideas that started trends. He created stuff that no other producer dared to attempt. Some might consider his work risqué, but if risqué meant good ratings, Damon didn't mind.

Reality television was a different kind of beast to tame. With normal television, actors knew what was expected of them. On reality television, there were no scripts. However, off camera, there was an art to producing people to do whatever you wanted them to do. Damon was a master manipulator. Right now, his most popular show was a dating show. Damon had mastered the art of playing mind tricks on his contestants so that his show was interesting. He made sure there was lots of drama and cat fights. With the combination of alcohol and mental suggestions, he could get anyone to do what he wanted them to do. Most of the time, all he wanted was sex and drama. He wanted ratings.

Damon had a classic psychopath personality type. Damon felt no remorse when he persuaded people on his shows to do something that they didn't want to do. He used charm and manipulation to get his contestants to have sex, just to boost the show's ratings. Sometimes, he would tell a female contestant that one of the male contestants was confessing his love for her off camera, but was too shy to tell her in real life. Or he would get into one of the guy's heads, by telling them that another guy was after his girl when they weren't around. Once, there was a virgin on the dating show. After she had a few cocktails, Damon pulled her aside and told her that she would be single for the rest of her life because no man wanted to date a virgin. That very same drunk virgin lost her virginity in front of the camera. Damon got the good ratings for his show that he wanted.

Damon wasn't always a psychopath. When his son died, something inside of Damon died. There was a time that Damon was a happy man. Not that he was unhappy now. All he ever did was work. He kept himself occupied by working. He enjoyed his job. He got a thrill out of being good at what he did. Damon sat behind his large oak desk and looked at the one single photo that he had on display. A photo of his deceased son. He only had the one child.

Damon pushed the button on his phone intercom. "Mary, where's my coffee?"

As with many successful narcissists, Damon was a difficult man to work for. When Mary took the position as assistant producer, she hadn't known that it would also entail being Damon's personal assistant, tending to his every beck and call. Mary knew that she was learning from one of the best, but the more that she got to know Damon, the more she realized that she did not want to be like him.

"I am on my way to your office sir. I have coffee and a ratings report." Mary rushed to Damon's office and set the coffee and papers on his desk.

"This is the fancy coffee. Are the ratings that bad?" Damon examined his coffee cup and eagerly awaited his assistant's response.

Mary had worked for her employer long enough to know that today was a good day to splurge on the fancy coffee. "The ratings aren't bad. I just know you. And I know that when the ratings aren't great, you consider them to be bad."

Damon thumbed through the report. Mary sat silently on the huge black leather couch in the corner of the room. She hated waiting around for Damon's usual angry rant, but it was part of her job. He always needed someone to be angry with, and that person was usually Mary.

"Our ratings are staying pretty steady. What can we do to better our ratings?"

Mary sat silently. She knew that Damon had not directed the question to her. He was talking to himself.

"Week 8, we had a peak of viewers. Mary, refresh my memory. What happened in week 8?"

Mary sat up straight. "Sir, that was the week that John fell off the horse when they went horseback riding on a date. He broke his arm. We promoted the ambulance during the commercial for that week's episodes. Just like you suggested. An ambulance ride and an injury always seems to pull in more viewers."

Damon put his pointer finger to his lips. "Interesting."

Damon sat in his large chair, rocking back and forth. Even though he was looking in Mary's direction, he wasn't looking at her. Mary could tell by his eyes that Damon was deep in thought. She sat quietly and still and waited for him to unleash his anger.

"We need that spike in viewers every week. Apparently, we are doing something wrong. Why didn't we retain those viewers? C'mon Mary. What's the solution here?"

"Sir, we can't have an injury every week it's…"

"Shut up Mary. Leave me alone. I need to think."

Mary stood up and walked out of Damon's office. She was relieved that he hadn't screamed at her too much. It was peculiar that he hadn't. She would gladly leave Damon alone. On a normal day, Damon would have gotten much angrier at Mary. He would have blamed her for not having more viewers. They still had more viewers than most of the other shows on the network, but Damon was a perfectionist. Everything had to be done perfectly. Damon wanted his shows to have the best rankings. He wasn't happy settling for mediocre.

Mary sat patiently at her desk outside of Damon's office. She looked at all the awards on the walls that her employer had won. She agreed that he did have some talent, but at what cost? He had publicly ruined many people's reputations on television.

Turning someone into a villain on television was great for rankings. Mary realized that the people they were producing were people. They were human beings with real lives. It wasn't as hard as one would think to instigate a fight between 2 contestants on a reality television show. But it just didn't settle well with Mary. These contestants had to go home to their real lives when the show was over. After enough editing and instigating and turning people into bad guys, you could potentially ruin their lives. Mary wasn't ruthless like Damon. Mary had a conscience.

Mary did need a job. Working for Damon was a great life experience and would look wonderful on her resume. She would just have to endure his mental abuse. Mary's phone buzzed.

"Get me legal on the phone. Right now."

"Yes sir, Mr Dahmer."

Mary pushed the button for the extension to legal to connect her boss. She wondered what he was up to.

Damon stormed out of his office in a hurry. "Walk with me Mary."

"Yes sir. Where are we walking?"

"Have you been paying attention? What do you do while you're here Mary? Sit around and daydream all day? We are going to legal."

Mary walked behind Damon and rolled her eyes. Luckily, he couldn't see her. He was walking so fast that it was hard for Mary to keep up with him.

"Sir, may I ask why we are going to legal?" Mary knew that producers didn't work directly with the legal department. Unless maybe Damon was in his own personal legal trouble. Maybe someone was trying to sue him. If they were, it would serve him right.

"I am going to pitch them a show idea. I need you to take notes." Damon continued to walk with determination.

"Don't you need to pitch a new show idea to the network?" Mary was confused.

"We will get to that, Mary. We need to speak with legal first. Walk faster. Keep up."

Mary shook her head and rolled her eyes. She knew that it was going to be a long day.

URN had a great legal department. The lawyers had many responsibilities, such as writing contracts for the reality show participants, studios, and workers. For whatever reason that Mary couldn't figure out, Damon had an urgency to speak with them.

Damon opened the door and walked in. He didn't bother to hold the door for Mary. Mary reached for the door as it was shutting. She almost got her fingers pinched between the door and the jamb. Damon was standing at a secretary's desk.

"No, I don't have an appointment. He was busy when I called. I need to speak with him now." Damon was just a rude person.

"Well, sir, you have to wait. May I ask what this visit is regarding?" The secretary obviously didn't care that Damon thought of himself as an important person. She was going to make him wait anyways.

Damon took a deep breath. "Regarding? How about regarding an injury on a show? Yes, I need to speak with someone regarding injuries."

Mary raised her eyebrows. She still couldn't figure out what Damon was planning.

The secretary was quick to apologize. "I am so sorry. Was someone hurt on the set? We weren't informed. Did it just happen? Yes, I have someone who will see you. Please, follow me."

Damon muttered under his breath. The only audible word was 'finally'.

Mary and Damon followed the secretary to an office. "Mr. Roberts, I'm sorry for the interruption but I have a Mr. Dahmer here to see you."

"Yes, thank you. Hello Damon. How are you doing? Have a seat. What do I owe this pleasure? It isn't everyday that I get a visit from an executive producer. Please don't tell me that you have bad news."

Damon did not sit. He stood. "No bad news. Just some questions. What happens legally when one of our contestants gets injured?"

Mr. Roberts looked puzzled. "Why? Did someone get hurt?"

"No. Not yet. Not recently. A few weeks back, someone was injured. A horse accident. What was the legal protocol for that?" Damon had questions and he wanted answers.

"Naturally the network pays all medical expenses..."

Damon cut off Mr. Roberts. "Mary, write down medical." Damon motioned to Mr. Roberts to continue.

"His contract pretty much stated that the network isn't liable for accidents, as long as the accident isn't due to negligence of an employee. The horse is a wild animal, not an employee. So the network isn't liable. Why do you ask?"

Damon did not answer Mr. Roberts' question. "Okay, so they can't be injured by another person, or from negligence. Hmm... What if a contestant hurt themselves?"

Mr. Roberts shook his head. "Are they mentally ill? Why are you asking? Did someone hurt themselves?"

Damon ignored Mr. Roberts. "Mary, write down a shrink. Psychologist. Psychiatrist. Something like that. Thank you for your time Mr. Roberts. Come Mary. We have work to do."

Mary shrugged her shoulders at Mr. Roberts and followed Damon back to his office.

CREATION

Mary was looking out the window in Damon's office. Men in business suits were rushing to wherever they were going. With their briefcases in hand, people were scurrying to their offices, or perhaps a studio. Mary always played a game in her mind. She would try to put stories with the people that she watched. She saw a woman walking behind a man in a suit. Mary imagined that this woman was like her. She felt sorry for this woman as she pictured the man in the suit berating her for every little thing she did that wasn't pleasing to him. Maybe this woman didn't walk fast enough, or maybe she didn't always know an answer to her boss's question. Mary watched as the man in the business suit approached a door. Business suit man held the door open for the woman following him. Mary had been wrong. Not once had Damon ever held a door open for Mary. Why couldn't Mary work for a man like that?

Damon strummed his fingers on his desk. "Mary. Are you paying attention? What's in your notes?"

"Yes sir. I am sorry." Mary glanced at her notebook with only a couple of items written in it. "Medical and psychiatrist. Maybe psychologist."

Damon shook his head. "Do you know that when I started working in television there were strict rules? Cursing, violence, and nudity were taboo. Then television evolved. People want to watch violence and nudity. I have given the people nudity. That just doesn't seem like enough. Viewers want more. I intend to give them more. Violence. Reality television violence. Something that television has never seen before." Damon smiled. He seemed pleased with himself. Damon strummed his fingers faster and harder on his desk.

"Sir, how can we incorporate violence into reality TV?" Mary was confused. She thought that Damon had officially lost his marbles. Her boss had gone crazy.

"Premium TV was a success when we were the first without commercial breaks. Then the internet started streaming apps that also cut out commercial breaks. We need something fresh. A new idea. Videos trend all over the internet. Videos of people getting hurt. When people watch the car races and the cars drive the same circle for several hundred laps, it doesn't get exciting until there's a car crash. Those videos go viral online. We, me and you Mary. We are going to create that for reality television."

Damon's continued ramblings confused Mary even more. Sometimes it was as if Damon spoke just to hear himself speak. The man could speak for hours without making a point. Mary tried to analyze the way Damon's mind worked. She was quickly called back to reality.

"Hello? Earth to Mary! Any ideas?" Damon snapped his fingers, as if he were calling to a dog.

"Yes sir. We can incorporate more dangerous dates into the reality dating shows?" Mary wasn't quite sure as to whether she just formed a question or a statement.

"No. Wrong! Wake up. We will have a show that is nothing but injuries. Let's give the viewers what they want." Damon was always so stern.

"So you think that people actually want to watch human beings getting hurt?" Mary was sure that time she phrased a question.

"Yes. We promoted an ambulance on the show and saw a spike in ratings. Let's give the people what they want." Damon looked so smug and so sure of himself.

"Right. Yes. Ambulances. Injuries." Mary agreed just to please her boss.

"How can we format a show that revolves around people getting hurt?" Damon glared at Mary. "I'm feeding you the answers. And you still can't get it right. C'mon Mary. Think. Think!"

Mary shook her head. She knew that Damon had gone crazy. "Okay, I get it now. How about a game show? A game show with dangerous stunts. Cash prizes. But the contestants would have to sign a waiver. Some sort of legal release, where the network isn't liable." Mary was proud of herself, even though she couldn't believe the words coming out of her own mouth.

"Exactly. That's my girl. Pay people to hurt themselves. People like money."

Mary cut Damon off. "No, that's crazy. People won't hurt themselves for money."

Damon continued his rant. "The whole purpose of the show will be to see what lengths people will go to for money. We will pay cash prizes. We will need sponsors. We can pay medical expenses. We will have a shrink on staff to ensure that the contestants are mentally stable. This is genius."

Mary couldn't believe her ears. Damon was officially crazy. Maybe he was the one that needed the head doctor. "First of all, nobody wants to watch people get hurt. Second, the network will never sign off on this. Third, no company would ever sponsor such a crazy idea."

Damon stood up, and walked to Mary. He raised his pointer finger and pressed it to Mary's lips. "Shh. Yes. Everyone wants to see people get hurt. Viewers are bored with normal television. The network will agree to any show that will get great ratings. Companies will sponsor. This is the next big thing in television. I will be the showrunner. With you being my assistant, we, me and you, have a ton of work ahead of us. Trust me, this will be huge."

Damon had the nerve to tell Mary to trust him. He was the last person on earth that she would ever trust.

"What are you waiting for? Wake up Mary! Chop chop! Get on it. We need to start polling the audience. Ask them on our web page what they want to see. Set up a meeting with the network's most creative writers. What am I paying you for? Get to work. Now." Damon's eyes looked almost diabolical.

Mary jumped up. "Yes sir. I will start an online poll. I will get you a meeting with writers." Mary shook her head and walked out of Damon's office. Sometimes she thought that Damon may be the devil himself.

RESEARCH

Mary spent 2 full work days at her desk looking up injury videos online. Sports injuries, daily life injuries, car accidents etc... She couldn't believe how many views some videos got. Every gross video made Mary sick to her stomach. There was a video of a teenager jumping off the roof of a house into a swimming pool. This video really caught her attention. The kid undershot the jump, and missed the pool. The boy landed on concrete from at least 15 feet high. As the boy's feet hit the concrete, the video played in slow motion. The boy's right foot inverted, and seconds later he was screaming for help. The camera focused on the boy's mangled leg. There appeared to be a bone protruding through the skin. There was a ton of blood. The boy's leg was twisted in an unnatural way and looked deformed. The other kid who had been recording the jump just laughed at his friend. The video had several hundred thousand views.

Her internet search yielded more videos of injuries than she could possibly watch in 1 lifetime. There were many skateboarding injuries that resulted in broken bones. Mary watched car accident videos, and many of those resulted in bloody faces. Several broken noses. Apparently, the human nose could bleed heavily. Videos of people's faces full of glass after car accidents, from a broken windshield made Mary cringe. It was as if she could feel their pain.

Mary wondered why people filmed this stuff. She especially wondered why people were watching this stuff. With each video that she watched, her stomach churned just a little bit less than it did earlier. Was she becoming immune to watching people get hurt? However, maybe Damon wasn't as crazy as she had originally thought. The numbers didn't lie. People were viewing these videos. She couldn't believe how high the number of viewers were, but there was obviously an audience for gore and injuries. Many people really did enjoy watching people get hurt.

An online poll on the network's website resulted in more than half of the viewers agreeing that John falling off the horse in week 8 was the most interesting thing that had happened on their show. John breaking his arm was apparently more interesting than watching people have sex. It was a dating show. It was as if the audience almost expected sex. They didn't expect injuries.

Mary just stared at her computer screen after hours of research. Damon was right. Television had evolved. Sex wasn't enough anymore. Viewers wanted gore. Viewers didn't care that they were watching real life people get hurt. They just wanted to see pain. Pain wasn't something that they got to see everyday. Television didn't have shock value anymore.

Mary wondered what had happened to humanity. She had always thought of the world as a compassionate place. Shouldn't people be concerned about each other? As bad as Mary didn't want to admit it, her boss knew what people wanted. It was her job to help him produce his desired outcome. It was logical, even though it sounded crazy.

Mary gathered her papers on the results of her poll,

and the views on all the videos of the broken bones. It was time to go tell her boss of her findings. She knew that Damon would relish in the fact that Mary no longer deemed this idea absurd. Their viewers were sick. Damon was even sicker. If anyone could create this vision, Damon could.

"More than half is better than I expected." Damon was very pleased with himself.

"Yes sir, more than half of our viewers think that John breaking his arm was exciting." Mary was still trying to ease her brain of all the videos she saw of people getting hurt.

"We need good writers. And sponsors. We need to find out how much pain people will endure and for how much cash. It sure sounds like easy money to me." Damon knew that he was going to leave his mark on the television industry. He would be the first man to do reality television in a way that no other person had ever done before.

For Damon, creating exciting television wasn't for the money. Damon had a rush of adrenaline every time one of his shows produced something of shock value. He got high on life just thinking about his show which would be nothing but shock value.

"We'll get writers on board. Then the network. Then we have to promote this thing in a mysterious way. We are going for shock value here. Let's make this thing so big that even the people who don't want to watch it, will watch it." Damon leaned back in his chair. He kicked his feet up on his desk.

Damon was an award winning producer. He didn't have many friends, but he did have many achievements. He smiled as he thought of this idea turning into a show, it would be another entry on his list of accomplishments.

Damon was a divorced man. His marriage had fallen apart after the death of his son. He was now married to his work. He didn't need a wife. Even though he slept alone most nights, he had ideas of exciting television shows to keep him company. Damon did not need people in his life. He preferred success over people.

Damon amused himself. Even though he preferred to spend the majority of his time alone, he seemed to know what people wanted. People wanted to see pain. He knew that he was the perfect man to give them that. People wanted to watch television to see what they couldn't see in real life. Reality television was full of shows that they could see in real life. If people wanted to see people dating, then they could date. If people wanted to see drama, they could start an argument between roommates or co-workers.

Damon's show of pain would be something that people couldn't watch in their humdrum lives. Damon knew that it wouldn't be hard to get contestants who were willing to hurt themselves for cash. People liked money. In the real world, people did many things that they didn't want to do, but they did it anyways for money. No person wants to punch a clock 40 hours a week, but they do it. For a paycheck. It wouldn't be hard at all to find people to hurt themselves for cash. Damon was very pleased with himself. This might be easier than he thought.

His dream of producing the highest rated show on television would soon be a reality.

DAMON'S RESEARCH

Damon got into his expensive sports car. He felt his fingers melt into the luxurious leather steering wheel. At the push of a button, he heard the engine roar to life. Damon felt alive as he exceeded the speed limit the whole drive home. He was making plans in his head. Tonight would be an exciting evening.

Following his normal routine, as soon as Damon walked into his home, he removed his suit jacket. He put the garment on a hanger, and hung it perfectly next to all of his other suit jackets. Normally, he would turn on his television and watch (criticize) whichever show URN was airing at the time. Not tonight, Damon had other plans.

It wasn't unusual for Damon to hire himself a woman for an evening to keep him company. He picked up his cellular phone, and called the usual 'dating' service. Tonight he had a special request. He asked that the service send him an open-minded woman. A woman with the least inhibitions. Tonight would be his own special experiment.

Less than half an hour later, Damon's doorbell rang. He was told on the phone about Lydia. Lydia was highly recommended due to the fact that she was known for pleasing her clients, no matter the lengths she had to go to. However, he was warned that extracurricular activities, of course, cost more. Money was no object to Damon. He was conducting research for his upcoming television show.

Lydia walked in. Her body was thin and sleek. When she smiled at Damon, her eyes sparkled with curiosity. She complimented his home, and said that she now understood why he was considered a VIP for the company she worked for. She could tell by his huge home that he was a successful man.

"I was told that you may have some special requests for me tonight. Let me assure you that I am highly professional. You do not have to be shy. I am very experienced in pleasing even the kinkiest clients." Lydia removed her jacket and exposed her plump breasts. Her black dress was classy, yet it revealed just enough skin to intrigue any man with a wandering eye.

"First, let's just talk. Tell me about yourself." Damon's smile had a charm to it. Yet his eyes were a bit mysterious.

"We can talk if you want. I doubt you are paying me $500 an hour to talk. As you know, I'm Lydia. I love my job." Lydia rubbed Damon's shoulders. Her long hair gently brushed against his ear. She talked slowly, as if she was trying to seduce her client.

"No. Tell me about the real you. I'm sure that you love your job. Blah blah." Damon looked up at Lydia. "If women loved servicing men it wouldn't cost $500 an hour. You love money? Am I right? What's your story? College student? Single parent? Do you have a sick parent?"

Lydia stopped rubbing Damon's shoulders. "Once upon a time, I planned on becoming an actress. As you can see, that didn't pan out. Yes, I have a kid. This job affords me a way to give him a nice lifestyle. Plus I work limited hours. I get to spend plenty of time with him. With that being said, it doesn't mean that I don't love my job." Lydia sighed and looked Damon in the eyes. "Anything else you wanna know?"

"Yes my dear. Would you like a drink?" Damon grabbed Lydia's hand and pulled her into his chest. "Please relax. I mean no harm."

Lydia finally smiled. She put her mouth close to Damon's ear and whispered. "Sure, I will have whatever you are drinking."

"Make yourself comfortable, and I will be right back."

Damon returned carrying a couple glasses of bourbon. He was pleased to see that Lydia had removed her dress. She wore a black lace bra and panties. The garter belt attached to her silk stockings was a lovely sight. Her legs were crossed and she licked her lips as she glared at Damon. "Tell me what you desire. Tell me what turns you on. Let me guess. You like bondage? A little BDSM? I am here to please you. Anything that you want." Lydia flipped her long hair over her shoulder as she took a glass from Damon.

Damon sat down in a chair opposite from Lydia. "Actually, I'm a watcher."

Lydia uncrossed her legs. She spread her legs and used her right pointer finger to rub her lace panties. "That's not an unusual request at all. I love to be watched."

The bright red fingernail attached to Lydia's finger caught Damon's attention.

"I like what I see. Hold that thought. I'll be back in just a minute." Damon walked out of the room to gather supplies. He returned, this time carrying a towel and wire pliers.

Lydia was still rubbing the sweet spot between

her legs. Damon could see that her panties were now slightly moistened. Lydia raised her long, bright red fingernail to her mouth and slowly licked the tip of her finger. Until Damon raised the wire pliers.

Lydia stopped licking her finger. "What are those for?"

Damon placed the tool and the towel on the couch next to Lydia. Damon sat back down. "Like I said, I like to watch. I want to sit over here. I want to watch you use those pliers and pull out your pretty little fingernail."

"This is a joke right? This is crazy. I thought you wanted weird sex. This is just absurd. There is no way that I'm letting you use a pair of pliers anywhere on my body."

"Shh. Calm down Lydia. I am not going to touch you. You are going to do that to yourself."

"No. I'm leaving. Just so you know, the service will still bill the whole hour to your credit card." Lydia picked up her dress.

"I will pay you $1,000 extra. Cash money right now." Damon began the bargaining.

Lydia stopped in her tracks. "You are crazy. Like I said. There is no way."

Damon dug into her pocket, and pulled out a wad of $100 bills. "I have $3,500 cash. Right here. Right now. It's yours. Plus, the service can bill my card for however long you want. All you have to do is pull out 1 fingernail. Your real nail. Not the false nail."

Lydia stared at Damon and the spread of money.

"Lydia, think of how many toys, how many meals, how many school clothes you could buy for your kid. Afterwards, you can wrap your finger in a bandage. Your fingernail will grow back out." Damon knew that his words had Lydia thinking.

Lydia slipped into her black dress. Fully dressed,

she sat down and took a sip of the bourbon that Damon had poured for her. Lydia took a deep breath, and spread the towel out in front of her.

"That's a good girl. I believe that you can do this." Damon felt a tickle in his pants. He was starting to get turned on. He wasn't sure whether it was his power of persuasion or his thoughts of success turning him on, but either way he was happy.

Lydia spread her left hand on the towel and looked at her fingernails. She picked up the pliers with her right hand and squeezed them. She looked at Damon and shook her head. "I don't know if I can do this."

"It's okay baby. Pick a nail. Any nail. You can do this." Damon comforted Lydia.

Lydia placed the cold metal ridges of the tool on her pinky fingernail. She squeezed the pliers tight to get a good grip. She made a tug and yelped in pain.

"I only see a little bit of blood Lydia! You have to pull harder. That nail is still attached to skin. Try again."

Lydia's eyes were full of pain as tears formed in her eyes. Lydia gritted her teeth. She once again placed the pliers on her fingernail. The nail was partially raised from the skin from the first tug, and was even more sensitive to touch now. She squeezed with her right hand, and screamed as she yanked up on the pliers. The nail separated from the skin even more. A small line of blood ran down the side of her hand onto the towel. Lydia quickly raised her finger to her mouth and tried to suck the pain away.

"That's fine. You can use your teeth. As long as I see a fresh layer of skin where that nail used to be. You are so close to earning $3,500." Damon rubbed his crotch through his pants. He was even more excited than expected. Maybe it was the blood that was turning him on.

Damon watched as Lydia mangled her mouth to bite her fingernail. Lydia quickly pulled her hand away from her mouth and spit the red fingernail onto the towel. She held up her left hand to show Damon. There was only skin and blood where her fingernail used to be. The skin was pink. The fresh skin was not smooth. It looked almost like wrinkled skin after sitting in water for too long. Lydia tried to suck the blood from her finger before it ran down her hand.

"Good girl. This is your money. You may leave now."

Lydia wiped the tears from her face and sucked on her little finger. She collected her cash and her jacket, and left without saying a single word. Damon had never been happier in his whole life. He was right, people were willing to do anything for cash.

CASTING

It took a full 3 months for Damon to get approval from URN for such an extreme television show. Mary wrote a very thorough report on how many viewers were online viewing gore injuries. Legal assured the network that they could write contracts that would release the network from any liability of injuries that were self-inflicted. The board at URN wasn't convinced that the show would be a hit. They agreed to give Damon one show. If it produced good ratings, they would give Damon a recurring show. Damon was given a limited budget, but he didn't worry. He knew that one episode would be what he needed, then sponsors would gladly contribute to the budget. The next task was casting.

Legal wrote up a disclaimer that the network would not cover any medical expenses except immediate medical care. The disclaimer was written in such legal jargon that it wouldn't make sense to the common person without a law degree. In layman's terms, the contract pretty much stated that you were responsible for any harm that you did to yourself. Plus, you must be deemed mentally competent by the network's psychiatrist.

Damon thought of maybe scouring homeless shelters for contestants, but he knew that a lot of the homeless population would be deemed mentally ill. He needed to find people who needed cash, but weren't crazy. He weighed the pros and the cons from finding contestants online. The biggest con was that the internet always yielded replies from crazy people. The largest pro was that it was free marketing. The more people who were talking about his pain show meant that more people knew about it.

Damon wasn't quite ready yet to disclose full details. He wanted to market this show in a mysterious manner. He wanted to put it out there on the internet that this would be the first pain reality show of all time. He would leave it to people's minds to wonder for themselves what a reality pain show was. He was going for shock value. If he wanted people shocked for the world premiere, he would have to market vaguely.

Damon scribbled out a list of 3 simple questions:

Casting Call Reality Game Show

1. Do you want to be on television?

2. Do you like easy money?

3. Does your love of money outweigh your fear of pain?

Damon deemed the questions vague enough. Legal could include their full disclaimer. From experience, Damon learned that this world was full of idiots willing to do anything to appear on television.

Damon buzzed Mary on the phone intercom. "Mary, I need you in my office. Pronto. Now."

Mary ran into Damon's office. "Yes sir. How can I help you?"

"I need this casting call on the network's web page, yesterday. ASAP. And make fliers. I want fliers for the show distributed around every college campus within a 300 mile radius. We only need 2 contestants for the first show. Since I'm the showrunner, and you're my assistant, we will hand select our contestants." Damon handed Mary the paper.

"Sir. We could get thousands of replies. Are you sure that you don't want to delegate this to a casting producer?"

"I'm sure Mary. Are you the executive producer? No. You're the assistant producer. Last time I checked, that means I am your boss. Don't ever ask me again whether or not I'm sure of anything. I wouldn't say something if I wasn't sure of it. That's all. Now go"

Mary hung her head and exited Damon's office. "Yes sir. Online. And college campuses. I will get right on this."

Damon looked on his desk at the photo of his boy. His son was only 16 years old when he was killed by a drunk driver. Damon wondered if his son was still alive, would he be so full of malice? He missed his boy. He didn't really miss his wife who left him. But he missed his boy.

Damon shook his head and chuckled to himself. Here he sat worrying over things that he couldn't change. It didn't matter why he was the man he was today. Reasons wouldn't change who he was. He did however contribute his son's death to his success. If Damon were busy playing family man, he wouldn't have time to be a businessman.

In 2 weeks time, Mary presented Damon with nearly 8,000 applicants for the casting call. Each page included a picture and a short biography. Damon had Mary separate the contestants by sex. Damon would pick a male contestant. Mary would pick a female contestant.

As Damon sifted through the pages, he scammed the biographies for words that screamed desperation. Unemployed. Medical bills. Single father. People who may be more willing to go to extreme lengths for money.

One particular applicant caught Damon's eye. Marty Blevins, a local college student. Damon shook his head and laughed. He couldn't believe what he was seeing. He set Marty's application aside. The man's face appeared rather thin, and years older than the age in his bio. Either the man was a drug addict, or he was sick. Damon could not believe his luck in coming across this applicant.

Damon looked at the man's picture. "I will come up with a special show just for you Marty. Just be patient. You won't be on the premiere, but I will get to you soon enough."

Damon selected a handful of applicants and passed them along to Mary. Most of them were tough guys with muscles. Most of them were unemployed. He could trust Mary to select the first 2 contestants. She knew to pick people who needed money.

Damon never showed his appreciation for Mary. She was competent enough to complete tasks to Damon's liking. She reminded him of his younger self. The young man that he was when he started producing. Back then he knew when to keep his opinions to himself, but he also knew when to interject. Mary was very much like that. He hated it when she questioned whatever he was doing professionally, but it kept him in line for the most part. He enjoyed her dedication to him. One day, Mary would be successful.

Mary arranged a group meeting with 10 possible candidates to be on the game show. She was surprised that Damon wanted her to carry out such a task. Her boss was stubborn and always wanted to be in control of everything. Most executive producers hired people, like assistants, to carry out menial tasks. She was flattered that Damon trusted her with such a huge responsibility.

"Hello group! I am an assistant producer here at URN. My name is Mary. We are creating a game show called 'Easy Money'. I would like to take a moment to welcome each and every one of you here today. Please take one packet off the top, then pass the rest of them around."

Mary looked around the room. Out of the 10, more than half were young college student types. A couple of the men looked like they lived at the gym due to their muscles. Strong men were expected to know how to endure pain. The rest just looked like your typical everyday person that you would see shopping in a market.

"I am going to review this packet with you today as a group. Then, I will meet privately with each and every one of you, 1-on-1. Are there any questions before we begin?" Mary rubbed her face as she saw 2 hands raise in the air. She pointed at the plain man in the front row.

"I love money as much as the next guy. Pain, well, not so much. What kind of pain are you talking about? Fake TV stunt pain? And how much cash are we talking?"

"Full disclaimer, which we will cover in this packet. The pain will be real. However, it will be self-inflicted pain for an agreed upon price. Yes, your injuries will be very real. The cash will also be very real. How much cash you win will depend on how much pain that you suffer. The example used in the packet is cutting yourself with a straight razor for $1,000. Your wounds, should they be deep enough to require stitches, would be treated by medical professionals provided by the network. Any other questions?"

The same gentleman who just asked the question raised his hand again. Mary pointed at him.

"That sounds ridiculous to me. I just assumed that since it's on television, it would be fake stunts. And I thought there would be more cash involved. Am I free to leave?"

Mary shook her head yes. "Yes, any of you are free to leave at any time. Cash prizes do get larger. In our first episode, the contestants will have a chance to win $50,000. However, that would require a lot of pain. That's a huge cash amount though. At no point are you obliged to participate in any activity that you do not wish to participate in. There's the door. You are free to go."

The gentleman who asked the question stood and walked out of the room. Another guy followed. Now, Mary was looking at a group of 8.

A girl in the second row, who had 6 facial piercings, booed as the men left. "They are wusses. I love pain. There's not much that I wouldn't do for 50 grand."

Mary made a mental note in her head to cast the girl with the metal in her face. She only hoped that the girl could pass the psych evaluation.

"Okay group, open the packet to the second page. Let's cover the legalities first." Mary stared at the lengthy packet. She was in for another long day.

After a long group casting session, Mary was now into the individual interviews. She had decided to begin with Amy, the girl with the metal in her face. The girl was exactly what Mary was looking for in a contestant.

"So, you say that you love pain. As I explained, to be on the show you have to pass a psychological evaluation. Does your love of pain extend into a mentally unhealthy realm?" Mary couldn't keep her eyes off of all the piercings in the girl's face.

"I'm not a cutter, if that's what you mean. But I do love tats and piercings." Amy raised her shirt to show Mary her nipples. "Getting these puppies pierced was the best feeling that I have ever felt in my whole entire life. Do you want to touch them? You could even pull on 1 of them, if you'd like."

Mary turned her head. Seeing the metal protruding the soft pink skin made Mary's stomach churn. "No. Thanks though. Please, lower your blouse. I don't need to touch them. I just can't believe that they didn't hurt."

Amy smiled. "Hurt? Hurt is a state of mind. It felt good. When I got my clit pierced it was a sexual hurt in a good way. Getting my nipples done was a more pleasurable kind of hurt. It was like extreme foreplay. I loved it."

Mary was fast to speak. "There's no need to show me that other piercing from down south. I take your word for it. What else can you tell me about yourself?"

"Not much to tell. I'm a college student, so I'm broke. Like, I'm broke all of the time." Amy paused for a second to think. " Oh yeah, and I like money. That's what you want to hear, right?" Amy was extremely satisfied with how she had answered the question.

Mary smiled. "That's great Amy. I'm going to get you set up with a psychiatrist. If you pass the evaluation, it's safe to say that you will be 1 of the first contestants on 'Easy Money'. Congratulations."

Amy gave a thumbs up and a big cheesy smile. "Yay. I can't wait."

The first interview was easy enough. Only 7 more to go.

When Mary interviewed the other women, she kept an open mind, but she knew that she had already found the female contestant that she wanted. She told them that if she needed them, she would be in touch. If Amy made it past the head doctor, Mary knew that she wouldn't need to contact another female.

Since 2 men had already left during the group interview, Mary only had 3 men to choose from. Only 1 of the 3 had left an impression on her. His name was Bill. Bill needed money for his sick child. He had been having problems with his health insurance, and needed money to cover his kid's chemotherapy treatment costs. He had even made that remark that if he had life insurance, he would kill himself so that the life insurance money could save his child's life. Unfortunately, he didn't have health insurance. Mary knew that this man was desperate enough for money that he could make an interesting show. Mary set up the appointments for Bill and Amy to advance to the next stage of the interview, and see the shrink. She kept her fingers crossed and hoped that Damon would be happy with her selections. Mary did not want to disappoint her boss.

DAMON'S OBSESSION

Getting the new show up and running was Damon's main focus. It had preoccupied most of his time. He had begun working with writers to create 'stunts' for his pain show. Whenever they discussed how the participants would be hurting themselves, Damon would get slightly turned on. He was also reminded of his brief time with Lydia.

Even though Damon had tried to get another appointment with Lydia through the dating service, Lydia refused to see him. They offered to send him another girl. Damon thought it would be best to use another strategy to find himself a companion. With Lydia refusing to see him, he dreaded to think of what his dating service had thought of him. Lydia had barely even bled on their 'date'. Damon craved to see more blood. He decided to get creative and find a new companion.

Since Damon wanted privacy, he decided to rent a car. His car was way too obvious. Just way too flashy. He typically wasn't a low-key, hidden in the background kind of guy. Now, he wanted to blend in with the normal people. Damon removed his suit and tie, and slipped into a nice pair of designer jeans and a t shirt.

Damon drove downtown to an area that he never visited. He drove to the run-down part of downtown. This area was known for drugs, crime, and prostitution. This would be a first time experience for him. Damon had never picked up a street prostitute in his life. He figured that it couldn't be too hard. He had a pocket full of cash. Prostitutes liked cash.

Damon felt like he had hit the jackpot when he found an underpass with 3 scantily clad females standing on the corner. He watched them from a distance. None of them were as attractive as the girls that worked for the dating service he had used in the past. However, their bodies were young and fit. The most attractive girl was smoking a cigarette. Damon watched each time as the girl raised the cancer stick to her mouth. He loved the way that her lips slowly enveloped the cigarette. He was fascinated with her mouth. The shape that her lips formed when she exhaled was sensual and seductive. He started to imagine the things that he could do with her mouth.

Damon slowly drove up to the smoking hooker. She threw her smoke to the ground, and extinguished it with her high heel shoe. He watched as she twisted her leg pressed to the ground, and noticed how great her legs looked in the short skirt. She glanced up at Damon and slowly made her way to his car.

"Hey cutie. Oh, you really are cute. Are you looking for a good time?" The hooker smiled, exposing her smoke stained teeth.

Damon noticed that up close, the woman looked much older than she did from a distance. He couldn't believe how nasty her teeth were. They weren't just yellow, but some of them looked almost rotten. "Yes, I like having a good time. But I've never done anything like this. Never ever in my whole entire life. How does this work?"

"For $50, you can have anything you want. Your wish is my command." She smiled again, but this time she smiled so that her lips covered her teeth.

"$50? I have more than that. What can I get for more than $50?" Damon couldn't believe how cheap a street walker actually cost.

"Whatever you want, baby. Everything is for sale." The woman got into Damon's rental car.

"So, where are we going?" Damon flashed his charming smile at the lady.

"Right here baby. Nobody will bother us under here." The hooker began to rub Damon's leg. "Cash up front."

Damon reached into his pocket and produced $200. He held the cash out in front of her. "I'm not comfortable here. I wanna go somewhere private. Maybe your place. I'll pay you even more when we get there."

The woman snatched the money out of Damon's hand. "Just drive. I'll give you directions as we go."

As Damon drove, he was thinking about how glad he was that he had rented a car. He would have never let such a skank in his own car. The woman smelled of cigarette smoke. Damon kept flashing his charming smile at the woman. He wanted her in a good mood. He didn't want her to know what he was really thinking about.

She directed Damon to a fleabag motel. As soon as they got out of the car, she lit up a cigarette. She opened the door to her room. There were clothes and food wrappers scattered all around the room. This was apparently where the woman lived.

"I never bring a john here. So I hope you feel special." The woman held her hand out.

"Right. I do feel special. I told you that I'd pay you more. Here's another $100." Damon got the money out of his pocket.

She grabbed the money from his hand. She pulled her tank top from the bottom seam, and raised the shirt over her head, exposing her bare breasts. Her tits were plump and firm. Damon was impressed. He hadn't expected her to have such a nice chest. The woman unzipped her skirt and lowered it. She wasn't wearing any panties. Damon liked her thin bush. Wearing nothing but her high heels, the woman laid on the bed. "How do you want me baby?"

Damon turned around and cleared some dirty clothes from a chair. Damon took a seat and looked at her on the bed. Damon pulled a pair of wire pliers from his pocket and held them in the air.

"So you like kinky stuff?" The naked lady sat up. "I don't like torture myself, but if you pay me, I will torture you all night long."

"I want to watch you torture yourself." Damon was sure of what he wanted. He originally planned on the fingernail thing, but this hooker's smile gave him another idea. "I will pay you $100 for every tooth that you pull out of your head."

"You want me to pull my own teeth? I can't do that." The woman looked at Damon like he had 2 heads.

"I believe you can. For $200 a tooth." Damon tried raising the price. "You have a lot of teeth. You could make some serious cash here." Damon was amazed by himself. The street hookers were a lot cheaper than his escort service. Damon pulled a wad of cash out of his pocket and showed it to her.

Her eyes got huge when she saw all of that money. She reached for the pair of wire pliers. The hooker put the pliers to her mouth. She shook her head no. "No, I can't do this."

Damon urged the woman to continue. "You can do this. I have $1000 here. I will pay you $500 per tooth. Your going rate for usual services is $50. You could afford to take some time off work. You could buy yourself something nice. Say, you could even upgrade your hotel room. What do you say? You pull a total of 2 teeth. That's $500 per tooth. Pain is temporary. You can do this." Damon fanned out the cash on the table in front of him. He hoped he had raised the price high enough.

The woman eyed the cash. She appeared to be deep in thought. She was still naked as she sat on the edge of the bed. She took her fingers, and rubbed her front teeth. The prostitute shook her head yes, and smiled. Damon heard a slight clank as she gripped the tool and closed the ridged metal onto her front tooth. The woman's breasts plumped up as she took a deep breath.

She moved her wrist forward with a quick motion. Her eyes instantly filled with tears. With her mouth gaping open, she couldn't scream. Instead she made a gurgling noise.

Damon lowered his head to get a better look inside the woman's mouth. "That tooth is still attached to the gum. You didn't try hard enough. That's okay though. You can keep trying. Just take your time." Damon shook his pointer finger back and forth to indicate that her effort wasn't good enough.

The woman raised her lip to expose the root of her tooth. She grabbed the tooth with 2 fingers and wiggled it. It was loose, very loose. She looked at her finger and saw a thin stream of blood.

Damon loved the sight of blood. He grabbed his crotch as he felt his member stiffen. "Yes, it's loose. But you haven't pulled it yet."

"It hurts pretty good. It hurts so bad that I can't believe that it's still there. I heard a crunch in my head. I would've sworn that I pulled it!" Little specks of blood splattered out with saliva as the street walker spoke. "Give me a second."

The hooker stood in her nakedness, and walked to a piece of furniture beside the bed. Damon enjoyed the view of her naked butt. She opened the drawer, and pulled out a small black zippered pouch.

"What's that? What are you doing?" Damon couldn't quite make out what the woman was holding.

"I'm making myself better for you." The hooker held up a pipe. "Do you want some?"

Damon chuckled. "No, I'm good." At least he had figured out why her teeth were so nasty. He had always heard that drugs were bad for teeth. No wonder her teeth looked so rotten.

Damon watched as the woman raised the thin glass pipe in the air. She put something in it, and grabbed her lighter. He watched her naked breasts plump up as she held the flame to the pipe and inhaled the smoke. She looked towards Damon as she exhaled a huge smoke cloud.

She took a couple more puffs and smiled. "This will be easy now." The hooker squeezed her tooth with the wire pliers. She slowly twisted the tool. She smiled as she held the tooth in the pliers and displayed it for Damon to see. She rubbed her tongue in the bloody gap of her gum. Blood ran down her tongue.

Damon was almost disappointed that she didn't even flinch. Whatever she was smoking must have blocked the pain. He did love the sight of her blood. "Good job. Do that again, then you get $1000."

The woman grabbed for her glass pipe.

"No, I will pay extra if you pull this tooth without drugs." Damon wanted to see her flinch in pain.

The woman raised the pliers once again to her other front tooth. She wiggled the tool back, and then forth. "Please let me smoke."

"Shh. I'll give you an extra $500 if you don't." Damon continued to rub his crotch through his clothing.

The metal clanked onto her tooth. She moved the tool. Back, forth. Back, forth. One forward quick motion and she was holding her tooth in her hand. She showed the tooth to Damon. A trail of tears fell down the hooker's face, even though she was smiling. The woman sat down the tool, and reached for her pipe.

Damon left the cash on the table. It was time to go home. He was satisfied. Today was a good day.

EARLY MEDIA

"Mary! Get! In! Here! Now!" Mary's intercom on her desk buzzed. Damon did not seem happy. She dreaded whatever he was going to be mad about today.

Mary walked into Damon's office and stood. She was almost fearful. Damon turned his computer screen around for Mary to see. He clicked a button. Mary saw a video buffering. It was Bill. The man that she was trying to cast in the first episode. The circle in the center of the video stopped spinning, and the video began to play.

"I'm mad because I really needed to be on that show." Bill began explaining. He appeared to be sitting with a familiar local news reporter. "But they told me that I can't." Bill continued. "They made me see a head doctor, and the head doctor told me that I wasn't of 'sound mind'. They are only accepting applicants that can pass mental tests."

"Okay Bill. What do you know of the show?" The reporter began the questioning.

Bill looked into the camera. "It's a reality game show. They pay you to hurt yourself."

The reporter made a frown. "Why would you want to be on a show if it entailed you hurting yourself?"

"I need money. My kid is sick. I would endure any

kind of pain if it helped get my kid better." Bill began to tear up.

"What exactly do you mean that they pay you to hurt yourself?" The reporter wanted to get to the root of the story.

"The example that they gave us was cutting yourself with a straight razor. They said in the first episode, there would be over $50,000 in cash prizes." Bill looked away from the camera.

"To clarify, Bill, URN is paying cash to people who hurt themselves on a game show? That can't be real, can it?" The reporter shook his head in disbelief.

"They say it's real. There was even paperwork about receiving medical treatment for the self inflicted injuries. I don't know." Bill shrugged his shoulders.

"So people, you heard it here first. URN is planning a reality game show paying contestants to self-inflict harm. Tell us what you think. Is this real, or some publicity stunt? Would you watch a game show of this nature? Go online and click the link with our game show questionnaire. We will let you know the results on Friday's show." The reporter waved bye to the camera.

Damon clicked the video off. "What do you have to say Mary?"

Mary honestly didn't know what to say. "I don't know what to say sir."

"That's what you have to say for yourself? This was genius. We are getting tons of free publicity. That news station is getting people to talk about our show, to think about our show. This is exactly what I wanted! I probably don't tell you this enough but I'm proud of you, Mary." Damon actually complimented Mary.

Mary's boss had never said anything nice about her. She was in shock. Not once before had he ever told her that he was proud of her.

Damon continued, not waiting for Mary to speak. "But they think this is a fake show. Like we are pulling some fake publicity stunt. I guess since Bill decided to sell them his story, they automatically assume that URN is behind it. I gotta figure this one out. I don't want people thinking that our show is fake. But we could use this to our advantage. We can urge viewers to watch it, to decide for themselves whether or not it's fake."

"Live." Mary managed to verbally produce the single word.

"Live? Please continue." Damon looked impressed.

Mary had never impressed her boss until today. "Live. We air the game show live. In front of a live studio audience. We can't edit fake stuff into a live show. Then afterwards, we persuade our contestants to do interviews about the show. What their experience was like being on 'Easy Money'."

"Genius. Pure genius. Give yourself a raise Mary. Do you have any other ideas for me?" Damon wanted more from Mary.

"Do you want me to make a public comment to that news channel? I can go public with a statement confirming that the show will be 100% real. Do you want me to start stirring the media pot?" Mary was full of ideas today. She was actually proud of herself.

"Yes. That's perfect. But don't get so busy that you forget to replace the applicant that our doctor rejected. I just can't believe this. I couldn't have planned this any better myself. I can't believe that I didn't plan this. This is the first sign of how huge our show will be. Thank you for helping me make television history."

Mary stood stunned. Not only was Damon proud of her, but now he was thanking her. Mary couldn't believe her ears. She wondered why Damon was in such a good mood. She did notice that when he came into the office that morning, he had a smile on his face. She wondered if something had changed in Damon's personal life to make him so happy. Maybe he had met a woman? Anyways, that didn't matter. All that mattered was that she was getting a raise.

Mary checked the email from URN's psychiatrist. Bill failed the exam, but luckily Amy had passed. Mary couldn't wait to tell Amy that she was going to be on the first episode of the show. It would be a coin flip between the other 2 male contestants. Neither one of them seemed desperate for money. Just your typical unemployed status. One did seem to be a tough guy. Tough guys have reputations to protect. If they're tough, they should be able to handle a little bit of pain. The show was coming right along. Soon enough, it would be time for the world premiere. The very first episode. Mary was actually excited.

THE FIRST EPISODE (MARY'S POV)

Finally, all of this hard work was becoming a reality. Thanks to news channels, and social media, 'Easy Money' was the most anticipated show of the season. Some people claimed they only wanted to watch it to see if it was real. Some people claimed they only wanted to watch it to see exactly what it was. However, very few admitted to wanting to watch the show to see people suffer in pain. With that being said, it wasn't hard to fill the live audience with 500 viewers. They had so many show up to be in the audience that they had to turn some people away. It didn't matter why people watched it, as long as they watched it.

Damon actually wanted to watch the show. He put Mary in charge of everything else. He was really starting to trust Mary with real responsibilities. Mary did not want to disappoint Damon. The first snag of the night that Mary hit was that the earpieces the crew used to communicate with each other were not working. They improvised by sitting Damon up front so that at least he could hand signal the host.

The host, Peter Conway, was a staple at URN. He had successfully hosted many shows for the network. He was known for his charm. Women loved him just because he was so easy on the eyes. When he flashed his smile, it instantly raised the female demographic watching the show. Mary just hoped that Peter had a strong stomach, and could handle the blood in tonight's episode.

Mary made one last pit stop backstage to the contestant waiting area. Damon instructed her to give them a pep talk. Damon told Mary to get in their head. She was going to try and convince them that they were invincible. Damon even told her what to say. Pain was temporary. Pain was a state of mind. Money was real. Money was what mattered.

Mary had already spoken with the director of photography. She wanted the cameramen to show the actual injuries. She wanted a full view of the contestants hurting themselves. Then she wanted the camera to zoom in on the blood. Mary wanted the viewers at home to know how real this was. The audience members would really get a good view as to how real it was. Mary told the gaffers (lights) to make sure that there was enough light to see everything clearly. There would be music on the game show, but no sound effects. They wanted every yelp of pain to be real. They didn't want an injury to appear fake by trying too hard to liven it up with sound effects.

Mary crossed her fingers and hoped that everything would go as planned. She only hoped that this episode would live up to Damon's standards. She watched on a screen as it flashed 'Viewer Discretion is Advised.' She heard Peter welcome the guests. 'Easy Money' was now live. Mary had a view of the show from backstage. The music sounded good. The lights looked perfect. Everything seemed to flow together perfectly. She knew that Damon would be pleased.

Mary heard the audience applaud. They were pumped up. She watched on the monitor as the camera did a sweep of the audience. It was a rush, seeing all those people in the audience. All of these people came to see something she had helped create. It was a full house out there. And to think, at first she thought Damon's idea was crazy. Seeing it come to fruition was very exciting. Mary wanted to take a bow, right then, right there. Damon was right, hard work does pay off.

Mary watched as Amy climbed into the first glass cube, and began piercing her ears with the staple gun. Mary flinched with each pop sound the staple gun made as it ejected a staple into her soft flesh. Amy was perfect for this. She only hoped that with episodes going forward, there would be more people like Amy to apply.

A thought hit Mary. Something she hadn't thought about since they had first started working on the show. The network had only given them 1 episode. What if URN didn't like the show? 'Easy Money' hadn't even aired yet, and it had already gotten more publicity than any other show on the network ever. Surely the network would add more episodes of 'Easy Money'.

Mary pushed her panic aside long enough to catch Amy stapling her shirt to her shoulder. Amy was a trooper. Obviously, she did love pain. Out of the corner of her eye, Mary saw a cameraman cringe with pain.

"No. You do not get to cringe now. You are working. Zoom in on that. Show how real it is." Mary screamed at the worker.

Mary hadn't realized that they didn't take the time to prepare the crew for what they were about to see. She had been too busy orchestrating everything else. Mary could kick herself. She had seen so many gore injuries in the online videos that she was prepared for the show. At least she could scope the cameraman's reaction, somewhat, to real viewer's reactions. At least none of the crew was vomiting. Mary remembered wanting to vomit after she watched some of the bloody online videos, but she never did. Is it physically possible to be so disgusted that you actually vomit? Mary never had. She hoped there wouldn't be any viewers at home retching out their guts.

Mary pulled herself out of her head long enough to watch Stephen attempt to pierce his ear with the nail gun. Stephen did not impress her in his casting interview. The camera zoomed in on Stephen's bloody torn ear lobe. It was torn right where the earlobe meets the jaw line. There was blood. Lots of blood. Mary almost gagged as she watched Stephen try to wipe the blood off his neck. The blood just kept running down his neck, there was no wiping it off. Mary was impressed with Stephen. She didn't expect much out of him, but when he decided to complete his challenge, she was impressed. Apparently, he was a tough guy. Despite the fact that he now had a severely opened wound on the side of his head, Stephen decided to go on with the show. At least the audience was still applauding. The people were liking the show.

Mary panicked when Stephen decided to quit after completing his challenge. They hadn't planned on a contestant not finishing the show. Hopefully, Amy would be open minded to the last round. It's only a gun. Surely, she would agree to shoot herself for $50,000. That sounds extreme, but $50,000 was a lot of cash to a college student. Mary kept her fingers crossed that Amy would complete the show.

Mary watched as Stephen cried real tears, real hard. Backstage. The man sobbed with every step that he took. He didn't look like such a tough guy now. Mary felt bad for him, for about half a second. He literally did it to himself. Stephen literally shot himself with a nail gun. Nobody forced him to do it. He didn't shoot himself just once, he shot 5 nails into himself. It was harder to feel bad for someone when they made the decision to hurt themselves.

Finally, Mary heard Amy agree to shoot herself with a real gun. Damon had wondered if $50,000 was enough to tempt someone to hurt themselves so severely. Mary had convinced Damon that $50,000 was a lot more money to a college student than it was for someone like Damon who had such a large salary. Thankfully, this first show had worked out. Mary knew that the network would give them more episodes. Then she wondered about sponsors. Mary's curiosity was killing her to know the show's ratings. How many TV's were turned on to 'Easy Money'? Hopefully, a lot of them were. With a lot of viewers, they could get sponsors. With sponsors, they would have a larger budget. With a larger budget they could pay their contestants more money. Of course, the challenges would be more difficult though.

Mary watched as Amy shot off her little finger with a real bullet. That was the perfect ending to the show. If people wanted blood and gore, then they got it with the splattered pinky finger. Amy looked like she was in pain, but not as much pain as Stephen. Hopefully, she could cheer them up for their interviews with the media the next day. The happier the contestants appeared to be, then the happier the viewers would be. Even though the first episode had ended, some of the work had just begun.

AFTER THE FIRST EPISODE

"Mary, walk with me." Damon appeared to be happy tonight.

"Yes sir." Mary scurried to her boss's side.

"Intros. We need to add intros on each contestant." Damon did know how to make good TV. "I want to make our contestants human. We need to explain why they are on the show. Do they need money? And for what? Do they just enjoy pain? Blah blah."

"Does that mean that the network has agreed to give us more episodes?" Mary could barely contain her excitement.

"Well, unofficially, no. But it was a hit. They will give us more episodes. I am sure of it. The audience loved it. Some of them wanted more." Damon stopped at his office door.

"Intros. Got it. I think we need more contestants." Mary shrugged her shoulders as she said it. She was sure when it was a thought in her head that it was a good idea. When she said it aloud, and Damon looked at her funny, she wasn't so sure anymore.

Damon glared at Mary intensely.

Mary found her confidence and began to explain.

"Stephen quit after just 1 challenge. What if both contestants had quit after just 1 challenge? We wouldn't have seen our grand finale. Nobody would've shot the real gun." Mary was sure of herself this time. She did sound confident.

"Good thinking, Mary. I expect to get sponsors after tonight. With more of a budget, we can make harder challenges with higher cash prizes. So I agree. We need at least 1 contestant per round. Now, go back. Find whichever hospital Amy and Stephen are in. Prep them for interviews tomorrow. Make sure they are happy. Good night. I'm gonna surf the web and see what our viewers are saying." Damon went into his office and fired up his computer.

He didn't even have to run a search. 'Easy Money' was the main topic of conversation on his homepage. There were mixed reviews. Some people loved it. Some people hated it. Many still questioned the authenticity. Every platform of social media was buzzing with people's opinions of the show.

Damon clicked on a live stream of a local news channel.

The computer speakers clicked on full volume. "'Easy Money' is the most disturbing thing I have ever seen in my life. Why would anybody need money so bad? I still don't believe that it's real. We're live, with callers. Phone us and give us your opinion. Hello, thanks for calling, caller 1. What's your thoughts?"

The person on the phone line sounded muffled. "I think that $50,000 would change my life. I want to be on the show. How do I apply?"

The news reporter cut the phone call short. "Check URN's website. Let's take another caller. Hello, you are on the air."

A man with a deep voice gave his opinion. "Hi. Yes, that show is a disgrace. People are hurting themselves for cash. How degrading is that? However, with that being said I couldn't turn it off. I kept waiting to see what happened next."

That was exactly what Damon had wanted to hear. Even the people who hated it were watching it. As soon as Damon turned his computer off, his phone rang.

It didn't take long. The network was calling to give Damon more episodes. Damon knew that they would, he just didn't know that it would happen so fast. Damon relished in the fact that his absurd idea was a hit. With all of the internet buzz, he knew that the sponsors would be coming to him, and soon. Damon propped his feet up on his desk. He smiled, enjoying his success. He would have to make a free evening sometime soon so he could have himself another night of enjoyment. He enjoyed his personal private shows.

Mary went to the hospital to check on Stephen and Amy. Stephen was in surgery. Mary assumed for his blown off ear lobe. However, Amy had refused surgery. Amy's finger was nothing but a nub. All Amy had let them do was stitch it shut and give her some pain pills.

"Mary! I am so glad to see you." Amy was sitting on her hospital bed. "I'm not staying here. I'll be outta here in no time."

Mary was surprised that Amy was in such a good mood. "Aren't you chipper? Are you in any pain?"

Amy laughed. "Of course I'm in pain. But I'm also $50,000 richer. I'm gonna pay off my student loans and buy myself a nice car. Do you know how good it feels to get out of debt? I want to thank you for this experience."

Mary gave Amy a hug. "You were a star tonight. Are you gonna feel up to doing interviews tomorrow?"

"Of course. I wanna tell the world how good I feel. How happy I am. I want everyone to know how rich I am!" Amy was genuinely happy and laughed.

Mary wasn't sure how happy that Stephen was gonna be. The doctors wouldn't tell Mary anything due to confidentiality. She waited for him to get out of surgery. After surgery, she waited for him to get out of recovery.

"Hey Stephen. You were great on the show. How are you feeling?" Mary tried to sound as happy as she could. Even though he was bandaged, she could still see part of the side of his head. The skin surrounding the bandage was purple like it was bruised. Stephen's whole jaw line looked swollen.

"How do you think I feel? I hurt." Stephen was very short and rude.

"Are you gonna feel up to doing any interviews tomorrow? Or do you want me to put that off for a couple of days?"

"Do I have to? I don't want to do any interviews." Stephen turned his head as a single tear fell down his cheek.

"No, you don't have to do anything that you don't want to do. Why don't you want to do any interviews?" Mary rationalized his decision. She would rather him not do an interview instead of giving a bad interview. The show did not need any negative publicity from a contestant.

"I looked like a baby on national TV. I let that girl upstage me. Plus, I only made $10,000. I can't believe that I quit. I didn't look like much of a man on television." Stephen sniffled trying not to cry more.

"I think that you did a great job. You didn't look

like a baby from where I was standing. You completed your task, even after pretty much blowing your ear off your head. If that's not manly, then I don't know what is." Mary squeezed his arm. He needed an ego boost.

"I'm tired. Can I just go to sleep?" Stephen turned his head away from Mary.

"Of course you can. Get some rest." Mary could finally go home.

At least neither 1 of the contestants were mad at the network. There would be no negative contestant interviews to contribute to the naysayers thinking even less of URN.

All in all, Mary had a great day. She was completely exhausted, yet sleep did not come easy for her. Even though neither contestant was mad at her, Mary's conscience was getting the best of her. Even though the show was legal, was it moral? Mary was almost ashamed of herself for what she had helped create. She had definitely changed.

She was mad at herself about the visit to the hospital. She didn't go to the hospital to check on the 2 human beings who hurt themselves. She went to the hospital to ensure that the reputation of the show would not be marred even worse. There was a time that Mary thought about the well being of people. Not success. Maybe Damon had started rubbing off on her.

Since she couldn't sleep, she decided to do an internet search. Pictures of the show were all over the internet. There was even an article about how watching violence promotes violence. Was Mary promoting violence? Luckily, she didn't find any 'mimic' videos yet. She dreaded copycat videos of people (especially children) shooting themselves with staples or nail guns. Surely, children wouldn't have access to real guns.

With all of the social media platforms still

buzzing about 'Easy Money', she did feel a small bit of pride for being such an integral part of such a hit show. But something wasn't right. Nothing was necessarily wrong, but there was definitely something that didn't feel right to Mary. She wasn't breaking any laws. The contestants weren't mad at her. The whole internet was talking about the show. Mary wasn't as proud of the show as she should be. This was probably the most successful day of her entire career, but it just didn't sit right with her. She should be ecstatic, but she wasn't.

The world that she was living in now scared her. Wholesome TV of fake gore had evolved into reality gore. What were the viewers like if this was what they wanted to see. What happened to good, old fashioned, family oriented TV? Nobody wanted to watch that anymore.

Mary turned out the light, and decided to try and get some sleep. Starting the next day, they had to start planning new episodes. Their work had only just begun. Mary and Damon made an unlikely duo, but something about it worked.

OPPOSITION

"We had more viewers than the championship game! Do you know how exciting that is?" Mary was actually starting to get the feel for success, despite the fact her conscience wouldn't let her sleep.

Damon smiled. "Yes, I'm aware. But have you read any of the negative reviews? Actually, most of them are negative reviews, but yet the people still watched it. Welcome to television. Instead of turning the channel, they give you bad publicity. Bad publicity is better than no publicity. Just in case there's someone living in a cave somewhere, I'm sure that they have heard about 'Easy Money' by now. 'Easy Money' is like a car wreck. You can't look away."

Mary had skimmed through Amy's interview with a local reporter. There was a picture of Amy's stump pinky finger. The sight was disgusting. Luckily, Amy was happy. She gave the show good publicity. She actually encouraged other people who were in need of cash to apply for the show. So not all of the publicity was bad.

Damon continued his rants and Mary got bored. Even though he had started giving Mary the respect that she deserved (sometimes), his rants still bored her. She played her usual look out the window and daydream game. Today, Mary picked 2 women who were standing and talking to each other. She decided to give them a funny story. She imagined the women speaking of last night's episode.

Woman in green: I perform oral sex on my husband for a lot less money.

Woman in red: Sure, I do too. Pulling a trigger would be much faster, and maybe even more enjoyable.

As if right on cue, Mary watched as both of the women raised their heads to laugh right at that moment.

"Right, Mary? I mean to call it truth. This is what they want." Damon was still talking.

"I'm sorry. I missed that last part. Come again?" Mary started to pay attention.

"Calling 'Easy Money' truth was the highest honor. This is what people want to see, even if they're too ashamed to admit it. People enjoyed watching them suffer last night. The viewers have never seen anything like this before. Truth. I agree. The show is truth. Our show is truth." Damon had finally stopped talking. Or not. "That means that we are truth. We are crossing television barriers we didn't even know existed yet. Pat yourself on the back."

"Yes sir, I agree with everything." Mary still wasn't entirely sure what she was agreeing with.

"Okay. Meeting with the writers at 5:00. Be there Mary, I value your opinion." Damon gave Mary a pat on her shoulder.

Mary looked at her shoulder to make sure that she wasn't on fire. Damon would try to extinguish her if she was on fire, right? Mary was not on fire. Damon had just chosen to touch her. That was a first.

"I will be there boss. I wouldn't miss this meeting for the world." Mary was impressed with this new side of Damon.

Damon sat at the head of a large oval table. The meeting was comprised of writers and Mary. Even though the first show was a success, Damon wanted to revamp the show to a more interesting viewing experience.

Damon began the meeting. "Last night's episode was huge. But it was dry. Kinda boring."

One of the writers cleared his throat and shook his head in disagreement.

Damon did not look pleased. "It was boring. Yes we saw people get hurt, but there was no heart. No story. If we just keep pumping out shows with injuries, trust me, people will get bored with it. We need to add some fluff. Any ideas?"

A man that Mary had never seen before in her life raised his pointer finger in the air. "The characters, um contestants, is all that we have to work with."

Damon cut the man off. "Yes. Character introductions. Maybe a little bit of a backstory. If they have some sort of sob story, we show it to the world. The media has been questioning what kind of person wants to be on our show. In our next episode, we will answer that question for them. What else can we do to make it a little more spicy?"

The room was silent. Damon looked around the room at all of the blank faces.

"I might have an idea." Mary decided to speak up. "Let's focus on the actual injuries. I don't mean to zoom in on the injuries with the camera. I mean have Peter talk to them. Ask them how they feel. I don't know. Maybe he could ask them if the money was worth it. Amy's interview with that reporter went viral. Why can't Peter do exit interviews?"

"I can't believe this." Damon nodded his head. "I am in a room, surrounded by what are supposed to be URN's best writers, and my assistant is the only 1 with an idea."

A small voice came from the far end of the table. "We write reality TV. There's a big difference between writing reality TV and a game show. There are a few shows on the network where we have weekly competitions that eliminate participants, but those competitions are completely different. And I think it's safe to say that most of the writers don't agree with 'Easy Money'.

Many heads shook in agreement.

"What do you mean by don't agree? What is there to agree with? Or even disagree with? This is a show. It was the network's most watched show."

Another writer decided to chime in. "Mr. Dahmer, this show is sad. You are preying on poor people. For amusement."

Damon had heard all that he wanted to hear. "Fine. If you don't agree, then I don't need you. There's the door. You are free to leave."

The writers sat very still. Damon was known for having a temper. In their faces you could see that they were wondering what Damon was up to. After a few seconds of silence, a few of the men left the meeting.

Damon threw his coffee mug at the door and it shattered into tiny pieces. "Fine! I don't need you then!" Damon was very upset with the writer's resistance.

Damon looked around at the few writers that remained. "Put on your creative thinking caps. Let's come up with an improved 'Easy Money'.

Damon didn't care that people opposed the show.

All he cared about was that they watched the show. He had bigger, better future plans for 'Easy Money'. He didn't need people to agree with his idea. For every person that didn't like the show, there was a person that did like the show. The numbers didn't lie. They had a ton of viewers for the world premiere. Lots of discussions were being had about the content of the show. He wanted people talking about the show. He wanted to leave an impression with his show.

Damon sat and looked out his office window, deep in thought. He was making history. Plus, he had plans with the show that would satisfy his inner needs. He had more plans to make. It was time for Damon to get to work. All that mattered right now was 'Easy Money'.

Soon, Damon would need his own personal release. He craved to see more blood. He felt so powerful when women made themselves bleed for his pleasure. With some cash, he could make anyone do anything. He had plans of revenge for 1 particular contestant. He thought of Marty Blevins. It was pure luck that such a man applied to be on the show. Now, all he had to do was get the stars to align in his favor.

He looked at the photo of his boy on the desk. When he looked at his son's picture was probably the only time Damon felt emotions. Even those emotions had slowly begun to fade with the memories of him being a father. Over time, Damon didn't have too many 'feelings'. Emotions were for the weak. Life was about power and making money. Right now, Damon had both. Life was good.

DAMON'S PLANS

The network had agreed to give 'Easy Money' 2 more episodes for now. So much of the publicity was bad that the higher executives weren't sure if the ratings would stay so high. Naturally, people had tuned in to see what this game show was that everyone was talking about. Now that people had seen it, would they tune in again? Damon was happy with having 2 more episodes. That was all he needed to prove to the network that this world was full of viewers that loved this type of thing. Sure, this show wasn't for their normal everyday viewer, but there was definitely a demographic for it.

Mary had become flooded with way too many applicants. Tons of people wanted to be on this show. Had people become so lazy that they would rather make a quick buck rather than get a job? At least they were sure that the people who applied to be on the show would watch. Damon decided to help Mary by giving her more staff to help with the casting. Of course, he would have the final say as to whom they cast, but Mary couldn't do it alone. She could oversee a casting crew. Mary knew what Damon was looking for in a contestant. His assistant understood his vision.

Damon knew that the ratings were so high because the show had been brand new. He now needed more shock value. The challenges would have to be more daring. More entertaining. Eventually he would take things to another level. He hoped that the network would give him a full season of episodes, but they didn't. He had to work with what they gave him.

Damon looked at the lucky contestant he picked from the pile of the first episode's applicants. Marty Blevins. Blevins was a name he hadn't thought of in such a long time. Even though he didn't have a direct history with Marty Blevins, he was aware of who he was. After hiring a private investigator, a very discreet private investigator, Damon learned more about Marty Blevins.

Marty was a college student. A bad college student with bad grades. He was a known drug user, having a couple arrests for drug possession. Mostly heroin. Damon wondered if it was heroin that the streetwalker who pulled out her teeth had been smoking. Damon couldn't help but for his mind to wonder. He thought of the couple of women he had power over, that succumbed to his desires. Even though he was trying to plan future episodes, his mind was obsessed with these women.

He redirected his mind back to Marty. He had preparations to make. Meanwhile, he had an inner beast that desired to see more blood. He desired to feel power. Maybe it was more about the power than it was the blood? Damon wasn't sure, but it also didn't matter. He just knew that he needed a release. He needed a release very soon. An idea a writer came up with for the second episode gave Damon an idea. Heat was painful. Not necessarily bloody, but painful all the same. He wanted to see his street walker in pain.

With a pocket full of cash, Damon drove to the spot where he found his streetwalker. He was very disappointed that she wasn't there. There were other women standing around, but Damon wanted his girl. He had laid his claim on her, and it was time to make it official.

He only hoped that she was still staying in the same hotel room. What was the worst that could happen? If he knocked, and she didn't answer, he could go home. Hopefully she would answer the door. She was a drug addict. Surely she spent all the cash she made from pulling her teeth on drugs, and not on getting a permanent residence.

Damon pulled into the run-down hotel parking lot in his rental car. There were very few cars in the parking lot. This was one of those places that offered weekly rates. Luckily, it did not attract tourists. It mostly attracted homeless people and prostitutes. There was not a car parked in front of his woman's room. Hopefully, if she was inside, she would be alone. She told Damon that she never brought any of her clients here.

Damon looked around again to make sure that nobody was outside to see him. He knocked on the door. A light came on.

"Who is it? I'm busy in here." It was her voice.

"I'm back to see you. How are you?" Damon never told her his name, nor did he want to.

Damon waited. He stood back from the peephole so if she looked out she could see him. Instead he saw the curtain pull aside in the window. He waved and smiled his charming smile. She opened the door immediately.

"Hi. You're back. You're lucky that I'm here. Get inside quick." When she smiled, Damon looked at the gap in her gum where her front teeth used to be.

As soon as Damon walked into the room, she shut the door behind him and locked it. Damon saw the glass pipe laying beside the bed.

"I didn't think you would come back. I'm kinda glad that you did." The woman sat down on the bed.

Damon looked around the dirty hotel room. Her existence was no doubt a sad existence. Of course she was happy to see him. He offered her a way to make money and pay for her drug habit. He had always heard that drug addicts cared about nothing but drugs. Apparently, that was true.

"I wanted to see you. I just now realized that I know nothing about you. What's your name?" Damon wanted to talk to her. He knew that she had been smoking since her pipe was out. He liked it better when she could feel it. If he could talk to her for a few minutes, maybe she could feel a little bit more for what he had planned for her.

"What do you want my name to be?" She tried to be flirty.

"I want your real name. I don't want your name to be anything. I'm just trying to get to know you a little bit." Damon realized that he sounded rude. He tried to correct that. "I've thought a lot about you, ya know, since last time."

She was in thought. "You are very unique, aren't you? Okay, I'll play along, my name is Destiny."

"Destiny? That's your real name?" Damon stopped himself. It was hard to not be rude. "That is such a pretty name. Well Destiny, it's nice to officially meet you."

"Did you bring anything for me?" The hooker didn't bother asking him for his name. All she cared about was money.

"Of course I did. I want to keep you happy." Damon reached into his pocket. He pulled off a couple of bills. He didn't want her to see how much cash he had with him, at least not yet.

Destiny took the money from his hand. "Nice. I've missed you too." Lie. She missed the money.

"Do you still want to play with me? I didn't know if you would be happy to see me or not. You were such a good girl last time though." Damon thought about the last time. The images of the blood dripping down her mouth excited him.

"I like to play. What do you have in mind? What else did you bring for me?" She smiled. Destiny didn't care that her 2 front teeth were missing.

"I have some toys in the car. I'd rather show you than tell you. If that's okay." Damon got his car keys out of his pocket.

"Wait. I'd rather know first. How do I know that you're not some weirdo? You're not here to kill me or anything are you?" Destiny was in thought. Maybe the drugs she had smoked were starting to wear off.

"It's me. You can trust me. I didn't touch you last time, did I? I promise that I won't touch you this time either. I am a watcher. That's all. You don't have to do anything that you don't want to do. If you say no, then I'll leave. Simple as that." Damon was great at comforting people.

"Okay. But if I say no, I mean no." Destiny tried to sound stern.

"Of course. You have that right. I will never make you do anything that you don't want to do. I'm a man of my word. I don't want to make you mad. I want you to keep seeing me." Damon was genuine when he said that he wanted to keep seeing her. That was probably the only truth to his words.

"You want to make this a regular thing? I can't pull too many of my teeth. I need them to eat. After I saw you last time, I had to numb the pain before I ate for a few days. My mouth was sore. Plus, it was an occupational hazard for me. I use my mouth for my job. I had to take a few days off." She pointed to her missing teeth.

"No teeth. Not this time. Yes, I do want to make this a regular thing. Actually, I brought extra cash in case you agreed to keep seeing me. I need a way to find you. I brought money to pay for this room for 2 months. Under certain conditions." Damon had actually put thought into this.

"What conditions?" Destiny was interested.

"First, you go pay the hotel clerk now. Then you bring me back the receipt. I don't want you to accidentally smoke up all of your rent money. I'm only thinking of your well being. Then I want it to be made clear that you bring no other man here. If I show up, I don't want to run into a client." Damon was sure that would be enough to satisfy him.

"How about I just give you my cell phone number? Wouldn't that just be easier?" Destiny was actually making sense.

"That works too. But I may not always call first. I think it's fair that if I pay for the room, you do not work for any other man in this room. You can still do the conduct business in a car thing. Just not here." Damon didn't want to call Destiny from his number. He didn't want anything to be traceable.

"Deal. I don't bring men here anyways. I already told you that. You were special." Meaning that he paid more than most clients. "I do sometimes have a friend over. She works the corner with me. Can she still visit?" Destiny looked at Damon.

"Of course. That would be fine. Did you tell her

about me? Have you told anyone else?" Damon hadn't thought of that. He couldn't risk her telling anyone about him. He wanted privacy.

"Yes, I told her, but not anyone else. She didn't believe me. Until I showed her all of the cash you left here. She told me that I was lucky. She was actually working the same night that I was. She was bummed that you didn't pick her up from the underpass." Destiny was being honest.

Damon couldn't believe that another streetwalker actually envied Destiny for pulling out her own teeth. I guess there was no shame in being a drug addicted hooker. Cash was the only thing that mattered to them.

"Maybe someday, I can meet her too." Damon's head reeled with ideas.

They agreed upon their deal. Destiny went to prepay for the room, and Damon reminded her to bring him the receipt. He had plenty more cash for her that night. He went to his car to collect his own toys.

THE BIG D

Damon returned to the hotel room after getting the items from his car. Damon sat in his usual chair across from the bed and waited. Destiny shortly returned with the proof that she had paid her rent in advance. As Destiny entered the room, she saw what Damon was holding. It looked like a long pole. There was a small butane torch lighter setting on the table.

"What is that?" Destiny almost got scared. She did not know what she was seeing.

Damon held up the pole. It was a few feet in length of hard metal.

"I got this off of one of those auction internet places. It's actually an antique. I bought it special, just for you. If you look closely, you can see that it forms the letter "D" on the end." Damon held the object for her to see.

Destiny was anxious and did not sit on the bed just yet. "I see what it is. I just don't know what it is."

Damon turned on his charm. "It's okay. Trust me."

Destiny started speaking before Damon could elaborate. "What I see is a pole, and a lighter. Maybe I agreed to this way too soon. I knew that you were strange, but I didn't know how strange you were. What kind of kinky stuff is this?"

Damon tried to calm her down. "It's not kinky.

Just let me explain. You can always say no to it if you want. This is a brand. Like what they use on cows. You get it hot, and it leaves behind something like a tattoo. There are actually some tattoo parlors that do something very similar to this."

"How bad does it hurt?" Destiny reached for her glass pipe.

Damon wanted her to feel this. He didn't want her smoking. "Please, don't do that just yet. You can smoke all you want after this. It's my understanding that it only hurts for a few seconds. Your nerve endings should eventually numb the pain."

"How much are you gonna pay me to do this?" Money was Destiny's top concern.

Damon was happy. The negotiation had started. "I was thinking that $500 would be a fair price. What do you think? And remember, you can always say no. I will never force you to do anything that you don't want to do."

"Double that. I need $1000." Destiny thought that she was getting the upper hand in the deal.

Damon knew to start his price low. He anticipated her wanting more money. "Sure. I can do that." Damon fanned out the money on the table.

"Sex. What about sex? Do you ever want sex?" She was a hooker. The question made sense because that was the usual service that she was used to providing.

"Maybe. I don't know, not yet. I just want to watch you do this for the time being." Damon really hadn't thought about having sex with her. Maybe one day. Not right now. He had more important desires to fulfill.

"So how do you want to do this? I have no clue what I am doing, so you're gonna have to tell me what to do." Destiny was ready to earn the money.

"First, we need to heat up the brand. We are improvising here, so I brought this lighter. It might take longer to heat up. But that's okay. You aren't in a hurry are you?" Damon spoke slowly and calmly. He saw Destiny getting jittery.

"You do that part, okay?" Destiny couldn't believe that she had agreed to this.

Damon pulled out a pair of heat resistant gloves. "We both need to wear 1 of these. Safety is top priority." Damon laughed at his own little joke.

Destiny looked at Damon in disgust. "Sure. Whatever you say."

Damon turned on the small butane torch. He held the blue flame to the end of the metal shaft. He wasn't sure about this part. He didn't know how long it would take to heat it up. He had brought extra butane just in case he needed more. He moved the flame around the metal shaped "D" in small circular motions, hoping to heat it evenly. As he held the flame to the rod, it began to glow a dim orange color. Destiny watched, and shed a small tear. The heating process felt like an eternity to her.

Damon saw her getting scared. "It's okay. This won't hurt for very long. I am so proud of you for doing this. You are so brave."

The pole's tip began to glow a brighter orange.

"Take this with your gloved hand." Damon handed her the pole.

She held the pole. "Where do I do this? It's so long. It's kinda hard to handle. I don't wanna do it wrong."

Damon flashed his comforting smile at the hooker. "Just press it into your skin, firmly. Hold it there for a few seconds. Easy as that."

"I wanna do my thigh. I guess we didn't think this through." Destiny handed the long stick back to Damon. She stood and removed her pants. She was shaking with fear.

Damon ignored her trembling and put the small

torch to the "D" again. He wanted it hot enough to work. He wanted for her to feel this.

She sat back down on the bed in her little red lace panties. Damon handed it back to her. Destiny raised the pole. It was so long that it was almost awkward for her to get a good position over her thigh with it. She seemed afraid to hold it anywhere other than the handle. She saw the tip glowing with heat and gulped. Real fast she lowered the metal down onto her fresh thigh flesh. Destiny screamed in the highest pitch Damon had ever heard before in his life. Damon heard a quick sizzle. Destiny jerked back on the pole and dropped it beside the bed onto the carpet. The carpet also sizzled. Damon quickly picked the pole up with his gloved hand.

Damon voiced his disappointment. "That wasn't long enough. Half a second isn't long enough." Damon examined her wound. Her skin was flush. Small bits of skin were falling off. He wasn't sure if he was imagining it or not, but he thought he smelled a strange odor. Maybe it was burnt carpet. Melted plastic smell.

Destiny cried large tears. "It hurts so bad. I can't do it again. I won't do it again."

Damon could barely make out the image of the "D" on her red skin. It was sloppy. She hadn't held it still long enough in position for the "D" to form. It just looked like a mess of skin. Destiny reached for her glass pipe, and Damon didn't stop her this time.

Destiny inhaled a few lungfuls of the pipe smoke. Her crying began to slow down. "You're still paying me right? I did what you asked."

Damon tried to remain calm with his response, even though he was angry that she hadn't done it properly. "Of course I will pay you. Why don't you smoke for a little bit? Calm down. Then maybe you will let me do this to you. I will give you another $1000 if you let me brand you."

Destiny ignored him as she sucked on the piece of glass. It was as if he wasn't even there. All she cared about right now was the drugs. Damon got a thrill thinking about it being his hand that would hold the tool that hurt her. He had never done that before. He felt that same tickle in his pants, but now it was intensified. His excitement was magnified.

Destiny sat the pipe down. "How long will you hold it on me?"

"Not long. Just a few seconds. It won't hurt for long. Then you can smoke as much as you want to feel better. Just think of how much dope you could buy with all that cash." Damon held the lighter to the "D" again. It began to heat up. Damon's crotch grew.

"Okay." Destiny's speech was much more relaxed. She was obviously high, and ready to do anything to earn some drug money. She laid down on the bed and waited.

Damon got onto the bed and straddled the lower half of the hooker's legs. He held the branding iron with both hands above his head. He slowly lowered the tool. He wanted this to be perfect. Destiny could feel the heat from the iron before it made contact with her skin. Damon made sure to hold the tool still as he pressed it into her flesh.

He began counting. "One…"

Destiny tried to jerk, but since Damon was sitting on her legs she could only move the top part of her body. He made sure the tool was pressed deep enough into her skin so that even if she flinched it wouldn't mar the shape of the "D". Destiny released a sharp cry of pain.

"Two…" Damon was counting extra slow. He enjoyed the sound of her sizzling flesh. It sounded similar to a loud, constant snake hiss.

Each second felt like years to Destiny. Even though she had gotten high, she wasn't high enough to numb this kind of pain.

"Three..." Damon smelled a rancid smell. Almost like charcoal, but not quite. It was the smell of burning flesh.

"Four..." His counting was even slower with each number. Damon felt so powerful. This hooker was at his mercy. He was in full control.

Destiny writhed in pain. "Stop!" Destiny began to wail.

"Five." Damon raised the poker off her leg and carefully climbed down off of the woman.

He looked at her on the bed. She had quickly sat up and was looking at her leg as she cried. It didn't take her long to reach for her pipe and begin smoking.

Damon looked around the room and found an ice bucket. It appeared to be made of chrome, or some sort of other metal. He put the hot end of the iron into the bucket and propped the handle up against the wall. As she sat and smoked, Damon got down on his knees to examine her traumatized skin. The smell was still putrid. Damon breathed in deeper to get the full effect. Even though her flesh was red, he could see a perfectly formed "D". Damon was proud of himself. Where the letter had raised in her skin, he could see the top layers of dermis sloughed away. Damon rubbed his crotch.

Destiny paid no attention to Damon as he investigated her leg. All she cared about was getting high. Damon didn't mind. He had done what he had come to do. Damon felt his hardened manhood through his blue jeans. He had never been more turned on in his entire life.

Damon dug into his pocket and pulled out the largest wad of cash Destiny had ever seen. She stopped smoking long enough to look at all the money. Damon threw the cash on the bed.

Destiny called to Damon as he was walking out of the door. "You'll be back right? I hope I made you happy."

Damon confirmed with a head nod that he would be back. He shut the door behind him. This had been the most thrilling night of his life. Damon couldn't be happier.

THE SECOND EPISODE

"Welcome back ladies and gents to 'Easy Money". I am your host, Peter Conway. For those of you who missed our last episode, let me assure you that you are in for an exciting show. I wanna say thanks to all of our returning viewers. We have a very exciting show in store for you tonight. Our challenges will be harder, and cash prizes will be larger! Before we begin, do not try this at home. Viewer discretion is advised. Every task performed tonight is live, in front of a live studio audience. These are not stunts. What you are about to witness is real. We have medical staff here. Do not attempt this at home. Now, on with the show." Peter flashed his award-winning smile that the ladies loved.

The camera panned out across the audience. Once again, every seat was full. People cheered and clapped. The background music was drowned out by the crowd's excitement.

Mary watched from backstage. Tonight, at least their headsets worked. Peter had an earpiece in his ear. He could hear everything that Damon and Mary said.

"Okay, that's long enough. Lights on Peter." Mary directed her crew as to what to do. It was another responsibility that Damon had trusted with her.

Damon could of course hear everything that she said, so if he needed to correct her, then he would. However, he wanted to sit back and enjoy the show.

"Once again, we have special clear, glass blocks on stage, but we will get back to that later. First, let's meet our contestants." Peter turned to look at a huge screen behind him.

A video began playing. "I'm Joy. A widower."

The video showed Joy petting her cat. The video was filmed in Joy's home. The couch was worn. The walls were faded.

"Not much to say about myself. I'm in a lot of debt. When my husband died, that cut off most of my income. His funeral was expensive. I'm really close to losing my home. I do not want to be homeless. I think I have what it takes to win some 'Easy Money'. I loved watching Amy on the show. I want to be as good as her. She was so happy after the show. I want that to be me."

Joy walked onto the stage and waved to the crowd. Peter directed Joy to her podium.

"Welcome to the show Joy. Glad to have you here." Peter was a great host. "How do you feel?"

Joy smiled into the camera. "I feel good. I think this is gonna be great. I can't wait to meet my competition."

Peter turned and pointed to the screen behind him once again.

The character intro started playing.

"I'm Willy." Willy was dressed in overalls, in a big field. "I'm a farmer. Well, I was a farmer. The bank took my fields from me, and I have a baby on the way. I'm used to physical pain. When I was farming, my body ached everyday. Now, I gotta provide for my baby. I hope to make enough money to get my farm back, or at least buy another farm."

The redneck walked up to Peter and shook his

hand.

Peter was told to question each contestant. "Willy, do you have what it takes to win some easy money?"

Willy shook his head yes. "I sure do. I have plans for the future. Some cash would make it easier to make those plans come true."

Peter looked into the camera. "On this episode, we will have 3 contestants instead of 2. Let's meet our last player."

The video began to play. "I'm Ken. I know that I can win some 'Easy Money'. I used to perform in bodybuilding competitions. I made my body hurt on a daily basis. I can do this. You know what they say. Pain is just weakness leaving the body. I'm not weak. I need some money. I recently lost my job and the job market isn't looking too good right now. I have a family to support." The video showed pictures of Ken from some of his muscle man competitions.

The huge muscular man walked onto the stage and straight to his podium. He seemed to be overwhelmed by the lights and the noise. He looked around, dumbstruck.

"Ken, you're our last contestant today. Are you ready to play?" Peter didn't want to ask the man any difficult questions. By the look on Ken's face, Peter wasn't sure if he could even speak or not.

"Thank you for having me here." Ken's deep voice was shaky.

Peter began explaining the rules. "Contestants, as you can see, there are buzzers on your podium. I will give a challenge. You will buzz in to place a bid on said challenge. The lowest bidder gets to do the challenge and win the money. Easy enough. So the premise here is to do it cheaper than your competitors. Does everyone understand? Good. Let's see what we have in store for our competitors today."

Peter walked up to 3 large rectangular glass blocks. "As you can see, each block is 30 foot in length. The theme of tonight's episode is walking. Things that you walk on. Each round gets harder, and the cash amounts get higher. The first glass block is full of gravel. The second one is broken shards of glass. And for the last challenge, we have a raised metal plate. That looks easy enough right now, but when it comes time, there will be flames under the metal plate making it hot. Just to be clear, all challenges will be performed barefoot tonight. Let's get on with the show."

The crowd roared with excitement. Ken still looked kind of confused. Joy and Willy cheered along with the live audience. They looked excited and happy to be on the show.

Peter flashed his pearly whites. "Our first task is considered to be simple. Remember contestants, you need to buzz in before bidding. Our bidding will begin at $25,000! Walk on 30 feet of gravel, and you can win some easy money. Begin bidding now."

Ken buzzed in first even though all 3 of them had hit their buzzers.

Peter acknowledged him. "What's your bid Ken?"

"I'll do it for $26,000!" Ken was confused. He was bidding in the wrong direction.

Peter corrected him. "No Ken. You need to bid lower if you want to win."

Ken laughed at himself, along with the audience.

Joy and Willy both went for their buzzers.

"Yes Joy. What's your bid?" Peter asked.

"$24,000"

Willy buzzed in. "I'll go $23,000."

Ken buzzed in. "I get it now. $22,000"

Willy buzzed in again. "I will go as low as

$15,000"

Joy and Ken looked at each other. They shook their heads no.

Peter asked the contestants if anyone else wanted to bid. They both agreed that Willy could have it.

Willy sat on the chair that Peter provided. "I walk barefoot in many creeks at home. I've done this before. This shouldn't be so bad." Willy commented as he removed his shoes and socks.

Willy entered the glass block and took his first step. "Ouch! These rocks are more jagged than the creek bed at home."

Peter intervened. "It's okay Willy. Take your time. You are on your way to earning some easy money."

The man in overalls placed his other foot in front of him very gently. "That wasn't so bad. I can do this."

The camera zoomed in on the gravel. It did appear that a lot of the pointy edges were pointed upward. Mary had made sure to not let the prop guy rake it too smooth. Damon had instructed her to make it as difficult as possible. On Willy's next step you could hear him yelp. He jumped up, only to realize that jumping up made it worse. He had all of his weight impact the gravel with a high force. Willy screamed. Then he stood completely still. The camera zoomed in on the bottom of Willy's foot as he raised it across his opposite knee to examine it. The sole of his foot was beet red. There was a slight tear in his foot, which was barely bleeding.

Mary chimed in on her headset. "Peter, the audience is getting bored. Say something."

Peter began talking. "As you folks at home can see. Willy is not a professional gravel walker."

The live audience laughed.

"C'mon Willy. You're about halfway there. You say you have a baby on the way? $15,000 is a lot of diapers."

Peter looked at the audience. They didn't look bored to him. They were watching this man trudge along the gravel.

Peter must have said what Willy needed to hear. Willy inhaled deeply, and sped up. One foot forward. Next foot forward. The man was practically running. He made it to the other end of the block in practically no time. You could see the pain in Willy's eyes. His feet weren't as tough as he thought they were. Willy walked on his tiptoes back to the chair where he left his shoes. He rubbed loose pieces of gravel off the bottoms of his feet. There was a small mixture of blood in the loose gravel.

"How do you feel, Willy?" Peter was told to entertain the audience. He was also told prior to taping to conduct some sort of unofficial interview with the contestants after each challenge.

"I'm okay. I tell you what. I feel $15,000 richer is what I feel. Do I have to put my shoes back on?" The redneck knew that putting his shoes on would be painful.

Peter looked backstage at Mary for an answer.

"We have disposable shoe covers for them. We can't have the contestants bleeding all over the stage." Mary was borderline upset. She would've sworn that she already had told Peter about that, but maybe it had slipped her mind earlier.

Peter listened to his earpiece. "No. We have something for you."

A man ran out on the stage carrying the paper shoe covers. Willy slipped them onto his feet and tiptoed back to his podium. He stayed on his tiptoes for the rest of the show, not wanting to apply anymore pressure to his feet than he had to.

Music started playing and the audience cheered.

"Congratulations Willy. You have won $15,000 of

'Easy Money'. Let's get on with the next challenge." Peter approached the second block. "Full disclosure, that glass looks sharp. Just looking at it makes my own feet hurt. But since this task is harder, the price gets higher. For this task, the bidding begins at $100,000."

The audience gasped. The contestants looked at each other. That is a lot of money.

"Thanks to our sponsors," Peter directed the viewer's attention to adverts behind him, "we have more money to pay for these challenges."

The audience members whispered among themselves. This was the highest cash prize yet seen on the show. They were paying more to walk on glass than they paid Amy to shoot herself.

"Do any of our contestants have experience walking on glass?" Peter looked at the players.

Each player shook their heads no.

Peter began the bidding. Willy started bidding with them in the beginning, but his feet still hurt. As the bids got lower, he kept his mouth shut. He was willing to hurt his feet even more for such an obscene amount of money, but Joy and Ken kept lowering their bids. Joy and Ken were like rabid dogs fighting over a last piece of meat. They kept buzzing in and underbidding each other.

Joy had won the bid at $75,000. Ken finally gave up when he realized that she wasn't gonna stop bidding lower than him.

Joy was happy. "I'm getting ready to lose my home. My payoff price is $66,000. I can pay off my home! I can't believe this is really happening. Is this for real Peter?"

"Yes, this is real, Joy. But you must first complete the challenge. That means you have to walk barefoot, 30 foot, across broken glass." Peter tried to sound chipper and not worried.

"I can do this in a matter of minutes. That means that I will own my house for the rest of my life! I can do this!" Joy looked at the crowd.

The live audience whooped and hollered.

Joy removed her shoes and entered the block. She stood frozen as she looked at the tiny pieces of glass that laid before her. "I've seen people do this on TV. It can't be too bad."

Peter shook his head in agreement. "I believe in you Joy. Just think about your lovely home. You're a short walk away from being a proud homeowner. That has to be exciting."

Damon watched the crowd. People in the crowd shook their heads yes in agreement. Damon knew that this show would get great ratings now. He only imagined how many viewers would want to be on the show because of the huge payouts. He knew then that their ratings would be good enough to get a permanent time slot from the network.

Joy very slowly took her first step onto the glass. The studio was quiet, and due to great microphone placement, you could hear a slight crunch as she lowered her foot onto the clear pieces of pain. Joy let out a grunt of discomfort. Joy decided to take a long stride. She put her other foot forward and tried to distribute her weight evenly on her foot. After hearing the slight crunch, Joy shrieked in pain. Her face cringed.

"Talk to me Joy. How are you feeling?" Peter decided to break the silence.

"It's a bit uncomfortable, but I can do this." Joy remembered that Willy went fast over the gravel. Maybe it would hurt less if she went fast. Joy took 3 quick steps, yelping in pain with each step. She began to cry. "I don't think I can do this, Peter. Do I have to do it?"

Peter shook his head no. "You don't have to do anything that you don't want to do. But you are a good way into the block. Almost halfway. If you exit through the door that you entered, you leave with no money. If you make it to the other side, you can pay off your house. The choice is yours."

Mary's face turned red and she started hyperventilating.

"Just breathe. Take your time. Calm down." Peter tried to coax her to the other door.

Joy wedged her fists on both sides of the narrow rectangular block. She started breathing slower and talking to herself real low. "I can do this. I'm almost halfway there. I can do this. I can do this."

The crowd began chanting Joy's name in unison. "Joy. Joy. Joy."

Joy looked into the crowd. The camera zoomed in on the tears streaming down her face. Joy balanced on one foot and extended her other leg as far out in front of her as she could. She tried to place her foot down gently, but instead she had overstepped. Joy fell forward into the glass. She caught most of the fall on the palm of her hands. She was sobbing at this point. She quickly stood up and looked at her hands. The camera zoomed in on the shards of glass protruding from the tender skin of her palms. Small lines of blood flowed off her hands. The blood dripped on the glass at her feet. She had also fallen on a knee, which was also bloody.

The audience went quiet.

"Joy, are you okay?" Peter knew it was a stupid question as soon as he asked it.

Joy couldn't answer due to all the crying she was doing. She mustered what little bit of will that she had left and ran to the other end of the trail of glass, screaming every time her feet hit the glass. The crowd rose to their feet and cheered. Peter quickly opened the glass door. Joy collapsed onto the stage screaming like a crazed woman.

Medical rushed onto stage. The cameras zoomed in on the soles of Joy's feet. Glass sparkled in the lighting. The bottoms of her feet were riddled with broken pieces of glass and blood. Medical staff did not wear microphones, and Joy's microphone was only picking up her crying.

Mary quickly went to work. "Turn Joy's mic off. Peter, comment, say something."

"Let's take a second here and discuss what a daring task Joy just completed." Peter was thinking of the right words to say. "She was so brave. I couldn't imagine walking across all of that glass. She earned that money. She can now pay off her house, isn't that great?"

The medic gave Mary a thumbs up. She had Joy's mic turned back on.

"I (deep breath) choose to quit.(Deeper breath) But I won $75,000 right?" Joy tried to get the words out between sobs.

Peter shook his head. "Yes. Congratulations Joy. You won $75,000 of 'Easy Money'! Audience, let's hear it for Joy."

As the crowd roared, a man in scrubs came out on the stage with a stretcher. The 2 medical men helped Joy onto the stretcher and wheeled her away.

"As they say, the show must go on. Are we ready contestants?" Peter looked to Ken and Willy. Willy still stood on his tiptoes from the pain.

Both contestants cheered, ready to get on with the show.

"Our next, and last challenge is the hot plate." Peter turned to the last block. Flames started under the metal plate. "As you see, fire is heating up that metal plate. The rectangular block is very well ventilated through the roof. We don't want any of our players suffocating in there. However, it will be very hot. I'm not a scientist, and I don't know degrees of heat, but that plate will be hot and painful."

The audience laughed. Peter was told to keep the audience entertained. He felt like he was doing his job well.

"This task is considered to be very difficult. The bidding will start at $150,000." Peter looked at the audience and they gasped once again at the high cash prize.

Ken and Willy kept buzzing in, trying to underbid each other. This amount of money could possibly be life changing for these contestants. It would certainly make their lives easier. Ken went as low as $100,000 and Willy went silent. He looked at his feet and the small amount of blood that had soaked through his disposable shoes.

Willy shook his head no. "I might regret this, but I won't get any lower."

Ken jumped up and down. "Yes! That's a lot of money."

Peter agreed. "It sure is. I wish you the best of luck."

The crowd was silent as the muscle man removed his shoes.

"So, Ken what are your thoughts?" Peter used the quiet time for a brief mini interview.

"Fast. Speedy and swift. I'm gonna move as fast as I can. Then be rich. Those are my thoughts." Ken was ecstatic.

Ken approached the glass block and opened the door. He could feel the heat before he even stepped inside of the rectangle. The door closed behind him as he took off running on the hot metal plate. He twisted his face in pain and grunted as he sprinted as fast as he could. It was over in seconds, and kind of disappointing. Ken exited the other side of the glass block in what felt like mere seconds. As soon as Ken stepped onto the stage he dropped down onto his buttocks and looked at his feet. The camera zoomed in on the oozing skin. His flesh was black and mangled, as if it was falling off the bone. A clear fluid was oozing out.

Peter sniffled his nose. "What's that smell? Do you smell that? Oh, that's gross. Ken, how do you feel?"

Ken smiled. "I feel rich. I can barely feel my feet anymore. That can't be good can it?"

The gas flames turned off, and the camera zoomed in on the metal plate. Skin deposits were left behind. The camera zoomed back in on what little skin was left on Ken's feet. There were blisters already starting to develop.

Ken was hysterical. He was possibly in shock. "Are those my feet? Where's my feet? Why can't I feel my feet?"

Mary had Ken's microphone cut off. Medical took a stretcher on stage and a curtain lowered.

Peter turned to the camera. "Do not try this at home. What you have seen tonight is totally real. The challenges were not faked by smoke and mirrors. There was no costume makeup involved in any of this show tonight. Thank you for watching. And if you think that you have what it takes to win easy money, please check out our casting call on our website. Do not, I repeat, do not send us videos of you injuring yourself. We will not pick you as a contestant if you do. Until next time, I'm Peter Conway. Goodnight viewers." Peter waved bye to the cameras as the credits rolled.

AFTER THE SHOW

Damon pushed the button on his headset. "Mary. I need you, now."

"Yes sir, I am coming your way." Mary did not want to leave her boss waiting. She rushed to him.

"That show was boring. I could have went to sleep! Gravel was stupid. The glass was okay. It was great when she fell down, but that hot plate! Who's stupid idea was that? It was over so fast! And Peter. Someone needs to train Peter on how to entertain a live audience! I'm so mad that I can't even see straight." Damon's eyes glazed with contempt.

"I'm sorry. But we don't know how these challenges are gonna work out. It's not like we have a rehearsal. We can't practice this stuff in real life. The audience seemed happy. I think they liked what they saw." Mary tried to say anything to make her boss happy.

"The money." Damon stopped talking to think. "They liked the money amounts. That's probably the only thing that impressed them. And that guy's feet at the end. They looked like they were in bad shape. Maybe that will keep the viewers hooked. The network only gave us one more show. We need to make it a good one! Do you hear me?"

"Yes sir. I hear you." Mary hung her head as she walked away. She didn't think the show was that bad.

Mary went to her office before heading to the hospital to check on the players. She turned on her computer, to see what people were saying about the show. The big buzz was the large money amounts. 'Easy Money' still had a chance. It wasn't as bad as Damon had made it out to be in his head.

She knew the drill. She had to go to the hospital and try to prep the contestants for the interviews that were coming. She remembered that Willy hadn't gone to the hospital. She called Willy's cell phone to see where he was. He didn't answer. His pregnant wife answered instead. Mary found out that Willy was already speaking to a reporter inside the studio. Mary rushed to hear what he had to say. Damon would kill her if he said anything that would make the show look bad.

"No, I didn't make enough money to buy a farm, but I think I could maybe make a down payment on one. My feet don't hurt that bad. I told them that I don't even need a doctor. I've suffered worse than this." Willy was giving a multiple reporter interview. Apparently, the reporters were waiting outside the studio for a chance to talk to a contestant. Reporters were screaming questions, each reporter louder than the last reporter, so that their question would be heard.

Mary rushed to Willy's side, and ushered him and his wife back inside the studio. Mary turned into a person for a minute. She finally stopped being a producer long enough to be a human being. She convinced Willy to go to the hospital. She was truly concerned with his well-being. She told him that he should at least let them disinfect his wounds. Maybe get something for the pain.

Mary loved her job, and she wanted to keep it, but her conscience would feel better if she was concerned about these people's well beings. A man had practically melted all the skin off his feet, and Damon called the episode boring. Her boss had turned into a monster. She had helped create a monster.

Mary would have to navigate a fine line, between pleasing her conscience and her boss.

There seemed to be no pleasing Damon. He had seemed so happy with Mary before the episode. Mary was sure that she hadn't done anything wrong. Damon's mood swings were getting to her. He seemed to slowly be changing to an even worse version of himself. Damon had never been pleasant to be around, but now he was just extremely irritable.

Mary didn't have time to worry about Damon. She could only do what she needed to do. Her top priority was checking on the contestants. She decided that in order for her to feel good about herself, she had to start caring more about the players. Mary went to the hospital to see Ken and Joy. She told her herself that she wouldn't even worry about discussing interviews with them. Their health care would be her only concern.

'Easy Money' was just a show. Ken and Joy were people. People who willingly hurt themselves in exchange for cash, but people nonetheless. Maybe the show did prey on poor people. Mary felt bad for the widow who was only trying to save her home. If Damon had never come up with this idea of a pain show, Joy would have surely found another way to save her home.

What had become of this world? Mary didn't know who was crazier. Damon for coming up with the idea, or the contestants? Damon just wanted ratings. At least Joy had earned the money to save her home. Mary tried to think of the good things the show did. If she dwelled too long on her conscience, she just might go crazy herself. Mary tried to push her conscience aside. She had to work. Mary kept telling herself that it was just a job.

For all she knew, Damon's mood would swing back to happy. Trying to figure that man out was like trying to decipher something written in some alien language. There was no figuring Damon out. She would just have to tolerate his childish outbursts. The only thing she had control over was herself. That was all that she could focus on right now. If that meant pleasing her conscience, that's what she would do.

DAMON'S PLANS IN MOTION

Damon made sure to get Mary to cast Mr. Marty Blevins.

"I don't understand. Who is this guy?" Mary was confused as to why her boss wanted this guy.

"He was in with that first group of contestants for the first episode. His bio stuck with me. I just think that he will make a good contestant. Contact him. Cast him. Ensure that he passes the psych evaluation. Coach him I guess." Damon thought of his plans and was actually filled with joy.

"Coach him? Is that ethical? I haven't helped anybody else pass their evaluation. Why start now?" Mary wasn't sure what Damon was up to.

"Just give him a heads up about it. Tell him to get his head on straight before he sees the doctor. What I'm asking of you is basic. Simple. Do it." Damon got frustrated with Mary's questions.

Mary sat at her desk and skimmed Marty's short bio. Nothing stood out to her. He was a college student, trying to make ends meet like any other college student. Nothing screamed desperation. He wasn't losing his home. He didn't have a sick kid. This didn't make sense to Mary. His bio was pretty much the same generic bio that they received from the average person.

Mary picked up the phone and called Marty Blevins. She set up an initial meet and greet. Maybe after meeting this guy, maybe then it would make sense.

Damon had also asked that Mary sit out for the writing of the next episode's challenges. He said that everything they had come up with together had made a boring show. Mary didn't mind. It would give her more free time to concentrate on her other duties.

Damon sat with the writers that would still work with him.

"The feet episode was boring. We need more blood. More excitement. We have a huge budget for this episode. Ideas? Go." Damon asked for them to help liven up his show.

The first writer spoke up. "Knives are classic."

Damon vetoed the idea. "Boring. Not creative enough."

"How about jumping from heights? That could be grotesque." Another writer thought he had a good idea.

"Maybe." Damon just wasn't sure of that one.

The writer tried again. "Hands. Bloody hands. Something to make bloody hands. You'd have to pay well if they are risking losing a hand, but it could be exciting."

Damon thought for a second. "I like it. I'm thinking over the top. How about a wood chipper?"

A writer laughed. "No way would someone be dumb enough to stick their hand in a wood chipper.

They would most definitely lose a limb."

"Not even for a half million dollars?" Damon smirked at the writer. "A man just burned his feet to the bone for a fraction of that."

The writers shook their heads. "That could work. I was thinking more like a garbage disposal."

Another writer gave his idea. "I was thinking a fan. Like a metal one. What are they called industrial fans or something? I don't know, I'd have to check with a hardware store or something. That could injure a hand."

"Finally. We are getting somewhere. These injuries sound pretty interesting. We can work with this. You check into the garbage disposal. See if the prop guy thinks he could get it on stage." Damon pointed at another guy. "You look into fans, get something that looks painful. Mark out all name brands. Nothing with a logo. I'm not sure on the wood chipper yet. Let me look into it. Tentatively, I think this could be a good episode. Good work guys."

Damon decided to research wood chipper. He didn't know much about them, but there was recently a news story about a guy who tried to kick tree branches into a wood chipper. The machine somehow sucked the guy in, and it killed him. After watching videos of how wood chippers turn trees into tiny mulch like chips, he only imagined what it could do to a person. This was the gore that the show needed. This would be perfect for Damon's plan.

After a long day of planning, and trying to set up the third episode, life kept throwing Damon curve balls. First he got a phone call from his boss. Ken gave a bad interview. His feet were so burnt up. He had several skin graft surgeries ahead of him. This made Damon mad to no end. It was a boring challenge. It didn't give the vigor to the show that he expected. In Damon's eyes, it was Ken's fault for agreeing to do it. An adult man made a decision to do something stupid. Damon did not feel responsible.

Then the writers kept calling Damon. According to legal, an industrial fan would not be feasible for a prop on the show. In order for it to cause injury, the safeguard would have to be removed. Legal said that was a no go. Also, the writers voiced their concerns about using a garbage disposal. They said it would be hard to set the perimeters of the challenge. That it was too hard to stipulate how deep the contestant would have to insert their hand into the garbage disposal. BLAH BLAH. Damon was tired of hearing all of the negativity.

"Mr. Blevins, thank you for meeting with me today." Mary eyed Marty Blevins up and down. He looked years older than he actually was.

"Sure." Marty did not seem like a talkative man.

"As I said on the phone, we reviewed your application to be on 'Easy Money'. Are you still interested?" Mary did not see anything special about Marty.

"I sure am." Once again, Marty answered in a very short response.

"Okay. Tell me about you." Mary decided not to ask a question. She wanted something with an open ended response.

"Umm... I'm a college student. And I'm local." Marty was good at skirting questions.

"Right, I see that here on the application. I need to

know what would make you a good candidate for the show." Mary was getting fed up.

"Money. I need money. Simple as that." Marty shrugged his shoulders and raised his hands up on both sides.

"Is there a reason why you need money?" Mary tried to dig deeper.

"Yes." Once again, Marty gave a one word answer.

"Okay. For what reason?" Mary hoped to finally be getting somewhere.

"I don't know you well enough to tell you." Marty got smart with her.

"Well, if you want to be on the show, I need to know. This is unofficial. Everything you tell me today is private. It will not be on the show, I promise." Mary wondered if she had maybe stumbled upon why Damon was so interested in this contestant.

"Let me be hypothetical. What if someone had a bad habit? A bad habit that costed money. Then what if said person owed bad people money for that bad habit." Marty looked at Mary to see how she would respond. He decided to forgo the fact that he was also behind on child support. He feared the people that he owed money to more than he feared jail. He needed Mary to understand the seriousness of his debt.

Mary shook her head yes. "Now, we're getting somewhere. That makes sense. Have you ever been declared mentally ill?" Mary wondered how Damon had known of this man's debt, and his bad habit. As far as she knew, her boss didn't gamble or have any involvement in drugs.

"No. Never." Marty shook his head no as he spoke.

"Good. I have to have you see a psychiatrist. They have to declare you as a sane person before you can appear on the show." Mary didn't know how to coach someone to pass a psych evaluation like her boss instructed her to.

"I need money. Along with a hypothetical bad habit, comes lying. Trust me, I know how to say what a doctor would want to hear." Marty finally smiled.

Mary was relieved. Marty did not need coaching. Now she had a little bit of information on Marty. She decided to try to connect that information to Damon. She didn't know how she was going to do it, but she could try. Maybe Damon had some secrets of his own. Mary placed a phone call to a trusted friend that owned a private investigation company.

DAMON'S OBSESSION EVOLVED

Work was too stressful. The show wasn't doing as well as he had expected. This was not easy. Damon was losing his mind trying to make everything perfect. He had to keep his eye on the prize. There was a bigger picture here, that would not only benefit the show, but also his own inner monster.

Damon rented a car and drove to the seedy motel across town. He didn't bother to call even though he had Destiny's phone number. He had cash. She wanted cash. Luckily for him, she had a habit that consumed a lot of money. It worked in his favor. Destiny would never have enough money. She needed Damon's money to feed her growing habit. That meant she was weak to all of his requests.

Damon pulled his baseball cap over his face to try to conceal his identity, just in case anyone was watching him. He didn't want to be recognized. Even though he was never on camera for the show, in his own mind, Damon was a known and recognizable man. Damon put more importance on himself than he deserved.

He stopped outside of Destiny's door. He heard her talking to someone inside her room. It was a female's voice. Damon stood and listened, but he couldn't make out what they were saying. Instead of knocking, Damon turned to leave. As soon as he turned around to walk back to his car, Destiny's motel room door opened. She was saying her goodbyes to her friend, and saw Damon.

"That's him. He's here." Destiny told her friend.

Damon turned around to look at Destiny. He wanted to know who she was talking to. He needed to know who knew about his visits to Destiny. There was a woman standing with Destiny. She looked familiar. Damon recognized her as one of the street walkers he watched the first day in the underpass.

"Hi. Is this a bad time?" Damon smiled innocently at the women.

"It's never a bad time for you. This is my friend. Would you like to come in and meet her?" Destiny was truly happy to see Damon.

Damon's day had just gotten better. He knew that this would be a good night.

"I'm Amber. I work with Destiny if you know what I mean. Like sometimes we work with the same client at the same time, if you catch my drift." Amber put her arm around Destiny's waist. The woman's teeth were just as rotten as Destiny's had been when she pulled them.

Damon's attention was directed to the raised skin on Destiny's thigh. It was a scabbed over letter 'D'. He pointed to it. "That looks good."

Destiny looked down at her thigh. "Well, it hurt

like you wouldn't believe. It's still kinda sore, but it's nothing that I can't handle."

Amber looked at Damon. "What's the d stand for?"

Damon hated it that she was asking questions. "Nothing. I just got it cheap online."

"When Destiny told me about you, I thought she was lying. I thought her teeth just fell out, and she made up a story. Until I saw this." Amber pointed at the brand. "I told her this reminds me of that new game show."

"What new game show?" Damon played dumb.

"I dunno. I think it's called 'Easy Money'. People get paid to hurt themselves. Do you live under a rock or something?" Amber was getting smart with Damon.

Damon did not like Amber's tone. "No. In a house. I don't watch television. Maybe I should check that show out."

Destiny quickly changed the subject. "I'm so glad that you're back. You have good timing. Do you wanna play with the both of us?"

Damon shook his head no. "I actually came to ask you for a favor. I need something. I was wondering if you could hook me up with some of that?" Damon pointed to the nightstand. He knew her drug kit was in there.

"You're in luck. That's why Amber is here. I just filled up myself…"

Amber abruptly put her hand over Destiny's mouth. "Shut up. He could be a cop."

"Trust me I'm no cop. Look at her teeth, and her leg." Damon flashed his charming smile.

"I guess maybe. But I don't know." Amber still wasn't sure of Damon.

"What can I do to prove that I'm not a cop? I'll do anything. I just need a hookup." Damon was convincing.

"Shut up Amber. He's my best client. Trust me, he's not a cop." Destiny was starting to get mad.

"Prove it." Amber was stubborn. "What's your name anyways?"

"Amber, I said shut up. Stop now. Or I want you to leave." Destiny got madder.

"You said that he doesn't even want sex. He sounds like a cop to me!" Amber got tense.

Destiny stood up and opened her door. "Leave now, Amber. Right now!"

As Amber walked out the door she looked at Destiny. "Don't call me from jail. I won't bail you out." Amber left in a huff.

Destiny quickly apologized to Damon for her friend.

"It's okay." Damon did not like how Amber had questioned him, but he didn't want to appear upset to Destiny. "It's a shame that we couldn't have set a play date with the 3 of us. Anyways, I'm short on time. Like I said. I just want a hookup. I'll pay double."

"I didn't even know that you smoked. I would share with you, ya know." Destiny smiled and rubbed her tongue in the gap of her missing teeth.

"I only smoke sometimes." Damon lied. "And I never drive when I do. I've been arrested before. I try to play it safe. Can you help me out?"

"Anything for you. She didn't scare you off did she? I can talk to her. She's moody. I'm really sorry. This gig is the best thing that's happened to me in a while." Destiny was worried that she had blown it with her best client.

"I assure you, this is perfect. You are great. I love our time together. I will be back, but now I have to run."

Destiny sold the drugs to Damon. He had somewhere to be. It was time for him to leave.

Damon drove to the underpass. Luckily, Amber was there standing on the corner. There was nobody else around. He guessed that even hookers had slow days at work sometimes.

Damon slowly drove up next to Amber. "Hey, I'm sorry. Things didn't go well back there. Let me prove to you that I'm no cop. I was hoping the 3 of us could set something up. I'm sure Destiny told you that I paid well." Damon held up $500 for Amber to see.

"What's that for?" Amber kept her eyes on the money.

"I'd like to spend some time with you. Actually, I like how your legs look in that short skirt. You turned me on. I was thinking maybe we could spend some time together." Damon turned on his charm.

"I don't have any drugs on me. So if you are a cop, you know that a prostitution charge is no big deal." Amber was still leery of Damon, but she wanted that cash.

"I'm not a cop. Get in." Damon handed Destiny the cash. "I know a little private spot on the beach. Let me prove it to you that I'm not police."

Amber reluctantly got into the car.

During the short drive to the beach Damon was lost in his own thoughts. It was dark. He was in a rental car. She was a drug addicted hooker. She could go missing. Nobody would notice. Or maybe they could just talk. Maybe he could pay her off, and make her a part of his favorite past time. He didn't know how he was going to handle this situation.

Damon drove to a secluded spot and decided to play things by ear.

"I love it here. I come here sometimes to be alone." Damon took Amber by the hand, and led her down a trail that led to the water.

"And how does this prove that you're not a cop?" Amber still had an attitude even though he had just given her $500.

Damon looked around. They were completely alone, with nothing but the sound of the waves and the darkness.

"Would a cop do this?" Damon started unzipping his jeans.

"I don't know. From what I hear, you're not into sex. Right?" Amber was still questioning Damon.

"You're partly right." He pulled his pants completely off. "I'm not into sex with Destiny. You though, you turn me on. You look younger. You're just sexier than she is." Damon looked at her. She wasn't more attractive than Destiny, but he knew that was what she wanted to hear. "I like you. You play it smart and safe. I was hoping maybe I could get to know you." Damon reached for his pants on the sand and pulled out more money. "How much do you want, I'll pay you well."

Amber eyed the money. "For what? I'm not into all that stuff you make Destiny do."

Damon knew that this girl just wouldn't play along with his game. Still, he had to control his temper and play it cool. "I want you. No games. I want you naked, right here right now." Damon rubbed his crotch through his boxer shorts.

"Straight sex. No pain." Amber tried to set some boundaries.

"Well, I was hoping for more than straight sex. I

like oral too. But of course, no pain." Damon agreed to her rules. "Please, I'm begging. Look at this." Damon pulled down his boxers to reveal his hard on. "Can you undress, extra slow for me?"

Amber started swaying her body. Maybe she used to be a stripper. She slowly raised her shirt, like Damon instructed. After she removed her bra, she squeezed both of her breasts.

"Oh, you're good. That's great. What else do you wanna show me?" Damon acted interested.

Amber turned her back to Damon, and bent over as she lowered her skirt.

"You have some nice legs. I like how you tease me. The panties, lose the panties." Damon started to stroke himself.

Amber looked Damon in the eyes. "Yeah, how much are you gonna pay me?"

"How much do you want? You like money? Are you sure you aren't up for any games?" Damon tried flashing his charming smile.

Amber stopped swaying. "No. I said no pain. I can leave right now."

"Shh. It's okay. Just please take your panties off." Damon was begging.

Amber cautiously looked at Damon. He stuck cash in her panties. Amber removed the bills, and slowly lowered her panties.

"I'm so turned on right now. Are you sure you don't want to play?" Damon didn't want sex. He wanted to see blood.

"Yes! I'm sure! Quit asking!" Amber picked up her panties and started putting them back on.

Damon could no longer control his temper. She had asked him too many questions. He couldn't risk her putting it together that 'Easy Money' was his show. Damon didn't know what to do. He didn't think. He just acted.

Damon wrapped his hands around Amber's thin neck. She tried to beat him with her closed fists, but he was just too strong. Damon stared the hooker straight into her eyes as he strangled her. She tried to speak, but her sounds came out as gurgles. She tried to kick, but that didn't stop Damon. He squeezed harder, until her lifeless body fell limp. Damon dropped her body to the ground and stared at her. He laid next to her.

"I gave you an option. I just wanted to play. You were just too smart. But I want to thank you. I have never felt so powerful in my life." Damon was actually talking to her dead body.

Damon knew he had to weigh down her dead body so she would sink in the ocean. Damon went to his car, and got a knife. He knew that when gas builds up in a body, it makes it float in water. He took the blade and made several stabs, until her body was riddled with gashes and holes. The wounds leaked, but they didn't bleed in a way that Damon expected. He flipped the body over and made more holes in her body with the sharp blade. By the time he was done stabbing her, his arms were tired. He guessed that he had made a few hundred holes in her body. He used her clothes to tie heavy rocks to her body. Just for kicks, he shoved small rocks down her throat, and into her vagina. He started putting rocks in some of the wounds that he made, wedging stones between muscle and flesh. He even embedded stones in some of her inner organs. He looked at her lifeless body, slowly leaking blood. Her gaping wounds were stuffed with stones. Damon hoisted Amber into the water and watched her as she sank. He got into the water, and washed the blood off his own body.

Damon got dressed. He was so far down the beach, hopefully, she wouldn't be found for a very long time. Plus, she was a streetwalker, and a drug addict. She probably wouldn't be missed for a very long time.

BEFORE THE SHOW

Damon had planned a great show for tonight. Even though this was the last episode the network had given him permission for, Damon knew that after tonight, the show's ratings would skyrocket. This would be huge. He looked around at the live audience, his audience. They were there to see him. These people wanted to see his creation. Damon felt like the most powerful man in the world. All of these people were his followers. His life's work was finally appreciated. These viewers understood the importance of what Damon was doing.

Damon was proving that people didn't care about other people. People cared about money. People cared about amusement. He was giving people the freedom to finally be who they wanted to be. They wanted to watch people get hurt. It was nothing to be ashamed of. It was entertainment. Just like any other mind-numbing television show. 'Easy Money' was different. It wasn't. It did the opposite. It made people think.

Damon basked in his glory. He knew what was in store for the season finale. This episode would have the shock value that Damon craved. The fact that it would give him self gratification in another way was just an added bonus.

Mary was backstage. She still had to go to each of the contestants waiting areas to give them the usual pep talk. It was her job to fill their head with dreams of huge cash prizes. Pain was temporary, money was real, blah blah.

Mary had called her private investigator friend several times to try to figure out Damon's bond with Marty Blevins. Her friend hadn't answered the phone, and she had left several voicemails. She did see his value as a contestant, but she still couldn't figure out how Damon knew. People with expensive habits need money. That made him willing to do anything for a buck. Unfortunately, they couldn't put that in his character introduction video. The other 2 contestants looked promising too. They almost reminded her of Amy, the star of the first episode. They were willing to do anything for cash.

As Mary entered Marty's waiting room, she was greeted with a cloud of smoke. She waved her hand in front of her face to try to see in front of her. She cleared the smoke and saw Marty with a pipe.

"What are you doing? We're going live very soon!" Mary coughed as she tried to speak in the cloud.

Marty sat perfectly still and didn't say a word.

"Marty! Are you okay? Should I call medical?" Mary didn't know if she was mad or worried.

"No. I'm fine." Marty finally said something.

"What are you doing? You can't smoke in here. What is that drugs?" Mary panicked. She needed 3 contestants tonight. She couldn't lose Marty. Damon really wanted Marty on the show.

"It was sitting here. On the table. I thought maybe

you left it for me. Ya know, like to loosen me up before the show." Marty tried to act innocent.

"No. I did not leave drugs in here for you! Are you crazy? I can't put you on now. What am I gonna do? Why am I asking you? You're high!" Mary thought about telling Damon.

"I'm fine. I wanna be on the show. I can still do it. I won't smoke anymore, I promise." Marty was making sense.

Against her better judgement, Mary agreed to let Marty still be on the show. Her job was on the line, and she could not afford to disappoint Damon.

SEASON FINALE

"Good evening folks! I'm Peter Conway, welcoming you to another episode of 'Easy Money'. Viewer discretion is advised. Don't try this at home. Tonight's episode is an exciting episode, with the highest cash prize we have ever offered! Like I've said before, I cannot stress this enough, do not try this at home. Who's ready to play 'Easy Money'?"

Damon watched as his supporters cheered. It was all because of him. He couldn't wait until they saw how exciting tonight's episode would be.

"We have a theme with each show. Tonight's theme is hands. Oh, I just shudder when I think about something happening to my hands. But we have some brave people here tonight. Let's meet our players." Peter turned to the video screen.

There was a video of a woman sitting next to a hospital bed. "I'm Laura. This is my mom. She's been sick for sometime now. I just can't imagine life without my mom." Laura began to cry. "The insurance company refuses to pay for her surgery, so I'm gonna win for her."

Laura walked out on the stage and heard the audience let out sounds of sympathy. "Aww."

Laura tried her best to smile. When the crowd started applauding she took a bow, and assumed her place behind the podium.

Peter offered his best heartfelt smile. "Welcome Laura. That's just a shame about your mom. I wish you the best of luck."

"Thanks for having me Peter. If anyone needs money, it's me." Laura tried to sound optimistic.

Another video started playing on the huge screen. There was a woman standing in front of a huge house. A really expensive car was in the background. The attractive woman looked into the camera. You could tell that she wasn't shy. "I'm Kelly. I'm going through a really bad divorce, and I'm gonna lose all of this." Kelly motioned her hand behind her. "I like money. That's all there is to it. When the show started doing huge cash amounts, I decided that I wanted to be on the show. I'm materialistic. If those other people can do it, I can too. I don't want to have to get a job."

Mary shook her head about this contestant. She just loved money. She didn't have a sob story. After a solid interview with Kelly, Mary was convinced that Kelly would do anything for cash. The network thought it would be a good spin for the show. They wanted the world to see that the show wasn't just targeting poor people.

Kelly walked on stage, dressed in what was obviously an expensive dress. The audience laughed, and Kelly did not look pleased.

Peter didn't know what to say. "Welcome Kelly."

"I'm glad to be here Peter. I just want to make money. I don't necessarily need money. I'm just spoiled. And for all those people who laughed at me, I'm gonna prove to you how much I love money. Watch. I know that I can do this." Kelly was spunky.

The audience laughed, but eventually cheered for Kelly.

Next was Marty's video. Marty was in a library,

presumed to be a college library. "I'm Marty. A college student. I do not want to start my life out in debt. School is expensive. I need some 'Easy Money' to pay tuition. I don't have parents to help me out. Plus, I have a kid to feed. I have watched the show since the very beginning. I'm a huge fan. I'm just glad that I'm on the show now, with the higher cash amounts. I'm excited about this."

Marty walked out on the stage. Mary hoped that he could still do the show. He wasn't obviously high, but Mary knew that he wasn't in his right mind.

"Good to meet you Marty. Do you have what it takes to win 'Easy Money'?"

Peter was starting to sound like a generic host with the usual questions. Damon told Mary to help Peter be a better host. It was just another shortcoming that Damon noticed in Mary's work performance. It didn't matter. Tonight's episode would be all the excitement the viewers needed. Damon sat back and got comfortable, ready to watch the show.

"Like I said Peter, I'm a huge fan. It's great to be here."

Mary was relieved that Marty was capable of answering a simple question. She didn't know what to expect after he was smoking whatever he was smoking.

"The rules are simple. There will be 3 challenges tonight." Peter held up 3 fingers. "The contestants will bid and the lowest bidder gets to complete the given challenge. Buzz in with the buzzers atop your podium. After you complete the challenge, you win 'Easy Money'. Simple enough?"

The contestants shook their heads in agreement. They understood the rules. The audience roared with anticipation. Lights directed the viewer's attention to 3 glass cubes on the stage.

"As you can see, we have 3 glass cubes on stage. Each task will be completed in the cubes. With the theme being hands, each challenge revolves around hand injuries. In the first cube we have a vat of deep fryer grease. I believe that it is warmed up to about 350 degrees. Next we have a drill press. Then we have a wood chipper. Wait, is that right? A wood chipper?" Peter couldn't believe his eyes. He turned to Mary for confirmation.

Mary spoke into her headset. "Yes. It's a real wood chipper. Recover from this. You're not looking too good in Damon's eyes right now."

Peter smiled into the camera. "That's right. It's an actual wood chipper. What did I tell ya folks? Tonight's episode will be the best episode ever. Stay tuned because you just won't believe tonight's cash prizes."

Mary spoke into her headset. "You're being too informal Peter."

The contestants looked at the glass cubes, then at each other. The crowd roared.

"We're going to start with the grease. The challenge is to stick your hand in the vat of hot grease. You must insert your hand into the grease to your palm." Peter held up his hand. He pointed to his palm. "Your fingers must be fully immersed in the grease to win this challenge. The grease must be at least to the palm of your hand. Are we clear on the rules?"

The 3 contestants shook their heads yes.

"Now this task is considered 1 of our simpler tasks. The bidding will start at $75,000. Contestants, you may now start the bidding." Peter pointed at the contestants.

Each contestant was hitting their buzzer. Marty must have just been slow. He didn't buzz in fast enough. Mary knew that it was because he was high. She hoped that he didn't make her look like a fool tonight. The bidding war was back and forth between Laura and Kelly. Marty eventually got frustrated and just quit trying to hit his buzzer. Kelly placed a bid of $44,000. Laura shook her head no. Marty didn't try to go any lower either.

"So Kelly, that's a lot of money. What do you plan to buy with it?" Peter tried to be the host that Damon expected him to be.

"I can do a ton of shopping with that cash." Kelly walked across the stage to the cube.

"So I'm gonna clarify this again. You have to really stick your hand in the grease. Not just the tips of your fingers, and trust me, we will be able to tell. Are you ready Kelly?" Peter opened the cube door.

"I'm ready, this will be over in just a few seconds. Of course, I can do this." Kelly entered the cube and looked down at the bubbling grease.

A camera was positioned in the top of the cube. The crowd went silent as Kelly held her hand above the grease. She lingered in the same position for a few seconds. Kelly shut her eyes. Very quickly, Kelly shoved her hand into the grease. She shrieked in pain. Even quicker, she pulled her hand out of the vat of 350 degree grease.

"Lower her microphone. She's too loud." Mary instructed her crew as the woman's cries of agony hurt her ears.

Kelly held up her hand and looked at it. Her hand was mangled to what resembled a claw. It did not even look like a hand anymore. Her hand was pink and red and oozing fluid. It appeared as if some skin had dissolved, but what little skin was left was unrecognizable. Her hand looked like a huge open wound. She continued to scream. Peter opened the cube door.

Medical came on stage and ushered Kelly offstage.

Even though she was backstage, and her microphone was practically silenced, the audience could still hear her screams.

"On with the show." Peter pointed to the next cube. "Here we have a drill press. In this challenge, the contestant must drill a hole completely through their hand. To be clear, we must see the end of the drill bit under the platform on which their hand lies. Are we ready contestants? The bidding starts at $100,000. Begin the bidding."

Marty looked like he was the first person to hit his buzzer, but Laura's podium lit up. Laura looked at Marty. "My mom's surgery costs $72,000. I really need this money. I will do it for $72,000."

Marty couldn't believe that she dropped the bid that low that quick. She must really need that money. Marty shook his head. He would give this challenge to Laura.

Laura approached the cube. Peter opened the door and Laura entered. She looked at the machine.

"I know this looks confusing, but I will walk you through it. Laura, do you see the blue platform?" Peter was told how to instruct her. "You place 1 hand on the blue platform. Use the other hand to grab the red lever. As you lower the red lever, the drill bit will drop. And remember, you must go completely through your hand. Are we clear?"

"Yes. Can I do either hand?" Laura sounded shaky.

Peter shook his head yes. "Either hand is fine. Flip the black switch on and the machine will start."

Laura flipped the switch and the machine screeched to life with a low pitch roar. It sounded like a piece of machinery. Laura laid her left hand on the blue platform. She put her right hand on the red lever. Laura gritted her teeth and squinted her eyes.

Laura pulled down with her right hand as quick as

she could. The spinning drill bit lowered, penetrating her flesh. Small specks of blood splattered on the interior of the glass cube. Laura hit resistance, and she had to pull down harder on the red lever.

"For mom!" Laura screamed as the sound of the machine changed. It sounded slower. The camera zoomed in on the bottom tip of the drill bit, which was spinning below the blue platform. Laura raised up on the red lever, and blood splattered everywhere as the drill bit exited her skin. Blood dripped from the drill bit. Laura pressed the black button to power off the machine, and stood very still. She didn't even scream.

"Laura? Are you okay?" Peter was concerned. "Laura, talk to me."

Laura stood frozen, just staring at the hole in her hand. She was obviously in shock. Medical came out and helped Laura offstage. The crowd applauded as Laura was escorted away.

THE MAIN
EVENT

Damon looked around at all the happy faces in the audience. They were like him, they wanted to see this. Watching people in pain was a pleasure. He knew that the main event was still to come. The audience was in for a treat tonight. One last round. It was a great challenge.

"How unfortunate for Laura. I'm sure that she will be fine. At least now she can help her mom. Let's give her another round of applause." Peter encouraged the crowd to show appreciation for what Laura had just done.

Mary's phone buzzed. She had a text message. Finally, her PI friend was getting back to her. The text read 'Sorry, I've been busy. Marty Blevins is a drug addict. He owes back child support. His dad is a drunk. Actually served time for DUI and manslaughter. I hope this helps.'

Mary shook her head. That still didn't connect Damon to Marty. Was Damon doing drugs? Was he a drug dealer? She didn't have time to figure this out now. She was in the middle of a live show.

Peter looked to Marty. "Well Marty, you sure are lucky tonight. There is one challenge left, and you have no competitors to underbid you. How do you feel?"

Marty looked lost. "I don't know Peter. It's a wood chipper. I don't think I will stick my hand in a wood chipper. I'm allowed to quit, right?"

"Sure. You can quit at anytime. You don't have to do it, but do you at least want to hear how much the cash amount is for this challenge?" Peter questioned the last remaining player.

"I really don't think it matters. I think I'll just go home." Marty was sure of himself.

"Well, Marty that's a shame. But it is allowed. For this challenge the amount was going to be $500,000." Peter had gotten Marty's attention with that amount.

"A half a million dollars? You're kidding right?" Marty thought he had just heard the amount wrong.

"No. I'm not kidding. A half a million dollars to stick your hand in this wood chipper. To your wrist. What do you think about that?" Peter couldn't believe the grand prize either. It was an obscene amount.

"Basically, I would lose my hand. But that's a lot of money. Probably more money than I would make in 10 years." Actually, Marty knew with his drug habit that he would never get a real job and keep it. Plus, he owed some bad people money. They could kill him. Losing his hand wouldn't be as bad as those bad guys killing him.

"That might be so. But if you want to quit, I understand." Peter kind of hoped the guy would choose to quit. He didn't know if he could stomach that much blood. He knew that this machine would essentially devour the hand, and spit it out on the other side of the cube. Just the thought of it made Peter cringe.

Damon was so mad that he could spit nails. He didn't need the host to talk the contestant out of doing this. He needed Marty to do this. He needed Marty to do this not only to liven up the show, but for personal reasons also.

Marty weighed the pros and cons in his head. He decided that it would definitely be better to lose a hand than be murdered. "I'll do it. You said to the wrist right? Then I get rushed to a doctor, right?"

"Yes we have medical staff here, then I would be willing to bet that you might end up in the hospital." Peter couldn't believe the kid was considering this.

"I'll do this. I can do this." Marty was thinking of his drug debt, and that he was behind on child support. If his debtors didn't kill him, the police would eventually arrest him. He didn't want to go to jail. He needed this money.

Damon smiled. He knew that Marty would do it.

Peter approached the cube and opened the door.

Marty stood behind the machine. It had wheels. The machine stood about the same height as Marty's waist. There was a large rectangular apparatus that resembled a square funnel about the size of a welcome mat. A spout on the opposite side of the machine was where it ejected wood chips. Marty took a deep breath. In this case, it wouldn't be ejecting wood chips. It would eject small pieces of his hand.

"That piece you are staring into is called a feed funnel. That is where you will insert your hand. Pretty simple. Have you ever started a lawnmower before? On the opposite side, there's a string to pull that powers the machine on. Don't worry the cube is well ventilated. Take your time." Peter stood to the side of the cube, checking out the machine for himself.

Marty walked around to the other side of the machine. He recognized the pull string, and gave it a couple of tugs. The machine powered up, just like a lawnmower. The engine made a whirly choppy loud hum. It was louder than Marty had expected. This was too real. Marty stood and stared into the machine. He was almost in a trance, hypnotized by the machine's singing motor.

The crowd began chanting. "Marty! Marty!"

In one motion Marty raised his arm and placed his hand into the feed funnel. Marty let out a scream. He saw it, but he was too late. The sleeve of his shirt was mangled in the machine's grinding blades. It happened too fast. The machine started sucking him in. The force was so great. The other side ejected so much blood and composites of flesh onto the glass of the cube.

Peter rushed to the door. "How do I turn it off? Tell me now!"

Mary couldn't believe her eyes. The machine was devouring this man. "Drop the curtain now. Drop it!"

The machine did not let go of Marty's arm. It pulled him into the blades, ejecting small pieces of him out the other side. Marty tried to push away with his other hand, but he wasn't strong enough. Peter stood and watched as Marty's head got stuck above the feeder funnel. It instantly snapped his neck.

Damon was proud of himself. They had officially experienced their first death on live TV. The screen faded to black.

AFTERMATH

Damon and Mary sat in a quiet, dark office. They did not speak to each other as they waited for Damon's boss.

After a few minutes Mary broke the silence. "How did that happen? I don't understand."

Damon smiled. He had the nerve to smile after watching a man publicly die on television. "Don't worry about it. Everything will be okay."

That wasn't good enough. "A man is dead. He died on our show. How did we let it come to this?" She looked to Damon for answers.

Damon did not answer her. He wasn't nearly as traumatized as Mary. He was actually enjoying every minute of this whole ordeal.

Mr. Styles entered the room. He walked around the large meeting table to the end seat. He looked at Mary, then Damon, and just shook his head.

"We are waiting for Mr. Roberts, from legal, to come so we can sort this out. We'll all be lucky tomorrow if we still have jobs. I can't believe that I went along with this stupid show. They're gonna shut the whole network down, I just know it." Mr. Styles just kept shaking his head.

"It's okay. There will be no legal repercussions. I'm sure of it." Damon sounded too confident.

"Why would you think that? A man died." Mr. Styles was too sad to even be mad.

Mr. Roberts walked in. "I'm sorry it took me so long to get here. I was at home. Not watching that ridiculous show. What do you need me to do?"

Mr. Styles' sad eyes looked to the attorney for help. "I'm sure you heard that a contestant died on live TV. What does that mean for the network? What's gonna happen to us?"

Mr. Roberts was calm. "Nothing. Marty Blevins signed a contract. Fortunately, his contract had a death clause. In the event of his death, he left a beneficiary for his cash prize. His toddler son it was, I believe. The contract he signed released the network of any liability."

"A death clause!" Mr. Styles finally began to show his anger. "When did we add a death clause to the contract? I never approved such a thing."

Mr. Roberts looked to Damon. "Damon asked me to add it to this contract. It's a good thing that we did. There is nothing that can be done legally. You need to let all the news stations aware of this. He knowingly signed off, knowing that death was a possibility."

"You said this was added to his contract. Did any other contestant have a death clause?" Mr. Styles asked his legal friend.

Mr. Roberts' eyes looked up at his forehead while he was thinking. "Actually, no. He was the only contestant, ever, to have a death clause. I didn't think anything of it."

Damon smiled. "See, crisis averted. Everything is okay. Trust me."

In disbelief, Mr. Styles looked at Damon in disgust. "Mary, did you know about the death clause?"

"No sir. I had no idea. But I did catch Marty smoking drugs before the show. If they test his blood can they see that? Will that make our show look better?" Mary was concerned.

"Yes, maybe. But this isn't just about making the show look good. A man died. I feel like a broken record repeating myself! Do you understand that? A man is dead." Mr. Styles didn't know who to release his anger on.

Damon smiled. "Everything will be fine. Trust me. If anything, the show will be better. This is what the viewers wanted. They will want more of this. I know how to make good TV."

"A man is dead! You think viewers will want more of that?" Mr. Styles shook his head. "For now, there is no more show. Damon, it sounds like you need a break. You are suspended. I need to figure all of this out. I will get with the network's publicists to clean this up. You are dismissed. Leave me alone!"

Damon was sitting in his office looking at the picture of his son on the desk. He knew that his suspension would be temporary. The network would need him. Damon knew this show would be the show with the highest ratings. The network wouldn't be willing to walk away from such a popular show just because a man died. A worthless man, who wouldn't be missed. A drug addicted, deadbeat dad.

Mary came into Damon's office stomping her feet. "What was that about a death clause? Why didn't you tell me? And why Marty? You should have told me! I knew when you wanted to specifically cast him that something was off! I should have stopped you!" Mary had never spoken to her boss like that ever before. It felt good.

"Calm down. There's no need to be mad. Everything will be fine. The show will be back on in no time. They just have to go through with the formalities." Damon was calm and collected.

"Who was Marty? Why him?" Mary questioned her boss. She was going to demand answers even if he didn't answer.

Damon flipped the photograph of his son around for Mary to see. "An eye for an eye."

"What does that mean?" Mary hated it when Damon spoke in riddles.

Damon thought for a moment. "I was so happy when I found Marty's application. Remember when I told you to put casting calls out on college campuses? I was hoping that Marty would apply. Marty's father was the drunk driver that killed my son. I was only doing to him, what he had done to me. The difference is that Marty's dad is a drunk. And he probably won't care. I cared when I lost my son."

Mary couldn't believe what she was hearing. "That doesn't add up. How did you know that he would die on tonight's show?"

Damon put his pointer finger to his lips to hush a chuckle. "It was easier than you would think. First, I knew he was a drug addict. I put drugs in his waiting room. I needed him to be high, so he would be stupid enough to stick his hand in the wood chipper. I had the props guy mess with his buzzer. Marty couldn't have buzzed in if he wanted to. I knew the other women would quit, and that would leave Marty with the wood chipper. He was high. And it's hard to say no to a half of a million dollars. I had a few modifications made to the chipper. It was so easy. Plus, it's good TV. Wait, you'll see. People will want more." Damon was callous and cold. He was actually pleased with himself.

"I can't believe this. I'm gonna tell." Mary's eyes filled with tears.

"Who are you gonna tell? The network? They would cover it up. The police? I would tell them that you were in on it. You were the person to cast Marty. You handled him before the show, not me. You knew that he was high tonight, yet you let him go on the show. I'm not the only person at fault here. Maybe you would go to jail. Maybe you wouldn't. Either way, it would be professional suicide for you. You can't tell. Legally, we are covered. There's nothing to worry about." Damon tried to be comforting to his employee.

"I can't believe you. I can't even look at you right now." Mary stormed out, leaving Damon all alone. Mary knew that Damon was right. She couldn't tell anyone, no matter how bad her conscience would haunt her. She knew that he was high on TV. She admitted it to Mr. Styles and Mr. Roberts. What had she gotten herself into?

Mary was so mad. She was mad at Damon. She was mad at herself.

DAMON

Damon was having a great night. Everything had worked out perfectly according to his plan. He gave the viewers what they wanted. Death would be the next step for the show. The ratings would be huge! He was covered legally. Damon had already prepared what he would say publicly if ever questioned about the show. How could he have possibly known that the machine would cause death? Marty willingly stuck his arm into a wood chipper. Peter had given Marty the option to quit. Damon could pretend to be sad about the loss of a contestant. But he wasn't. Marty's dad was the reason Damon had lost his son. This was only fair in Damon's eyes. The fact that he could profit from Marty's death was just icing on the cake. Damon was proud of himself. He managed to get revenge, and great ratings both at the same time. Only a mastermind could orchestrate such a feat.

Damon went straight from his office to Destiny's hotel room. He didn't care that it was late. He was in the mood to play. He just experienced the greatest night of his entire life. He wanted to end it perfectly.

"I'm glad you're here. I didn't wake you did I?" Damon saw the pipe on the nightstand and knew that she hadn't been sleeping. She had been smoking.

"Come in. I'm always happy to see you." Destiny

hugged her sugar daddy.

"I was hoping that Amber would be here. I was hoping the 3 of us could work something out. She could add some excitement to our little arrangement. Did you tell her how generous I am?" Damon turned on his charming smile, pretending he didn't know that Amber was fish food.

Destiny rolled her eyes. "I think she's mad at me. I haven't seen her. She won't answer my calls. She has some nerve. To be mad at me for kicking her out of my room. I didn't like it that she was being rude to you. This is my room. I won't allow her to run you off. You are important to me." Destiny reached for her glass pipe. Damon's cash was important to her. She needed easy money to keep up with her smoking habit.

Damon would usually stop Destiny from smoking, but not tonight. He was so happy, he didn't care what she did. "I'm going on vacation. I wanted to see you before I left. I will miss you when I'm gone. But don't worry, I won't be gone too long."

Destiny exhaled the smoke. "A vacation? Where are you going? I want to go." She whined like a little child.

For a second, Damon thought of taking her with him. She could be fun to have around. They could play together often. On the other hand, she could also put a damper on him finding someone new to play with. "I'll think about it. I'm not leaving this very second."

Destiny placed the glass pipe back on the nightstand, and turned to Damon. "Do you wanna play tonight? Did you bring anything for me?"

Damon pulled out a wad of cash, and spread it across the small table.

"What do you have in mind?" Destiny was eager to earn that cash.

Damon was stumped. He hadn't come here with

a plan. He was too busy enjoying his night of revenge. "Actually, I don't have any ideas tonight. There's a lot of money here. You know what I like. Why don't you surprise me?"

Destiny looked around the room, like a lost puppy. "Surprise you? I don't know. Um. I could... I don't know."

Damon encouraged her. "If you want this cash, you'll come up with something good. I'm sure."

Destiny walked to a small closet on the far side of the room to come up with an idea. "Can I pull more teeth?"

"No." Damon shook his head.

"Okay." Destiny sounded disappointed. She continued to look for inspiration. She threw out a wire hanger and a high-heeled shoe. "What about these?"

"I don't know. I'm not going to watch you beat yourself with a shoe. What would you do with the clothes hanger?" Damon was interested.

"I could spank myself with it." Destiny knew she wasn't very good at this.

"No." Damon shook his head to be clear.

"I've got it. I know something that you'll like." Destiny walked into the bathroom, and returned with a small knife. It was maybe 4 inches in length.

"Why do you have that in your bathroom?" Damon was intrigued.

"I carry it when I work. I undressed in there earlier." Destiny acted as if it was no big deal that she carried a knife at work. In her line of work, it was actually a smart idea.

"What do you plan to do with it?" Damon urged her to talk dirty to him.

"I guess I could cut myself." Destiny smiled, proud of her idea. "You tell me where and how. I'll do it."

Damon thought about how crazy this woman

was. She was willing to do just about anything for money. As she sat on the bed, he admired his handiwork on her thigh. The scarred "D" he branded her with was a lovely sight.

Damon pointed at her opposite thigh. "You could carve another 'D' into your other leg. But I want it deep. I want to see it bleed."

Destiny grabbed her glass pipe and put a flame to it.

"I want you naked when you do it." Damon had demands.

As Destiny exhaled she shook her head to acknowledge his command.

She stood, and removed her shirt. Damon had forgotten how perky her breasts were. She lowered her skirt. She did not have on any panties. Damon rubbed himself. He approached her as she sat on the bed. He traced a "D" in her thigh with his finger.

Destiny took the knife and slightly inserted it into her soft flesh. A small line of blood ran down her leg. "Ouch. I can't. I can't do it to myself."

"Do you want the money or not?" Damon sat back on the chair to enjoy the show, waving his hands over the cash.

"It's not fast enough. Do you want to do it?"

She did not have to ask Damon twice. He took the knife in his hand and examined it. It didn't have much of a tip on it, but the side of the blade looked sharp enough. That didn't matter to him. Destiny laid back on the bed, and tried to relax. Damon stood and enjoyed the view of her firm body laid back on the bed. He got on his knees on the bed straddling her. He took the blade, and rubbed the dull side between her breasts, down her belly. He paused as he got to her bush. He shook his head no. He had other plans. Those plans were not sexual. He wanted to mark her.

He pressed the metal to her thigh. He pressed hard to ensure that it was deep enough in her skin. She began to shriek. Damon shushed her. She reached for her pipe. She wanted to smoke again.

"No. I have an idea." Damon took a pair of leggings and tied them around her mouth to muffle her screams. He once again inserted the blade into her leg, and quickly made the straight line of the "D".

Even though Destiny squealed, it wasn't loud. He looked up at her. She wasn't trying to fight him, she was just in pain. He watched as the blood ran out of her leg like a small stream. He dipped his finger into her blood. He ran his bloody finger around her nipple. Destiny liked that. Damon looked at her bloody nipple, and got an idea. He untied her mouth.

"I don't like this idea. I know what I want. I want you to cut off your nipple." Damon would be satisfied with that.

Destiny shook her head no. "I can't."

"Destiny, there's $3000 on the table. Do you want it or not? It would be fast. Just put the knife here, and cut." He put the blade at the top of her nipple against her skin. "It would be over in seconds."

"You do it. You can do it. Let me smoke." Destiny was scared as she shivered in fear.

Damon hated how much she was smoking, but he was in a good mood. When she finished, he tied the leggings around her mouth again. He situated the blade along his pointer finger. His thumb was below her nipple, the blade was on top. He pinched the knife to his thumb, and he felt the edge of the blade slightly dig into his thumb like a paper cut. Destiny screamed and started hyperventilating as she watched her nipple fall to the bed. A streak of blood flowed down to her navel, which pooled up with blood.

Damon was pleased with himself. He left into the

night, wondering where it might lead him.

Turn the page for Deadly Reality TV Series Book #2: Pain for Gain

DEADLY REALITY TV SERIES BOOK #2

Pain for Gain

By Sea Caummisar

PAIN FOR GAIN (FILMING OF THE FIRST EPISODE)

"Good evening ladies and gentlemen! I am your host tonight for the exciting debut of 'Pain for Gain'. I'm Peter Conway. We listened to the viewers and have come up with an exciting game show. I know, a lot of the viewers were sad when 'Easy Money' was cancelled. But we have now come up with a kinder, gentler show to appeal to our audience. With that being said, do not try this at home. Viewer discretion is advised. Let's get on with our show."

Music played and the lights were bright. Peter was standing on a stage with 2 podiums. There was no audience for this show. This show would not be filmed live like 'Easy Money'. 'Easy Money' was cancelled due to the death of a contestant, that happened on live TV in front of a live studio audience. The network, Uptown Reality Network (URN) was cautious to never have an accident like that ever happen again. Peter Conway had also been the host on that show, and had watched a wood chipper murder a man. The machine actually devoured the man, and spit chunks of his flesh out the other side. Peter had been traumatized by the incident, but readily accepted the invitation to do this show after he had gotten the raise he had requested.

Mary, who had been assistant producer on 'Easy Money', was now working under a new executive producer, William Hendricks. William had a reputation that preceded him. He had plenty of experience, but not with this kind of show. He also had plenty of friends in high places. He knew network owners and board members.

"Let's meet our contestants! Come on out." Peter welcomed his players onto the stage.

"Welcome to 'Pain for Gain' Sara and Evan, they are a married couple. In this show we play in pairs. Are you excited about being on the show?" Peter was an inquisitive host.

Sara began speaking. "We are excited, Peter. As long as there aren't any wood chippers on the show." Sara laughed.

"Next we have Greg and Jeff. Best friends for over 20 years! Welcome." Peter watched as the men walked out on the stage.

"Thanks for having us Peter! We are ready to win some cash." Greg was talkative.

"Let's start with how the game works. As you see we play in pairs. All challenges will be performed by both couples. Now let's start 'Pain for Gain'!" Peter looked at the players as they shook their heads letting him know that they understood his words. "Are y'all good at darts? For the first challenge, 1 partner will stand in front of the dart board. The other partner will throw darts at them. These darts have very sharp tips on them." Peter held a dart up for the camera to see. "You get paid according to which part of the body you hit. Limbs are worth $500. Abdomen and shoulder area is $2,000. Facial area is $5,000. There are a total of 5 darts to throw. That's a potential of winning $25,000. "

Peter looked at the best friends first. "Greg and Jeff. Who is throwing? And who is getting hit by the darts?"

Jeff spoke up first. "I've won plenty of dart games before. I think I should throw."

Peter stopped Greg before he stood in front of the dart board. "First, put these on." Peter handed a pair of safety goggles to Greg.

Mary looked at her new boss, William. The safety goggles were William's idea. Mary thought safety was important too, but she knew that it wouldn't make good television.

Mary was imagining in her mind what it would be like if someone got hit in the eyeball with a dart. She could picture the dart sticking straight out of their sight organ, and as the person pulled it out of their eye that it would start squirting blood. Maybe she was jaded from working on 'Easy Money'. However, today she would not see anything of the sort. This show was tame compared to 'Easy Money'. Too tame, probably.

Greg put on the safety glasses, and stood in front of the dart board and waited. Jeff picked up a dart and examined the tip. He stabbed his finger with the tip, and found out that it was sharp. Jeff squinted and aimed the dart at his best friend. Jeff released the dart and it flew through the air, heading directly towards Greg's face. Plink. The dart bounced off his safety goggles.

Peter commented so that the players would be clear on the rules. "In case I didn't stipulate it, the dart must stick into the skin to win the money. That dart did not stick, so that's zero dollars. At least you have 4 more tries."

Jeff raised another dart in the air. He wanted to hit Jeff in the face, but he was afraid of hitting the plastic glasses again and not winning any money. Instead he aimed a little bit lower. Jeff threw the dart, and it hit Greg in his cheek. The dart was sticking out of his skin.

"Dangit! That hurts." Greg quickly removed the dart from his cheek, and there was only a small speck of blood. "Can we trade positions Peter? Can I throw now?"

Peter shook his head yes. "You can trade positions as often as you'd like. As long as someone gets hit by darts, you win money. So far you have won $5,000."

Jeff and Greg switched positions. Greg pinched the dart in between his finger and thumb. The dart went flying through the air. The dart pierced Jeff in his forehead, but bounced off due to there not being enough flesh to hold the dart in place.

"Ouch." Jeff rubbed his forehead. "Am I bleeding? That hurt? Peter does that count? Please tell me that it's worth $5,000."

Peter shook his head no. "Like I said, the dart has to stick and that dart did not stick. It bounced. Try again Greg."

Greg took more time to aim for his friend's fleshy cheeks. When he was sure that he had his aim correct, he let the dart fly. Before Jeff had time to react, Greg let the last dart fly.

Jeff stood very still. "They stuck! That's another $10,000 right?" Jeff pulled the darts out of his face.

Peter congratulated the contestants for winning $15,000. It was time for Sara and Evan to try. After a quick bicker about who was going to throw, they decided to let Sara throw.

She did not want to be on the pain end of this task. Evan removed his shirt, and told his wife to take her time while she was aiming. Even though Sara aimed at her husband's face, the dart fell shy and stuck him in the chest.

Peter congratulated the guests on their $2,000 win, and urged Sara to try again. Once again, she threw a dart that hit him in the chest.

"Sara, please let me throw. All I have to do is hit you in the face with the last 3 darts to win $15,000." Evan begged his wife, to help them win more money. "I can aim better than you."

Sara reluctantly agreed. Evan threw a dart at his wife, and it landed right beside her little nose.

"Bullseye!" Evan was proud of himself.

"No! Stop this hurts. This isn't worth $5,000." Sara shed a tear down her cheek.

Quickly to shut his wife up, Evan threw another dart that stuck into his wife's cheek.

Sara cried out in pain and walked to her husband. "Stop it now! I won't let you hit me again! It's my turn!" Sara grabbed the dart from her husband.

Evan saw how mad his wife was and decided not to push his luck. Sara was so mad at him right now. She never agreed to him throwing the second dart. Sara wiped her tears aside, and raised the dart. She patiently aimed. She released the dart, which landed in the center of her husband's throat. Evan plucked the dart from his neck, and rubbed it. He found out what his wife said was true, it did hurt.

"Stop production!" Mary interjected. She was speaking out of turn. She was only the assistant producer.

"Why?" William, her new boss asked.

"It's boring. We can't air this. The viewers will not watch this. We need something better." Mary knew that her job was on the line.

"Keep filming. Go ahead Peter. Set up the second task." William instructed Peter to keep going. "Mary, I'm in charge. This is my show now. I like it. If this doesn't suit you, then you can leave."

Mary didn't say a single word. She had worked for stricter bosses before. Damon, her previous boss, was a difficult boss to please. William did not scare her. Mary gathered her belongings and went to exit the studio. She turned around to see part of the second stunt. Evan and Sara were on stage with paintball guns preparing to shoot each other. Mary laughed. Sure, paintballs sting, but that wasn't the kind of pain their viewers wanted to see. This was child's play compared to 'Easy Money'. She could do better than this. Why did they have to bring William in on her territory?

WHERE IS DAMON?

"Put me in charge of the show. William's ideas are horrible. He's way too safe." Mary begged Mr. Styles, president of URN, to give her the show.

"You don't have his experience Mary. We're lucky that he agreed to work on 'Pain for Gain'. I'm confused. First you refused to work for Damon. I agree with you, Damon was too hardcore. Now you say that William isn't creative enough. You think William is too kind. Make up your mind Mary." Mr. Styles was fed up with Mary.

"Damon was too hardcore. A man dicd on 'Easy Money'. Damon luckily secured the network legally for it, but he is extreme. William doesn't have what it takes for a show like this. We have to think about our viewers. I don't care how much experience he has, or how much stock he owns in URN, he isn't cut out for a reality pain game show. I can be the compromise between Damon and William. I'm creative, but not cold hearted." Mary put her sad eyes on display, hoping to charm her boss.

Mr. Styles thought for a moment. "Let me watch what he tapes. I will think it over. I'm not making any promises. Anyways, have you heard from Damon? I hate to say it, but we got so much hate mail when we cancelled 'Easy Money'. We do need something with an edge to it. No death shows, but definitely an edge."

"Damon disappeared after you suspended him. We don't need Damon, we have me. Just please think about it." Mary left her boss's office, hoping that he would see things her way.

Damon Dahmer, who used to be executive producer on 'Easy Money', stood on the balcony of his apartment looking at the ocean. It was a pretty day outside. He had recently relocated somewhere in Mexico. He loved Mexico. The laws weren't as strict, the women were cheap, and the weather was lovely. He wondered why he hadn't moved here sooner.

"Please. Please help me!"

Damon heard a woman scream from inside his apartment, and smiled. His newest playtoy was currently waiting for him. He walked inside and saw the woman hanging, with her arms spread, tied to the banister of the stairs. He smiled as he looked at her naked body. She was young and beautiful.

"Can I get down now? My arms are sore." Maya looked at Damon, wishing that he would agree to untie her.

"I will let you down anytime you please. I guess it depends on how much money you want to make." Damon looked at her feet. She was on the tips of her toes. Damon had tied her up to the perfect height so that she could only reach the floor with her toes. He did not want her to be comfortable during their playtime. "You've only been there a couple of hours. Are you quitting?"

"I want to make money, but my feet and arms hurt too bad. I can't do this anymore." Maya begged for mercy. She was very poor. She had a family to feed, but she couldn't endure this kind of pain any longer.

Damon walked over to the banister and loosened the ropes around her wrists.

Maya collapsed to the floor. "I'm sorry, but I can't do that anymore."

"Are you open to play another game?" Damon looked at the naked woman on the ground. "I will pay you very well."

"I don't know. I hurt so bad." Maya groaned as she spoke, and rubbed her shoulders.

Damon enjoyed his time with Maya because her english was almost perfect. He disliked that she was weak. "Wait here one moment." Damon left Maya laying on the floor momentarily. When he returned he was carrying pepper spray. He held the bottle up for her to see.

"What is that?" Maya eyed the item that he was holding.

"It's a spray of toxins. I believe it has hot pepper in it. It's very similar to mace, like the police use." Damon smiled thinking of what he planned to do.

"Police? There was a time when they arrested me and they sprayed me. My eyes burned for such a long time. How much will you pay me?" Maya remembered her experience with the substance. It hurt, but she could do it again, for enough money.

Damon pulled out American money. "This is $500 dollars. What is that here? Over 9,000 pesos?"

Maya's eyes got huge. She had never had that much money ever in her life. She closed her eyes tight. "Okay, spray me." She was eager to earn some money.

Damon shook his head no. "Not your face. I wanna spray it somewhere private." Damon bent down to the floor and ran his hand between her bare breasts. He slowly moved his hand lower, until he got to her trimmed pubic bush. "Here, inside your forbidden area."

Maya shook her head no.

Damon pulled out more money. "What if I

add this to it?"

Maya cried. "You're so mean. You know that I need money. Why torture me?"

Damon smiled. This was music to his ears. "I won't torture you without your permission. Actually, I want you to spray yourself. I won't even do it. I will sit back here and watch."

"You're so mean." Maya raised her tired arm, which was still sore from being tied to the bannister, and reached for the can of pepper spray. Maya spread her legs and gave Damon a good view of her womanhood. She turned the nozzle towards herself. She slowly pushed down on the button. Liquid spewed onto her private parts. She quickly dropped the can. "AH! AH! AH! It burns so much! Make it stop burning!"

Damon laughed. He did love Mexico.

FINDING
DAMON

"I was not trying to undermine you. I just have history with this kind of thing. You don't have the heart for it." Mary was trying to explain to William why his version of the show wasn't good enough.

"I'm in charge here. I was told to make a pain show, that ensured there wouldn't be any deaths. I doubt anyone would die from a dart or a paintball gun. I'm still producing pain. The viewers want to see pain, not extreme torture. Plus, I have a conscience." William wasn't going to change his opinion.

"I have struggled with my conscience. But then I get thank you letters from past contestants. Take Laura for example. She used a drill press to make a hole in her hand, but she used that money for her mom's surgery. Her mom is alive today because of our show. These people consented to hurting themselves.

They benefited from being on our show." Mary did still struggle with her conscience, but her career had started to take off. She tried to focus on the positive things that became of the show. She tried to ignore all of the negativity. It was the only way she could live with herself.

"What about Marty Blevins?" William looked at his underling with a sneer.

Mary remembered Marty Blevins. He died on the finale of 'Easy Money'. Mary also knew that it wasn't an accident. Damon had only made it appear to be an accident. "That's a totally different topic."

"No, it's not. An accident caused a man to lose his life. We can't let that happen again."

Mary's phone rang. It was Mr. Styles.

"I watched that taping Mary. It was boring. I found Damon. I think if the 3 of you work together, we will have the perfect balance of producers. William will be cautious, Damon will be the entertainment, and you can be the voice of reason. Good luck." Mr. Styles hung up the phone.

Mary's jaw dropped. She was speechless.

William saw that she looked like a lost child. "What was that Mary? Who was it? Are you okay?"

Mary started trembling. "Damon. They have called Damon. He's coming to work with us."

Damon was packing up his belongings from Mexico. He had enjoyed his time in the foreign country, but he did miss work. Plus, his habits were expensive. Women didn't torture themselves for free. He had been suspended after a contestant 'accidentally' died on 'Easy Money'. He had stayed away long enough. After Marty Blevins' death, groups were created to boycott the show. Marty's family did not partake in the boycotting. Which was what Damon had essentially wanted. He wanted Marty's father to feel how it felt losing a son. Unfortunately, his hard work was fruitless in that department.

According to Mr. Styles, for every boycotting viewer, there were 2 viewers that missed the show. The network ultimately saw that it was in their best interest to keep a reality pain show on the air. That was why they needed Damon.

Damon was carefully placing an expensive suit in his luggage, when he was distracted by a moan coming from the bathroom. Maya, Damon's personal playtoy, kept coming back for more. Despite all of her pain, she kept coming back for more.

Maya walked out of the bathroom. "No matter how many cold baths I take, it still hurts when I go to the bathroom. I will never even be able to look at a can of pepper spray without reliving the pain of spraying it in my privates."

"You were such a good trooper. I'm proud of you." Damon did enjoy his time with her.

"I wish that you weren't leaving. Will you come back and see me?" Maya sat on the bed that was covered with all of Damon's belongings.

Damon thought for a moment. "I'm sure that I will. Eventually, maybe I will come here to live permanently. Who knows? Maybe one day I will stir up enough trouble at home that I will have to leave. Maybe. Of course, I can visit on vacation." Damon winked at the beautiful woman.

"I don't know why, but I will miss you." Maya looked sad.

"You will miss my money, not me." Damon knew that she didn't care for him. She couldn't care for him. He only caused her pain. She only needed his money. "Before I leave, do you want to play for a last time?"

Maya eagerly shook her head yes. "What do you have in mind this time?"

"This should be grandiose due to my going away. I don't know when I will see you again. We should really step it up this time. What do you think?" Damon was thinking over the top.

"It depends on what you are thinking." Maya started to get a little scared.

"I would like to do something that would help you remember me forever. But it won't hurt too bad." Damon lied.

"Just tell me what you are thinking." The suspense was killing Maya.

"I like to leave my mark. The letter 'D', real large on your back. With an iron. I will heat it up, and iron you just like I iron my shirts. It won't kill you, it will just make a scar on your back."

Maya thought for a moment. She knew that whenever she refused to do something, Damon always raised the price. "No. No way. I won't do that."

Damon knew that she was negotiating. They had played together many times before. "Let's just skip the game. $10,000. That's probably enough for your family to live on in this country for a year. I feel like I am being generous."

"More." Maya was not thrilled with the idea of being scarred for life.

"10,000. I won't pay a penny more. Don't test me. Or I will leave and you will get nothing." Damon's threats were not hollow. He was thinking that he could just kill her and do anything with her that he pleased. But he was in a good mood today. He was happy that URN needed him. Plus, he did like Maya.

Maya sat silently. She did need the money. She shook her head yes. They didn't speak as

Damon cleared the bed. He put the rest of his clothes into his luggage.

"Undress real slow." Damon was demanding.

Maya stood and raised her dress over her head. She did not wear undergarments. She knew that Damon liked it better when she could get naked quickly.

"Lay face down on the bed." Damon motioned to the bed, almost like he was welcoming her.

Maya slowly laid face down on the bed. Damon looked at her soft skin and ran his finger down her spine. When he got to the bottom, he looked at her firm buttocks, and appreciated the fact that she took care of her young body. He grabbed 2 pairs of pantyhose from a drawer. He tied each wrist to a bedpost.

"Struggle for me." Damon watched Maya as she wiggled her arms and tried to get loose. She was unable to free herself.

Damon went and got the clothes iron. He plugged it in next to the bed, and set it on the nightstand. While he was waiting for it to heat up, he traced a large 'D' on her back with his fingers, that spread across her shoulders, all the way down to her buttocks. "This is where I will leave my mark. Are you okay with that?"

"I don't know. Maybe I don't want to do this. Untie me. I think I'm changing my mind." Maya began to panic.

"Shh. It's okay. The cash is on the table waiting for you. I'm sure that your family will appreciate you doing this for them." Damon smiled thinking about how she would have something to remember him by. A scar for life.

Maya began to struggle against her pantyhose restraints. "I do not want to do this. Please untie me." She began to scream at him.

Damon hushed his subject. He didn't care if she struggled. He actually enjoyed it that she was fighting him. She was helpless right now. Damon held his hand in front of the metal plate of the iron. He could feel the heat from it, and knew that it was hot enough to do with what he wanted to do. He held the small appliance in his hand and put it close to her back. He pushed a button to release a spray of steam on her vulnerable skin.

"Stop. Now! That's too hot! I do not want to do this!" Maya struggled harder. She had changed her mind, yet he wouldn't untie her. "Please. I'm begging!" She began to cry.

Damon placed the hot object into her skin by her left shoulder blade. Her skin began to sizzle. She screamed in agony. Damon ignored her, and very slowly glided the iron down her back to her buttocks. He raised the iron and admired the first stroke of his work. Maya was crying out in pain. He loved hearing her screams. He straddled her thighs, and felt himself get aroused as she wiggled her firm rump against him. He placed the iron on her left shoulder blade, again, and pressed down harder. He very slowly made a gracious curve to form the 'D'. Maya was screaming and crying harder, begging him to stop.

Damon stood, and admired his marking from the foot of the bed. "Your cash is on the table. I have a plane to catch." Damon grabbed his luggage and left, leaving the woman tied to the bed wailing in pain.

WELCOME HOME, DAMON

Damon felt right at home as soon as he set foot on URN's property. He hoped that he would get his old office back. He loved that office. He strolled through the parking lot, smiling as he breathed in the fresh air. The air did feel different here than in Mexico. Everything somehow seemed fresher. As he opened the door to the building of his old office, he realized that his awards were no longer lining the hallways. Damon was not happy.

Damon quietly approached Mary's desk. "Hello. How are you?"

Mary looked at her former boss in dismay. "You really came. Why?"

"Mr. Styles says that you need me. The show needs me. The network needs me. I'm home." Damon smiled. "Where's all my awards?"

"You have some nerve coming back here

after what you did." Mary was angry.

"What I did? What did I do, Mary? Did you tell anyone of importance? No, you didn't. So whatever I did or didn't do, must not be too important. What I did was breathe life into reality television. What I did was give this network great ratings. What I did was amazing." Damon was proud of the fact that he managed to 'accidentally' kill someone on live television.

Mary's phone buzzed. "Yes sir. I'm here. I have those reports. We also have a visitor."

Damon was intrigued. "We. You are part of a we. Who is the other part of the team? This is interesting." Damon did not wait for Mary to reply. He walked right past her desk, into his old office.

"William. William Hendricks. It's been years. How have you been?" Damon had been an assistant to William many years ago. Damon hated seeing the man sitting behind what used to be his large oak desk. Damon sat down on the large couch in the corner of the office.

"Damon! You're back. I didn't believe it when they told me. You shouldn't be here. You're too reckless. I do not want to work with you. Don't get too comfortable." William never did like Damon. He always had a feeling that Damon wasn't normal. He thought that Damon was hit by the crazy stick.

"Well, like it or not, Mr. Styles has welcomed me back. It looks like we will be working together, whether or not you like it. I have 2 goals. The first is to make good television. The second is to reclaim my office." Damon did settle in. He made himself comfortable on the couch and welcomed the challenge.

The meeting was comprised of the 3 producers (Damon, William, and Mary) and a couple of writers. William and Mary did not look happy that Damon was there.

Damon began the meeting. "Okay, Let's play catch up. Who wants to fill me in on what I've missed?"

William and Mary sat silently. They did not want to speak to Damon.

Finally, a writer began to speak. "The show is now called 'Pain for Gain'."

"Weak. That's a horrible name. Who came up with that?" Damon looked to Mary and William, but did not get any answers.

The writer continued to update Damon on what he had missed out on. "The tasks are friendlier and less violent. The only interesting aspect of the game is that it is played by teams of 2. Apparently, legal worked something out with a contract stating that the network isn't liable if they agree to let their partner hurt them. I'm pretty sure the contract also absolves the partner from any legal punishment. We must have some great lawyers."

It was as if a light bulb lit up above Damon's head. "Teams. Pairs. I can work with that."

Even though it had been a few months since Damon had been around, he hoped that he could find Destiny, his former playmate, in her usual shady motel room. With any luck, she was still a drug addicted prostitute. He hoped that she hadn't done anything foolish, like checking herself into some drug rehabilitation. He rented a car and drove to the crime infested part of town.

Damon approached the door to her room, and crossed his fingers. He raised his hand to knock, and waited.

"Who is it?"

Damon immediately recognized her voice. He didn't need to say much. "Me."

Destiny looked through the window to make sure that it really was Damon. Despite his sick, twisted fantasies that he imposed on her, she had missed him. She opened the door and gave him a hug.

"I am so happy to see you. I have missed you so much. Get in here." Destiny welcomed Damon into her room. Finally, he had found someone who was happy to see him.

Destiny was as happy as a small child at a birthday party. "How are you? Where have you been? I was worried about you. You didn't even bother to call."

Damon looked around the small room. It was the usual mess, with dirty clothes and used food wrappers scattered everywhere. He noticed that her drug kit was laying on the nightstand. It didn't look like too much had changed.

"I honestly missed you. I've been in Mexico, trying to keep myself occupied." Damon smiled when he thought of the ways he had been occupying himself. "I have to say, being away from you was the worst part of my vacation. You really are a special woman." Damon looked at her missing front teeth. Below her short skirt, he could see the bottom of the letter 'D' that he had branded into her delicate skin. He did have some good memories with Destiny. "How did your nipple heal?" Damon remembered that he had sliced off the tip of her nipple, and he really wanted to see it.

Destiny raised her shirt. She wasn't shy. She displayed her breasts to Damon, so he could see what he had done to her. "It bled. A lot. I put some of that glue on it, you know it's like bandage glue. Anyways, that made it stop bleeding. It doesn't hurt at all now. Other than it looking funny, it isn't a problem. None of my clients seem to mind."

Damon knew why none of her clients minded. None of her clients cared. They weren't hiring a street hooker to care for her. They hired her for sex, and sex only. Damon however, did care for her in his own sick way for his own sick reasons. "How have other things been?"

Destiny looked sad for a moment. "Not good. Do you remember Amber, my friend? They found her dead in the ocean. So we have been cautious at work. I only see my regulars now. I don't get in the car with strangers. They said that she had been mutilated."

Damon tried to look sad, even though he loved his fond memory of stabbing Amber several hundred times. "Oh, that's a shame. You need to be careful out there. Did it happen while she was working?" Damon was being nosey, wanting to see if maybe the police were on to him.

"The newspapers just said that she had been in the ocean for so long that they didn't have much evidence as to why or when it happened. They said that her body had been stabbed multiple times. I miss her. I think that she had to be working. I don't know anyone else who would want to hurt her." Destiny was getting sad remembering her friend. "Since I've been careful at work, business has been kinda slow. I'm so glad to see you."

Damon smiled, relieved that he wasn't a suspect in the murder. "Daddy's home now. Are you in the mood for some playtime?"

"Always." Destiny was ready to make some money. The hooker reached for her glass pipe, and offered drugs to Damon.

Damon shook his head no. "I have some toys in the car. Can I bring them in?"

Destiny shook her head yes. Damon went to the car, and returned with a small cardboard box.

Destiny peeked inside the box. She saw a ball gag and a blindfold. "Those actually are toys. That's not what I was expecting of you at all." She was used to Damon having toys that were more torturous. Do you have anything else for me?"

Damon smiled. "Of course I do. I want to make sure that you are taken care of." Damon placed a stack of money on the table. "I thought today we could just have some fun together. Let me show you how much I have missed you."

Destiny took one last puff from her pipe, and shook her head yes. She stood to remove her clothes. Damon feasted his eyes on the parts of her body that he had mutilated. He was turned on by her breast with the absent nipple. He loved the 'D' he had branded on her thigh.

Damon felt his growing crotch through his blue jeans. "Do you trust me?"

Destiny obediently shook her head yes.

Damon put the blindfold on the hooker. Destiny shivered as he ran his finger along her breast and her missing nipple.

"I'm not a fan of the ballgag. I like hearing your screams, but these rooms have thin walls. I don't want to disrupt your neighbors." Damon placed the ball gag around the woman's face. "Try to scream."

Destiny tried to scream but the sound came out as muffled gurgle. Damon stood admiring the naked hooker who was now vulnerable to him. He was getting ready to do something that he hadn't done in a very long time. In honor of missing Destiny, he was going to have sex with her. He put his mouth close to her ear and shushed her. He raised her arms above her head and pinned them to the bed. He lowered himself over her thin body, and treated Destiny like the prostitute that she was.

Destiny was in shock. Damon had never wanted sex before. Destiny was blindfolded, so she couldn't see what he was doing, but she could feel what he was doing. Destiny kept waiting for Damon to throw some kind of sick fantasy into their sexual act, but he didn't. Instead, he just used her body as a sex toy.

Damon removed her blindfold when he was finished. "I hope this shows you how much I missed you. Don't get used to this. I still like to play. Come up with something for me next time I visit." Damon left the cash on the table, and said his goodbyes.

RIVALRY

Damon looked at Mary and William. He knew that there was a time that Mary respected him. He needed her respect again. Lucily, Mary had kept his secrets, so she must not despise him. William, on the other hand, had never liked Damon. He knew that it would be difficult working with him.

"The darts were okay, but paintball guns? That's not pain." Damon had just finished watching the first tape of 'Pain for Gain'.

William defended his position. "Have you ever been shot with a paintball gun at close range? It stings. It even leaves welts."

"The show has pain in the title. Not stings. Not welts. Pain. Pain is the objective. C'mon Mary, we're a team of 3 working together. What do you think?" Damon looked to his underling, hoping that she would side with him.

Mary took a moment to think before she spoke. She did not like William's ideas, but she did not want to side with Damon either. "I think William did his best to ensure pain without death. I'm sure that Mr. Styles told you that we can't have another death on the show."

Damon smiled at Mary. She was just being difficult. He was used to that, and liked the game. "I was told. No more deaths, but what's wrong with it if people are willing to die for money?"

William did not like what Damon was saying. "I'm not going to even acknowledge that you just said that out loud. How about this? We need applicants. Not too many people wanted to be on the show after Marty died."

Damon offered a solution. "We can find the people willing to die, and do special episodes with them. I assume we still have a budget. Did our sponsors pull out?"

"Not all of them. We had to promise them a show without death to keep them." Mary shot a piercing glare at Damon.

"Okay. No death. Not yet at least. But we do need ratings. Our viewers don't want to watch paintball fights. That's why Mr. Styles brought me back. We just need ideas. Ideas that don't result in death, just extreme pain. Mary, I know you. You shouldn't let your conscience get the better of you if people are willing to hurt themselves. What other ideas do you have?" Damon looked at both of his colleagues.

William was the only person to answer "I was thinking the next episode they could shoot each other with water guns full of boiling water. Nobody would die of little streams of hot water." William was proud of his idea.

"You're thinking too small, William. Boiling water isn't bad, but not water guns. Take it to the next level. What are your thoughts, Mary?" Damon looked at Mary.

"As bad as I hate to admit it William, he's kinda right. He did make a hit show off of extreme pain. Maybe we should listen to him. We should also monitor him for our contestant's safety. But he isn't entirely wrong. And we can never let him be in charge of casting." Mary hated agreeing with Damon, so she had to mention the casting part just to undermine him in some way.

"That's fair. Good. Now that we are all onboard, I'm thinking hammers and knives for the first episode. Huge cash prizes will keep the viewers hooked, and it will ensure that people will still want to be on the show." Damon was happy with himself.

"No. I put my foot down. That's too extreme." William disagreed with Damon.

Damon knew that Mary wasn't going to be a problem, but William was. Damon would have to find a way to change William's mind.

When William walked into his office, he was greeted by Damon. Damon was sitting in William's chair, with his feet propped up on

William's desk.

"Hello William." Damon's smile exposed his teeth. "I was hoping to run into you here."

William laughed. "Aren't you a lucky man? Running into me in my own office. What are the odds?"

Damon did not like sarcasm, unless it was his own. "Let's compromise here. I'm not trying to be a difficult man, I just want to make this show the best that it can be."

William shook his head no. "Do you remember years ago, when you used to work under me? I always felt that there wasn't something right about you. Now you just keep proving me right."

Damon did remember what it was like working under William. William did not give Damon the freedom to have his own creative ideas. Damon and William never got along. At one point, William abused his power of being Damon's boss and turned him into an errand boy. Damon was a producer, not an errand boy. Damon had to go to the network himself, to get himself out from under William's thumb. Luckily, that was when Damon convinced the network to give him his own show. That was when Damon's career had really started to advance.

"Anyways, how about you get to pick a challenge, and I get to pick the other challenge. After the show airs, we do an online poll. That way we can see which challenge our viewers liked best." Damon was trying to compromise. He knew that he could beat William in a friendly competition.

"You're just as hard headed now as you were back then. That's why I never liked you. You always think that you're right. I have news for you. You're not always right. Sure, let's try things your way. Just this once. Then, we'll go from there. Now, get out of my seat." William made his way for his desk.

Damon was happy. "Just for kicks. Let's add a kicker to the pot. Whoever's challenge wins the online poll gets this office."

William shook his head no. "I don't agree to that."

"Are you scared of a friendly competition? I don't blame you. I would be scared to compete against me, too." Damon was trying to intimidate his opponent.

"Sure. Winner gets this office. Now, I have work to do. Please, leave me be."

Damon and William shook hands to make the friendly wager official.

As soon as Damon left the office, Mary went to William.

Mary wanted to know what had happened in that office. "What did Damon want?"

"A competition." William shook his head in disbelief. "I'm going to produce a challenge, and he's going to produce the other challenge.

Then we do an online poll asking the viewers which challenge was better. Winner gets this office. I'm not so as much worried about the office, but which direction the show is taking. I want it to be a relatively safe show. Something tells me that he doesn't."

Mary was mad. "Do I get a say in this at all? I'm involved here too."

"You're still an assistant producer. That's just the way it is. Get used to it." William was a stern man.

Mary wasn't sure who she liked the least. She didn't care much for Damon or for William.

PAIN FOR GAIN (THE SECOND EPISODE)

"Hello! Welcome to an exciting episode of 'Pain for Gain', where contestants can win big money! We have a great show planned tonight. I'm your host, Peter Conway. In this game show our players compete in teams. Let's meet the pairs for tonight's episode."

The contestants walked out onto the stage. The podiums were marked 'Red Team' and 'Blue Team'.

Peter walked up to the first podium. "On the red team we have Alfred and Wanda. How long have you been married?"

Wanda smiled at the camera. "We have been married 15 years."

Alfred chimed in. "Yeah, she's the love of my life. She wanted to be on this show to help out with our finances. Money has been a little tight. I agreed because it's something she wanted to do. As all married men know, you have to give the woman her way."

Peter laughed and agreed with Alfred. "Welcome blue team. Pam and Jason. You're also married. Newlyweds, right?"

Damon watched and got bored. He really didn't care to meet the contestants. It was his idea to give the teams colors. That way it would be easier for viewers to remember who was who. Damon just wanted for Peter to get on with the show. Lately, he had a short attention span.

"For the first challenge, we have water guns filled up with boiling water. Do not try this at home. These water guns are specially made to contain the hot water. For this challenge, we are paying $250 dollars per second that water is sprayed directly to the skin. These tanks are limited in size, so don't expect to get more than 60 seconds of spray time. That's a possibility of earning $15,000!" Peter held up a water gun for the camera to see.

The red team, the long time married couple started talking amongst themselves, trying to figure out who would be on the hurting end of the boiled water. The husband agreed to let his wife shoot him with the water gun.

"Honey, just try to not stay in the same place for too long. Spray and keep moving. It won't hurt me as bad. Spray all of it on my skin." The husband removed his shirt to give his wife a broad target.

The wife began spraying her husband above his right shoulder, and was slowly moving the hot liquid across his entire chest. The husband screamed as she was spraying, but it didn't seem to hurt him too badly.

Damon looked at Mary. "Is the water really boiling? It's not looking like he's in too much pain."

Mary shrugged her shoulders. "I don't know. William did everything for this challenge. He's the only person who knows how hot the water really is. Knowing him, it's not that hot. He's super worried about safety."

"There's no room for safety in a show like this. You know that don't you Mary? Don't tell me that you like this guy. We made a good team, me and you. We don't need him." Damon was trying to be genuine with Mary.

"We made a good team? You didn't tell me that you had planned on murdering the son of the man that killed your son. What kind of a team is that? You like having a pushover around. Someone that will do whatever you want." Mary was still upset with Damon.

"I was just testing the boundaries of television. I wanted to see how people would react to a death. Who better to test it on than Marty Blevins? Yes, I had a personal agenda, and I kept it a secret from you. For that, I'm truly sorry." Damon tried to put on his most charming smile.

Mary studied Damon's face. "Are you sorry? Do you even know what that word means?"

Damon winked at Mary. "Of course I do. Why didn't you tell anyone what I did?"

"Because I felt responsible too. It wasn't just you. I allowed the show to spin out of control. I won't let that happen again." Mary made a promise to herself, and she was going to keep it true.

"Shh. It's time for my challenge." Damon hushed Mary so she could watch his challenge.

"For this challenge, we are offering $100,000 for a pinky toe." Peter tried to make the challenge sound exciting. "All we need is 1 pinky toe. We have supplied knives and cleavers, and even an axe. $100,000. That's a lot of money. For this challenge, the blue team will go first."

The newlywed team looked at each other.

The husband spoke first. "What do you think, honey?"

"No. No way. We won't do that." The young wife looked at her husband lovingly.

"We need that money. That would help us buy a home. Cut my toe off. Just do it fast." The husband urged his wife to cut his toe off.

The wife shook her head no. The husband

didn't stop. He whispered into his wife's ear, until she agreed to do it.

The young man sat down on the chair and removed his shoe and sock. "There's a medical team here, right?"

Peter assured the young couple. "Yes, we have medical here on staff. I was told that they have ice ready so they can try and preserve any toes, just in case they can be reattached."

The couple decided to use the meat cleaver. The young woman held it in her trembling hand and raised it in the air. The husband grabbed onto the chair that he was sitting on and closed his eyes. She swiftly lowered the cleaver, and made contact with his little toe.

"No! No! Ow! No! Not again! Stop!" The husband screamed in agony.

His wife picked up the little toe and held it in the air for him to see. "It's over. We just won $100,000. I won't do it again. It's okay now."

A medic rushed onto stage carrying an ice cooler. He took the toe from the woman and placed it into the ice. A pool of blood collected at the screaming man's foot. Another medic brought out a stretcher and wheeled the man off of the stage.

Peter smiled into the camera. "Isn't that a great way to start a marriage? With $100,000. Congratulations to the blue team."

Damon turned to Mary. "See no chance of

death, but it's still in the range of what viewers want to see. What do you think?"

Mary walked away from Damon shaking her head. She was still mad at him. Damon knew that she would come around, eventually. He just had to be on his best behavior. He needed Mary as an ally to get rid of William.

"Red team, what do you think of this challenge?" Peter questioned the long term married couple.

"There is no way I'm letting my wife do that to me. We'll go home and..."

The wife cut her husband off mid-sentence. "We need that money. We could send our kids to private school. We could give them a better life. You heard Peter, they might be able to reattach the toe. No big deal."

The husband looked at his wife like she was crazy. "No way. Our kids will be fine."

"Then cut my toe off." His wife offered him a suggestion.

Her husband shook his head no. "I won't hurt you."

"I want that money." The woman kicked off her shoe, and walked over to the challenge area.

"No, babe. I refuse." The man did not follow his wife.

Like a crazed woman, she picked up the axe and raised it in the air.

"Babe, stop!" He turned his head so he

couldn't see what his wife was getting ready to do.

She swung the axe down on her foot. Clank! She dropped the tool to the ground and wailed in pain. Her husband rushed over to her, and looked at the ground in horror. Not only did she chop off her pinky toe, but she over swung the axe and also chopped off the neighboring toe.

Damon smiled. Once again, he was giving the viewers what they wanted to see.

A GOOD DAY TURNED BAD

Damon waited what felt like an eternity for the show to air. He liked it when they filmed live. It was instant gratification. He hated it that the network had imposed the rule on them that they couldn't do live shows anymore. They had to film it first, then air the episode. Finally, the episode aired, and Damon had Mary put a poll on the website asking which challenge was better.

Damon turned on his computer to see what social media had to say about 'Pain for Gain'. Obviously, the first episode (darts and paintball) got horrible reviews. Their target audience wasn't looking for such simple challenges. Viewers liked the second episode better. Hopefully, with any luck, Damon hadn't lost viewers yet. He was so mad at William that he could scream.

Damon found a video posted by someone

with the screen name 'Pain Lover' and turned his speakers up. The video began to play. "That first show, 'Easy Money', was awesome. Now they give us this crap!" The video showed a short video clip of Marty Blevins being sucked into the wood chipper. "That was the best show ever! Now they give us a show full of teenage pranks. They can't take good TV away from us. I am starting a petition. Sign it. I will send it to URN, requesting a better pain show. At least we got to see people cutting off toes. Maybe it will get better. Click the link below the video to sign the petition."

Damon clicked his computer off. He was right. People wanted to see more deaths.

Damon walked right past Mary's desk. "My office now."

Mary closed her laptop and followed Damon into the office.

William looked up. "Thanks for knocking, Damon. Can I help you?"

"This is my office now. Leave." Damon was demanding.

"Whatever do you mean?" William looked lost.

"Mary, the online poll results?" Damon beat his hands along the side of the desk for a drumroll.

"People liked the cutting off of the toes.

Sorry, William. Damon won the bet." Mary looked at the ground.

Damon was happy. He now had his office back. Now all he had to do was get rid of William.

Damon drove straight to Destiny's hotel room. He was walking on air. He had a great day. Now he was hoping that Destiny had come up with something playful for him.

"I'm so glad to see you. Your last visit was incredible." Destiny smiled at her sugardaddy.

Damon recognized that it wasn't only his work performance getting good reviews. "I'm so glad to see you, too. Have you done your homework? I'm anxious to see how creative you can be." Damon smiled at the hooker.

"Actually, I have. But the problem is, you didn't tell me how generous you were willing to be. I have 2 ideas. Which idea I follow through with will depend on you."

Damon was intrigued. "What will $1,000 get me?"

Destiny held up a stun gun. It was small and fit perfectly into her hand. It had 2 metal prongs on the tip that would shoot electricity into Destiny's body.

Damon had never experimented with electricity before. "I like that idea. Do I dare ask what the other idea is?"

Destiny set the stun gun down, and held up her pointer finger. "Wait just a second. The next idea, is a big idea. It would require more cash."

Damon smiled. He enjoyed playing with Destiny. He pulled out more money.

"I watched a television show where a woman cut off her own toe. But I would need more money for that. A lot more money." Destiny was proud of her idea.

Damon did not like it that Destiny was watching his show. He couldn't chance her figuring out who he was. He had a professional reputation to protect. "What kind of television show is that? I guess we watch different kinds of television."

"It's a game show. People get paid to get hurt. It's on that reality network. They get paid big money though. I think she won $100,000. I would do it for a quarter of that." Destiny smiled, hoping he would be willing to fork over that kind of cash. Apparently, he was rich. She was sure that Damon had that kind of money.

Damon's heart broke. He actually liked Destiny. He really did miss her while he was gone. Now she was asking for large amounts of money. And she was watching his show. He wanted complete anonymity in this situation. Damon didn't usually have emotions. Why did he care for her? She could be a problem.

Damon pushed his emotions aside and

turned on his charm. "I don't have that kind of cash on me, at least not right now. I do like the stun gun thing. Why don't we have fun with that for now." Damon winked at Destiny.

Destiny picked up her new toy and held it up. "The guy at the store said it has 50,000 volts. He said it's pretty much the same kind as the police use." She handed it to Damon to examine. "Plus, I thought it would be smart for me to carry it after what happened to Amber." Destiny crossed her heart, thinking about her murdered friend.

Damon eyed the small weapon. He had never seen someone shot by a stun gun. Damon pressed the small object into Destiny's stomach. "Are you sure about this?"

Destiny nodded her head yes. Damon squeezed the object and activated it. The weapon made a zapping noise. Destiny flopped down on the bed and began jerking like she was having a seizure. Damon did not let up. He kept zapping her, until he saw that she was unconscious. He spread her arms above her head and tied them to the legs of the bed. He placed the ball gag in her mouth, and secured it around her head. Damon sat down and had a good cry, something Damon hadn't done in sometime.

DESTINY

This was Damon's first visit to Destiny's motel that he didn't rent a car. He was starting to feel safe with Destiny. He had some sort of attachment to her. He couldn't figure out what that attachment was, but he didn't like it. He did not like it at all. He knew that he couldn't kill Destiny while he was in his own car. He left Destiny tied up to the bed and gagged while he went to get a rental car.

As Damon entered her motel room, he saw that she was awake.

"Mmmmm. Hmmmm." Destiny was trying to speak, but she could only make noises due to the ball gag in her mouth.

"You're awake. I'm glad to see you." Damon smiled at his victim.

"Mmmmm. Hmmmm!" Destiny tried to wiggle but her hands were tied to tight. She couldn't move. He hadn't tied up her legs, and she was kicking at him.

"Calm down. I'm just playing with you. You know that I'll pay you. If I take that out of your mouth will you not scream at me?" Damon smiled, hoping it would make Destiny feel better about the situation.

Destiny nodded her head yes. Damon removed the ball gag.

"I won't scream. I just have to use the bathroom. Will you untie me?" Destiny asked her captor with an urgency.

Damon thought about the situation for a moment. If he was going to kill her, he didn't need her urinating everywhere and leaving behind evidence. "Of course, but can we still play afterwards?" Damon was trying to sound sincere.

"Yes. But I have to potty now!" Destiny was getting frustrated.

Damon untied her arms, and watched her as she went to the restroom.

"What do you have in mind for this playtime session? You know I didn't like that stun gun. I still feel weird from it." Destiny was screaming from the toilet.

Damon was relieved that she didn't suspect anything. Damon studied her movements as she walked back into the room, and grabbed her pipe. Destiny started inhaling the toxic fumes of the drugs. For a second, Damon started thinking that maybe he didn't have to kill her. She didn't care who he was. All she cared about was her drugs. She wasn't even mad at him for keeping her tied up while he left.

"Did you go get more money when you were gone?" Destiny took another puff from her glass pipe.

"Yeah, actually I did." Damon sat down on the bed next to her. He didn't like it that she asked him for more money.

Damon reached into his pocket and pulled out the stun gun. He zapped Destiny until she faded out of consciousness once again. He tied her hands behind her back, and her feet together. He looked out the window. He didn't see anyone outside. It was really dark in the parking lot. He hoisted Destiny over his shoulder, and carried her to his car. He knew an isolated place in the desert where he could take her. It was only a few hours drive.

Destiny woke up in the passenger seat of Damon's rental car, tied up. "Where are we?"

Damon looked at her, trying to keep his eyes on the road. "We're going for a drive."

"Why? I didn't agree to this. You didn't tell me that you would be taking me somewhere." Destiny was confused.

Damon was just glad that she wasn't getting mad at him. "I'm sorry, but I don't think I can do this anymore." Damon's eyes swelled up with tears. He was going to miss her after he killed her.

"Can't do what? I have tried to do anything that I can to please you. You're starting to scare me." Destiny tried wiggling free from her ropes. "Where are we? How long have I been unconscious? This road doesn't look familiar. Why did we leave the city?"

Damon was silent as he continued to drive. He was trying to remember all the good times he had shared with Destiny.

Destiny refused to give up. "Please talk to me. I have enjoyed our play times, but this doesn't feel right." Destiny shed a tear. She knew that Damon was taking her to kill her. "Just talk to me. We can figure this out."

Damon knew that she was lying. "You don't enjoy our time together. How could you? It was nothing but pain for you. You enjoyed the money! That's all I am to you. A paycheck!"

"Kind of. You are also the most generous man that I have ever met. I had already told myself that if you agreed to pay me big money, I was gonna start a new life. All I do is sit in my small motel room, and get high. I'm miserable. My only friend is gone. You were gonna be my way out. All I wanted was a new life." Destiny started sobbing. "I don't want to die!"

Damon pulled the car to the side of the road and looked at her. "I'm alone too. I don't sit around and get high all day."

"No, you just torture women. Dangling money in front of them, so that they will do anything you want. You're not any better than me. You just have more money than I do. Yes, I wanted money. I'm only human." Destiny was angry and scared. "You don't have to kill me."

Damon entered a different address into the GPS on his phone, and drove while Destiny cried.

Damon pulled up in front of a large building.

"What are you doing? Why are we here?" Destiny looked shocked.

"It's an inpatient drug recovery hospital. Rehab. I'm offering to help you. Under certain conditions." Damon looked at Destiny's face, trying to judge her reaction. "First, you should know that I have a professional reputation to protect. We are a few hours outside of the city, so it should be safe for me to bring you here. Noone will know who I am. I will pay for your rehab, but you can't tell anyone about my habits. If I find out that you told anyone in there what I have done to you, it will be bad. But you do need to really try to get off the drugs."

Destiny was scared by Damon's threat. She promised to keep Damon's secrets, and agreed to get off drugs. Damon was happy. Maybe he wasn't alone like he thought.

OFFICE POLITICS

Damon had a little spring in his step. He had his old office back, and a friend, assuming that Destiny really would get off drugs and keep his secrets. He believed that she would hold up her end of the deal. He walked into his office, like he was walking on air. Things were looking up for him. He was so happy that he was back at work. Even though he had enjoyed his stay in Mexico, he had missed his job. He was good at his job. It made him feel powerful.

Damon called Mary into his office.

"William is fighting me about planning the challenges for the show. What are your thoughts?" Damon knew that he would need Mary's help if he wanted to force William off the production of his show.

"He's careful. Which is what the network wants. I find his ideas boring, but maybe it's good that he is careful. The network approves of him. The network was going to cancel our show, which would leave me without a job. I need my job. They agreed to keep the show on the air, as long as he was part of the production." Mary did not want to give Damon too much information.

"The network wouldn't cancel our show. We have better ratings than any other show. We were bringing in huge money from our sponsors. The network isn't stupid. I think there's more to it than that. What are you not telling me? What happened while I was suspended? This is me. You can tell me anything, Mary. We have history together. I value us working together." Damon did like Mary. Damon needed to get information from Mary. "I may not always be rational. And I really am sorry that I didn't let you in on my plans of killing Marty Blevins, but I knew that you were already struggling with your conscience. I did it to better our show. Our careers. I did it for the both of us. I couldn't have created 'Easy Money' without your help."

"After you were suspended they canceled 'Easy Money'. They even talked about taking me off of the other show I was working on. I had to beg and plead just to stay on with the network. William pitched them a new idea. A 'kinder, gentler' pain show. They told me he was the only person who would agree to do such a show. But I saw a lot of the fan mail.

People didn't want a safer show. They wanted 'Easy Money' back. The network thought he had a good idea. Then, the network waited for lawsuits after Marty died. There were no lawsuits, only a handful of protests and boycotts. Nothing legal. I think that's why the network brought you back." Mary hoped she hadn't made a mistake by telling Damon the truth.

"Essentially, William took it upon himself to try and take my job?" Damon asked his assistant.

Mary shook her head yes.

"How can we get rid of him?" Damon wanted William gone.

"We can't. He's been with the network for a very long time. He's a huge stockholder." Mary shrugged her shoulders. "Mr. Styles doesn't want to make William mad. He wants to keep him on the show. It's not a bad thing having him around."

Damon disagreed with Mary. He didn't like it that William had tried to take his position away from him. He wanted William gone. He had a vision for the show, and that vision did not include William.

"I would like to begin this meeting by discussing the future of 'Pain for Gain'." Damon sat at the head of a large table.

The meeting was being held by 3 people. Damon, William, and Mary. Damon had insisted on a formal meeting of all the producers.

"Fine by me. You're taking this show down a bad road." William didn't mind opposing Damon.

"We are losing viewers. Our ratings are only half as good as those of 'Easy Money'. We have lost a couple of sponsors. It's not too late. We have to get this show back on the right track." Damon brought paperwork to support his claims. He handed packets to William and Mary.

William flipped through the packet with ratings reports and the list of income generated by the sponsors. "This doesn't mean anything. Viewers don't know what they want. Give it time, 'Pain for Gain' will top the television charts in time."

Damon agreed with William. "Yes. I plan to do for 'Pain for Gain' the same as I did for 'Easy Money'. I will get it back to number 1."

"No." William stopped Damon from speaking. "As a representative of this network, I refuse to let you ruin the network's reputation worse than you already have."

Damon ignored William. "If you turn to the third page, you will find my proposals for the show. Just a few minor changes."

"Wait just a minute. You can't come back

here after your leave of absence and force your ideas on us." William did not like it that Damon was taking charge of the meeting. Nor did he like the direction the show would be taking.

Damon smiled. This was exactly what he expected. "Well, there's 3 of us here. The right thing to do here is to have an official vote. Mary's vote will be the deciding factor." Damon turned to face Mary.

Mary sat without saying a word as she read the packet. She didn't know that the ratings were so low. She also saw the money they were losing by losing sponsors. As bad as Mary didn't like it, Damon was right. 'Pain for Gain' needed to become more like 'Easy Money'. Mary also remembered that 'Easy Money' resulted in the death of a contestant. Even though she didn't like it, she had to side with Damon. She liked it that she was part of such a successful show. She had to think of her own career. She hoped with William also working on the show, that Damon would be on his best behavior.

"I'm sorry William. Damon is right. These ratings are bad. We need Damon to work his magic."

PAIN FOR GAIN (THE THIRD EPISODE)

"I'm Peter Conway, welcoming you to 'Pain for Gain'. The only reality game show where contestants hurt each other to get paid. Do not try this at home. Let's get on with the show."

While Peter was busy introducing the guests, Damon took the opportunity to thank Mary.

"I'm glad that you have decided to side with me. I know that William isn't happy with you right now, but he don't matter. I'm just trying to do what's best for the show." Damon was proud of Mary. He knew that she would side with him.

"I didn't do it for you. I did it for the show. I did it for my own career. This doesn't mean that I like you." Mary walked away so she could watch the show in peace.

Damon directed his attention back to Peter.

"Welcome red team. What made you decide to be on the show?" Peter asked the couple standing behind the first podium.

"My husband here decided to take all the money that we had saved for retirement, and invest it in stocks. We lost everything. All of our savings. We have no chance of retiring anytime soon without money. We need a cash infusion into our bank account." The wife of the red team looked at her husband, like she was blaming him for losing everything they had worked hard for their whole life.

Peter offered his sympathies and moved onto the next team. "Blue team. How about you? What do you plan to do with the money that you will earn today?"

A man spoke up. "We've been business partners for years. The economy hasn't been too good on our business. I know that if we had some money to put back into our company, then we can get back on the right track." Both of the men clapped.

"Okay. I wish both teams the best. You aren't competing against each other. All you have to do is complete the challenge to win the money. Simple enough. Let's get on with our show." Peter walked over to a meat slicer and waved his hands over it. "This is a meat slicer.

The same kind of meat slicer that you see in a deli at a supermarket. It's typically used to slice sandwich meat. This slicer has 3 adjustable settings. The first setting is the thinnest, the second setting is medium, the third setting is the thickest. Meaning it cuts a thicker slice of meat. One person will stick their hand in the slicer, The other person of the team will secure their partner's hand in place while they slice off a piece of their partner's palm. The setting the slicer is set on determines how much money you will earn. The thinnest setting earns you $2,500, the middle setting earns you $7,500, and the thickest setting will earn you a whopping $20,000. Do we all understand? Good. The blue team will go first."

The first man looked at the meat slicer, then his business partner. "I don't know. There's a big difference between $7,500 and $20,000. We need that higher cash amount. I say we do the thickest."

His business partner agreed with him. "Okay. Fine by me. If you let me slice your hand in this challenge, I'll take the pain in the next challenge. Deal?"

The man stuck his hand on the cold metal of the meat slicer. "Okay, let's do this." He shut his eyes and took a deep breath.

His business partner pressed the man's palm firmly onto the blade of the meat slicer.

Peter instructed the other man what to do.

"Just press that tray onto the back of his palm. Clamp it down to lock it into place."

The man did as he was instructed.

"Now, when you hit that power switch, the blade will start to turn. Glide the tray with your partner's hand forward, then back to you. Pretty simple." Peter made an uncomfortable face as he told the man how to work the machine.

The man powered up the machine. His business partner grimaced his face and closed his eyes when he saw the blade spinning. The man glided the tray forward, and sliced off a piece of bloody palm flesh fell next to the machine.

"Stop it! Turn it off! No!" The man was in excruciating pain.

His business partner quickly turned the machine off. When he saw how thick the slice of meat was, he went into shock.

Peter approached the men to take a closer look. "I think we need a medic now!."

The screaming man pulled his hand out of the tray and looked at his palm. "My bone! I can see my bone! I can see the bones in my hand!" Blood ran down his arm. A medic came and escorted him off the stage.

His business partner watched as his partner left with the medic. "I'm so sorry. He told me to. I'm sorry!"

Peter tried to comfort the man. "Yes, he

agreed to do this. You didn't do anything wrong. Do you want to leave with him? Or do you want to stay for the second round?"

"I told him that I'd do the second challenge. I think I would feel better if I stayed and earned money."

"Congratulations! The blue team just won $20,000. Red team, are you ready? We have your very own meat slicer over here. We knew that this would be a messy challenge." Peter looked at the machine as it dripped blood.

"No way! I'm not doing that." The husband refused.

"It's your fault we lost all of our money in the stock market. You have to do this!" His wife was not happy with him.

"Did you see his hand? No way!" The husband shook his head no.

"What if we do the thin setting?" The wife offered a solution.

"No. No way. Let's wait for the next round. The second round is always worth more money." The husband still refused.

"Fine. But you have to promise to do it. No matter what it is." The wife wasn't happy, but she understood her husband's reasoning.

"Promise. Anything but the meat slicer." The husband begged his wife, hoping she would be happy.

"Peter, can we skip out on this round, and only do the second challenge?" The wife asked the host.

"Sure. You don't have to do anything that you don't want to do. Are you sure?" Peter did not want the red team to feel pressured to do anything they didn't want to do.

The husband spoke up loudly. "Yes. We're sure."

"Okay then. Let's get to the next round." Peter continued on with the show. "In the second round we will be using drills." Peter walked over to a table with 2 handheld drills. "All you have to do is drill a hole completely through any body part of your choosing. This challenge is worth $50,000. Red team, you go first."

The wife already started nagging her husband. "You promised to do this. Where do you want me to drill?"

The husband shook his head. "I don't know. Maybe we shouldn't."

"You promised. We need this money." The wife was not happy.

"Okay. Okay. Drill my hand. Stay in the center of my palm." The husband reluctantly agreed to let his wife put a hole in his hand.

The wife started smiling. She looked as if she was actually going to enjoy doing this to her husband. Her husband laid his hand flat on a piece of wood.

"Just squeeze that red trigger. Then push that drill bit through his hand." Peter instructed her how to use the drill.

The wife placed the tip of the drill bit on the back of her husband's hand. She smiled as she squeezed the trigger. The drill bit started spinning, and she pressed down hard to make it spin through his flesh. Her husband started screaming, and she started laughing. It took at least a full 4 seconds before the drill bit penetrated completely through his hand and hit the wood. Those 4 seconds felt like an eternity to her husband. She pulled the drill bit out of his hand and squeezed the trigger. It spun and blood flew off the small tool in multiple directions as she laughed.

Her husband held his hand up and screamed. Then he screamed some more. A medic came and ushered him off the stage.

"Congratulations red team! You just won $50,000." Peter tried to put on his best smile, but it was hard after seeing what he just saw. "Blue team. Well, there's only 1 of you left, so I guess you'll have to drill yourself. Are you ready?"

The man shed a tear, knowing how painful this would be. "Can I do my shoulder? I think that would be easiest. I use my hands everyday at work."

Peter shook his head yes.

The man picked up the drill, and held it up to his shoulder. He shook his head no, and blew out a large breath. The man squeezed the trigger, and the drill bit started spinning. The man gritted his teeth and screamed as he pressed the drill further into his shoulder. Seconds later, the camera zoomed in on the drill bit exiting the back of the man. The man was yelling in pain as he quickly pulled the drill out his body. The man dropped to his knees and cried.

"Congratulations blue team. You just won $50,000!" Peter looked into the camera. "Thanks for joining us tonight folks. I'm Peter Conway, wishing you a goodnight."

Damon found Mary and approached her. "We're back. Wasn't this great? I knew teams were a good thing. If 1 person quits, the other person can still complete the next challenge. This was wonderful. That wife, she was loving what she was doing. Did you hear her laughing?"

Mary shook her head yes. William saw Damon and Mary talking.

"You should be ashamed of yourself. That show is a disgrace. I will not stand by while you do this! I'll make sure they take this show off the air before I let you ruin this network! What are you thinking?" William did not approve of this episode.

Damon spoke in a calm manner. "I'm thinking about ratings. The ratings will go up, I just know it. This show will be a hit. They won't take it off of the air." Damon wasn't worried. He knew how to make good television.

VISITATION

Damon drove the few hours to visit Destiny in rehab. He was really proud of her for staying there. She was there willingly, she could leave anytime that she wanted. Maybe she really did want to change. She had been in there for a couple of weeks, and they finally allowed her to have visitors. When she called Damon, she told him that she didn't have anyone else who would want to visit her.

Destiny looked better since she stopped smoking drugs. Her face began to fill out a little bit. She had put on a few pounds, and it looked good on her. Even her hair looked healthier. Damon looked at her missing front teeth, and remembered the day she pulled them out. He realized that she was actually kind of pretty now.

"When we get you out of here, we'll take you to a dentist. I'm sure you could get implants or something. You look nice now, when you get your new teeth, you'll be really pretty." Damon smiled at the woman. He always had a feeling that he was alone in this big world. He didn't feel alone when he was with Destiny. She really knew him. She even knew his flaws, but she seemed to still like him.

"For real? Seriously, you think so? I'd love to get new teeth." Destiny smiled, but when she did she covered her missing teeth with her upper lip. She was self conscious of the gap. "This whole thing still seems crazy. I didn't even know your name until you dropped me off here. Now you're turning into a really sweet man."

Damon had never been called sweet before. He didn't want to be sweet. But he didn't want to feel alone either. "Have you had to talk about... stuff?"

"They have me talking to counselors almost constantly. Mostly about drugs, and working the streets. Nothing about you. I promise." Destiny remembered Damon threatening her the day that he dropped her off. "Thanks for coming to see me. I'm thinking a little better now. Like I have a clearer head. When they told me I could have visitors, I didn't have anyone else to call. I felt alone."

Damon grabbed Destiny's hand. "You're not alone. You have me." Damon meant what he said. Now they would have each other.

On the drive home, Damon passed a little

strip club and decided to stop in. He wasn't the kind of man that went to those kinds of places, but he was happy. He figured that it wouldn't hurt to stop in and have a bourbon.

When Damon walked in, he was overwhelmed by the smell of cigarette smoke and loud music. He was turning around to leave, and out of the corner of his eye, a woman carrying around a whip caught his attention. He decided to stay, so he ordered himself a drink. The woman with the whip was walking past him. He eyed her up and down. She was wearing a leather bra, with a short leather skirt.

She noticed Damon checking her out. "Hey. You're new here. Do you like what you see?"

Damon shook his head yes. His eyes scanned down to her feet. She was wearing shiny black boots that had a very thin, tall, pointy heel.

"Something tells me that you're into the same stuff I like. Can I interest you in a dance?" The woman took her gloved finger and ran it across Damon's cheek.

"A private dance? I'd actually like a private show. Somewhere really private." Damon winked at the stripper.

"Sorry, honey. I only work here, at the club." The woman winked back at Damon.

"Okay, how much is a private dance?"

Damon rubbed his hand across her whip.

"$50. That gets you 3 songs." The woman took the end of the whip and tickled Damon's hand.

Damon reached into his pocket and pulled out a stack of cash and showed it to her. "What can I get for $500?"

The woman thought for a moment. "You a cop?"

Damon shook his head no.

"Meet me here, at this address. In 3 hours. That's when I get off work. Bring the cash." She reached into her bra and handed Damon a business card.

Damon sat and sipped his bourbon. Tonight was going to be a good night.

Damon drove to the address on the card. It appeared to be a little run down apartment. Damon knocked on the door.

"Hey. Welcome. I'm glad that you're here." The woman was now wearing normal clothes. Blue jeans and tennis shoes.

Damon looked around the apartment. Even though it was small, it was clean and tastefully decorated. "You look different."

"I dress like that at work. I just got home." She let her black hair down from her ponytail. Her hair swallowed her face in a messy way. She ran her hand through her long hair. "Did you bring the money?"

Damon shook his head yes.

She took Damon by his hand. "Come with me." She led Damon to her bedroom.

Damon saw a wall full of different kinds of whips, wooden paddles, and floggers. In a small display case there were multiple clamps. She also had an array of ropes and chains.

"Welcome to my playroom. Where your pain is my pleasure." The woman raised her shirt over her head. She was still wearing the black leather bra. She lowered her blue jeans, to reveal her black leather panties.

"Actually, I don't like pain myself. I'm more of a giver."

"Well, I have some ground rules. There's different price packages with different types of whips. I also charge more for the electric nipple clamps. Just tell me what you want. I aim to please." She smiled at Damon.

"I'm a bit unconventional. Do you like pain?" Damon whispered in her ear as he felt of her soft hair.

"I do." She whispered back to him and turned her face to his.

"Will you hurt yourself? I want to watch." Damon took a finger and lowered the leather bra strap from her shoulder.

She placed her hands on Damon's hips. "Have a seat." She lowered Damon onto the bed. She walked across the room and grabbed a candle and lit it. The flame flickered. She stood in front of Damon, hypnotizing him with the flame. The wax began to melt. She raised the candle and poured the hot wax on her chest, smiling as she did it.

"That's not pain. That's pleasure. I want to see pain." Damon teased his new toy.

She walked over to the nipple clamps and grabbed the pair that had a remote control attached to 2 wires. She removed her bra, and clamped the pinchers onto her perky nipples. She handed Damon the remote. He turned the power all the way on high. She giggled.

"That's pleasure. Show me pain." Damon requested of the stripper.

"What do you have in mind?" She smiled at him, playfully.

Damon reached into his pocket. He showed her a wad of money. "I want to see you hurt. All you have to do is hurt yourself."

"How?" She looked into his mysterious eyes.

Damon looked around the room. He was surrounded by different forms of sexual torture toys, but that just wasn't his thing. "I want to see you bleed."

"I can't do that. I show a lot of skin at work. Any open wounds would not be good at work." She gently sat on his lap and wrapped her arm around his neck.

Damon motioned for her to get up. He

stood and walked over to a lamp. "How about heat?"

"Like the hot wax?" She looked confused.

"No." Damon started unscrewing the lamp shade. He touched his finger to the bulb. It was very hot. "Let's get creative." Damon unplugged the lamp from the wall. The room went dim. He picked up the lamp, and carried it to her. "Touch this."

She gently put her finger to the bulb and giggled in a flirty way. "Okay. How much are you paying?"

Money. All these women ever wanted was money. Damon quickly dug into his pocket and threw the wad of cash on the bed. He didn't want the bulb to cool down. "There's $2,000. How's that? Hurry up, before it gets cold."

She laid back on the bed. "You can rub it on me if you want for that kind of money."

Damon carefully maneuvered the light bulb gently in between her firm breasts. She giggled each time the bulb made contact with her skin. He rubbed the hot bulb on her nipple and she moaned with pleasure. This wasn't hurting her. Damon wanted to see her in pain. Damon quickly raised the lamp in the air, and swung it down on her chest. The light bulb shattered into tiny pieces piercing her delicate skin.

"Get out! Now!" She sat up and tiny pieces of glass shimmered in the dim light, stuck to her breasts. Tiny streams of blood ran down her chest to her abdomen.

Damon stood and admired the blood.

She reached for her shirt. "Get out!"

Damon turned and left. Tonight was a good night.

MEETINGS

Damon had gotten a call from Mr. Styles requesting a meeting. Damon had barely spoken to his boss since he had returned to the network. He wondered what his boss wanted. Damon was looking good in his expensive suit. He confidently walked into his Mr. Styles office.

"Good of you to meet me today. I appreciate it. Once again, I'm sorry that we parted on such sour terms. I hope you understand my position." Mr. Styles wore a friendly smile.

Damon did remember when his boss had suspended him. It was the night that Marty Blevins had died on 'Easy Money'. Damon didn't see what the big fuss was about. He made sure to have all the legalities covered in Marty's contract. There were no legal repercussions. All he was doing was his job. He was making exciting television.

Damon tried to push his negative feelings for his boss aside. "Sure, I understand completely. What is this about?" Damon wasn't big on small talk. He wanted his boss to make his point soon.

Mr. Styles shifted around uncomfortably in his chair. It was almost like he could feel the tension radiating from Damon. "I called you here today about William Hendricks. He has filed a formal complaint against you."

Damon was suddenly interested. "A formal complaint? What exactly does that mean?"

"It means that he wants everyone on the board of the network to know that you are difficult to work with. He thinks you're being reckless in your professionalism." Mr. Styles was getting frustrated.

"I assure you that I'm doing nothing but my job." Damon tried to control his anger. "I have given this network the best ratings they have ever had. My shows are hits. He was in charge of that first episode of 'Pain for Gain'. He got horrible publicity. Why do they want to keep him around anyways?"

"He's been with this network for a very long time. He has a lot of friends in high places. You'd be wise to not make him mad, Damon. I'm telling you this as a friend. Not a boss."

Damon knew that Mr. Styles was not his friend. He had given Damon the boot the first chance that he had gotten. He didn't come to Damon and ask him what happened when that contestant died on live TV. He just got mad at him, then suspended him.

Damon stifled his emotions. "I appreciate that. I'm in a situation with William. He doesn't see things my way. He is trying to stop me from making good television. I'm only trying to give the viewers what they want. These contestants aren't forced to do anything. They do everything by their own free will. But William is trying to be safe. Too safe. He's actually concerned about safety on my pain show."

"Let me stop you there. This isn't your show. Your show, 'Easy Money', was cancelled. Technically, 'Pain for Gain' is his show. He stepped up in your absence. You're going to have to learn to work with him." Mr. Styles' patience had worn thin.

"Give me my own show. He can have his, I can have mine, then we can see which show gets better ratings." Damon's solution made complete sense to him.

"I can pass that along to the board, but I doubt it. If your show hadn't had such great ratings, we wouldn't have any pain shows. The network is still on the fence about airing that kind of a program. If I were you, I wouldn't push my luck. I would just play nice with William. This is your job we are talking about." Mr. Styles tried his best to give a comforting smile, but it was obviously fake.

"Please, just try to get my show back. In

the meanwhile, I will try to work with him. But what about the ratings? I can't give in to his weak challenges if I know the show won't get good ratings." Damon was actually asking his boss for advice.

"I don't know. You're Damon Dahmer. Work it out. You always do. Like I said, he has a lot of pull around here. I wouldn't make him mad if I were you." Mr. Styles' words of warning meant nothing to Damon.

Damon went straight to William's office. He didn't care who William knew, or how much time and money William had invested in the network. Damon was a professional. He would not let William ruin his professional career. Damon knew that he was good at his job.

Damon laughed at the fact that William was now in a smaller, less desirable office. Damon had won the nicer office, fair and square in their friendly bet. IIe didn't bother to knock, even though the door was closed. Damon walked right in. William was on the phone.

"William, you placed a formal complaint against me? That's absurd. You had no grounds!" Damon was very angry.

William looked up at Damon. He was obviously irritated. William spoke into his phone. "This is exactly what I was telling you about. He just barged into my office. Screaming at me. Let me call you back." William hung up the phone. "You're only proving my point. You're acting like an irrational child. There's no talking to you."

Damon closed his fist and slammed it down on William's small desk. "Are you trying to take my job away from me? This is my show. I won't let you take it away from me. Your work will never be as good as mine. Deal with it. This is war." Damon stormed out of the office, slamming the door behind him. He said what he had come to say.

ALONE

Damon got into his fancy sports car, and sped home. He walked into his large home and threw his suit jacket on the couch. He couldn't believe that William made a complaint against him. It didn't worry Damon, he knew that the network needed his professional creativity. It was just the fact that William went behind his back, and took matters into his own hands. William was acting like a school child, tattling to the teacher. They were adults, and Damon intended to resolve this like adults.

Damon needed his job. He looked at his home full of expensive, luxurious items. He had worked hard his whole life to afford such a lavish lifestyle. Someone was threatening to take that away from him. He could not allow that to happen.

Even though he had worked hard to give himself a good life, Damon looked around and realized that he was alone. There was a time before his child was killed by that Blevins man, that his home was full of love. A drunk driver killed his son. Damon thought that killing that man's son would give him the contentment he needed out of life. He was wrong. Damon felt alone.

Damon had tried hard to convince himself that he didn't need love in his life. He didn't need people in his life. He had his career. He needed a distraction. Damon checked the clock. It was perfect timing for a perfect distraction. He knew exactly what would make him feel better.

Damon rented a car, and drove for a few hours. He knew that his new friend would be getting off of work soon. He could make it to her apartment parking lot as she was coming home, and meet up with her. Afterall, he did owe her an apology. Damon pulled his baseball cap over his eyes, and sat in the dark car waiting for her arrival.

Eventually, he saw a car pulling into a parking spot in front of her apartment. It was dark outside, but it looked like her driving. He got out of his vehicle, and approached her.

"No. You cannot come in! Plus, you shouldn't be here. I don't need my neighbors to see this. They don't know where I work, or what kind of business I conduct in my apartment. Plus, I don't want to see you after what you did to me. Please, just go away." Even though she was angry, she was trying to be quiet. She didn't want to draw attention to herself. The woman turned her back to Damon and started walking away.

Damon looked around. The parking lot was practically deserted. He saw no lights on in the other apartments. It was late. "I came to apologize. I was wrong the other night. Let me make it up to you. I was out of control. What I did was wrong. Let me at least give you more compensation. I brought more money. I remembered what you said that you having wounds would hurt your business at work. I owe you."

The woman paused. She turned back around and looked at Damon. "Okay. Fair is fair."

"It's in the car." Damon walked over to his rental car. He opened the back door and pulled out a large bag, and began digging through it.

The woman walked up to Damon, and he pulled out the stun gun, and quickly zapped her. The woman's body jolted, then she went limp. He stuffed her into the backseat of his car, and drove away.

Damon pulled over just a couple of minutes later into an abandoned gas station. He had his ropes handy, and began to tie her up before she woke up. Damon drove into the desert. He wanted to be alone with his new friend. She was going to be his distraction from work stress.

The woman woke up laying in sand. The wind was blowing. Her hair was covering her face. She tried to look through the hair that was covering her eyes. She was laying on her belly. Her legs were folded up behind her, and her wrists were tied tightly to her ankles.

"Hello. Welcome back. I'm so glad you're awake."

She saw the evil man who had smashed the light bulb on her chest. The woman tried to speak, but she had a gag in her mouth and could only make muffled sounds.

Damon bent down, and gently used a finger to get the hair out of her eyes. "I wanted you awake for our playtime. Isn't it beautiful out here in the desert? We're so isolated. So far away from civilization. I especially like it at night. In the dark,like it is now."

Damon wanted her to watch as he spread his tools out in front of her. He wanted to see the terror in her face. He wanted to hear her gurgled screams. This was his favorite form of playtime. He held up each item before he placed it on the ground in front of her. He held up what looked to be a large pair of scissors. They were hedge shears. He held up some kind of a gardening tool that resembled a claw, with 3 sharp fingers on it. He also had a hammer.

The woman looked around. She saw a shovel covered in sand and dirt. There was a large, deep hole next to the shovel. The woman struggled and screamed, but she couldn't break loose from her bindings. This man was crazy. She knew that this man was going to kill her.

"Shh. I just want to see how much pain the human body can endure. It's just a game that I like to play. I tried to hire you as my new play toy, but you were stubborn. This is so much more fun for me anyways. I needed this in my life. So I'd like to thank you." Damon flipped the wiggling woman over on her side and slowly unbuttoned her shirt. He enjoyed the throaty sounds that she was making.

The woman tried to struggle against him, but there was no use. She was tied too tight. The woman was crying so hard that she started to hyperventilate. She was so uncomfortable, and now she was having a hard time breathing.

"Shh. It's okay. It will be over soon." Damon comforted the woman.

Damon took the claw and felt the sharp points of the tool. He flipped the struggling woman over on her side. He stabbed the 3 sharp tips of the claw in the thin flesh between her breasts. He pressed the tool firmly into her skin, and raked it down to her belly button. Her skin instantly opened up, and blood was leaking from the wounds.

"What did you tell me? That you didn't want to bleed? It was bad for work. My goal is to see you covered in blood, from head to toe." Damon revealed his plan to the crying woman.

She started shaking her head no. She was begging him with her eyes to release her.

Damon picked up the hedge shears, and snapped them together right in front of her face. He shoved her back over on her stomach. Even though she was squirming, he managed to get a good grip on her index finger. The woman shrieked in fear as she felt the metal on her hand. Damon positioned the blades around her frail finger, and quickly snapped the blades shut. Her finger fell down on her back. The remaining nub squirted blood like a water fountain. The woman had a small pool of blood on her back.

"This is fun." Damon laughed and looked up at the moon. He was finally free to enjoy himself. Damon hadn't felt this free in quite some time. "I have an idea."

Damon flipped the woman over on her side, and positioned the blades of the shears around the woman's nipple. The sharp blades sliced through the nipple like a knife cutting butter. A stream of blood started pooling up in the sand. Damon used the shears to cut off the woman's pants, "Stop moving. You don't want me to cut you, do you?" Damon laughed at his own joke.

Damon put his hand on the woman's knee and spread her legs, to expose the essence of her womanhood. The woman shrieked and squealed. Damon enjoyed her sounds. He took the shears, and positioned each blade on the sides of the exposed skin of her woman parts. He snapped the tool together, and the flaps of skin fell to the ground. That bled a lot. The woman passed out from the pain. Damon took the sharp claw and took his time raking it along her body. He wanted her to bleed, and he made sure that she did.

When he was finished slowly scraping the skin off of her, he used the hammer on her face to make her extra pretty. He swung the hammer uncontrollably until her head splattered like a cracked egg. When he was done with her, practically every bit of her body was covered in blood. Damon looked at his work of art. He couldn't figure out why he enjoyed this, but he did. He felt powerful in this moment. Damon stood, admiring her bloody body, and the mess that he had made.

Damon was happy. When he was finished admiring his work, he rolled her body over into the grave that he had already dug. He was all alone in the desert. No one would ever find her body here.

PAIN FOR GAIN (THE FOURTH EPISODE)

"Welcome back for another episode of 'Pain for Gain'. I am your host Peter Conway. Tonight's episode has very daring challenges and some great contestants! Also, we have some huge payouts to our lucky winners. Hang onto your seats, ladies and gents. Let's play 'Pain for Gain'."

Damon got comfortable in his seat as he watched the filming of the episode. Writing this episode was difficult on Damon. William would not let Damon do the challenges he wanted to do. Damon compromised with William, and went along with the not so interesting challenges. Damon was secretly plotting in his head ways to get rid of William. Damon didn't like this show. He wanted it to be done his way.

"For the red team we have James and Lori. What made you want to be on our show?"

Lori looked down to the ground and didn't speak.

James spoke up for her. "I'm in between jobs. We don't currently have health insurance, and our baby is sick. We need cash for doctor bills."

Peter looked at the players with compassion. "I wish you the best of luck. Blue team. Hello Steve and Sara. Welcome to the show. Why did you want to compete on our show?"

Sara was loud and energetic. "We're just fans of the show, Peter. We watch this show all the time. We need money to pay off some bills, maybe even go on a vacation if we win enough."

The husband and wife duo cheered and gave each a big hug.

"Okay. The rules are simple. All you have to do is complete the challenges to win money. If you suffer pain, you gain some cash. Easy enough. Let's see what the challenges are tonight." Peter walked over to a display case. "Our first challenge is usually the easiest, and pays less. The next round is harder, but worth more money. For the first challenge, we have a light bulb. It looks harmless enough. But one player will wear a safety glove, and smash the light bulb into the skin of their partner. The bulb must break on the skin. This challenge is worth $10,000."

William had vetoed all of Damon's good ideas. Damon suggested blow torches, table saws, and knives. William refused. When William agreed to the light bulb, Damon didn't mind. It was his way of paying homage to his friend that he buried in the desert. Anyways, he had a secret plan in play for the second challenge that would make William mad.

The red team got excited as Peter invited them to come play out the challenge.

"This is easy. Lori, smash it into my back. I can handle it. It's only broken glass. This will put a dent in some of our medical bills. This is easy." James reassured his wife that it was okay to hurt him.

Damon got bored. He thought this challenge was weak. He already knew that people would do this for way less money.

Lori slid her hand into the protective glove, and held the light bulb away from her like it was a grenade. Damon laughed at her. It's not like the light bulb itself was dangerous. James removed his shirt, and turned his back to his wife.

"Now, just smash it into his skin real hard Lori. Press it on there real good. It has to break into his skin." Peter instructed the contestant what to do.

Lori rammed her arm into her husband's back until the glass bulb shattered into tiny pieces. "Dang it!" James yelled.

She saw small streaks of blood begin to run from his skin. "Honey, I'm so sorry are you okay?"

Peter ignored the couple as they made small talk with each other. "Congratulations red team. You just won $10,000! Isn't that exciting? Blue team, are you ready?"

Steve and Sara ran over to where Peter was standing as they got ready for the challenge. Steve removed his shirt. Sara put on the safety glove.

Damon laughed at the safety glove. Of course, that was William's idea.

"Sara, ram it into my chest! It can't be that bad. If they can do it, so can we!" Steve was hyping his wife up, getting her ready to embed tiny shards of broken glass into his skin.

Sara raised her arm with the light bulb and approached her husband. He took a deep breath and shook his hands by his sides. As he exhaled, Sara shoved her hand into his chest and pushed the light bulb into his chest. You could hear the crunching of the glass.

"Whooo! Whooo!" Steve screamed with excitement. "'Pain for Gain' baby! We did it!"

The husband and wife duo jumped up with excitement.

"Congratulations blue team! You just won $10,000!" Peter was just as excited as the players.

Damon knew that his part was coming up. He leaned forward in his chair, watching the monitor closely. He couldn't wait for William to see what he had planned.

Peter walked over to a small display, and reached down and grabbed a gun. "What we have here is a bb gun. Not a real gun. This weapon shoots small plastic bbs. In this challenge, each team gets 5 bbs. Where you shoot your partner, depends on how much you get paid. Limbs are worth $2,500. The actual body is worth $5,000. And the facial area is worth $7,500. That means if your partner takes all 5 pellets in the face, you could earn $37,500. Just for getting shot by pieces of plastic. Okay, blue team you get the privilege of going first."

Steve and Sara practically ran over to Peter.

"Babe, I can take 5 pieces of plastic to the face. Get as close as you need to. Make sure your aim is good. We're going home with that money!" Steve was excited to win.

Sara looked at her husband. She was a pretty good aim so she knew that she didn't have to stand too close.

"Oh, yeah, Steve, you need to wear the safety goggles." Peter reminded the player.

Damon rolled his eyes. Safety on a pain show. So foolish of William. Damon went along with such weak challenges hoping that

William's show would get bad ratings, and eventually get cancelled. That would be 1 step closer to getting 'Easy Money' back on the air.

Sara raised the toy airsoft gun to her face and squinted her eye to get a good aim. Sara exhaled and squeezed the trigger. A small hole formed on her husband's face, on the upper part of his cheek bone. He held a hand up, motioning for his wife to stop for a second. He rubbed the area of the hole in his face.

"Stop. Stop production. Cut!" William lunged out of his chair and approached the stage. He walked up to Sara. "Give me the gun!"

Sara looked stunned, but she did as she was told. William fiddled with the weapon, and held up a tiny metal bb.

"Plastic. It was supposed to be plastic! Who loaded this with metal?" William looked around the room. He scanned everyone at the filming. His eyes landed on Damon, who was trying not to laugh. "What do you have to say for yourself?"

"Me? Why do you think it was me?" Damon tried to look innocent. "You can still save this. Just edit it, have Peter say it's metal, not plastic. Finish up the show. It's getting late."

"Get off my set now!" William was so angry that his face was turning red.

"Fine. I'm bored anyways." Damon collected his stuff and walked outside.

Mary followed Damon out. "What are you doing? I have really tried hard to be on your side. Why did you do that?"

Damon looked at Mary and saw an opportunity. "Do you miss 'Easy Money'?"

"I don't know. Maybe. Parts of it." She hated to admit to Damon that his previous television show had been genius.

"William's show is bad. I was trying to help get good ratings, but he fought me. So now I just gave in to him. His show will get cancelled, then we can go back to doing our thing." Damon thought his idea was brilliant.

"No, he'll get you fired first. What you're doing is stupid. He's not the kind of man to play games with." Mary didn't know why, but she was concerned for Damon.

"I'm the kind of man you don't play games with. We were a great team, Mary. Let's do it again." He was hoping that his words were registering to her.

"If we're a team, that means I'm in on your plans. No surprises this time. No Marty Blevins. But let me ask you something. Why do you think I need you? Maybe I want my own show." Mary cocked her head sideways at her boss.

"You're too good a person to do this kind of thing, Mary. That's why I need you on my team. That's why you need me. You balance me out. I balance you out. It's perfect." Damon walked away, knowing that what he told her was the truth. She was a good person. She couldn't do this type of show alone.

HOMECOMING

Destiny was finally getting out of rehab. Damon had thought about it, and he decided that he wanted her with him. As long as she agreed. Maybe it was time for Damon to try something new. Maybe he didn't want to be alone anymore. It was time for a change. The car ride would be plenty of time to talk about it, and see what she thought.

While she was an inpatient at the hospital, he had paid for a dentist to fix her pulled out teeth. She actually looked pretty with her plump cheeks, and healthy hair. Damon almost didn't recognize her. She no longer looked like a drug smoking, strung out hooker. Damon made sure to compliment her on her new looks. He was a gentleman and opened her car door for her.

When he looked at Destiny, he saw a blank slate. She was fresh off the streets, fresh off drugs. She was also looking for a new life. Maybe at this point in their lives, they needed each other. Luckily, she was also happy to see him. He feared that maybe she held a grudge against him for the pain he paid her to inflict upon herself. She wasn't angry at him at all. She was thankful to him for paying for her rehab.

"What are your plans?" Damon thought he would just ask her a few questions, to see what her thoughts were.

"I don't know. I don't want to work the streets anymore. I guess I will get a real job. I probably lost my motel room. It's not like I had anything of value there, anyways. I made a mess of my life. I need to fix that. Starting now." Destiny looked out the car window.

"I paid for your room. I didn't want you to lose your stuff." Damon smiled at her to get her attention.

"Why are you so nice to me?" She smiled back.

Damon ignored the question. "Are you sure about not wanting to do drugs anymore?"

Destiny shook her head. "I am so sure. I haven't felt this good in ages. I was slowly killing myself. Doing dreadful things for money." She raised her skirt to see the brand on her thigh.

"Look, I'm sorry about that. It was work related." Damon tried to explain.

"Work related? I don't understand. Are you some sort of pain police?" Destiny laughed at her own joke.

"I'm a producer. Executive producer. I created 'Easy Money'. I currently work on 'Pain for Gain.' I feel awful for the things you did to yourself. The things I did to you. Remember, you can't tell anyone."

"Holy crap! That makes so much sense. I won't tell anybody. You made it right. You fixed me. You're the person that saved my life by taking me to rehab. You got me off dope. I'm forever in your debt. So I guess you have a really great life, huh?" Destiny really was indebted to him.

"I was thinking maybe we could go to your motel, and gather your things. Do you wanna come stay with me? I have plenty of room." Damon was serious as he asked the question.

Destiny laughed. "Are you serious? Of course I do. But wait. Do I have to hurt myself anymore?" Her laughter quickly stopped as she became worried.

Damon nodded his head no. "Of course not. It's different now." Damon was happy. His house would no longer be empty.

When he pointed out his house from the street, Destiny couldn't believe how big it was. Damon led Destiny around and showed her the house, room by room. She was in shock when she found out that he had a gym, a library, and a pool.

"You really want me to stay here? With you? What's the catch?" Destiny was confused. She knew that if something seemed too good to be true, then it probably wasn't true.

"No catch. Honest." Damon took Destiny by the hand. 'I'll show you to your room."

"My room? My room isn't your room?" Destiny was even more confused.

"No. Not yet. It's just very sudden. I want to get to know you." Damon really was charming.

"You're rich, cute, and have a good job. Why me?" Destiny wasn't very trusting. She had only recently learned his name. Now he wanted her to live with him. Something didn't add up.

Damon thought for a moment. "I'm a very private person. I don't have many people in my life. I only have work. I thought we could be good for each other." It seemed simple to Damon.

Destiny knew that for now, she would sleep with her bedroom door locked, and with her eyes open.

Destiny did exactly that. She didn't sleep too well, hoping that she didn't make a mistake by moving in with this stranger. It made sense to her that their time together originally started because he was seeing what people would do for cash on his television show. However, she still wasn't quite sure whether or not she could trust him.

When she woke, Damon greeted her in the kitchen with a cup of coffee. He seemed so warm and kind. He was the exact opposite of the man in her motel room that paid her to inflict pain on herself. She couldn't figure out if he was crazy. Maybe he was just misunderstood. For now, she decided that it was best to push that out of her mind, and try to enjoy it. Anyways, she had no money, and nowhere else to go.

"I have a spare car in the garage. Here's the keys. And here's some money. Why don't you go get a new wardrobe today?" Damon was being generous.

"Why are you being so nice to me?" Destiny looked at the money he had just laid out on the table.

"You deserve it. I think I'm going to enjoy having you around." Damon gave her the softest peck on her cheek. "I have to get to work. Enjoy your day." Out the door he went.

Destiny stood in the middle of the kitchen trying to figure out her life. She didn't know why, or even how, but things were looking up for her.

BUSY, BUSY, BUSY

The office was buzzing with workers doing their jobs. Writers were rushing to meetings. Assistants were answering phones. Video editors sat at their desks with their eyes glued to computer monitors. Everyone seemed busy.

Damon had decided to stop into the breakroom to get his own coffee this morning. He wasn't in the habit of asking Mary to perform such menial tasks anymore. He remembered how it had felt when he worked under William, and William asked him to get coffee.

There was a group of people gathered around the network bulletin board. A flier had been posted for the company's annual party. Every year, the network had a fancy party for all employees. It was an opportunity to dress up, and share food and drink with your colleagues outside of the work environment. Damon hadn't been to a network party in ages. He had no desire to mingle with the people that he saw everyday. He didn't get along with most of them.

"William Hendricks is coming this year. Can you believe it?"

Damon overheard a couple of the secretaries talking about the party.

"I know. I would love a chance to get on his good side. He's almost infamous around here. He's best friends with 1 of the owners. But he went from having such great shows, and now he's working on that pain show. It's almost a disgrace for him."

"I heard that the network offered him a big raise to do that show. They thought he could turn that show around after Damon Dahmer was fired."

Damon tried to blend into the background. He hadn't been fired. He was only suspended. He was just gone for a long vacation.

"You didn't hear? Damon's back. Not for long. William is trying to get him fired."

Damon had heard enough. This was enough to make Damon mad. He was the center of the office gossip. Maybe he would have to go to URN's party this year. He had to show William that he wasn't going anywhere.

Damon was staring at his computer seeing how the ratings for 'Pain for Gain' had plummeted. When 'Easy Money' was on the air, it was rated the highest watched show on the network. "Pain for Gain' was very slowly becoming the network's least watched show. There was no way that the network would fire him. They'd be more likely to give Damon his old show back. The network wanted good ratings.

Damon's phone rang. He saw on his caller id that it was his boss, Mr. Styles.

"Well good morning Mr. Styles. It's a lovely day isn't it?" Damon tried to make small talk out of pure sarcasm.

"This is not a social call, Damon. William is upset over what you did. Changing plastic pellets with metal bbs. What were you thinking?" Mr. Styles was mad.

"What makes you think I would do that?" Damon stifled a snicker. "Perhaps the prop crew made a mistake?"

Mr. Styles sighed loudly into the phone. "He's not playing. He's serious. He wants you gone."

"Me? I didn't do anything, and he can't prove anything. Here I was, hoping that you were calling to tell me that the network agreed to give 'Easy Money' back to me." Damon was not going to hold his breath waiting for that. Not yet, at least.

"If you want your show back, learn to be a team player. You're only making things harder on yourself." Mr. Styles hung up the phone.

Damon leaned back in his chair, and thought for a moment. He decided that he wasn't making things harder on himself. It was time to make things harder for William.

With 'Pain for Gain' getting fewer viewers, there would be no way that the network would stand behind William's work. If Damon were to be patient, the show would inevitably get cancelled, eventually. That would open a time slot for another reality pain game show. It shouldn't matter who William was best friends with.

Unfortunately, that wasn't always how the real world worked. Plus, Damon did not have patience. He knew that even though the network liked good ratings, 'Easy Money' was a controversial show. If he had any hope of getting it back on the air, he would have to somehow get William out of the picture.

HOME LIFE

Damon couldn't wait to tell Destiny about the office party. He hoped that she would join him. He would love to have her on his arm for the event. He told her that it could be their first official date. Destiny was excited, but overwhelmed at the same time. She was used to her old life of sitting in her motel room and getting high after she made some money selling her sex to a guy on the street. She had never rubbed elbows with the professionals in the entertainment business. Well, she had only rubbed elbows with Damon, and she was still getting to know him. Damon assured Destiny that everything would be fine. She would be perfect. As long as she was with him, he would make sure that she was completely comfortable.

Damon had never revealed any of his private life to his co-workers. He wanted to try being human again, like he was before the death of his son. He had a plan for this party. Of course, he had an ulterior motive. Destiny didn't know it yet, but she was a part of this plan.

It took a few days, but Destiny started settling in at Damon's home. He didn't expect much from her. He hadn't minded that she was still unemployed. He didn't ask her for rent money. She didn't have to clean house, he had workers come in once a week to keep his home clean. He didn't expect sex with her. She had her own private bedroom. Destiny was especially happy that he didn't request anymore pain shows. Now that she was off drugs, she didn't think that she could hurt herself, or even allow Damon to hurt her physically.

Damon was a perfect gentleman around the house. He would spend time with her, and talk to her about work stuff. He hadn't told her anything about his feud with William, because he felt like she didn't need to know about that. They watched movies and television together. They were both trying to lead normal lives.

Damon got bored with the mundane life of boring normal stuff. He was full of rage, even though he was great at keeping it a secret. Destiny had no clue that deep down inside of Damon was a constant urge to see blood. There was a quiet voice in his head begging for power and control. That voice wanted to see people in pain. Damon had experienced enough emotional pain in his life, that he thought it was fun to see others in physical pain. That, combined with the feeling of being in control and powerful, was what drove Damon. Damon couldn't shut out that voice in his head any longer.

In the middle of the night, when Destiny was deeply sleeping in her private bedroom, Damon snuck out for some play time.

Damon pulled out his untraceable prepaid cellular phone from his pocket. He had conducted several searches online, and had found an underground world of prostitution. Women willing to sell their sex to strangers for money. Damon assumed they must do it for drug money, or whatever bad habits they might have. He didn't care why they did it, as long as they were willing to play with him. He set up a play date.

Bambi (as if that was her real name) greeted Damon at her door wearing sexy lingerie. It was a lacy red one piece, resembling a see-through bathing suit. She obviously wasn't shy. Damon noticed that she wasn't beautiful, but she wasn't unattractive either. Her body was young and curvy. She wore way too much makeup. Her lips were overly plumped, like maybe she had them injected with collagen. She charged $200 an hour.

Damon had a pocket full of cash. He wanted to play with her.

"Welcome sweetheart." Bambi rubbed her tongue around her thick lips. "I've never seen you before, have I?"

Damon shook his head no.

"Get comfy." Bambi motioned for Damon to sit down. "I like to go over the rules first with all of my new clients." Once again she licked her lips trying to be seductive. "Cash up front. Some things cost more than others. And you never show up here without calling first. Got it?"

Damon shook his head yes.

"Okay, now that we have the business part out of the way, why don't you tell momma what you like, and I can tell you what it costs." Bambi flipped her hair over her shoulder.

These women were always wanting money. Damon reached into his pocket and pulled out the originally agreed upon $200. "What does this get me?"

"Your foot in the door. If you want to get in further than the door, it costs more. I should let you know that I'm known for how well I can work my mouth." She made a circular shape with her mouth. "I've been told that I'm very talented in that department."

"So, do you have a pricing menu?" Damon tried not to laugh at his sarcasm. Anyways, he knew that what he wanted wasn't on the menu.

She pointed at her mouth with her long manicured finger nail. "This costs another $100."

"You sure are expensive, aren't you?" Damon was focused in on her mouth.

"And I'm worth every penny." Bambi got closer to Damon and put her hand on his thigh.

Damon put his hand on top of hers. "What if I want something that's not on the menu?"

"Most anything is on the menu, honey. Money talks, if you catch my drift."

How could Damon not understand what she was saying? She liked money. He knew that coming here. Why else would she be in this business?

"Your lips are beautiful." Damon lied. "I have a friend that just got a piercing called a tongue web." He lied again. He didn't have any friends other than Destiny. Maybe Mary was his friend. That was debatable. However, neither of them had a piercing.

"Never heard of it." Bambi was not impressed with all of this talking.

Damon ran his finger gently around her large lips. He pointed inside of her mouth. "It's a piercing under the tongue. On that little flap of skin under the tongue."

"I've heard of normal tongue piercings. I've heard that it can increase sexual pleasure. What's the purpose of that piercing?" The hooker was now interested. He was speaking of a topic that she liked.

"It's not sexual. My friend told me that it's a painful piercing, yet it's harmless. It's a common thing for that flap to tear. The mouth is miraculous. It heals itself in no time." Damon looked at her to see if she was paying attention. She was. "I am just fascinated with that part of the mouth right now. Raise your tongue. Can I see yours?"

Bambi shrugged her shoulders and opened her mouth wide. She raised her tongue to expose her frenulum. Damon had researched this. It was a part of the body that was capable of bleeding a lot. He desired to see blood.

Bambi closed her mouth and swallowed. "Does that mean you want oral? Like I said, that's extra."

Damon smiled at her and softened his eyes. "I'm willing to pay. I will pay plenty extra." Damon removed her hand from his knee so that he could reach into his pocket. Damon pulled out a small pair of shiny, surgical scissors.

"Wait a minute. What's that for?" Bambi backed away from Damon, yet she was still facing him.

Damon held the scissors by the sharp end, handing the looped finger holding end to Bambi. "Here, you can take them. I want you to use them."

Bambi quickly snatched them from his hand. "What do you mean by use them?"

"I want you to cut that tiny flap of skin under your tongue." Now, Damon was happy.

"Nope. Not happening." Bambi refused. She held the scissors close to her. She didn't want Damon to have them. She feared what he might do with them.

Damon dug into his pocket, and pulled out a wad of cash. "I have $4,000 here. All you have to do is cut that flap. It would be over in seconds. Like I said, the mouth heals itself. You will bleed. But that's all."

"I have been working for a few years. I must say, you just took the cake. This is the craziest proposition ever. You can't be serious."

"I am."

"Are you crazy? No, wait, you're crazy and rich, right? Is this some prank? Are you part of some fraternity or something? I know this isn't really happening." Bambi started to laugh.

Damon did not like being laughed at. "I am serious. I made a simple request. I offered you money. How is this any different than how you degrade yourself daily at 'work'? This just happens to pay a lot more." Damon tried to remain calm and logical. He hoped she was a drug addict and really wanted the money. He didn't want to have to kill her. He hadn't been cautious enough to kill her. He was sure that his fingerprints were already in this room. He was in his own car. Even though his phone was disposable, he bought it at a store with a camera. Damon began to panic.

"I'll play along. What is this, some sort of role play fetish? Sure, honey. Give me that money. I'll cut the bottom of my tongue." Bambi tried to keep a straight face, but she couldn't.

Damon handed her the cash. She counted all $4,000 of it, and her eyes got wide.

"You're serious, aren't you?" Bambi stopped laughing.

Damon shook his head yes.

Bambi shook her head no. "I don't know about this. This is absurd!"

"As I stated earlier, it is not a serious injury. Just a painful injury. There's a lot of money in your hand right now. What do you say?"

Bambi walked over to a mirror hanging on the wall and looked at her mouth. She walked over to a drawer, and pulled out a bottle of pills. Damon wasn't surprised. Prostitutes who used drugs seemed to be the norm. She swallowed a couple of the pills and chased them with a sip of water. Damon loved knowing that there were people in the world willing to give in to his every whim. Damon really started missing 'Easy Money'. He couldn't wait until he got his show back on the air to get his dosage of pain viewing.

"Okay. Can I do it in the mirror?" Bambi looked at Damon, then back at the mirror.

"Sure. Anything you want. I'll just stand behind you." Damon walked up behind Bambi and placed his arms on her shoulders, as she examined the underneath of her tongue.

Damon positioned his head so that he had a good view in the mirror. "Just a little snip. Then you're $4,000 richer."

Bambi spread her mouth as wide as she could. She curled her tongue onto the roof of her mouth. The tiny flap of skin under her tongue exposed itself. Bambi tilted her head back to get a better view. She placed her thumb and pointer finger through the loops of the scissors. She shook her head no. She closed her mouth.

"Hang on. I have to swallow." Bambi swallowed.

She got back into position. This was like foreplay to Damon. He was becoming very aroused. She placed the scissors to her tongue. She closed her eyes. She closed her thumb and pointer finger together, and wailed in pain. Bambi dropped the scissors, and started to cry instantly. It all happened so fast that Damon didn't get to see anything. Bambi was swallowing.

"I didn't see it." Damon was frustrated. "Open your mouth."

Bambi sat down and opened her mouth.

There was a puddle of blood in the bottom of her mouth. Damon could see the blood spurting. She covered her mouth with her hand. She kept swallowing her blood and groaning.

"What's it taste like?" Damon was curious.

"Warm." Bambi tried to speak through closed teeth. Blood began spilling in front of her teeth. "Salty. Pennies"

"You were a good girl tonight. You get a gold star for today. The bleeding will stop. You will be fine. I'll be in touch." Damon left her sitting on her bed, moaning in pain.

URN ANNUAL PARTY

Destiny looked stunning in her evening gown. She had turned into a real beauty in her long, shimmering sequined dress. She had never dressed so formal in her entire life. Damon looked equally nice in his tuxedo. Destiny was self-conscious in her new clothing, but Damon assured her that she was gorgeous. He wanted to do everything right tonight to keep her happy. He complimented her, he opened her car door, he held her delicate hand. Not only did he feel like he needed her in his life, he also knew that he needed to use her tonight to get William out of his life. Tonight would be a great night.

Damon wasn't surprised that most of his co-workers treated him like an outsider at the party. After the death of Marty Blevins on 'Easy Money', there were rumors that he had planned the death. They were only rumors. Mary was the only person who knew his secret. Luckily, she never told anyone. She couldn't if she wanted to keep her professional career.

Destiny was too busy being dazzled by the music, food,and drink to notice that people were avoiding Damon. She had never been to such a grand party before. Even though she felt out of place, she was confident with Damon by her side. She was impressed by him. Damon was a charming man. He made Destiny feel like the only woman in the world. He had given her a great life, and been a perfect gentleman the whole time. She wasn't used to being around gentlemen. In the line of work that she had retired from, she was always around men who only wanted sex from her. It was refreshing being around Damon.

Mary was also an outcast at the party. Mary wasn't comfortable with people at the party avoiding her. After unsuccessfully trying to find friendly co-workers to sit with, she scanned the room for William and Damon to see if they were also getting the cold shoulder. William was the center of attention, having conversations with owners of the network. It wasn't fair that William was still accepted into the popular circles of the network. It was just that he never worked on 'Easy Money'. William didn't carry the stigma of being responsible for a contestant's death. That burden was assigned to Damon and Mary.

Mary couldn't believe her eyes when she saw Damon with a woman. After working under Damon for some time now, she never knew him to have any sort of a personal life. He was quite secretive. As she watched him spoil this mystery woman with attention, she began to see Damon as a person. Mary shook her head. That couldn't be right. Damon didn't act like a person. Damon acted like an emotionless machine that only cared about his business success. Before 'Easy Money', Damon had been a very respected producer. When Mary began working under Damon, she knew that it was great for her career working under him. Damon killed that, at the same time when he killed Marty Blevins. Working for Damon was now like a curse. Of course, she still had a decent paying job, but it would now be hard to ever advance her professional career.

Mary made her way over to Damon and Destiny, and practically startled them when she spoke. They seemed to be lost in their own little world.

"Good evening Damon." Mary sat down next to Destiny. It was still weird calling him by his first name. Before he had messed up on 'Easy Money' and Mary lost respect for him, she always referred to him as sir or Mr. Dahmer. After he revealed his secret of killing a man to her, she felt it was appropriate to drop the formalities. "Who is this with you tonight?"

Damon was charming as he smiled at Destiny. "Destiny, I would like for you to meet Mary." Damon wanted to see how Mary would react towards Destiny before continuing the conversation. He hadn't been on the best of terms with Mary lately, and hoped that Mary wouldn't try to sour Destiny's mood.

Destiny and Mary were actually getting along. Damon made sure to keep his ear close to their conversation to ensure that Mary didn't say anything that he would disapprove of. As Damon listened, he realized that Destiny was actually a sweet person. He was actually enjoying the fact that they were hitting it off. He hoped that Destiny would leave an impression on Mary, and maybe Mary would stop holding a grudge against him.

Damon watched William closely from the corner of his eye. He tried to keep track of how many alcoholic beverages William consumed. Damon did start to get angry as he watched William having such a good time with their bosses. Damon tried to remain calm. He had to focus on the plan.

After a long evening of Mary and Destiny getting to know each other, the room started to empty. As people began leaving, Damon kept an eye on William. Damon excused himself to the restroom, and returned with 3 drinks. He gave a drink to Mary and Destiny, but told them that the last drink was a peace offering to William. He asked Mary to go introduce Destiny to William. He explained to Destiny that he and William worked together, and to offer the drink to William as a 'peace offering' from Damon. He knew that William would not be able to resist the charm of such an attractive woman offering him a drink. Plus, Destiny had experience accommodating to men. He was sure that William would take the drink.

"Peace offering? Seriously?" Mary didn't understand why Damon was concerned about William.

"We have to work with him. I just want him to meet Destiny. I've got to be honest, she's changed my outlook on life, and I want to turn a new leaf. It's best for 'Pain for Gain', if all of us could get along." Damon turned his sad eyes to Mary in hopes that she would take his new friend to meet their co-worker.

Mary liked this side of Damon. She agreed to do as he wished, in hopes that it would help their production of the show.

Damon watched as Mary approached William. He also watched as William's eyes focused in on Destiny. He did take the drink from Destiny. Tonight would be a good night.

Going Home

Damon watched as a tired William left the party. He said his goodbyes to Mary, and escorted Destiny to their car. As they were leaving the parking lot, they ran into William shaking his head, staring at a flat tire on his own car.

"Isn't that William? Maybe we should go and check on him." Destiny really was sweet.

Damon pulled his car in front of William. "Is something wrong? Can we help?" Damon was only trying to be courteous.

"Damon. Hello." William was slurring his speech. "Oh, hi there Destiny. Flat tire."

Destiny looked at Damon worried. "He's drunk. We should give him a ride home."

Damon couldn't have agreed more. William did not want to get in Damon's car, but Destiny had been nice enough at the party. Plus, he was really tired. He didn't think that he had drank too much, but maybe he did. Maybe he was drunk. William couldn't figure out why he was so tired.

William climbed into Damon's backseat, and thanked Destiny for the ride. Damon didn't mind that William wasn't exactly being friendly with him. Damon just wanted it to appear that he was being friendly.

Damon dropped William off at his house.

He continued on his journey home with Destiny. Damon stopped at an open all night gas station by his house to get some gum. He treated Destiny to some candy. Damon made sure to smile into the store camera while making his purchase. It would only help him establish his alibi, if in the event something were to happen and that he needed an alibi.

Damon led Destiny into the house by her hand and wished her good night.

"I want to thank you for taking me tonight. I really liked Mary. Tonight was very special to me, Damon." Destiny gave Damon a kiss on the cheek. "I was thinking tonight maybe you could sleep in my room with me. I would really like that."

Damon hated to say no, but the timing just wasn't right. "You're lovely. I wish I could, but I'm so tired right now. Let's wait until tomorrow night. I promise to make tomorrow just as special as tonight was." Damon was happy that Destiny thought so much of him.

Destiny went to bed, looking forward to spending the next night with Damon.

Damon very quietly snuck out of the house, so he wouldn't wake his sleeping beauty.

Damon drove himself back to William's house. He parked his car a couple of blocks away so that he wouldn't be seen. He carried a bag of toys, and crept into William's home. William was sleeping soundly, snoring on his couch. Damon propped William up in a sitting position, and began to tape his wrists together. As Damon was taping William's ankles together he almost woke up. Damon stood a few feet away from William, and launched a dart into his face.

William started waking up. William slowly opened his eyes. "Damon, is that you. Where am I?"

Damon pinched the tip of another dart, and aimed it for William's eye. Bullseye.

A slurring William woke up. "What the?"

Damon walked up to William and pulled the dart from his eye. Squish. "You should've worn your protective glasses. Safety is important." Blood ran from William's eye just like tears would. "Wake up William. Time to play. I drugged you hours ago. You should be able to wake up now." Damon threw a glass of cold water on William's face.

"I'm awake. What are you doing? Why does my eye hurt?" William was still half asleep. He tried to open his wounded eye, but he couldn't.

"I'm playing my favorite game with you." Damon looked at William with sheer joy.

William looked around, and started to realize what was happening. His face turned to panic when he saw that he had been tied up.

"Get out of my house, now!"

"First, we are going to have a little talk. I'm in control right now. Got it?" Damon spoke in a calm manner.

"I've got nothing to say to you. Untie me now!" William was screaming at his captor.

"I'd be nice to me, if I were you." Damon offered the man some friendly advice.

"I will have your job for this! What do you think you're doing?" William struggled against his bindings.

"You already tried to take my job. You weren't good enough to be my replacement. Now, you're filing complaints on me, trying to get me fired. Big mistake." Damon sat and watched as William tried to get free. "Struggle all you want. You aren't going anywhere."

"You're going to jail. You're going to prison!" William threatened Damon.

"Wrong. I have other plans. I'm home in bed, sleeping right now. I have a witness who would confirm that." Damon was proud that his plan had come into fruition.

"What do you want?" William tried to speak rationally.

"What I want is to not work with you, anymore. I want 'Easy Money' back. I hate your show. I hate working with you. I hate you for trying to take my job from me. Now, I just want to play." Damon was sure of what he wanted.

"Okay. I'll put in a good word at the

network. I'll try to help you get your show back. Untie me. Now." William hoped he had convinced Damon to free him.

Damon laughed. "Sorry. Too little, too late."

William was angered. "You won't get away with this."

"I was smart enough to drug you at the party, wasn't I? I was smart enough to slash your tire. I was smart enough to form an alibi. I'm smart enough to burn this house down with you in it." Damon loved his plan. "Of course, a candle will start the fire. Perhaps, I could leave the oven on for an explosion. Then, your body will be nothing but ashes. Hopefully, they never even suspect foul play."

"You're a maniac! I knew it all along. You never were right in the head!" William struggled harder.

Damon reached into his bag, and pulled out a meat cleaver, just like the cleaver used on 'Pain for Gain'. "Do you remember when you told me that this challenge was too extreme? I want to play that challenge right here, right now." Damon grabbed William's foot. William tried to wiggle out of Damon's grasp, but he couldn't. Damon raised the blade into the air, and swiftly swung it down on William's toes.

William howled in pain. "Please stop. I'm begging you." William looked down to see that Damon was now holding his detached toe in his hand.

"See, that's not too bad, is it? It's a shame that you won't get paid for this." Damon laughed again, and started shuffling through his bag.

William was crying. "I will beg. I will do anything that you want me to do. Please just don't kill me."

Damon ignored his victim. "There's something I always wanted to try on the show, but I couldn't monetize it. I couldn't measure it, to see if the contestant did it good enough. Now, I can try it on you." Damon held up a hammer. "I thought it would be great to have the players break their own fingers or toes. But it's not like we have x-ray machines on the set."

"Stop. You don't have to do this. I promise. I can get your show back." William was willing to say anything to stop Damon.

Damon looked at William's bleeding foot. "Let's start with the toes that you have left on this foot."

"They were actually talking about bringing "Easy Money' back. I promise. 'Pain for Gain' just doesn't get good enough ratings." William tried to stop himself from crying.

Damon paused. "Seriously? When?" Damon wanted more information.

"Next season, I think. They're talking about it. I can put in a recommendation. You do know that I have some pull with the network, right?" William was relieved that Damon was rethinking this situation.

FIREWORKS

"I know why they suspended me, but why did they cancel my show?" Damon wanted to know more.

"Huh?" William was trying to not concentrate on the pain in his eye and his foot. "A man died. So they cancelled the show."

"No. Wrong. Try again. I know a man died on the show. But the network was covered legally. They wouldn't cancel their highest rated show for that." Damon raised the hammer over his head, gripping it with both hands. He brought the tool down on William's large toe.

William screamed. "Stop. Stop. Don't." William had never felt so much pain in his entire life.

"Why did they cancel the show? They could've brought it back." Damon demanded answers.

"They were going to bring it back. But they approached me about doing a new show. Something similar, but not as hardcore."

William was trying to speak through his tears.

"Tell me the truth William!" Damon looked at William's other foot and aimed his hammer for the other large toe.

"AHHH! STOP! I wanted the show. It was my idea!" William was crying and screaming like a small child.

"Finally. You're being honest. What about Mary?" Damon thought this was a perfect opportunity to get any information that he could.

"What about Mary? What do you mean?" William didn't understand the question.

"Did Mary want me gone?"

"I don't know. She never told me that she did. She never told me much about you. Sure, I think she wanted a promotion, but she always said you were perfect to produce reality pain."

Damon knew all that he needed to know. Mary had kept his secret about killing Marty. Mary was on his side. He couldn't really tell by the way that she had been mad at him. Despite her anger, Mary was loyal to him.

"Thank you William. It was a pleasure doing business with you." Damon went into the kitchen and turned on the oven. He lit a candle and set it close to a window curtain. Damon picked up his bag of toys and left William crying, tied up in the house that would soon burn to the ground.

Damon had a good night. He had accomplished what he intended to do. He was another step closer to getting his show back. The network was already considering giving him his show back. Now, with William out of the picture, he could show the network what kind of ratings he could get for 'Pain for Gain'.

As Damon was sneaking quietly in front of Destiny's door, he felt the need to celebrate. He softly knocked on her door, to see if she was awake. She didn't respond, so he knocked harder.

"What? I'm sleepin'." Destiny said quietly through the door.

"I can't stop thinking about you." Damon was being honest. He felt the need to be close to her.

Destiny came to the door, and opened it. Damon saw that she slept in an oversized T-shirt, and she was looking very sexy. Damon grabbed her face with both hands, and pulled her in close to him. He took her by the hand, and led her to his bed.

Destiny welcomed his body. She couldn't help but to notice the softness in his touch. He was no longer the same man who paid her to do bad things to herself. She still saw the 'D' he branded on her leg everyday, but it no longer reminded her of the monster that he once was.

He was charming, sweet, compassionate, and tender with her in the bed.

Damon rubbed his fingers on the scarred initial on her leg. He laid his claim to her, and he had marked her. Damon felt powerful, like he owned her. He cupped her breasts, and was especially turned on by her missing nipple. The nipple that he sliced off with a pocket knife.

Damon knew that Destiny was aware of who he was. She knew what he enjoyed. Yet, she didn't reject him. She accepted him for who he was. He didn't have to pretend with her. That didn't mean that he should tell her all the evil deeds that he had done, it just meant that she gave him a feeling of comfort. Maybe he wasn't a monster.

They spent the night pleasing each other's needs. Life was good.

CONDOLENCES

Damon walked with a pep in his step into the office.

"Good morning, Mary." It was a very good morning for Damon. He had successfully gotten rid of William, and he had gotten closer with Destiny. He couldn't see any way that things could get any better for him.

"Damon. Quit smiling. You haven't heard yet, have you?" Mary was concerned about what other people in the office would think if they saw how happy Damon was.

"Heard. I haven't heard anything." Damon walked past Mary, and opened the window blinds in his office. He saw that Mary had followed him inside of his office. "It's a good morning to let the morning sun in."

"William is dead." Mary offered no explanation. Just a couple of words. Maybe she was testing Damon to see what his reaction would be.

"No. Dead? He was fine at the party. Drunk. With a flat tire. We gave him a ride home. But he's not dead. Probably hungover." Damon tried to show no reaction other than surprise.

"His house burned down. That's all we know. You gave him a ride home?" Now Mary was concerned, especially with Damon's history.

"Sure we did. It was Destiny's idea. She's so sweet. We dropped him off, then we went home." Damon quickly changed the subject. "Destiny is the best isn't she? She makes me want to be a better version of myself." That wasn't a lie. He didn't say that he wanted to change. He was just pretty much stating that he wanted to stay the same, just a better form of the same person.

"He's dead. And you want to small talk about your new girlfriend?" Mary hoped that there wasn't something that Damon was hiding from her. With his past, she felt that she had every right to be suspectful.

"Yes. That's sad. I was hoping that William and I could have formed a mature professional relationship, but that wasn't in the cards. Oh, what does that mean for the show?" Damon knew that didn't mean anything for the show, other than the fact that William would no longer hold him back on his creativity. William spilled the beans before he died that the network was already considering giving Damon his old show back, but Mary didn't know that.

"They haven't said anything yet. Right now, the office is just grieving for our co-worker." Mary tried to read Damon's face, but she was getting nowhere.

"Well, the network will not close over his death. We still have to produce a show. Television still lives on. I hate it that he died, but it's no secret that he didn't like me. It's a sad situation, Mary, but I'm not going to dwell on it."

Mary didn't want Damon to dwell on it. She just hoped that he would show some compassion.

Damon was sitting at his desk, when there was a knock on his office door. Damon very calmly told whoever it was to come in.

Damon looked up from his computer screen and saw a couple of police officers. He was not worried. He expected this.

Mary saw the officers and stopped what she was doing to try and listen in on the conversation. Mary heard the officers question Damon about driving William home. Apparently, someone else saw them leave together. Damon stayed calm as he told the officers that it was his girlfriend's idea to give William a ride. He also told them what time he dropped him off, and that they stopped at a store, and went home themselves. He gave the officers Destiny's phone number so that they could call her and verify what he had just told them. The police didn't seem suspicious, they just said that they were 'looking into' the incident.

Damon seemed sad about the whole William situation in front of the officers. He didn't appear to be rattled.

Apparently, Mary wasn't the only person suspicious about William's death. Something just didn't seem right to her. She was glad that the police questioned Damon. She didn't feel so bad about wondering if Damon had anything to do with William's death.

Mary and Damon still had to work together. Damon suggested that they make 'Pain for Gain' more like 'Easy Money'. Mary noticed that without William around, there was no one to object to Damon's idea. Mary agreed with Damon, she wanted a better show also. She just kept a mental note about how convenient it was for Damon that William was dead.

Mary didn't know if she was crazy or not. It would be a bit extreme for Damon to kill William over a television show. All that Mary had heard was that William died in a house fire. But if it were as simple as that, then the police wouldn't have questioned Damon. She tried not to assume that Damon was a cold blooded murderer, but she did know that he indirectly killed Marty Blevins.

Mary decided to keep a close eye on Damon. She would agree with his show ideas, but only for the advancement of her own career. Of course she wanted to work on a popular television show with great ratings. Luckily, she had made friends with Destiny. Maybe if she got to know Destiny better, then she could try to figure out exactly who Damon was.

PAIN FOR GAIN (DAMON'S VERSION)

"Welcome to 'Pain for Gain'! The only game show where you earn big bucks for pain. I'm your host, Peter Conway. Tonight's episode will be a little bit different than the past episodes. I promise you that it will be more exciting, with higher cash prizes. Tonight, our couples will only be offered 1 challenge to complete. Hang on to your seats! Let's play 'Pain for Gain'."

It was Damon's idea to only offer each team 1 challenge. He had to format the show in this way, because if the players chose to complete the challenge they would probably be leaving for the hospital upon completion. He also had Mary pick contestants who really needed money. People willing to do anything for money. Mary had willingly gone along with all of Damon's ideas, but she seemed rather watchful. Probably to ensure that there wouldn't be anymore mishaps like Marty Blevins' death.

"Come on out red team! Let's meet our first team of players!" Peter was full of energy.

As a couple walked out, a large screen behind them started playing a video. It showed the red team sitting at a desk sorting through various papers.

The man looked at the camera. "I'm David and this is my wife, Charlotte. We started a small business a couple of years ago, and business was great."

Charlotte started to speak. "We didn't plan ahead. We have gotten behind on our taxes, and we are going to lose everything. We owe the government so much money that not only are we going to lose everything that we own, we might go to jail."

David looked at his wife. "We do not want to go to jail, so I decided that we should play 'Pain for Gain'. We will do whatever it takes to get out of this bind." The video ended.

"David and Charlotte, welcome to the show. You are in a very complicated situation. It's a good thing that you're here. It seems that money could easily solve your problems." Peter was sympathetic.

"Yes Peter. If we could pay our taxes, then

everything would be fine." David tried to sound hopeful. "We're going to play hard, and win!"

Peter walked the couple over to a table saw. "I know this looks extreme. But wait until you hear this! For this challenge we will be paying $150,000! That's a lot of money. Would that get you out of your tax debt?"

"It sure would Peter! But I hate to think what we would have to do with a table saw." Charlotte looked like she was in distress.

Peter held up a marker. "First, you need to decide who is getting cut, and who is doing the cutting. Whoever is getting cut, place your hand flat on this table."

David bravely displayed his hand on the table. He didn't even bother discussing it with his wife. She did not argue with him. Charlotte was still frozen in fear.

"Spread your fingers. This won't hurt right now, it's only a marker." Peter drew a line below David's middle and index knuckles. "Here's what you gotta do. Keep your fingers spread, and your wife needs to help guide your hand into the saw blade. The blade needs to cut into the webbing of your fingers down your palm, between your first 2 fingers. You must cut down to this line. It's not like you're going to lose a finger. You're just gonna cut your hand practically in half. There's $150,000 at stake here. What do you think? Do you want to complete this challenge?"

Charlotte shook her head no. "No, we are not doing this challenge."

"Yes we are! This is the only way to keep me out of prison! If I don't pay those taxes, I'm gonna serve time!" David looked at Peter. "Yes, we're doing this."

Damon watched on the monitor as the camera zoomed in on the teeth of the saw blade. Each blade shined in the light, looking very sharp. He didn't bother to listen to the exchange between the married couple. He knew that they would do it. They needed money. It would be very hard to turn down that much money when you are desperate for cash.

Charlotte was sweating worse than David. David placed his spread fingers close to the blade. Charlotte got into position, holding her husband's wrist and elbow.

"Are you sure? We don't have to do this." Charlotte did not want to do this.

David shook his head yes.

"Just flip that red switch, and that blade will start spinning." Peter was not looking at the couple as he instructed them what to do. "Then glide your husband's hand into the blade." Peter was trying to not grimace his face.

David used his free hand to hit the red switch. The tool's motor came to life, and sounded like a high pitched screech. David shut his eyes, not wanting to see what was getting ready to happen to him. The camera got a close up of David's hand. Charlotte pressed forward on her husband's elbow, and the webbing of his fingers made contact with the blade.

"Stop! Now!" David looked like he was going to pass out.

The blade was spitting blood everywhere, on Charlotte's face and on David's body. Charlotte quickly turned off the power switch, but the blade still spun for a few seconds. She was looking very pale. The camera showed the torn flesh and that the cut had exceeded the line Peter drew. David tried to hold his hand up to look at it. His pointer finger fell sideways, flapping like a loose appendage. It looked unnatural. David instantly vomited. Charlotte was crying.

Peter did not look at the results of the torn finger webbing. "Congratulations, you've just won $150,000!" Peter tried to sound enthusiastic.

Damon watched the monitor. He had instructed the camera crew to zoom in on the injuries. You could see into David's hand. Damon was not a doctor, but he swore he could see tendons and cartilage. Medical ushered David and Charlotte off the stage.

Peter looked into the camera. "Viewers, you asked for more blood, and I think we answered you! For lack of a better word, let's give David a hand." Peter clapped.

Damon was happy with what he just saw,

and he hoped that he had made the viewers at home happy too. He was especially excited to see the next challenge.

Peter brought the second couple out on stage. Their video played explaining that their newborn baby was sick, and required medical help that they couldn't afford. Damon didn't even bother listening. He knew that they were just desperate for money. Parents would do anything to help their sick baby.

Peter handed the blue team a pair of bolt cutters. The husband held the tool examining it.

"This challenge is simple, yet very painful. It's also worth $150,000!" Peter maintained his enthusiasm. "Are you aware of achilles tendon?"

The wife scratched her head. "Do you mean that place behind the heel of the foot?"

Peter shook his head yes. "All you have to do is cut your Achilles tendon. I assure you, these bolt cutters are sharp. It will only take 1 snip. It will be over quickly. Who is doing the snipping?"

After a short discussion between the young married couple, it was decided that the wife would take the pain of this challenge.

"I don't want to hurt you baby, but I have to walk around at work. We'll still need an income after this. Maybe we shouldn't do this. It's too much." Her husband was reluctant to participate in this challenge.

"Our baby needs us! We have to do this." The wife pleaded with him. "It's a lot of money. If it comes down to my foot hurting or my baby dying, I can take the pain."

Damon hated this part of the show, but it was necessary. Boring, but necessary.

The wife sat down in a chair and gritted her teeth. Her husband knelt behind her, down on his knees.

"Just place the bolt cutter around that tendon. That little skinny part above the back of her heel. Just snip it shut, then you're $150,000 richer." Peter encouraged the players to win the cash prize.

The man placed the cold sharp metal around the back of his wife's ankle. "Are you sure about this? I don't think I can hurt you."

"Just do it already!" She gritted her teeth, trying to prepare herself for the pain. She grabbed both sides of her chair as hard as she could. She was sweating in the lights of the cameras.

He snapped the bolt cutters and blood instantly drained from the woman's foot. She fell out of her chair. Gripping her leg in pain. The camera zoomed in blood flowing out of her ankle.

Damon watched with extreme interest. He was back to making great television. All he wanted to do was give the viewers what they dared to see. He wasn't the only person curious as to what people would do for money. It was fascinating to see people in pain.

Damon wondered if his viewers were cruel or curious. It didn't matter to him, as long as he got his show great ratings.

HAPPINESS

"I watched some of your shows today. It's disturbing." Destiny greeted Damon at the door, and didn't even give him a chance to set his briefcase down before she spoke to him. She was obviously upset.

Damon walked past her, and dropped his keys on the table. "I'm so glad to see you, too. I missed you while I was working hard all day at work." Sarcasm was Damon's second language. Damon ignored Destiny as he went about his normal routine of coming in from work. He hung his suit jacket in the closet, and poured himself a bourbon.

"Why do you make these shows?" Destiny wanted to know more about her lover.

"Do you recall a time that you watched the show and were willing to cut off your toe for money?" Damon wanted to remind her who she used to be.

"I was a different person then. I was on drugs. I'm not on drugs now. The show... it isn't right." Destiny stood her ground firmly.

Damon sighed. He didn't expect this. "Do you see this nice home you live in? That show pays for it."

"So you're no better than the players. Willing to do anything for money?" It was like Destiny was accusing Damon of something.

Damon didn't make the show just for the money. He actually enjoyed watching it, but Damon wasn't going to tell her that. "It's a job. That's that. I don't force anyone to do anything. The players willingly hurt themselves."

"For money. At one time, I hurt myself for money. It's not a good thing." Destiny wanted Damon to hear her.

Damon ignored her as he sat on the couch, and turned on the television. "So, what are you saying?"

"I don't know what I'm saying. The show is disturbing. Why do people watch it?" Now she just seemed curious.

Damon thought for a moment. "I don't know. Maybe just to watch it. It's something they've never seen before."

"Do you enjoy the show? I think you used to enjoy seeing me hurt myself. I know you enjoyed it." Destiny changed her tone.

Damon looked at her. He had to try to regain control of this situation. "I already told you, I paid you to see how the show would be. To see if people really existed that would do such morbid things for cash. Simple as that. It's not like I enjoy making the show." Lie. Damon was good at lying.

"The police called me about William." Destiny finally said what she wanted to say.

Damon put down the remote control. "Well, that was very unfortunate wasn't it? Quite sad." Damon tried to read Destiny's face for an expression with no luck.

"Is there anything that you aren't telling me?" Finally, she found the nerve to just get to the point.

Damon put on his charming smile. "I don't understand. What could I possibly not be telling you?" Playing innocent was the right thing to do.

Destiny decided not to push the subject. "I was just asking." It was best to drop the subject. Between the shows Damon was producing, and the way they met of him paying her to hurt herself, she wondered if Damon was keeping secrets from her.

Destiny wanted Damon to be the man of her dreams, but maybe he was a nightmare. He had been so great with her lately. She only hoped that her suspicions were wrong.

Destiny had made friends with Mary at the party. Maybe she could spend some time with Mary to try and figure out who Damon really was.

Damon was happy when he learned that Mary and Destiny were planning a girl's night out. He knew that Mary was loyal to him, and Destiny was indebted to him. Mary's job depended on Damon's professional creativity. Destiny's livelihood depended on him. He thought it would be great if the 2 most important women in his life formed a relationship.

When Destiny left their home to meet Mary, Damon was not worried. Destiny would never admit to Mary that she used to be a prostitute and that Damon paid her to do horrible things to herself. Mary would never admit that she knew Damon planned a contestant's death.

When Destiny arrived home, she was in a good mood. That was a relief to Damon. He wished he could've been a fly on the wall listening in on Mary and Destiny's conversation. While his lover was gone, his ears had been burning like he was their topic of conversation. He hoped that he wasn't, but he knew that he was.

Even though he probed Destiny for intel,

he didn't get any information from her. At least she was now happy, unlike she was earlier, when she was questioning him about William.

Damon and Destiny had now been sharing a bedroom, and he took her to bed. Even though they had bonded, and Damon was no longer alone, something was missing. He enjoyed the sex with Destiny, but he would have much rather seen her hurt herself. Perhaps he shouldn't have helped her get off drugs.

Damon knew that he was doing what was best for him. With Destiny being part of his life, he now appeared to be leading a normal life. Which was important to him. Not only could she be his alibi, should he ever need an alibi, she was helping him build his relationship with Mary. He was really trying to be normal, it just wasn't in his nature.

Damon was mad at himself for not taking the opportunity to visit Bambi while Destiny had been out. Damon needed a release. He needed to feel powerful. He needed for a woman to submit to his bizarre desires. Maybe he could try to get Destiny to become his pain slave again, just like when they had met.

He was Damon Dahmer. He was charming, and good at convincing people to do things that they didn't want to do. Surely he could convince his lover to play with him. He stayed awake all night, trying to figure out the best way to get her to succumb to his needs of watching people hurt themselves for his own pleasure.

GOOD NEWS

Damon was busy in his office coming up with new challenges for 'Pain for Gain', when his phone rang. Mr. Styles had requested a meeting with Mary and Damon. Damon didn't know what to expect.

Mr. Styles, being the professional man that he was, was courteous and polite as they entered his office.

"With William being gone, there are going to be some changes around here. 'Pain for Gain' was William's show, and out of respect, his show is being cancelled. We will only air 1 more 'Pain for Gain'." Mr. Styles tried to look sympathetic.

Mary twisted up her face as she thought about this. "But we have worked so hard. That's not right." Mary was upset.

Damon chose to sit quietly and say nothing at all.

"The network thanks you for your hard work Mary. There's nothing to be upset over." Mr. Styles tried to defuse her.

Damon sat and waited.

"That last episode had higher ratings than any show that William ever produced. We worked hard, around the clock, getting that episode ready in time. What now?" Mary was still upset.

"You're right. The ratings got better. You and Damon make a good team. The network is considering bringing 'Easy Money' back. Or whatever you'd like to call your new show." Mr. Styles smiled.

That was partly what Damon was waiting to hear. "What do you mean considering? It was the highest rated show on the network ever."

Mr. Styles turned to Damon. "Conditions. The network wants me to get the 2 of you to agree to some things. They call them conditions. Conditions that would be in a written contract. Actually, they'd be conditions in your employment contracts."

Damon did not like being told what to do and how to do it. He was sure that would be what those conditions would do. Damon said nothing.

"Well, what are they?" Mary was impatient.

"First, the network is strict that there are no deaths on the show. In the event of a death of a player, the both of you would lose your job. The show will not be live." Mr Styles began explaining the conditions.

"You said conditions. Plural. What other conditions are there?" Damon hated it that Mr. Styles was speaking so slowly.

"Well, as you know, the network hates pain shows. But they love ratings. Your ratings will also have to remain as high as the first season. Otherwise you would lose your jobs. If the ratings fall at all, you're gone." Mr. Styles sounded almost threatening.

Damon strummed his fingers on the table and looked at Mary. Mary shrugged her shoulders.

"Let me clarify." Damon sat up and looked his boss right into his eyes. "If a player dies, they fire us? If we lose viewers, they fire us?"

Mr. Styles nodded his head yes.

"I have given all of my adult career to this network. This is the kind of thanks I get!" Damon realized that his temper was getting out of control and took a deep breath. "What if we choose to not sign this contract?"

"Then you are dismissed. The network is not willing to offer you any other types of shows." Mr. Styles sat patiently.

"Do you think you're the only network?" Damon tried to remain calm.

"We're the only network bold enough to offer pain shows, so in this case, yes. Take the offer, or don't. It's up to you."

Mary and Damon agreed to their terms,

but Damon didn't like it. He had wanted his show back, but he didn't like that his job was contingent on it. He also hated the part about no deaths. His plan was to eventually incorporate death into his show. That would be the next level that his viewers were expecting. Surely, there were suicidal people in this world willing to be on his show.

For now, Damon knew it was in his best interest to do what the network asked of him, but eventually he knew that he would have to get them to change their minds. He considered the network owners as hypocrites. They didn't mind getting good ratings, but yet they didn't approve of his show.

Maybe he could find another network to pick up his show. Maybe he could create his own network of different kinds of pain shows. For now, Damon would just keep quiet. But he would keep his eyes open to new possibilities.

THE LAST PAIN FOR GAIN

"Welcome to the series finale of 'Pain for Gain'. I'm your host, Peter Conway. Next season, we will be back with another painful reality game show. Tonight we have a very exciting 'Pain for Gain' planned for you! Hold on to your seats. Don't try this at home. Viewer discretion is advised. Tonight's challenges will offer our highest prizes ever on this show, but the challenges will not be simple. They're probably the hardest challenges we've ever had. Now, who's ready to play 'Pain for Gain'?"

The teams walked out on the stage.

"Mary, what do you think? Should we bring 'Easy Money' back, or something new?" Damon thought a little chit chat would cure his boredom.

"I don't know but whatever it is better be good. I need my job. I can't go anywhere else and make this kind of money." Mary was stressed out. She knew that if she stuck with

Damon, he could keep the ratings up. But she also knew that he was dangerous. She would just have to keep a close eye on him.

"We have 3 teams tonight for our special finale. We did a random draw backstage to see which team would get which challenge. The challenges start out easier, then get harder. Let's start with our first team. Hi Lois and Carter. How are you feeling tonight?" Peter smiled at the first team of players.

"I'm scared." Lois looked at the ground.

"It's okay honey. You can hurt me. It's okay. We are getting ready to lose our home. I will not let that happen." Carter was confident.

"The first challenge is the simplest challenge of the night, but it's worth $150,000." Peter was very animated tonight. He was also worried after William's death that he might lose his job. "Over here, we have a forklift. All you have to do is drive over your partner's foot. Simple."

"I can't do that." Lois shook her head no.

"We have supplied a very user friendly forklift. I assure you that it's just like driving a car." Peter tried to make Lois feel better.

"No." Lois turned to her husband. "I can't hurt you."

"We need this money. It will be over in seconds. I'll go to the hospital. I will heal. Please baby, we can do this." Carter tried to stay positive.

The man led his wife over to the forklift and helped her climb into the seat. Lois was crying, and Carter was telling her to be brave. Carter placed his foot under the tire of the forklift.

"Just turn that key, like in a car. Put it in drive, just like a car." Peter instructed the sobbing woman as to what she should do.

Carter turned his head, so that he couldn't see what was getting ready to happen. He looked at his wife and mouthed 'I love you'. Lois turned on the machine, and put it in gear. The forklift rolled slowly, and flattened Carter's foot, like it wasn't even there. Damon sat close to the monitor. The screen was split. There was a camera on Carter's foot, and another camera on his face. Damon concentrated on the side of the screen with his face. Damon loved seeing Carter's face in agonizing pain. The man was screaming and crying as he fell to the floor. His wife turned off the forklift and rushed to her husband's side. Medical came onto stage promptly.

Peter turned to the camera. "I wish them the best. Congratulations Lois and Carter on winning $150,000! That looked like that hurt. But the show must go on. Next we have Paul and Cindy. Welcome!"

"Mary, do you think that was too boring? I think it was kind of boring. We need better stuff than this next season." Damon was worried about keeping his job.

Mary agreed. She didn't think it was boring, but she knew that it was just best to agree with Damon. Damon was sitting and thinking about what he could do with his new show to make it spectacular.

"Your challenge is worth $200,000. Would that help?" Peter handed them a little tool. "This is a sander, normally used to smooth wood. Tonight, it will be used on skin, if you choose to play. This is one of our longer challenges. For a full 10 seconds, you must hold this sander to the skin of your partner. I must warn you, this sander has some very rough paper on it. I honestly don't know what it would do to skin."

Damon had missed the introduction of this team, but he knew that they were a married couple that loved animals. They were going to hurt themselves and use the money to help rescue animals. Cats and dogs. Damon was glad that this world was full of crazy people.

The man removed his shirt. After a quick discussion, they decided it would be best to 'sand' his back. The man turned his back to his wife. The woman powered up the small tool, and the engine came to life. It wasn't very loud, but she watched as it spun in fast circles. She gulped and pressed it to his skin. The man jumped away.

"We still have 8 seconds on the timer."

Peter reminded the players. "You must do it for the full 10 seconds."

The woman examined her husband's back. His skin was already dissolved where she had pressed the tool to him.

"I can't do it. I just can't." The man was crying, and a string of saliva was hanging from his mouth. "It hurts too bad. I quit."

Mary looked at Damon. "We can't have contestants that quit once we get our show going. That will kill our ratings. At least now we can edit this out."

Damon shook his head no. "Look, he's missing the top layers of his skin. I see blood, I'm not gonna edit this out. This will give people something to talk about. They'll say the man was an idiot for starting the challenge and quitting before he got paid. I think our viewers will like this. It makes it real."

Anyways, Damon saved the best challenge and the most desperate team for last.

Peter approached the last team who was horrified by what they just saw. "And last but not least, we have our highest prize of $250,000!"

Damon already knew their story, and he made sure that the challenge selected for them was not picked randomly. They were a brother and sister team, with a sick parent. When it came to healthcare costs, people would endure any pain presented to them.

Peter handed the team a hammer and a single nail. He pointed to a chair. "The person who is receiving the pain will sit on the chair, and remove their shoe. The person giving the pain will use the hammer and the nail, to nail their partner's foot to that board. This might take a few swings of the hammer, so it won't be done very fast. But it is worth a quarter of a million dollars! Understood?"

The brother and sister looked at each other. They were already mortified by seeing the team before them sand their partner's skin off.

"I'll do it. For Dad. Just hammer fast okay?" The brother took charge of the situation and sat down in the chair. He slowly removed his shoe.

His sister looked at the hammer, but it was almost like she was paralyzed. Damon watched her face. She looked more fearful than her brother.

"C'mon. Let's get it over with. We have to do this." A small tear ran down her brother's face.

She knelt down next to her brother and touched the tip of her finger to the sharp nail. She was trembling.

"We have no choice. What other way can we get this kind of money? You can do this." Her brother was not only trying to convince her, he was also trying to convince himself that this was a good idea.

As she was shaking, she held the nail in place on his foot.

"Closer to my toes. My foot is thinner there. It would be easier." Her brother corrected her nail placement.

She lowered the nail closer to his toes. The hand holding the nail was shaking. She raised the hammer to swing it, and closed her eyes. She swung the hammer swiftly. She missed the nail, and the hammer pounded down on his foot.

"Gosh dangit!" The brother looked at his foot. He took a deep breath. He wanted to scream at his sister, but bit his tongue instead.

Damon looked at Mary. "This is what we need. Challenges that prolong the fear and the pain. This right here is great television. This is golden."

The sister held the nail in place again, and lined the hammer up. She made contact with the nail this time. Her brother howled in pain. She ignored his cries of pain, and swung the hammer again, and again. The nail was slowly penetrating his foot. The camera zoomed in on the head of the nail, as the rest of the nail started disappearing into his flesh. Her brother's face was red. He was gripping the chair tightly.

Damon watched his monitor, enjoying every second of it. Mary was watching Damon.

He seemed to be enjoying this just a little too much.

GIRL TALK

Mary was so stressed out about work. She couldn't afford to lose her job right now, and her and Damon's careers were on shaky ground. Mary needed a night out. And she needed to get a scope as to where Damon's head was right now. Damon didn't talk much about anything other than work. The best way to get inside of Damon's head was to speak to Destiny.

Fortunately, Mary had already started forming a relationship with Destiny. She did genuinely like Destiny, but she had to question as to why anyone would want to live with Damon Dahmer. At work he was so mysterious. His show ideas were twisted. Plus, Mary knew he wasn't opposed to being responsible for someone's death. Mary needed to make sure that Damon had his business head on, and thinking clearly.

Mary arrived at an upscale bar and waited for Destiny's arrival. She was so glad that Destiny agreed to meet with her.

"I'm so glad that you're here. I really need

a night out with a friend right now. Work has me so stressed out right now." Mary made sure to buy a drink for Destiny. That was why she chose to meet in a bar. In Mary's experience, alcohol seemed to make people talkative.

"You and me both! I've been a little tense myself. Is something going on at work? Damon has been a little on edge lately." Destiny sipped her drink.

Mary explained that their jobs were on thin ice right now. However, that wasn't what Mary wanted to talk about. She wanted to know more about Damon, without it sounding like she was trying to pry out information.

A man glanced at Destiny from across the room, and Destiny looked a bit uncomfortable.

"You okay?" Mary saw the man eyeing Destiny. "Who is that man and why is he looking at you like that?"

The drunken man got up, and staggered over to their table. "You working? You look so good right now. I haven't seen you in a while."

Destiny picked up her drink, and drank every last bit of it. Her face turned red. "I'm sorry, but you must have mistaken me for someone else." Destiny looked at Mary and hoped that she sounded believable.

"You're not Destiny? You could be her twin. A better looking twin, but a twin still the same." The drunken man just shook his head. "Sorry to bother you." The man walked away.

"What was that about?" Mary knew there was something to it. The man called her by name.

"I need another drink. What about you?" Destiny didn't know what to say. How could she explain this to Mary without telling her that she used to be a prostitute?

Mary gladly went and got another round of drinks for her and her new friend.

"How well do you know Damon? I know that you've worked with him, and he only says good things about you. But you seem so different than him." Destiny chose her words wisely. "I just mean that you're so friendly and warm. Damon's good to me. But I have to be honest. I barely know him."

Now Mary was getting somewhere. "I'm your friend. As your friend, does that mean I can talk to you about Damon and you won't tell him?" Mary knew that if she opened up to Destiny, and showed her that she trusted her, maybe Destiny would be more willing to also tell her about Damon.

Destiny looked into her drink and shook her head yes.

"Damon is moody. He's a great boss, but he can be demanding. His mood swings almost daily. Don't get me wrong, he is great at making good television, but he's not the easiest man to work for." Mary fed her friend just enough information to seem trustworthy. She didn't want to tell Destiny too much more, just in case she did tell Damon. "I just couldn't imagine living with him."

"Was Damon always like this? I know that he takes his work very serious. That show you work on. Maybe it's getting to him. Does it drain you making a pain show?" Destiny also wanted information on her new lover.

"Pain shows are hard. But they pay well. Contestants usually leave happy. They come for money, they get money. It's almost a win-win situation. At first, I didn't think I was cut out for it, but Damon certainly is. I think he enjoys it, a lot." Mary studied Destiny's face for a reaction.

Destiny started to tear up. "I think he does, too."

"Hey, cheer up. It's okay. You know you can talk to me, right?" Mary was genuinely concerned. Mary grabbed Destiny's hand.

Destiny took a gulp of the alcohol and set the glass on the table. She was getting drunk enough to talk to Mary. She had to talk to someone. She didn't have anyone else to talk to, and she really needed a friend right now. "If you breathe a word about this to Damon, I'm afraid he'll kill me." Destiny looked scared.

This was the stuff that Mary wanted to know. Mary looked Destiny in the eyes. "Cross my heart, hope to die. You can tell me anything." Mary actually made the motion across her chest, drawing a cross shape. Mary got closer to her friend.

Very quietly, Destiny began to open up. She told Mary everything. She told Mary about how she met Damon working the streets. How he paid her to hurt herself. She even told Mary about Damon driving her to the desert, and she was afraid that he was going to kill her, but dropped her off at rehab instead. Destiny was so confused, because now Damon had turned into a great boyfriend.

Mary couldn't believe what she was hearing. She had no clue that Damon was hiring hookers and making his own personal pain shows. Mary knew that Damon was dark, but not this dark.

"You need to leave him, now." Mary gave her friend advice.

"I have nowhere to go. I can't go back to my old street life. I don't know what to do." Destiny was trying not to speak loudly. "He's good to me now. He has given me a good life. But after I mentioned William, he acted strange. I don't even think that he was really upset."

Mary was glad that she wasn't the only person suspicious of William's death. Mary told Destiny to come live with her, but not to tell Damon. It would be their little secret.

BAMBI

Damon was glad that Destiny had chosen to go out for the night. That meant that he had his own freedom for the evening. Damon needed an outlet for his stress. He made a phone call to Bambi, and was glad that she agreed to see him. Of course she had agreed to see him. She was a pill-popping prostitute, and Damon had a pocket full of cash.

Bambi greeted Damon at the door, wearing sexy lingerie. She ran her tongue along her full lips.

"I see that you've healed nicely." Damon tried to act like a nice guy, but he honestly didn't care as to whether or not she had healed.

Bambi opened her mouth wide, and showed Damon the bottom of her tongue. "That was probably the worst pain that I've ever felt in my life, but it healed just like you said. Luckily, I self medicate, so I could handle it."

Damon knew that she was referring to her

pill habit. Plus, he paid very well. Of course, she could handle it. Damon always hated going through with the formalities, but they made a few minutes of small talk. Damon hated small talk. He didn't care about how she was doing, or that the weather had been great lately. He wasn't in the mood to talk. He was in the mood to see blood. He wanted control over this woman. He had frustrations that he needed to release.

"I've been thinking. You said you got that idea of under the tongue from a friend's piercing. I also have a friend that just got a new piercing." Bambi was almost excited to tell Damon this news.

Damon raised his eyebrows. He was amused. "Tell me more."

"My friend just got her clitoris pierced. You know what a clit is, right? Anyways, I watched a video online. It's something that we can do here." Bambi opened her laptop on the table and showed Damon a video. "I have a piercing needle. My friend said that it hurt, but not too bad. Do you want to pierce my clit? You saw the video. All you have to do is guide the needle." Bambi had done her own research on types of pain that she could endure, in hopes that Damon would return to visit.

Damon looked at Bambi's face. She was almost too excited about this. He wanted to see her in pain. Her clit wouldn't bleed. He wasn't sure as to whether or not he liked this idea or not. "Do you have any piercings?"

Bambi shook her head no.

"Why not?" Damon looked at her suspiciously.

"I don't like needles. At all. But if you're paying, maybe I could learn to like them." Bambi tried to giggle.

"How much is this worth to you?" Damon found it strange that she had this idea. He wasn't willing to pay very much if it was something that she wanted to do. He had planned on paying her to do something painful to her eyelids.

"$2,000." Bambi had already decided how much she wanted to be paid to do this.

"Couldn't I just go see this at a tattoo parlor. Or perhaps watch videos of it online?" Damon was being stubborn.

"But here, you're the person doing it. You're not watching somebody do it." Bambi was trying to sell her idea.

Damon thought for a moment. Perhaps it could be fun. He always enjoyed it when it was his hand doing the hurting. "$1,000." He countered her offer.

"Deal." Bambi got the needle out of the drawer, along with the bottle of pills.

"Nope. No pills until after." Damon had rules.

Bambi set the pill bottle aside, and handed

the needle to Damon. She climbed up on the bed, and slid her panties off. She spread her legs, exposing herself to Damon. Damon looked at the woman, wondering why this wasn't enough for him. Most men would love to have a woman spread herself before him. This just didn't get his juices flowing. He was attracted to women, but he needed a twist to his arousal. He needed blood or pain.

Damon pricked the needle to the tip of his finger. He saw a drop of his own blood sponge through the surface of his skin. He raised his finger to his mouth and tasted it. Bambi was watching him intently, taking deep breaths. She took her own fingers and pulled the folds of her skin away from her clitoris.

Bambi's neck was raised just enough to try to see what Damon was doing.

"Lay back. Relax. I'm a professional. I just watched an online video." Damon chuckled at his own joke, but Bambi was not amused.

Bambi laid her head back on the pillow, and closed her eyes. Damon looked at her face, and saw that she was scared. He took his fingers and flicked her clit. Bambi jumped.

Damon laughed. "That's not even the needle. Are you sure that you want to do this?" He was glad that she dreaded this.

Bambi didn't say anything. She tensed up her whole body, trying to prepare herself for the needle prick.

Damon took the tip of the needle, and positioned it on her exposed pea shaped organ. He just barely pressed it to her skin for a reaction.

"Oh. Is it done? Was that it? Are we done?" Bambi craned her neck to try and see Damon's face.

Damon shook his head no, then quickly shoved the needle into her, and he very slowly guided it out the other side of her female anatomy. Damon laughed at the woman as she moaned in pain.

Bambi sat up. "It's done right? That was it?" A single tear ran down her cheek.

Damon found the whole event rather anticlimactic. "Lay back. Let me see it."

Bambi reached for her bottle of pills, and Damon did not object. Bambi laid back on the bed, keeping her legs spread so her client would have a good view. Damon heard her crunch the pills. She was obviously chewing them. Damon grabbed the needle on both sides, and pulled to stretch out her clit.

"Ahh. Stop. What are you doing?" Bambi jumped up into a sitting position. She tried to close her legs, but then she realized that she still had the piercing needle stuck in her. With ler legs partly open, she inspected herself. "I have a ring in that drawer over there. Do you want to put it in for me?"

Damon thought for a moment. He went to

the drawer to get the body jewelry. He walked back over to the bed, and got down on his knees so that he was eye level with her sex parts. Bambi spread her legs for him, once again. Damon raised his hand to the needle, and flicked it. It vibrated in her delicate flesh.

"Stop. That hurts!" Bambi started to get angry.

Damon handed her the body jewelry. "You can do it." Damon dug into his pocket and got out the cash and left it on the table. "I'll be in touch." Damon was excited. He wanted to take the tickle in his pants home to Destiny. He had a present for her. Tonight would be a good night.

HARD WORK (TENSIONS)

Damon and Mary only had a few months to prepare for their own show. They had so much to do. They had to decide if they wanted to stick with the old format of 'Easy Money', or if they wanted to change it. Damon had decided that he wanted to make some changes. He wanted to make it better and improved. After all, they were making history here. It should be perfect.

Mary was more interested in the small details of the show. She wanted to make it shiny and entertaining. She was busy focusing on lighting, music, and the host. Damon tried to tell her that the viewers didn't care about all of that, but Mary didn't listen. She could handle all the actual show stuff, while Damon handled the creativity.

After getting frustrated with Mary for not honing in on his expert creative skills, Damon decided to take a lunch break.

"Destiny was asleep when I came in last night. I actually missed spending time with her. She's just wonderful, isn't she?" Damon looked to Mary, trying to pry into her relationship with his girlfriend.

"She is. She's great. But she's kinda weird. How did you meet her?" Mary played stupid.

"What do you mean she's weird?" Damon was almost offended.

"At the bar, some random guy approached her, he even called her by name. She denied knowing him. But I swear I saw her talking to him before she left." Mary shrugged her shoulders. They had already set this up. They orchestrated a lie, so Damon wouldn't be suspicious of how close they had gotten.

Damon knew it was probably an old client. He was proud of Destiny by not telling Mary the truth about her past. "That is odd. I don't know, maybe she just didn't remember him. I don't know. I didn't get to speak to her last night. She was fast asleep. She didn't even wake up with me this morning. I figured she was drunk or something."

"She did have a bit to drink. But I do like her. She's very friendly. How did you meet her?" Mary asked her question once again, to see if Damon would tell her the truth.

"She didn't tell you?" Damon didn't want to tell a story different than whatever Destiny had told.

Mary shook her head no.

Damon thought of a quick lie, that wasn't too far from the truth. "I hired her. The more I got to know her, the more I started to like her. She was cleaning my house."

So now Mary knew that Damon was still lying to her. She knew not to trust Damon. Why did she have to be stuck working with him?

Mary tried to act like her normal self around Damon, but that proved difficult. She just hoped that she put on her best bluff face, and that Damon wouldn't notice her hesitations against him.

Damon and Mary actually were very productive at work. Damon was proud of the new show that they were creating. It took someone special to come up with such a great show. Damon had no references, or any other shows to compare his ideas to. He was embarking upon something very unique. He would make this show even bigger and better than 'Easy Money'.

The whole time, working with Damon, Mary noticed that he enjoyed this too much. Sure, she was helping to produce a pain show, but she wasn't enjoying it in the same ways that Damon was. Mary was still trying to wrap her mind around the things that Destiny had told her Damon paid her to do.

The night before, Destiny had even showed her the brand of the letter 'D' on her leg. Mary couldn't get the image of the scar out of her mind. She knew that her boss was sick. She only hoped that he wouldn't let this show spiral out of control like 'Easy Money' did.

Mary wondered if keeping her job was worth working with Damon. No other network would want to hire her if Damon gave her a poor work performance review. Mary decided that it was best that she was the person assisting Damon with his new show. This way, she could keep an eye on whatever he may or may not be planning for the contestants. She didn't want anyone else to die.

Mary hoped that she was a good liar. She hated to imagine the things her boss might do to her if he knew that his girlfriend was moving into her house. She hoped she was doing the right thing by letting Destiny move in with her.

DESTINY
SHATTERED

Damon rushed home from work. Not only had work been productive, but he also still had a tickle in his pants from the memories of his evening with Bambi. He wanted to spend some quality time with Destiny. He had a primal urge to be with his woman. Damon walked in the front door, and was surprised that Destiny wasn't waiting for him.

He called out her name. "Destiny. I'm home."

Damon stopped at the closet by the front door, and neatly hung up his suit jacket. He removed his tie, and started unbuttoning his shirt. He walked into the kitchen, and still found no sign of his lover. He figured that maybe she was hungover and still in bed. He checked his bedroom, only to find an empty bed. She wasn't in the shower either. Damon went room to room looking for her.

He looked out the window. His spare car was in the driveway. She had to be at home. He checked her old bedroom. The room where she kept all of her belongings. The bed was empty. He saw that her closet door was cracked, so he peeked inside. All of her clothes were gone. He sat on the bed, disgusted. He had done everything to help her change her ways and have a better life.

Damon saw a note on her dresser.

'Dear Damon,

I'm sorry. I have to go find myself. I will miss you.

Love, Destiny'

The note was too simple. What did it mean that she had to find herself? Did she leave out of embarrassment? Did she not know what to tell Mary about the man at the bar? Destiny had nowhere else to go. Was she with that man?

The letter said that she would miss him. That wasn't fair. How could she mess with his head like this? Damon picked up a picture of them and threw the frame across the room, shattering the glass. Damon was hurt.

He would try to find her, but he didn't know where to look. Maybe he could ask Mary about the man at the bar. Maybe he should check her old street corner. Maybe she was getting high again.

Damon tried to turn his head off from

thinking about all of these things. He didn't want to feel like this anymore. Damon needed a distraction.

KILLING THE DEAR

Damon drove recklessly as he dialed on his cell phone. Bambi could possibly offer him comfort. He didn't like the way that he was feeling. He was mad. He was sad. He was hurt. He was disappointed.

He knocked on her door, and skipped the formalities. He threw her on the bed and undressed her.

"I didn't expect this of you." Bambi ran her tongue along his ear.

She knew all of the right things to do. Where to touch him, and how to touch him. He was aggressive. She didn't mind, she liked it rough. Afterwards, they sat on the bed. She reached for her bottle of pills, and offered him 1. Damon had never done drugs before, but he thought maybe it would help him feel better.

"What's gotten into you tonight?" Bambi was curious.

"Nothing. Why do you ask?" Damon remained calm.

"You aren't yourself. You've never asked for that before, so it just shocked me. That's all." Bambi shrugged her shoulders and ate another pill.

Damon decided to open up. "I thought maybe you could help me feel better."

Bambi held out her hand for her payment. "I hope you do feel good."

Damon got angry as she held out her hand expecting money. Damon calmly reached into his pocket. Instead of pulling out cash, he removed his fist from his pocket, and punched her in the side of her head.

"Actually, I am starting to feel better." Damon repeatedly slammed her head into the headboard until she was bloody and unconscious. Damon looked outside. It was dark, and no one was out there. He wiped the place clean of all his fingerprints. He lugged Bambi over his shoulder, and quietly transferred her to his car. It was a perfect night for a drive to the desert.

When Bambi woke up, she was laying in the sand. Her mouth was gagged. Her hands were tied behind her back. She saw the man from her room, the client that liked pain, digging a large hole. She stood up and started running.

Damon looked up from his hole. She was running. That was exactly what he wanted. He wanted her to think that there was a chance of escape. But he knew that she couldn't escape.

He was full of energy and rage. He ran after her. It wasn't hard to catch up with her. He grabbed her by her hair, and led her back to his hole.

"Hmmm.ummm.ummm." Bambi tried to speak, but she couldn't because of the cloth in her mouth.

"You said you hoped I felt better. This makes me feel better." Damon kept a tight grip on her hair and held her head at a low level as he walked very fast. He threw her on the ground. "I was hoping that you'd run. Now, I'll teach you a lesson." Damon walked to his nearby stack of toys, keeping a close eye on Bambi.

Bambi was frozen. Paralyzed with fear. She did not try to run. Damon returned with his trusty hammer. He held up a nail. "I read somewhere that knee pain can be the worst pain that a human being can endure. Or was it the worst place to get shot? I can't remember. But I guarantee that you won't run after this." Damon held up a nail.

Bambi found the courage to try and stand up, but before she got anywhere, Damon was on top of her. He slammed her body into the sand. He sat on her chest, facing her feet. He pressed the nail into a soft indention on her knee cap. He took the hammer and hit the nail into her.

"AGH! MMMM! NN!" Bambi hurt so bad. She had never experienced so much pain in her entire life.

Damon finished hammering the nail into her knee and stood over her. "Do you wanna run now?"

Bambi was crying so much that the cloth in her mouth was soaking wet with tears. She shook her head no.

"For good measure." Damon raised the hammer and pounded it into her other knee. "If you run now, I won't chase you. Promise."

Bambi writhed in agony. She couldn't have stood up if she wanted to. At this point, it was physically impossible. Bambi tried to scream, to speak, to do anything. She was helpless. She could only cry.

Damon knelt down, and wiped a few tears from her face. "Are you in pain? I'm in pain too! So this is only fair, right?"

Bambi closed her eyes. She was scared to look at Damon. She didn't want to see what he was going to do with her.

"Look at me! Open your eyes!" Damon made demands.

Bambi closed her eyes tighter, refusing to obey him.

"Fine. Have it your way!" Damon stormed off to his car.

Bambi squinted to peek out of her eyes to see what he was doing. He was walking back to her holding up something. Whatever he was holding was little. Bambi closed her eyes shut.

"You're going to look at me!" Damon straddled her chest, this time facing her head. He took a hand and pried her eye open. "We'll do it the hard way then!" He held up the surgical scissors for her to see.

Bambi saw the surgical scissors getting closer to her eyeball. She felt Damon press the metal flush against her eye.

"Stop squirming! You're going to make this worse." Damon wedged the sharp point of the scissors between her eyeball and eyelid. Damon took his time and slowly snipped her eyelid.

Bambi was squirming, but it was no use. She could only cry and scream.

Between his finger and thumb, Damon held up a small piece of skin with hair on the edge. Bambi was looking at her own eyelid in Damon's hand. Bambi tried to blink, but she couldn't. She couldn't close her eye. She was in so much pain that she vomited. The puke ran out the sides of her mouth around the cloth. Damon jumped up off her.

"Are you going to open your other eye? Or do you want me to do that again?" Damon threatened her.

Bambi opened her eye.

"I want you to watch me hurt you. Just like I have watched people hurt me my whole life!" Damon was full of hatred.

Damon pulled Bambi's panties to the side. "Watch this!" Damon looked up to make sure she was watching.

The eye that was missing the eyelid was watering real bad, and Bambi had a hard time keeping her other eye open. She was trying her best to watch him, even though she didn't want to.

"Your idea the other night was a joke!" Damon pointed at the jewelry in her clit. "I didn't want to pierce you. But now I'm glad I did." Damon grabbed the little piece of jewelry, and yanked it.

Her clitoris stretched, and then it ripped. Damon held up the jewelry for her to see.

Damon's phone rang. He held up a finger, telling her to be quiet, and he stepped away.

"Hello." Damon didn't recognize the phone number, but he hoped it was Destiny.

There was no reply.

"Destiny? Is that you? Come home, we can fix this."

A strange voice came from the other side of the phone. "No, not Destiny. But perhaps I am your fate. For now you can call me Mr. Cyber. I have a business proposition for you, Mr.

Dahmer."

Turn the page for Deadly Reality TV Series Book #3: Hurt Bank

DEADLY REALITY TV SERIES BOOK #3

Hurt Bank

By Sea Caummisar

HURT BANK PREMIERE

"Good evening viewers! Welcome to the brand new game show 'Hurt Bank"! The only show on television that pays for your pain. I am Peter Conway, your host tonight into the journey of a brand new show concept. It is my pleasure to welcome you. First things first, what you are about to witness is real. I assure you, nothing performed tonight is a stunt. Do not, I repeat, do not try this at home. Viewer discretion is advised. Let the game begin." Peter smiled into the camera revealing his blindingly white teeth.

Damon Dahmer, executive producer and creator of the show, looked at his assistant Mary. They had worked tirelessly on this show, coming up with new creative ideas. Damon enjoyed thinking about new ideas on how contestants could hurt themselves. Mary did not. She did it for a paycheck, and for career advancement. She did not do it for pleasure.

"Let me explain the rules. We will offer tasks to the player. Each task will be worth money. We will start with an easy, less painful task. After completion of the challenge, that money will go into the player's 'Hurt Bank'. Before hearing what the next task is, the player must decide to go home with the amount in their 'Hurt Bank', or to try the next challenge. The next challenge will be worth more money, but it will also hurt more. If they advance to the next task, but do not complete it, they lose all the money in their 'Hurt Bank' and go home empty-handed. We will have 5 rounds. Just remember, the player can quit at any time before agreeing to the next mystery challenge, and choose to go home with their 'Hurt Bank' money. Let's see how much each round is worth." Peter turned around and pointed to display a large 20 foot electronic sign.

Round 1 $10,000
Round 2 $30,000
Round 3 $60,000
Round 4 $150,000
Round 5 $250,000

"As you can see, if the player completes all 5 rounds, they will go home with a total of $500,000! That's a half a million dollars! It just depends on how much hurting the player is willing to do to themselves. Let's meet tonight's player."

Music played loudly. The large sign with the cash amount prizes lit up and started flashing. Mary, assistant producer of 'Hurt Bank', made sure that this show was aesthetically pleasing. Her boss, Damon, was more worried about creating a painful and shocking show. Their jobs were on the line. The network, URN (Uptown Reality Network), was already on the fence as to whether or not to keep a reality pain show on the air. However, they agreed to keep a pain game show on the air if the ratings stayed high, and if the contestants didn't die.

The player walked onto the stage, looking very nervous. He was nervous and sweating. His name was Howard. Damon examined Howard. He appeared to be puny. He was just a thin man, but after interviewing him, Damon knew that he was desperate for cash.

"Welcome to the show, Howard." Peter extended his hand for a handshake. "Tell me a little bit about your situation."

"I've been out of college for almost a year now. I got a master's degree in library science. I have over $40,000 in debt, and I cannot find a job. I lost my apartment a few months back, and was living in my car. Then my car got repossessed. Now I'm just homeless, going from shelter to shelter, trying to survive." Howard wiped the sweat from his forehead, trying to not tear up.

"I'm so sorry to hear that. You're in the right

place to win some money. Are you ready to play?" Peter tried to sound sympathetic.

"I get medical care, right? Afterwards? I won't die?" Howard nervously stammered out a few questions.

Peter tried to comfort the nervous player. "We do have medical on staff, prepared to treat your injuries. You can quit at any time, and go to the hospital, all expenses paid. But if you quit without completing an accepted challenge, you lose all the money in your 'Hurt Bank'. Do you understand?"

Howard shook his head to show that he understood.

At this point, Damon wasn't sure about this player. Upon his interview, he seemed desperate for money. Now he just appeared to be afraid. Despite the fact that he was homeless, he had passed the psychological examination with flying colors. The network made sure to only accept contestants deemed mentally stable.

"Let's play 'Hurt Bank'!" Peter showed his enthusiasm and used his loud announcer voice to try and loosen up the player. "The first task is to make yourself bleed. Sounds simple, right? For $10,000, make yourself bleed. We have supplied a box cutter for this task." Peter handed Howard the tool.

"How much blood?" Howard looked confused.

"It doesn't stipulate. All you have to do is make yourself bleed." Peter tried to clarify the task.

Howard took the tool, and pressed on the button to reveal the shining, sharp blade. Howard delicately pressed the tip of the blade into the tip of his finger. A small dot of blood escaped the surface of the skin.

"Congratulations! You just put $10,000 into your 'Hurt Bank'! Do you want to go home with that cash? Or do you accept the next challenge? If you do not complete the next challenge, you lose the full amount in your 'Hurt Bank'." Peter tried to be clear on the rules.

Howard looked brave and sure of himself. "This is easier than I thought. I want to advance to the next round." Howard was smiling, relieved that his first task wasn't too painful.

Peter held up a large fish hook. "This next task is worth $30,000. If you complete this task, that will be a total of $40,000 in your 'Hurt Bank'. All you have to do is shove this very sharp fish hook through your cheek. In order for this challenge to be considered as complete, we must be able to see part of the fish hook on the inside of your mouth, and also on the outside of your cheek. Are you clear on the rules?"

Howard shook his head yes, and held the fish hook up to the lights to examine it. He used his other hand to rub his jawline. "$40,000 is a lot of money. This is just like piercing my cheek. I think I can manage this." Howard opened his mouth, and slowly guided the tip of the hook to the soft flesh of the interior of his cheek. His eyes welled up with tears as he pushed harder. His mouth was opened wide and he let out a high-pitched squeal of pain. Wiping a tear with his free hand, Howard exhaled loudly. He pressed two fingers on the outside of his jaw, to create resistance. The camera zoomed in on him pushing harder on the hook. Howard closed his mouth, and the hook stayed stuck in place.

"I don't think it went all the way through. I don't see anything on the outside of your cheek" Peter tried to crane his neck to get a closer view.

Howard just shook his head. He opened his mouth, and once again grabbed the hook with his fingers. Howard was breathing heavily as he tried to push the hook all the way through his cheek. The tissues in his cheek were stubborn. They were tough. The camera zoomed in an imprint of the tip of the hook trying to find an exit. Howard struggled harder with the hook, until a small tip protruded the outside of his cheek.

"Congratulations! You added more money to your 'Hurt Bank'. You now have a total of $40,000! Do you want to go home with your money? Or do you wish to advance to the next round?" Peter was still looking at the tip of the hook that was hanging out of the player's cheek.

Damon hoped that Howard would proceed to the next round. There hadn't been anything too painful yet. Damon wanted to see blood.

Howard shook his head yes. He tried to speak with the hook embedded in his jaw, but it was difficult and his words came out mangled. "Yes. I can do another round." Howard tried to fiddle with the hook and remove it, but it wouldn't budge. Each time he tried to pull it out, it hurt worse.

"That's a barbed hook. I don't think it's going to come out very easy. Once you get to medical, maybe they can get it out." Peter tried not to cringe as he watched the man fight back tears. "The next round is worth $60,000! If you complete this challenge, you will have a total of $100,000 in your 'Hurt Bank'! Are you ready to play?"

Howard decided not to speak. It was just too painful. Instead, he just nodded his head yes.

Peter held up a small object in the palm of his hand. "This is what is called a sting grenade. It's the same as a regular grenade, except it is full of rubber balls. For this challenge, you must go into that glass cube, and detonate this sting grenade. Several rubber balls will explode into your body at a very high force. These grenades have been commonly used for crowd control. They will not kill you, but they will injure you. Do you understand this task?"

Howard shook his head yes, and took the device from the host. Howard slowly entered the glass cube, unsure of himself. He closed the door behind him, and looked around the small cube. The cube was 12 feet wide, and 12 feet in length. Howard raised his arm. The glass panel above him wasn't very high. He could touch the ceiling.

"All you have to do is pull that pin, and the grenade will explode, releasing rubber balls. I suggest maybe you drop it as soon as you activate it." Peter offered advice to the player.

Howard held the grenade as far out in front of him as he could. He used his other arm to pull the pin, and he quickly dropped the weapon. Howard quickly pressed the front of his body to a glass panel, to protect the front of his body from the bouncing rubber pellets. His face was smashed into the glass, showing every cringing facial expression. A loud bang rang out throughout the studio. There was a small explosion, and the cube filled up with a small cloud of smoke. Howard flinched each time he was stung by the angry bouncing rubber balls.

Peter waited a moment for the smoke to die down. "Howard, talk to me. Are you okay?" Peter approached the cube to get Howard's attention.

Howard gave a thumbs up, and slowly limped out of the cube. He was shaking his head. He tried to speak, but he was screaming. "I can't hear you Peter. My ears are ringing."

Peter motioned for Howard to turn around. The camera zoomed in on Howard's backside. His clothes were torn, and he was bleeding from a few places. Primarily his lower legs.

Peter screamed at the player. "Congrats! You have $100,000 in your 'Hurt Bank'. Do you need to go to the hospital now, or do you want to play the next round for $150,000? You could leave now with $100,000, or you can try for a total of $250,000! What do you want to do?"

Howard tried his best to see the back of his legs. He looked confused. Maybe he was in shock. He was still screaming. "I want more money! I want to keep playing!"

"Okay. If you don't complete this task, you go home with nothing. Are you sure?" Peter tried to give this player a chance to change his mind.

"I'm sure Peter. I have another round in me." Howard wasn't talking as loud as he was before.

"Okay." Peter agreed in disbelief. "What I have here is a firecracker. A M-80 to be exact. You must light this fuse while the firecracker is setting on your palm. The challenge is to hold this, and let it blow up in your hand. Are we clear?"

Howard gulped. He wished he hadn't agreed to do this. "What if I decide to go home now?"

"Then you lose all the money in your 'Hurt Bank'." Peter sounded apologetic.

Howard thought for a moment. He should have left when he had money. Now he had no choice but to hold the firecracker. He wasn't going home with no money after all the torment he put his body through.

Peter looked at Howard closely. He realized that a rubber ball was stuck to the hook hanging out of the contestant's cheek. Peter tried not to think of all the pain he had witnessed while hosting pain shows.

Reluctantly, Howard took the firework and a lighter from Peter.

"We have another glass cube for you over here." Peter guided the confused player to the cube.

Howard stepped into the glass cube. Peter shut the door behind him.

Howard opened his palm in front of him. He gently placed the small explosive in the center of his palm. He raised the lighter with a shaking hand and lit the fuse. Bang! Howard looked at his hand beneath a small cloud of smoke. There was blood dripping on his shoes. He no longer had any skin on his palm. His hand was a large bloody wound of exposed muscle. He also lost a couple fingers in the blast. Howard stared at his laid open flesh.

"I quit! I want a doctor!" Howard screamed in pain.

"Congratulations! You are going home with $250,000!" Peter said his goodbyes and concluded the show.

Damon was disappointed that Howard didn't make it to the last round. He really wanted to see Howard play with the blow torch. Luckily, there would be a next show. There would be more players and more opportunities to see blood. Overall, Damon was proud of this show. He was only giving the viewers what they wanted. More violence and more gore.

Of course, Damon had his own selfish reasons for the show. He also desired to see people in pain. Damon felt alive and aware of himself whenever he saw blood. Sometimes, he felt superhuman. He was the controller of the pain. He had never felt so powerful.

UNEXPECTED SURPRISES

Mary went to Damon's office giddy with anticipation. She was curious to see how their new show fared with the viewers. Even though Damon's door was open, she knocked anyways. She didn't want to do anything to put Damon in a bad mood. Ever since his girlfriend, Destiny, had left him, Damon was even more irritable than ever. (Not that he was ever friendly to begin with.) Destiny had secretly moved in with Mary to escape her suspicion that Damon was an evil man. Mary hoped that Damon never found out that Destiny was living with her.

Damon invited Mary into his office. Luckily, he was in a good mood.

"By your good mood, I assume the ratings are good?" Mary questioned her boss and crossed her fingers for good news.

"Through the roof! We are getting just as

many viewers as 'Easy Money', if not more." Damon took a second to remember his first pain show creation. Unfortunately, it had been cancelled after the death of a contestant.

Mary was more than happy. 'Easy Money' had been the most popular show on television. If 'Hurt Bank' was getting more viewers, this show would be astronomical. "This is great. It looks like the network will keep us around! I've been so worried that they might cancel our show and fire us. This is the best news I've gotten in some time. Now, I can breathe easier."

This was also good news because Mary knew this would also influence Damon's mood. If Damon was in a bad mood, it ruined her whole day. He was the kind of boss that was all business, no personal life. It seemed that lately, Mary was the only person Damon had to vent his frustrations on. Maybe now she could take a break from worrying.

Their discussion was cut short by another knock on Damon's office door. Damon looked around Mary to see a delivery man holding a large envelope.

"I need your signature, please sir." The delivery man placed the large envelope on Damon's desk. He held out a clipboard, awaiting Damon's signature.

Damon glanced at the envelope. "There's no

return address. Who's that from?"

The delivery man just shrugged his shoulders, and put the clipboard closer to Damon. Damon sighed and signed the clipboard.

Damon redirected his attention to his assistant producer. "Yes, Mary, you, or should I say we, have done a great job. I don't think the network will be firing us anytime soon." Damon thumbed at the envelope, secretly hoping maybe it was from Destiny. He hadn't heard from her since she abruptly moved out. He had searched for her, but he hadn't found her anywhere.

After an awkward pause, Mary excused herself. Damon picked up the envelope and ripped it open. Damon stared at the contents in horror. It was pictures. Pictures of him, in the desert, burying a woman that he had just tortured and killed. He was extra careful the night he murdered Bambi. He made sure that there was no one else around. He didn't know how anyone was close enough to take pictures of him. Damon sorted through the pictures, looking for some sort of a note.

Whoever sent the package obviously hadn't called the police. Otherwise, Damon would be sitting in jail or prison right now. Damon flipped one of the photographs over. On the back were 2 words. 'Mr. Cyber'.

Damon remembered the night that Mr.

Cyber had called him. He was actually in the desert torturing Bambi. It had been a bad night for him. It was the same night that Destiny had left him. When Mr. Cyber had called, Damon wasn't exactly friendly with him. Mr. Cyber had told Damon that he had a business proposition for him. Damon told the caller that he was not interested. Damon was too busy at that moment killing a hooker.

Mr. Cyber didn't take no for an answer easily. He went into detail telling Damon about a show that he hosted on the dark web. A show where they kidnapped people and tortured and killed them for online viewers. Damon had hung up the phone. He hadn't cared to know anything about Mr. Cyber's web show. Damon was a reputable businessman, at a reputable network. If what the caller had said was true, Damon didn't need any involvement.

Even though Damon enjoyed seeing the pictures of Bambi's mutilated body, paranoia began to set in. He was being watched, closely. Despite the precautions he took to avoid being caught murdering her, they had found him somehow. He also remembered hearing the disdain in Mr. Cyber's voice when he told him to never call him again.

However, Mr. Cyber had really gotten Damon's attention now.

When Mary got home, she couldn't wait to tell Destiny the news that the show was already a hit, and could even be more popular than 'Easy Money'. Destiny had been kind of sad lately. Mary figured that sharing good news with her friend might give her a little pick up. Sometimes, good moods can be contagious.

Mary was busy trying to cheer her friend up with a glass of wine, but her friend refused. Destiny liked wine. She actually loved wine. Mary didn't understand why her friend was so sad.

"You know you can tell me anything, right? I'm your friend. I'm here for you." Mary offered her friend a shoulder to cry on. "Is it Damon? Are you still missing him? It's been a couple of months. I'm starting to get really worried."

Destiny poured her glass of wine into the sink. Tears welled up in her eyes. Mary rubbed Destiny's back, trying to comfort her.

"I went to the doctor today." Destiny didn't offer Mary anymore words.

Mary's mind was scrambling. Was Destiny sick? Was it serious? Would she die? "You have to tell me more. Now, I'm even more worried."

Destiny couldn't find the words. Her lower lip trembled. She turned around and wiped the tears from her face.

The suspense was getting to Mary. "Just tell

me. It will be okay."

Finally, Destiny found her voice. "I'm pregnant."

Mary choked on her wine, and set her own glass down. A million questions flooded her mind. "Are you sure? Is it Damon's baby?"

Destiny cut her friend off. "The doctor confirmed it. And yes. It is Damon's. He's the only man I've been with since I got out of rehab. What am I going to do?"

Mary had to think about that. Destiny left Damon for her own safety. Even though he had been good to Destiny, she had still seen the evil that he was capable of.

"You can't tell him." That was the only advice Mary had for her friend at the moment.

"I can't take care of a baby on my own. At times, I do miss him. He really wasn't mean to me. I don't know what to do." Destiny cried large tears from both of her eyes. She wasn't sure how she was going to handle this situation.

For now, she was thankful that she had Mary's support. It could be worse. She could be all alone. Mary had been the best friend that she had ever had in her whole life. Not only did they live together, they did everything together, except for work. They knew each other's secrets and accepted each other unconditionally.

Damon rushed home from work, and turned on his computer. He was panicking, wondering who this Mr. Cyber might be. How had he gotten pictures of Damon burying Bambi's body? Damon didn't even know how to contact this man. All he knew was that the man had mentioned the dark web in their brief phone conversation. Damon didn't even know what that meant.

Damon typed the term 'dark web' into his favorite search engine. He pulled up all kinds of information as to what it was, but not how to get there. Apparently, the dark web was a bunch of hidden websites. Most of them were geared towards illegal activity. Damon was not technologically savvy. Sure, he could surf the internet, but that was about it. Damon wasn't sure if he should even be searching the term 'dark web'. Damon's phone rang.

"Mr. Dahmer, I see that you got my delivery."

Damon looked around the room. He was alone. "Who is this? Can you see me?"

"Don't worry. It's Mr. Cyber. I come to you as a friend. I'm probably your biggest fan. I can't see you at this moment, but I suppose I could turn on your webcam if I wanted to. I have nothing but respect for you and your work."

Damon took his finger and covered the tiny lense of the camera on his computer. "If you aren't watching me, then how do you know that I got your package?" Damon wanted to know.

"Easy. I'm monitoring your computer. You won't find me with your traditional search engines. This is invite only. I monitor your phone, too. That's how I knew you were in the middle of the desert. Thankfully, you took your time there, with your 'work' that night. I had time to come see with my own eyes what you were doing. It looks like I missed the fun parts, but at least I made it before the party had ended."

Damon was paranoid. A complete stranger was tracking his every move with his cell phone. He made a mental note to buy a new phone. "What do you want?"

"I want to collaborate with you. Maybe you could make a guest appearance on my show. Not as a contestant, of course. But as a producer."

"I can't." Damon began explaining his situation. "I have too much to lose. I cannot be involved in any public illegal activity. What if I deny your request? Will you blackmail me? Maybe turn me into the police?"

Mr. Cyber laughed into the phone. "I assure you, this is not public. I'm good at staying underground. Your identity would also remain private. I am not the kind of person to go to the law. I might try to get your attention in other ways, but trust me, I have too much respect for you to turn you in to legal authorities."

"No. I am not interested. But thank you." Damon hoped that would be enough to stop this mysterious person from stalking him. Damon threw his phone across the room, shattering it into tiny pieces.

Damon felt vulnerable for the first time in a long time. This mysterious person knew who he was, what he was about. Damon felt exposed. He didn't like the feeling that someone had the upper hand over him. He had to figure out who this Mr. Cyber was, and he had to figure it out fast.

BUSINESS STRESS (AND RELIEF)

Damon's mood was running hot today. He had to buy a new phone this morning before coming into the office. Plus he dropped his computer off to have his security programs updated. Not only was he worried about whoever this Mr. Cyber might be, he was also worried about how to get this person out of his life. On top of everything else, he just didn't have time for any of this. He was too busy planning the next episode of 'Hurt Bank'.

Damon tried to push Mr. Cyber out of his mind. He would deal with him when the time was right. For now, Damon was not worried about the threat of jail.

Mary did not seem her usual self today. She was scatterbrained, as if her mind was somewhere else. Damon needed his assistant to have on her best thinking cap today. He relied heavily upon her.

"Mary, I need to leave early today. I have some personal stuff to take care of." He had to pick up his computer before the shop closed. "Could you run the supply list to the prop people later this afternoon?"

Personal stuff? Oh, no. Mary hoped that Destiny hadn't informed him of the news of being pregnant. She decided to pry. "Personal stuff? Sure I can do the prop run, but you're Damon Dahmer. You never leave work for anything personal." Mary also noted in her mind that he never mentioned anything personal. Outside of the time he brought Destiny to a company party (where Mary had met Destiny), he was very secretive about anything in his personal life.

"Yes. That's what I said." Of course, Damon offered no other explanation.

Mary also noted that Damon was making it difficult to pry into his personal affairs. Maybe she just wasn't asking the right questions. "Just out of curiosity, whatever happened to Destiny? I really liked her." Mary hoped for the best. She hoped that the mention of Destiny wouldn't unleash Damon's temper.

Damon just turned his head to look out the window. He said nothing. He didn't answer Mary. Mary took his silence as a relief. It was better than him getting mad at her.

"I've gotta run some files to editing. I'll see you tomorrow." Mary left Damon alone. She would sneak out, and place a quick phone call to check on Destiny. She only hoped that Destiny hadn't told Damon anything yet. Mary could not imagine what kind of father Damon would be.

After picking up his computer, Damon was still stewing over the mention of Destiny. He had even hired a private investigator at some point, who couldn't find her. Either Destiny was good at hiding, or he needed a new PI. She hadn't opened any credit cards. She hadn't rented a hotel or residency under her own name. She hadn't bought a car. Maybe she was just good at hiding.

Between the worry about Mr. Cyber and Destiny, Damon knew that a night out would cheer him up. He just planned to leave his cell phone at home, to ensure that he was untrackable.

He drove around in a rental car, until he found a woman walking along the street. He liked the idea of driving around the seedy areas of town to find a hooker. Maybe, with any luck, he would find Destiny. Damon tried to remain hopeful. He even made it a point to ask any street walker that he picked up as to whether or not they knew a Destiny working the area.

It was dark, but Damon could make out the shape of a curvy woman standing on the corner. Damon pointed his car in her direction, and his headlights lit her up. She was 1 of the more attractive hookers. She had all of her teeth, and she wasn't so thin that she looked sick. She appeared to be fairly young. She couldn't had been more than 25 years old. Damon found his date for the night.

Damon never came off as a creep with a pain fetish. Whenever he first met a woman, he always tried to be welcoming and charming. He knew that women were more open to doing what you wanted if they liked you. Plus, he always paid well. Hookers like cash. That was just a fact of life. Otherwise, they wouldn't have chosen that profession. Damon had yet to meet a woman that did this job purely for pleasure.

After paying the young lady the agreed upon sum, Damon drove to a rent by the hour hotel. Luckily, the woman was happy to rent the room in her name. This woman was different than the others. Damon didn't see any sign of drug abuse. Of course, he could be wrong, but she just didn't seem to be the type.

Drug addicts were always easier to give in to his twisted requests of watching them hurt themselves. Damon liked a challenge. He could've picked up the hooker without teeth, and was so skinny that she looked like she hadn't eaten in a year. That was too easy. Damon wanted to be the person that corrupted this girl.

"Tell me about yourself." Damon always acted like he cared, but he didn't. It was all an act. He just needed this woman to think that he cared. Instead, he was just trying to get into her head. He wanted to know what made her tick. He needed to know her motivations.

"Not much to tell. I'm kinda new in town. Moved here a few months ago. I'm kinda in between jobs right now. This puts food on the table for now." She tried to look at him with sad eyes, so that maybe she would get a better tip out of him.

She started to slowly undress, however, she saw that her naked body was not grabbing his attention. Usually a client, especially a client that sprang for a motel room, would have already been on top of her. This man was different. He didn't pounce on her. Instead, he sat at the table and asked her questions about herself.

"Show business? Was that your dream?" Damon was curious. He found that a lot of the prostitutes and escorts and call girls were in town to pursue an acting career.

"Sure, that's every little girl's dream. But I actually moved here for the weather. Where I'm from it snows often. I just needed a change of scenery." The woman looked like she was telling the truth. If she were lying, Damon couldn't tell by her facial expressions.

"Drug habit?" Damon needed to know.

"What are you, some cop? You want me to write you an autobiography? Can we just handle our business? I gotta get back out there and make some money." Now the lady just seemed to be defiant and rude.

"Business? Sure. Money? Sure. How much do you need?" Damon tried to get her to be just a little bit nicer.

The woman laughed. "A couple million would do me just fine."

Damon reached into his pocket and pulled out his wad of money. "I only have a few grand on me. What will that get me?"

"Anything you want." Suddenly, seeing Damon hold that much money, she decided to play nice.

"I want to see you hurt yourself." Damon made what seemed like a simple statement. It was simple to him at least.

She cocked her head to the side. She said nothing. She thought for a moment. "What do you mean?'

"I want to see you in pain." Once again, Damon made a simple, self explanatory statement.

"Oh, like the TV show?" It was as if a light bulb clicked on above the woman's head.

Damon pulled his ball cap tighter around

his face. His show was very well known. A blessing, yet also a curse. Damon nodded his head yes.

"Okay, I'll play along. What do you want me to do?" Now the girl was curious. She must be a fan of the show.

"I want to see you eat a light bulb. At least a portion of it. I have thousands of dollars here." Damon fanned the money out on the table.

"Nope. That would tear my mouth up. Won't do it. Try again." She blatantly refused.

Damon hated it when his toys would not play along. He decided to take it easy on her this time. He could come visit her again, and take her out on a suprise playdate. Perhaps, then he could force her to eat a lightbulb. Until that became a reality, he would have to be creative. Damon looked around the motel room. It was just a basic room. There was a bed, dresser, television set, and a bathroom. Damon continued to search the room with his eyes.

"This is easy enough. I want you to lick that wall outlet." Damon wasn't sure what that would do, but he wanted to find out.

The woman looked at the wall. "Are you serious? You'll give me all that money just to lick that plug in thing on the wall? What's the catch?"

Damon chuckled to himself, thinking that she must not be very smart. "Yes. Just get down there and lick it. Be seductive. Really stick your tongue in there." He didn't know much about electricity, other than the fact it would shock her. He assumed that it wouldn't kill her. If it did, he could easily dispose of her corpse.

The woman actually laughed. "This will be the easiest money that I have ever made." She was happy.

Damon watched as the woman got down on her hands and knees. She tried to be sexy as she stuck her rump in the air. She looked at him, then at the wall. She pulled her hair to the side of her head. She licked her lips, as if she was seducing him. She stuck her tongue to the small holes in the wall and Damon heard a small thud. The woman was jolted backwards. Her facial expression changed from sexy to fear. Her eyes were huge. Her tongue was hanging out of her mouth.

Damon laughed. "Are you okay?"

The woman sat perfectly still, and then felt the tip of her tongue with her fingers. Damon got down on the floor to get a closer look at her tongue. He could see that it had just a small red mark on it. It was a very minor burn. Damon was disappointed, but was glad that he had found a new playtoy. Next time, he would bring toys with him.

After paying the lady, Damon got her telephone number. Not only had Damon found a new playmate, but he had already planned a personal pain viewing for her. At least now he had someone new to play with. He felt satisfied despite this boring event. He had plans to come prepared for their next meeting.

He could bring along his own props. Who was she to deny his requests? Most people who had ever denied Damon didn't live long enough to regret it. He was going to make sure that she was not an exception to that rule. For now, she could enjoy her warm weather.

Damon smiled, very much looking forward to the next time that he would get to play with her.

MARY'S DATE

Being good at her job, Mary knew that Damon was on edge lately. He was actually almost always on the edge anymore. She knew the perfect thing to perk her boss up was his favorite coffee. Even though it was expensive, she knew that it would be worth her while to go out of her way for her boss. Perhaps Damon would repay her with kindness if she showed up at the office with some java for him.

Mary was very carefully carrying 2 cups of coffee, leaving the coffee shop, and a man bumped into her. She dropped both cups and her shirt was covered in hot coffee. Mary looked at the mess she had made, and held her blouse away from her skin. When she looked up at the man who had bumped into her, she couldn't believe how green his eyes were.

"I am so sorry. Let me help you." The man offered her some napkins. "I feel horrible. I'll help you clean up. I'll buy you more coffee."

Mary was too busy looking at his eyes. She didn't hear a word he said.

"Are you okay?" The man wondered why Mary wasn't responding.

Mary pulled herself out of her daze. This man was a perfect gentleman. He was clumsy, but very attractive and very nice.

"I'm David. Let me help you."

Mary allowed the man to buy her more coffee. He was so charming. Between work and Destiny, Mary was emotionally drained. Sharing a conversation with David was like a breath of fresh air. When David asked for her phone number, Mary felt like a teenager again. She had been too busy to date, but she couldn't refuse him. They made plans to meet later that evening after work.

Mary met David at a small cafe that wasn't far from the office. Mary smiled as she saw that David had arrived early, waiting on her.

"I'm sorry if I'm a few minutes late. I have the kind of boss that doesn't like knocking off from work early." Mary smiled as she stared into his emerald eyes.

"I would wait for you forever." David's smile melted her heart. He was trying hard to impress her. "What do you do?"

Mary realized that even though she spent all day dreaming about this man, he was still a complete stranger. She didn't know what to tell him. The fact that she worked on a pain reality show wasn't exactly a crowd pleaser. "I'm an assistant producer for URN. The reality network."

David's face almost frowned. "Is that the channel that airs that pain show?"

Mary saw that he wasn't a fan. She didn't want this man to judge her by her job. "It is." She thought that a short response would be best.

"Do you work on that show?" David squinted his eyes.

Mary decided not to lie, but to not tell the whole truth. "I have. It's a job." Mary shrugged her shoulders. "What about you? What do you do?"

David didn't mind that Mary quickly changed the subject. He told her all about himself. She found out that he worked on computers as an information technology security specialist. She noted that he must also be intelligent. They got along perfectly. Mary hadn't even noticed how long they had been sitting there, but they had already gone through a whole bottle of wine getting to know each other.

Mary's phone rang, and she looked at it to see that her roommate was calling. After a brief conversation with Destiny, Mary looked at the time.

"I'm sorry. That was Destiny, my roommate. She was wondering when I'd be home. I didn't realize how late it is." Mary didn't want him to think that she was rude by taking the phone call.

"Destiny. That's an unusual name. I used to know a Destiny." David tried to keep the conversation going. He wasn't ready to end his evening with her.

Mary knew that Destiny used to be a prostitute. She hoped that David didn't know her roommate. "How'd you know your Destiny?"

"Oh, years ago. We went to high school together." David smiled at her.

Mary felt a bit relieved. Before she said her goodbyes, David gave her a sweet kiss on her cheek.

David seemed to be perfect. Mary needed something good and perfect in her life. This man was what her life was missing.

Mary felt like a teenager again. She forgot how good it felt to date. She sang with the radio the whole ride home. It was so nice having a night out with a man. It was even better not thinking about work or Damon for a full evening. She only hoped that things would work out with David. She was excited about their next date.

She made a mental note to not neglect Destiny. Her friend was going through a rough time in her life right now. Destiny needed Mary's support. Mary was sure that she could make time for both David and Destiny. Hopefully, they could all get along.

HURT BANK (SECOND EPISODE)

"Welcome back to another exciting episode of 'Hurt Bank', the only show on television that pays for pain. I'm Peter Conway. We have even more daring challenges tonight. It is my pleasure to bring to you the most exciting hour of television! Once again, don't try this at home. Viewer discretion is advised. Who's ready to play 'Hurt Bank'?"

"Tonight we are with Emily." Peter put his arm around the young contestant. "Emily, tell everyone at home a little bit about yourself."

Emily was a college dropout. She spoke quietly and seemed very timid as she told the story about a house fire that changed her family's life. "We have lost everything. My parents are older, and they depend on me. They didn't have any home insurance. We are now homeless, moving from shelter to shelter. We only had the clothes on our backs. Fortunately, the community has helped us by giving us clothes. But we have pretty much nothing else. I plan to win and buy a new home for my parents."

"How unfortunate Emily. You can win up to half a million dollars today!" Peter began explaining the rules. He wanted the player to be clear that if she advanced to the next round, she had to complete the next challenge. Otherwise, she would lose everything in her hurt bank. "As you know, our challenges start out easy and get progressively harder. Your first challenge is worth $10,000! Are you ready Emily?"

Emily looked frightened as she shook her head.

Peter held up a hot glue gun. "This is a tool used primarily in arts and crafts. It melts glue. It actually makes the glue very hot. The first challenge is to put some of this hot glue under your arm, in your armpit. I'm told that it is very hot, and is guaranteed to irritate the skin and leave blisters. Are you ready Emily?"

Emily reluctantly took the gun from Peter. She looked the device over.

"Just squeeze that trigger and the glue comes out that nozzle. You need to line your armpit with at least an inch of hot glue." Peter instructed Emily as to what the rules were.

Emily looked at Peter, then at the small item in her hand. She rolled up the sleeve of her t-shirt and raised her arm over her head. She looked at her armpit as she raised the glue gun. She got the small nozzle close to her skin, and began to press the trigger. As the glue slowly made contact with her skin, she wrinkled her face. However, she moved the gun, and drew a straight line.

"Good job Emily! You made that look easy, like it didn't even hurt. Congratulations. You now have $10,000 in your hurt bank!" Peter was happy for the player. "Do you want to leave with your money, or do you want to advance to the next round?"

For the first time, since the beginning of filming, Emily smiled. "I'd like to advance to the next round. I think I can do this."

Peter held up a mousetrap. It was a simple device. A piece of wood with a metal arm that would slam down once the spring was triggered. "For $30,000, your challenge is to trigger this mousetrap with your tongue. Now, this metal will slam down on your tongue very fast, and very hard. It will hurt. But $30,000 would bring your hurt bank total up to $40,000!"

Emily smiled again. "I'm so relieved. This isn't half as bad as I expected. I need that money." Emily took the mousetrap from Peter, and without even thinking, she stuck her tongue out as far as she could. She pressed her tongue onto the small trigger plate. The metal arm quickly slammed down on her tongue. "Ewww!" Emily tried to scream, but it sounded funny due to her tongue hanging out of her mouth. Emily started to cry as she tried to undo the mousetrap.

Peter stepped in and helped Emily get the mousetrap off her tongue. "Congratulations Emily! You now have $40,000 in your hurt bank! How are you feeling? Do you want to advance to the next round?"

Emily was rubbing her tongue with her fingers. Her eyes were pointed down, trying to see the tip of her tongue. "Am(th) I(th) bleeding?" Emily tried to ask Peter a question, but her tongue was so swollen she had a hard time talking. Almost every word sounded like she was pronouncing a -th sound on the end.

Peter looked at her tongue as she stuck it out. "No, I don't see any blood. But it's really red and swollen. Just shake your head for me. Do you want to keep playing? Just remember, if you don't complete the next round, you go home with zero dollars."

Emily looked at Peter, her eyes full of tears. She shook her head yes. She wanted to keep playing.

"Your next challenge is worth $60,000. This will bring you to a total of $100,000! The challenge itself is pretty easy, but the pain will be bad." Peter walked across the stage to a ladder attached to some sort of a contraption. "All you have to do is climb up this ladder, and stick your hand in that noose like contraption. Then you jump off the ladder. Your hand will still be up there, but your body will be down here. We premeasured your height, so that for a couple of inches of falling, your weight will pull down on your arm. I'm told, that at the very least, this task will dislocate your shoulder. But we're not sure what else it will do. It's not like we can test this. Are you ready Emily?"

Emily eyeballed the ladder and the opening that she would be sticking her hand into. She shook her head no.

"So you're choosing to quit? You lose that $40,000 if you leave now." Peter looked shocked that a player would walk away from that kind of money.

"I'm(th) not quitting(th). I'm(th) just not(th) ready(th)." Emily's tongue was still too swollen to speak.

Peter looked relieved as Emily approached the ladder. She slowly climbed onto the first rung, then the next, until she was at the top. She held her arm away from her, and slowly guided her hand into the hole.

"That looks good. Now, all you have to do is jump." Peter looked away as he told her what to do next. He did not want to witness her jumping.

Emily took a few deep breaths. She looked down to where she would be jumping. Emily closed her eyes, and quickly lunged off the platform. It all happened so fast. Her arm was over her head, as her body was falling downward.

"AWWWW". Emily screamed in pain.

Peter heard a crunching sound, even though he wasn't looking at her.

Emily's hand came loose from the noose. She was crying loudly. Her shoulder was drooping towards the ground. She rubbed her shoulder with her good hand.

Peter finally looked at Emily. "Congratulations! You now have $100,000 in your hurt bank. This next challenge is worth $150,000. Challenges do get harder. But if you advance, you could go home with $250,000. Do you want to continue playing?"

Emily stopped crying long enough to try and answer his question. "My(th) family needs(th) a house(th). I want(th) to(th) play(th)."

Peter shook his head in disbelief. At the very least, this girl had a swollen tongue and a dislocated shoulder. Perhaps her shoulder was even broken. Yet, she wanted more money.

"Okay. You must complete this challenge, or you go home with no money." Peter wanted to clarify the rules for her once again. "This challenge is worth $150,000! That's a total of $250,000!"

A small curtain raised on a corner of the stage. Emily looked and couldn't believe what she was seeing. A bear trap! A large metal trap with angry, sharp teeth.

"All you have to do is step into this bear trap. It would be over in less than a second, but the pain will last a very long time. I'm not a doctor, but perhaps you could lose your foot." Peter wanted to make her aware of the possibilities.

Damon shook his head in disgust. He didn't need his host trying to talk a contestant out of playing. Perhaps he needed to have a talk with Peter. For now, he made a hand signal towards Peter. Letting Peter know to stop talking. Peter pursed his lips, and said no more.

Still rubbing her shoulder, Emily slowly walked over to the evil contraption that could eat her foot. She noticed how the steel jaws shined in the lights of the cameras, making it look even scarier. Larger tears fell down her face. She looked completely defeated. She was deep in thought.

Peter didn't dare voice his opinion. He knew that it was best to not make Damon mad. Instead, he offered her instruction. "All you have to do is step down on that metal plate in the center with a foot. Easy. And fast. We have a crew backstage ready to pry it open afterwards."

Emily shook her head. "I(th) can't(th) do(th) it. Can I(th) see a demonstration(th)?"

It took Peter a second to realize what she was saying. "You want to see how the bear trap works? Sure. Actually, we have a demonstration set up just in case you decide not to do it. Ya know, just to show the viewers at home. I don't see any reason why we can't do that now."

A man walked out onto the stage carrying a piece of wood that was as tall as he was.

"That's what is called a 4 by 4. Meaning, it measures 4 inches deep, and 4 inches wide." Peter gave the man a second to get to the bear trap. "He is gonna set that trap off, and show us what the bear trap does to that wood."

The man lowered the wood down onto the bear trap, and swiftly the jaws clamped onto the wood, instantly snapping it as if it were a twig. Emily jumped back as she heard the pop of the device and the crunching of the wood.

"While they're busy setting that bear trap back into position, why don't you tell me your thoughts Emily?" He knew she couldn't speak well with her swollen tongue, but he had to kill a few minutes of time anyways.

"It's gonna(th) rip my foot(th) off(th)! But that's a lot(th) of money to lose(th). My family(th) depends on me(th)!" Emily's tears were quieter, but still falling down her face.

"This is your decision. If you step into that

bear trap, you win $250,000 dollars total. Then you could even advance to the next round worth another $250,000." Peter felt like he was encouraging her to carry out the task, even though he didn't want to. Sometimes, he just didn't like his job.

Emily didn't say a word. She quickly ran over to the bear trap and lowered her foot onto the center plate. The sharp teeth raised, gripping her leg and she screamed maniacally. Emily instantly fell down to the ground. The camera zoomed in to show her exposed bone. It was probably the bloodiest task on any of the pain shows, ever.

Peter tried not to look at the girl as she sobbed. Medical staff came out on stage. Peter was informed that Emily had chosen to take the $250,000 home, and not advance to the next round.

Damon was disappointed. He feared that he would never see anyone use a blowtorch on themselves for the last round. At least he was proud of this episode. He had never seen a bear trap in action before. He embraced his own creativity. Damon gave himself a pat on his back.

He took mental pictures of the bear trap snapping the girl's leg into a tangled mess of flesh and blood. That would be an image that could cheer him up, if he ever needed a little pick me up.

BLOWING
OFF STEAM

After a hard day at work, nothing made Damon happier than playtime. He had to keep his mind busy. Otherwise, he felt like he was going to explode. He was still devastated that Destiny had left him. He had finally started to open up to another human being, and she left him. Once again, he was alone.

He still had his job, and he loved his job. He particularly enjoyed the fact that he could put most of the responsibility of filming on Mary, so he could focus on watching the show and getting the full effect. Nothing made him happier than seeing people in pain. Nothing except him being the giver of the pain. He wanted that feeling of being in control of another person's life.

Damon gathered his bag of supplies and went prowling for his new play toy. A quick phone call, and he had plans to go pick the hooker up. He was going to teach her a lesson about not playing along with his previous request. He threw the disposable cell phone out the window of his car, just in case Mr. Cyber had hacked into it. He needed complete privacy.

The hooker willingly got into his car. She was willing to play. She just wasn't willing to play the games that Damon wanted to play.

"Do you wanna fool around this time? In the car? Or do you wanna get another room?" The hooker rubbed on Damon's leg.

Damon did not want this woman touching him. He wanted to hurt her. He smiled anyways. Charm. That was his best asset.

"The car is fine by me." Damon flashed his teeth at her, as he drove into a dark secluded alley.

The street walker snuggled up to Damon and started licking his ear. Even though he wanted to, Damon didn't pull away from her.

"How much cash did you bring this time?" She licked his neck, hoping to arouse him.

"I have plenty of cash, don't worry your pretty face about that. Let's get in the backseat." Damon unfastened his safety belt, and slowly made his way out of the car.

The hooker willingly climbed into the backseat of the car. Damon watched her as she was pulling her shirt skirt up to her waist. Her silky red panties caught his eye. She was too busy undressing that she didn't notice that

Damon had pulled a rag out of a bag. Damon doused the rag with chloroform and raised the rag to the woman's mouth and nose.

"What are you doing? Get that out of my face!" The woman scrambled to open the car door, but it was difficult due to the placement of her half removed clothing.

Damon climbed on top of the woman, but didn't understand why she was still conscious. He held her down while she fought him. In every movie that Damon had ever seen the substance used, the victim instantly passed out. He had wondered if the man he had bought the chloroform from in Mexico sold him a false product. Damon was relieved when the woman stopped struggling after a few minutes, and went to sleep.

Damon quickly used thick tape to tie the woman's arms and legs. He climbed back into the front seat, and made the drive to the desert. Right now, he was high on life. He didn't think he could get any happier.

When the woman woke up, she was already lying in the sand. Damon had been watching her sleep. While he was busy preparing his play time, he made sure to periodically place the chloroform rag under her nose. He knew he had to study up on the substance, to ensure that he was using it properly. He didn't want to use too much and kill her. But he also wanted to make sure he was using enough to keep her knocked out.

Damon looked around to ensure that they were all alone in the desert. Mr. Cyber had made him paranoid. He had never been paranoid before.

"My head hurts." The woman tried to sit up, but she was very drowsy. "What are you doing? Please don't hurt me."

She had already started begging, and Damon hadn't even laid a finger on her. He was pleased with this victim.

"I asked you to eat a light bulb the last time I saw you. You told me no. Now we play on my terms." Damon remained calm.

"You're crazy! Untie me! I'll do anything! Please!" The woman struggled, but it didn't do her any good.

Damon enjoyed watching her squirm. He loved seeing the fear in her face. He said nothing as he held up a small glass light bulb.

"I can't eat that! It could kill me!" The woman started crying as she realized what this psycho was getting ready to do to her.

Damon was pleased with himself. This was the kind of foreplay that he enjoyed. He hadn't even hurt her yet, but he was already getting turned on. He tried to ignore the tickle in his pants, but promised himself that after she was dead he would then get his sexual gratification.

Damon placed his large hand around her cheeks and squeezed, forcing her to open her mouth. He raised the light bulb to her mouth and laughed. She closed her eyes tight, yet tears still fell down her face.

He shoved the bulb into her mouth until he heard the crunch of breaking glass. He punched the bottom of her chin, forcing her mouth closed. She struggled against him, and even tried to scream, but she couldn't because he was holding her mouth shut. Damon held his hands firmly around her face as blood ran down her sweet lips.

Damon watched her eyes. Her eyes were screaming out in pain. He swore that he could hear her eyes.

"Swallow. After you swallow, I'll let go." Damon spoke calmly, hoping to soothe his victim.

She shook her head no and made noises.

Damon got bored after a few minutes and let go. The hooker opened her mouth and spit shards of glass and blood into the sand. It was too dark for Damon to see inside of her mouth, but based on the amount of blood that she had spitten out, he knew she had many open wounds. She just cried hysterically. As much as he enjoyed the sounds of her pain, he found her sobs annoying.

"Shh. It's okay now. The hard part is over." He just wanted her to be quiet. But she wouldn't stop crying. "Okay. Have it your way."

Damon pulled a box cutter from his pocket, and the woman cried harder. He forced her backwards onto the sand and laid on top of the street walker. She spit in his face and he felt the warm red liquid on his cheeks. Not only was he now covered in her blood, but he felt small shards of glass in his face.

Damon pinned her head to the ground and glided the blade across her throat, from ear to ear. Blood spurted out as she made her last gargle sounds. It didn't take long for her body to go limp.

Damon went to the car for his flashlight. He opened her mouth, and saw the sparkling glass embedded in the delicate tissue of her mouth. Her tongue had several slashed open wounds. The small crevices of the insides of her cheeks harbored small pieces of broken light bulb.

Damon slid her pretty red panties down her legs. He was all alone with his play toy. Now he could satisfy that tickle in his pants.

When he was finished with her limp body, he admired her blood stained mouth, and sliced open neck. He looked down at his own bloody hands. They shimmered in the moonlight reflecting the most beautiful crimson color he had ever seen in his life.

MARY GETS PERSONAL

Mary had finally invited David for their first overnight date. She had been out with David several times, and she was convinced that he was the man of her dreams. She could see herself marrying this man. It was too sudden to use the word love, but Mary thought she could possibly be in love with David.

Mary had not been to bed with a man in a very long time. She wanted their first time being intimate together to be in her own bed. She would be more comfortable that way. Plus, David could meet Destiny. David was sweet and funny. Maybe he could help cheer Destiny up. She had been depressed ever since she found out that she was pregnant.

Mary cooked dinner for her roommate and her boyfriend, while Mary and David got to know each other. Mary could hear Destiny laughing as she went to the kitchen to get the dinner plates.

"Mary has a great roommate. I can tell. How do you know each other?" David tried to make small talk over dinner.

Destiny stared off into space for a moment. "I used to date her boss."

"You're kidding? He's not mad that you moved in with his employee? He must be a great guy. I know a lot of guys don't want their exes to be a part of their lives anymore." David thought his words were harmless.

Mary saw that Destiny was getting upset. "He doesn't know. He's my boss at work. Not the boss of my life. Destiny is my friend. I would want her living with me regardless of what he thinks."

Destiny smiled. "I don't know what I would do without Mary. Maybe if things don't work out with you, I can convince her to be my baby mama." Destiny winked at David.

"Whew. I'm so glad you're pregnant. I was afraid to ask. I asked a woman in an elevator when she was due, and she got mad at me. Turns out she was just fat." David's laugh resonated around the room. David looked at Mary. "So, is your boss the father?"

"Yes. But it's a secret. And yes Destiny, I'll be your baby's daddy!" Mary could be funny, too.

After wonderful dinner conversation, and

plenty of laughs, Destiny excused herself to leave the love birds alone. Mary was nervous. She knew what an overnight date entailed, but she wasn't sure if she was ready to take the step in her relationship.

Luckily, David was a perfect gentleman. He didn't rush anything. He said all the sweet things that men say to their lovers. He kissed her softly, and treated her body like it was a delicate flower. Mary knew that she was in love.

When he touched her, Mary felt feelings that she had never felt in her life. He was the most tender man she had ever been with. She knew she was lucky to have found such a sensitive man.

David was the exact opposite of Damon. Mary couldn't even believe that she was comparing her boyfriend to her boss. Maybe she was spending too much time at work! Damon demanded that she devote all of her attention to the show. It felt nice to be a person again. It was nice to have a life outside of the office.

She snuggled up into the safety of David's arms and drifted off to sweet dreams.

The next morning, laying in bed still cuddling, Mary could hear Destiny stirring about making coffee.

"I think it's great that you're so close with

your roommate. She seems wonderful." David started putting his pants on.

Mary was relieved that he liked Destiny. "She's an important person in my life. She's just going through a tough time right now. I don't wanna neglect her, just because I'm head over heels in love."

David paused and looked at Mary. He instantly smiled. "Love? Are you sure?"

Mary blushed. "I um. No. It's just. Um."

"I love you too." David gave Mary a tender kiss on the mouth. "I like her. She can hang out with us anytime. If there's anything that I can do to help you with her situation, I'd be more than glad to help."

Mary was convinced that this man was perfect. Her life couldn't get any better.

COLLAPSE

Mary spent too much time drinking coffee and enjoying her new man. She lost track of time and got to the office late. It was just that she was so busy making plans to meet David and Destiny after work. It was great that David was open to spending time with her roommate.

She hoped that Damon was also running late. Maybe her boss wouldn't notice. Damon wasn't the understanding type of boss. He was very demanding.

Mary rushed to her desk, with her fingers crossed that she beat Damon to the office. No such luck.

"Mary? Is that you out there? I need you. Now." Damon had his usual demanding tone.

"Yes. Coming." Mary set some papers on her desk, as she scurried into Damon's office.

Damon had an array of papers scattered on his desk. He waved his hands over the messy desk. "I have been here almost an hour. Sorting through all this by myself. Not only am I trying to plan the next episode and sorting through casting contestants, but now I'm bothered with all the network requests. Mr. Styles is breathing down my neck for reports."

"I had a flat tire." Mary lied.

"I didn't ask. Mr. Styles is requesting written reports on sponsors. We have so many sponsors, this will take all day. It looks like you will be working late tonight. Get busy." Damon spun his chair around. He didn't even want to look at his tardy underling. Damon wasn't really mad at her. He just liked to exercise his authority.

"Yes sir. I'm on it. But I have plans tonight. I'm sure the network will understand if…"

Damon cut Mary off before she could say another word. "The network doesn't need to understand anything. You will stay an hour late tonight. Longer if these papers aren't filled out. Now, go."

As Mary left Damon's office, he smiled. It never bothered him playing the role of a controlling boss. He actually enjoyed it. He did appreciate Mary's hard work, but he had to teach her how important it was to arrive to work on time. Actions had consequences. Such as being late to work. Her consequence was having to work longer that evening.

Damon had a busy day planned at work. Home viewers who were wanting to be on the show were sending in videos of self torture. Damon's boss (Mr. Styles) demanded that Damon discourage viewers from sending in such videos. Even though the network frowned on it, Damon always kept a few of the videos to watch for himself. He enjoyed watching people hurt themselves.

Damon pressed play on his computer. The video started out simple enough, a man telling his name, and why he needed money. He didn't bother to listen. Who the man was, and his financial hardships, were not of Damon's concern. Damon just desired to see the pain in the man's face. The man in the video held up a fish hook.

"How not original." Damon was talking to himself. He was disappointed that this man had not been more creative. He stole Damon's idea from the first episode of 'Hurt Bank'.

The man did surprise Damon though, when he raised the fishing hook to his nose. The man guided the sharp tip of the hook into his nostril. Damon had to lower the volume on his computer as the man cried out in pain from shoving the hook through the cartilage connecting his nostrils. It took a few minutes, but the man successfully pierced the frail piece of skin. The tip of the hook was in his right nostril, and the long straight shaft of the hook was hanging from his left nostril.

Damon loved this part of his job. He wished the network would let him cast the daring people who sent in these kinds of videos. But they firmly refused. Plus, the chances that these people would pass the mental tests were slim. Mary had mostly been in charge of casting, but Damon didn't mind helping out a bit here and there. He actually enjoyed it.

The hardest part of his job right now was getting someone who would play until the last round and use a blowtorch to hurt themselves. Damon wanted to see someone bake their flesh with the hot flame. He regretted not taking a blowtorch to the desert when he treated his hooker to a dinner of light bulb glass. Oh well, there was always next time.

Damon didn't bother saying goodbye to Mary as he left the office. He looked at her desk covered in scattered papers. It served her right. She was late. It was only fair that she would stay late that evening. He didn't care if Mary pouted or got mad. Actually, he didn't care what any of her reactions were to anything. He was her boss, and what he said was the way it was going to be.

Damon returned home to his empty house. He remembered what it was like when Destiny would be waiting for him to get in from work. She had filled the rooms with life.

Once again, he was alone. He also didn't have any current playmates. He had killed his last toy. At least he had the memories of killing each and every woman that didn't please him.

Damon was getting out of the shower when his phone rang.

"Mr. Dahmer. I have something you want."

Damon was trying to recognize the strange voice. "Who is this?"

"I am sending you a picture. I want you to look at it. Then listen closely."

Damon looked at the screen of his phone. A picture was very slowly downloading. Damon was not a patient man. "Who is this?"

"Look at your phone."

Damon's jaw dropped when he saw the picture of a pregnant Destiny. "Where is she?"

"I have something you want. I have a business proposal for you. Meet me in 2 hours. At the internet cafe by your house. Do not be late."

The phone went dead. Damon collapsed on his bed and cried. This Mr. Cyber had Destiny. And she was pregnant. It had to be his child. He wanted another child. It had been years since his only son had died. He would do whatever it took to keep her safe.

Damon pulled out a picture of his deceased son. His son, murdered by a drunk driver. Damon repaid the favor and killed the drunk driver's son, but it didn't give him the gratification that he thought it would. His son had been so innocent and so young. He had failed as a father by not protecting his son. It was his fault for not keeping his son safe. Damon would not let anything happen to his baby that Destiny was carrying.

Damon sat in his car across the street from the cyber cafe, watching every person who came out of the small building. There weren't very many people inside. The storefront was a huge window. He could see everything that was happening inside. There was a teenager sitting at a computer terminal, and a worker behind the counter. What was the point of an internet cafe? Coffee shops also offered internet. Damon couldn't understand how a place that like could even stay in business.

Figuring that since it was a public place, Damon thought he would be safe meeting Mr. Cyber here. Damon went in and sat and waited. After a few minutes, Damon was approached by a man in a long, dark trench coat.

"So kind of you to meet me." The stranger smiled.

"Where is she! If you..." Damon was mad and started to scream.

"Shhh. We're in public. We will have a civil conversation." The stranger looked over his shoulder. The teenager on the computer was wearing headphones and didn't hear Damon's outburst.

Damon tried to calm himself. "Where is she?"

"Funny that you ask. You do know I monitored your internet searches and phone calls? I knew you were looking for her. You just weren't looking in the right places. I can find anyone using my computer skills. I found her. Actually, when I took that picture, she was with another man."

It took every bit of control Damon had to not get angry. Another man? It couldn't be true. Jealousy surged throughout his entire body. "I will ask again. Where is she?"

"She is safe, for now. Her safety depends on you. Before I tell you where she is, I need a favor. I just want you to make a guest appearance on my show. Then I will tell you how to find her."

"I can't be on some underground dark internet show. I am a professional." Damon bit his tongue to control his temper.

"I am a professional too. My servers are untraceable. You can even wear a mask. I will tell you when and where to be. Wear all black, and bring a mask if you want to hide your face. I will bring you a woman. You can do whatever you want to her. I've seen your work. I'm sure you will make an interesting show." The man handed Damon a piece of paper with a date, time, and an address. "Be there. Then I will tell you where she is." The stranger left. Damon tried to watch the man. He wanted to see what kind of vehicle he got into, but instead the man walked around the corner into a dark alley.

Damon stared at the sheet of paper. He had to know where Destiny was. The thought of Mr. Cyber hurting Destiny made Damon hurt inside. For now, he had to play along with this man's game. He could play games with the best of them. He was the inventor of playtime.

HURT BANK (THIRD EPISODE)

"You won't believe what's on tonight's show. Welcome ladies and gentlemen. I'm your host, Peter Conway. This will be the most exciting show ever! First of all, parental discretion is advised. Do not try this at home. This show is very real. My producers want me to take a moment, and give you a special message. Even though these people are hurting themselves, they are getting compensated. Our players undergo various mental evaluations, to ensure that they are mentally stable. They willingly hurt themselves. They even get medical treatment, free of charge. If you think you have what it takes to appear on 'Hurt Bank', get on our website, and answer a few questions. Please stop sending us videos of you hurting yourself at home. We will not watch it. We will not select you to be a participant on our show. Okay, enough of that. Now, on with the show!" Peter was smiling into the camera, appearing to be the perfect television host.

Damon wished that Peter hadn't added that part about not submitting videos of self torture. It wasn't as if the public would listen to how Peter opened the show. The viewers just wanted to see the pain. Damon was sure that viewers would still submit videos for his own personal enjoyment. Watching the videos distracted Damon's mind of wondering where Destiny was, and whether or not it was his baby that she was pregnant with. However, since Mr. Styles demanded that Peter discourage viewers from sending in self torture videos, Damon had to oblige.

"Now, let's meet tonight's player. Welcome Mark. Tell us a little bit about yourself." Peter shook Mark's hand.

Mark was a middle aged man, who was starting to go bald. He had a stout frame, and looked like maybe he had been in good physical shape in his younger years. "I'm married, with 3 beautiful children. My family is my whole world. Well, I was married. My wife passed away about a year ago. I have been trying hard to provide a good life for my kids, but I've been out of work for a while. Children are expensive. If I did go back to work, I'd spend more in daycare costs than what I make! I don't know what to do. I'm getting ready to lose my home. I cannot let that happen."

Peter gave a sympathetic glance to the player. "I'm so sorry to hear that. Let's hope tonight you make enough money to get your life back on track."

While Peter explained the rules, Damon noticed that Mary was looking at her phone. They were in the middle of production and his assistant was busy texting or surfing the internet. Soon, he would have to talk to her about how she wasn't taking her job seriously.

"The first round is worth $10,000. It's the easiest challenge of the show." Peter walked over to a small table that had what appeared to be a small bottle on it. "This is pepper spray." Peter pointed at the small bottle, rather than picking it up. "All you have to do, to put $10,000 in your hurt bank, is spray yourself in the face. Of course, while I step way over here." Peter stepped away as he laughed at his own joke.

"Easy. No problem." Mark was confident. He could do this no problem. Mark picked up the bottle and aimed it for his face. He didn't hesitate as he pressed down on the button. A small cloud of smoke formed in the air, and Mark began to cough. When the cloud cleared, snot was running from Mark's nose and his eyes were watering.

"Congratulations. You just put $10,000 in

your hurt bank! We have an eyewash area set up for you over here. I'll give you a moment." Peter led the man to the water fountain.

Mary was still on her phone. Damon couldn't stand it anymore. He walked over to Mary and grabbed her phone, and walked back to his seat. He glanced at her phone. It took full self control to not smash the phone into tiny pieces. She had been texting with her new boyfriend. Mary just stood in shock. She knew that after production, Damon was going to give her a good tongue lashing.

Peter started the show after giving the man time to rinse his face ."If you decide to keep playing, this next round is worth $30,000! What do you want to do Mark?"

Mark's eyes were red and puffy. "I can keep playing!" Snot was dripping from his nose in long strands.

"Okay. For $30,000, all you have to do is drop this 16 pound bowling ball on your foot, from a standing position. I'm not sure if it would break any bones or not, but I'm sure it will hurt. Are you ready Mark?" Peter handed the heavy ball to Mark.

Mark didn't think twice. This was way too easy. He was determined to win money. As soon as he took the ball from Peter, he immediately dropped it onto his foot. Marked released a howl of pain, and jumped around on 1 foot.

Peter tried not to laugh at the hopping man. "Mark, are you okay?"

Mark said a few bad words they would have to bleep out during editing, and confirmed that it hurt, but he didn't think anything was broken.

Peter went on with the show. "Do you want to keep the $40,000 in your hurt bank, or do you want to play the next round to add $60,000?"

Mark decided to keep playing. Mark needed money.

"This will make a total of $100,000 in your hurt bank!" Peter sounded so ecstatic. He held up a tool. "This is a pipe wrench. It's not small, but it's not large either. You must clamp this tool onto your front teeth. And pull out however many teeth it's grabbed onto. By the looks of the tool, it looks like it's about the width of 2 of your teeth. All you have to do is pull your teeth."

"Does the show pay for new teeth?" Mark needed to know.

"No. You get medical care. For pain and disinfecting. But we don't buy you false teeth. You'd have to do that yourself. After this, you would have plenty of money to do so." Peter was trying to encourage the player to complete the task. He knew that the producers hated it when he tried to deter a player from going forward in the show.

"Okay. I can do this. Can I get a chair? My foot does hurt." Mark was hurting, but not bad enough to stop playing. He didn't know which pain was worse, his eyes that were still burning or his sore foot.

A prop worker brought a chair onto stage for Mark to sit on. Mark took a deep breath as he awkwardly placed the metal object in his mouth. The rigid metal platforms were wide enough to cover 2 of his front teeth. It took a second for Mark to get the tool into place and adjust it tightly to his teeth. Mark inhaled and his chest puffed up.

Mark closed his eyes while he secured his grip on the tool. Mark exhaled while he pulled the tool upward, away from his face. A single tear fell from his irritated eye.

"I did it! I win more money!" A string of blood drizzled from Mark's gums. He didn't seem to mind that he was bloody, he only cared about winning money. The camera zoomed in on the tool in his hand. The unattached teeth looked small gripped in the tool's jaws.

Peter was happy for the contestant. "Congratulations! You have $100,000 in your hurt bank. Do you want to go home with your money, or continue playing for another $150,000? Just remember, if you do not complete the task, you leave with nothing. Challenges do get harder."

Mark thought for a moment. He was in

pain, but not extreme pain. $250,000 was a lot of money. "I'm okay. I can keep playing." He ignored the taste of blood in his mouth. He was running on pure adrenaline.

"You are playing for $150,000, making a total of $250,000 in your hurt bank." Peter paused for dramatic effect. "All you have to do is shoot yourself with a nail gun, in your knee. The nail gun is loaded with 3 inch nails. That means that 3 inches of harsh metal will penetrate 1 of the most painful areas of the human body. Are you ready to play?" Even though it was hard, Peter tried to keep his smile plastered on his face.

Mark started sweating. He felt like the tasks went from fairly simple to difficult. "I guess I have to."

Peter carried the nail gun to Mark.

"Any part of my knee?" Mark wanted to be sure that he was doing it right. He would hate to be disqualified.

Peter looked to Damon, who was shaking his head yes. "Any part of your knee. You can pick the exact location."

"Is there a doctor here? Maybe he could tell me the least painful way to do this." Mark tried to make light of a bad situation, trying to find the easiest way to perform this challenge.

Peter ignored Mark. There was no possibility of doing this challenge without suffering pain. A nail in a knee meant pain.

There was no way around that.

Mark rolled up his pant leg and examined his knee. He began poking his knee in various spots, looking for the softest tissue to penetrate. Once he found a location he thought was suitable, he looked to Peter and shook his head. "Here goes nothing."

Peter heard the swoosh of the nail ejecting from the tool. Mark yelped a high pitch squeal and fell from his chair. A line of blood ran down to Mark's ankle. Mark started crying like a baby.

Peter ignored the man in pain. "Congratulations! You have $250,000 in your hurt bank. Do you want to play for another $250,000? For a total of $500,000?"

Mark was too busy screaming and crying. He only heard a few words that Peter had just spoken. He was pretty sure that Peter asked him if he wanted to continue playing. "You must be crazy! I'm taking my money and going home!"

Damon was disappointed. No one would ever advance to the last round and use that blowtorch. He was hopeful. Maybe the next player would advance to the last round.

ENTER THE
DARK WEB

Dressed in black pants and a black sweatshirt, Damon drove through a collection of back alleys that led to run down warehouses. Each building that Damon passed looked worse than the building before it. Windows were busted out. The metal sidings of the buildings were rusted. Damon's gps even alerted him that he was on an unmapped road. From the few building numbers that he had seen, he was sure that he was headed in the correct direction.

The road dead ended. Damon looked at the large, angry building in front of him. He wasn't scared, but he had carried a pistol just in case he needed it. He had to find out where Destiny was. Mr. Cyber was the only person with that information.

Damon stepped out of his vehicle, and heard a whistle in the distance. A figure appeared in the shadows. Damon turned around and found himself face to face with Mr. Cyber.

"Mr. Dahmer. Always a pleasure to see you. Did you bring any 'props' for tonight's episode?"

"Props? Episode? I just want Destiny." Damon kept a level head.

"On the dark web, I have my own show. It's just more extreme than your show. You are the guest host tonight. I already have a victim waiting for you. I assure you, everything is untraceable. Our audience is by invite only. And they pay me good money to keep this show running. Actually, my largest donor requested you be on the show."

Damon tried to make sense of everything. "Why me? How do you know I wouldn't tell the police?"

"Don't forget Mr. Dahmer, I have pictures of you burying a woman in the desert. You were chosen based on your television greatness. I followed you, and realized that you would fit right in around here. I, and the donor, are the only people who know who you are here. Again, I will ask, did you bring any props?"

Damon did. He happened to bring along a bag of toys that he had been dying to use. Damon retrieved his bag from the trunk of his car. "And Destiny?"

"I will tell you tonight where she is. Trust me. She is safe."

Damon knew that he would never trust this man. Never. Especially when it came to Destiny's safety. He had an obligation to protect her and his unborn child.

Mr. Cyber led Damon into what appeared to be an abandoned building. Upon entering, the large open room looked like any other warehouse. But after a small doorway, Damon was surprised when he saw a large well lit room, full of computers. There were multiple screens, cameras, wires and other stuff. Damon didn't know what the name for all of the equipment was, but he knew that it was all expensive technology stuff.

"Welcome to my laboratory, Mr. Dahmer. As you can see, my show is just as expensive to run as yours. Once again, I assure you, this is private, untraceable, and confidential. We are the only people here tonight. Well, other than the victim. Our viewers watch from the privacy of their homes, on their own private computers."

"How do you know that I won't turn on you? I could kill you now for blackmailing me." Damon tried to be civil, but he was not happy with this situation.

"Then you would never find Destiny. I'm sure, after your first show, you will love this! This is just like what you did in the desert. Only here, you have an audience."

"I do not want to be filmed." Damon pulled

out a black ski mask from his bag to hide his face. He slid it onto his head.

"You will be anonymous. This is fun, trust me. Plus it pays well."

Damon looked at Mr. Cyber with dismay. "Money? I do not want money. Money does not motivate me. Right now, I'm doing this for Destiny."

"Okay. Anyways. Have fun in there. She's right through that doorway, waiting for you. Keep it interesting. And she's all yours. Make sure to kill her." Mr. Cyber pointed to a door.

Damon made sure that his mask was fastened tightly against his face. He picked up his bag of toys. It was glorious when he walked through the door. A naked woman was hanging from chains, attached by handcuffs to her wrists. Her arms were raised over her head. Damon stopped for a moment to admire her body. She was beautiful. Her breasts were firm and plump, with a small waist. Her shaved bald pubic area revealed the essence of her womanhood. Her skin looked so soft.

"Hello. Is someone there? Please, remove my blindfold."

Damon did as the woman requested and removed the cloth from her eyes. The woman had been crying.

"Please don't hurt me. I'll do anything. Please. I'm begging you." Her requests came out as soft whimpers.

Damon did not respond. Instead he slapped her on the buttocks.

"You like that? I can do that. Just don't hurt me."

Still, Damon ignored the woman's pleas as he removed his toys from his bag. She continued to beg, but Damon didn't mind. It was foreplay for him. Her cries turned him on, but not in a sexual way. He was aroused mentally. Alive, awake, and alert. Mostly alive. Doing what he enjoyed the most.

He tried not to look at the cameras. He tried not to think about the fact that people were watching him. He had to remind himself that he was doing this to find Destiny. He had to find Destiny. He had to find his unborn child.

"Sex. Do you want sex? You don't have to rape me. Just untie me. I'll make you happy. I'll be the best lay that you have ever had. I see the cameras. I can help you make a tape that you will watch over and over." In her head, exchanging sex for her own life wouldn't be a bad deal. If only this man would take her up on her offer.

Damon held up the small blowtorch for the woman to see. He clicked a switch and turned a nozzle, until a blue flame grew from the tip of the device. There was a faint whooshing noise. He loved seeing the horror in her eyes. She began to scream louder.

For a little bit of foreplay, Damon raised the

flame to the cold metal around her wrists. He remembered that in an episode of 'Easy Money' a man walked across a metal plate heated by flames, and the metal had burned the flesh from his bones. He wondered if he could get the handcuffs hot enough to melt the skin from her wrists.

She tried to kick him, but he easily stepped to the side. He heated the handcuff until it was glowing an orange color. The woman was screaming, and then she even spit on him. Damon loved every minute of it. He wiped at the spit on his mask and then licked it off his finger. It didn't take him long to forget about the cameras that were watching him.

After heating up both handcuffs, and enjoying her squeals, Damon held the flame close to her eyes. He slowly lowered the blowtorch, not touching her, but just close enough for her to feel the heat from the flame. When he got close to her pubic region, he got closer with the heat. He could smell her burning flesh. He heard her screams. He was in his element. It was a beautiful moment.

Damon guided the fire between her legs. Then he pulled the flame away from her. He used his free hand to spread open the folds of her vagina. He wanted her opened up for this pain. He once again got closer with the fire. He got so close with the blowtorch that the nozzle was inside of her. She released high pitched sounds of pain.

Damon realized that he was enjoying this too much. His crotch had grown. He pulled the tool out from inside of her. He didn't want to damage her too badly, just in case he desired her dead body sexually after he was done with her. He extinguished the flame, and returned to his bag.

Damon pulled out a straight razor, and admired the shining blade. The woman didn't notice, perhaps she was unconscious. He ran the flat side of the blade along her pretty face. He wanted her to wake up. He didn't like it that she wasn't struggling. He could no longer see the pain in her face.

Damon slapped the woman until she woke up.

"Please. NO!"

Damon was now excited, sexually. He lowered his head to her chest. As he ran his tongue along her breast, he quickly used the sharp side of the blade and cut off her nipple. He sucked on the open wound, drinking her salty blood. Once again, the woman was unconscious. Damon was mad. He wanted her awake, but maybe he had already tortured her too much.

To try and wake her, he slid the blade inside of her vagina. She did not wake, but blood ran down her legs.

Frustrated, Damon wiped the blade clean

with his tongue, and packed up his toys. He exited through the same door that he entered.

Mr. Cyber was happy to see him. "That was wow! There was a hint of sexuality, with an equal amount of brutality! But, um, is she dead?"

"I don't know. I don't care. Where's Destiny?" Damon was not in the mood to mince words.

"Fine. I'll take care of her. Take my business card. Call me anytime. You're always welcome back here. Just give me a call. Oh yeah, I hacked Destiny's phone. I wrote an address on the back. She has plans to go there, and at that time." Mr. Cyber handed the business card to Damon.

Damon snatched the card from his hand and didn't say a word. He just left, hoping that what he had just done wouldn't get him in trouble. Even though he enjoyed what he just did, he knew that it was too risky. These people didn't play by the rules. Not only had they followed him, and blackmailed him with pictures of him involved in illegal activity, they were threatening Destiny.

Damon had no intention to get involved in this underground world of torturing women, no matter how easy they made it. This was a woman that Damon didn't have to hunt down on the street. Plus, he didn't have to dispose of her body. But none of that mattered. He had to find a way out of that life.

HAPPY?

Destiny was very aware of her belly. It was getting bigger with every passing day. She had been working a steady job at an office as a secretary. She had a great home with Mary. Plus, she had a baby on the way. Still, she felt like something was missing from her life.

Even though her time with Damon had been brief, she had enjoyed it. Yes, it was weird that their relationship started as him paying her to hurt herself. But she completely understood that it was only because he was doing research for a new television show that he had created. Over time, their relationship had blossomed into something beautiful. Ultimately, he was the person that had cared enough about her to put her in rehab and get her off drugs.

He even gave her a great life. He opened his large home to her. He treated her with respect. He seemed like a great guy most of the time. She realized that in the end, he made her happy. If it wasn't for the fact that she had suspected him of murder, she would still be living with him.

Destiny realized that she wasn't alone during her pregnancy. She had Mary and her new boyfriend, David, supporting her every step of the way. Still, something seemed to be missing from her life. She did miss Damon, but she wasn't sure if she missed him enough to tell him about the pregnancy.

Even if she decided to tell him that she was pregnant, she would have to explain to him that she was secretly living with Mary for the past few months. Not only would Damon be mad at her, he would also be mad at Mary. Destiny didn't want Mary to lose her job for helping her. She was in a pickle.

Mary was the best friend that she could have ever asked for. She would never do anything to put Mary's job in jeopardy.

"Watching you with David makes me so jealous." Destiny teased Mary about her relationship. "Seeing you with him makes me miss Damon even more."

Mary thought she had been helping Destiny by introducing David into her life. She never thought that it would make Destiny feel lonely. She thought it would help her friend realize that she had a great network of friend support. "I'm so sorry. I only wanted to help you. I had no clue that you missed Damon. What about William? Do you still think that he might have killed him?"

"I don't know. My hormones have been acting crazy. I'm up and then down. This is his baby. You don't think that I should tell him?" Destiny was lost.

"You have to do what's best for you and your baby. Just never forget that I'm here, no matter what you decide to do. But please, if you do call Damon, don't tell him that you've been living with me. He's already been on me for not being focused at work. He'd kill me if he knew that you've been staying here." As soon as Mary said the word kill, it occurred to her that she meant it literally. She knew what her boss was capable of, and at times she feared him. "I don't know. Maybe he murdered William. Maybe he didn't. But I know for a fact he planned Marty Blevins' death, even though he didn't directly murder him. Just because you're down right now, please please, don't forget how you met him."

Mary was starting to feel guilty that David's overnight stays had been happening more and more. She knew in her heart that she was in love with David. She didn't want to stop spending time with him, but she didn't want to make Destiny sad either.

Destiny was sitting all alone in her bedroom, trying to ignore the laughs of Mary in the next room. Of course, David was staying the night again. She stared at her phone, dying to call Damon. Many times before, she had picked up her phone, only to not dial the last digit.

She looked into the mirror at her blossoming belly. She had to think about what was best for her baby. Damon had been good to her, and she was sure that he would be good to their child also. She didn't know for sure that Damon was a murderer. What if he wasn't? Then she was a horrible person for thinking that he could be.

This baby deserved to have a father. Damon could afford to give this baby anything that it would ever want for. Who was she to deprive her child of financial stability? Her feelings towards Damon shouldn't affect her child's relationship with him.

Tonight was different. She found the strength to dial all of the numbers into the phone. Damon answered promptly, on the second ring.

"Hello." It was nice to hear Damon's voice. Just the sound of him answering the phone gave her some comfort. He didn't even have to say anything meaningful. Just his voice brought her peace of mind. She hadn't been at peace since she had left him.

Destiny had made the phone call, only to find that she didn't know what to say. She could kick herself for not planning some sort of speech or something. She could only think of one word. "Hi."

"Destiny? Is that you? Are you okay? Where are you? I've missed you so much. Why did you leave?" Damon's tone wasn't angry at all. If anything, he sounded concerned. "Are you safe? Please, just speak to me."

Destiny felt bombarded by all the questions. She wasn't sure which question she should answer first. All she could do was cry. She tried to find her voice, but she couldn't. She was too confused. She had no words.

"Don't cry. Please. It's me. I've been looking for you. I miss you so much. Please come home." Damon was actually begging. He had never begged anyone for anything. Now he was just a mess of a man, begging. "Are you okay? Please, baby. I have to know."

Destiny hung up the phone. She honestly had no words. What could she possibly say to fix the mess that she was in. She still wasn't sure if Damon would be a good influence on her baby. She wanted to know for a fact that he was a good man. She hated being suspicious that he was evil. Her thoughts were driving her crazy.

Damon's mind was scrambling. Finally, Destiny called him! He checked his phone. Private number. Why did she have to block her number? He wanted to call her back. At least she called. He wished she would've said more. He had many more questions. It was a shame that he couldn't ask her about the pregnancy. It was a secret how he had found out. He couldn't tell her about Mr. Cyber.

Staring at the business card from Mr. Cyber, he was hopeful that Destiny would be at the address written on the back. Apparently, Mr. Cyber was a hacker. With any luck, his information would be good.

Damon hated that Mr. Cyber knew about Destiny. Mr. Cyber was a monster. Hopefully, Mr. Cyber was pleased with Damon's performance and would leave him alone. If he ever hurt Destiny, Damon would have to kill him. Even if it was the last thing that he did, he would keep her safe forever.

CHANCE
MEETING

Time seemed to pass slowly. Finally, it was the big day. If Mr. Cyber was right, Destiny would be having dinner at an upscale restaurant on the other side of town. Dressed to impress, Damon made sure to look absolutely handsome in his new suit.

Upon entering the restaurant, Damon asked to be seated at the bar. Before he ordered his first drink, his eyes scanned the place for any sign of Destiny. He checked his watch. He was a few minutes early. Maybe she just wasn't there yet.

He was surprised when he saw Mary sitting with a man. The man's back was to him, but he figured that it had to be her new boyfriend. He hated it that this man was getting so much of Mary's attention. He needed Mary's full attention on work. But this was perfect. What were the chances of running into someone he knew? If he were sitting with them, Destiny wouldn't think that he was there to stalk her.

Damon approached their table, and sat down at the empty seat. Then his eyes raised to get a good look at Mary's new boyfriend.

"Damon! What are you doing here?" Mary was shocked to see her boss.

Damon just stared at the man, and didn't say a word.

Mary noticed her boss eyeing her boyfriend. "David, this is my boss, Damon. Damon, this is my boyfriend, David." Mary looked at David. "I didn't know he would be here tonight." She looked at Damon. "What are you doing here?"

David extended his hand to shake Damon's hand. "Nice to meet you Damon. Mary has told me so much about you. It's my pleasure."

Damon stared into the man's face. He was trying to make sense of it. Why was Mr. Cyber sitting with Mary? Mr. Cyber was Mary's new boyfriend? David/Mr. Cyber was pretending to not know Damon. Mary couldn't be involved in the online show, could she?

Damon decided it was best to play along with the charade. "It's nice to meet you too, David. Now I can put a face to the man that's been distracting my Mary from her work." Damon tried to control himself. What he really wanted to do was lunge across the table and strangle this man.

"Stay, have dinner with us. We have room

for another. We haven't even ordered yet." David actually invited Damon to stay for dinner.

Mary secretly kicked David under the table. David looked to Mary, not sure of what he had done wrong.

"I can't stay. I just saw Mary and wanted to say hello." Damon couldn't understand. Why was Mr. Cyber with Mary? Damon didn't like this at all. "Well, hello. I have to get back to my drink at the bar."

Damon stood to leave. As he turned around, he was face to face with Destiny. He couldn't believe it. She was a sight for sore eyes. He touched her, to ensure that she was really there.

"Destiny. I'm so glad to see you. I…" Damon was so confused.

Destiny was smart, and could think fast. "I was sitting over there. I thought I saw Mary. I was just gonna say hi. I didn't know you were here, Damon."

Mary played along. She stood up and hugged Destiny. "I haven't seen you in so long. How have you been?" She made sure to speak loud, hoping that David would catch on. Surely he would get the hint that they were pretending to not be roommates. Mary was pretending that she hadn't seen Destiny in a very long time.

Damon couldn't help but notice Destiny's

belly. "You're pregnant. Please tell me that it's mine." He reached out his hand, and placed it on his child.

Destiny tried not to cry, but she was overwhelmed. Plus, she was hormonal from the pregnancy. She thought she was meeting Mary and David for dinner. She wasn't prepared to see Damon. Destiny looked to her friend, hoping that Mary would know how to handle this situation. Unfortunately, Mary didn't know how to act either. Mary just shrugged her shoulders.

"What a shock! You are pregnant!" The only thing Mary knew to do was act like she didn't know. "Congratulations! How far along are you?'

Destiny did the only thing that she could think to do. She hugged Damon. She put her mouth close to his ear. "We should go somewhere private and talk."

Even though Mary encouraged them to stay for dinner, Destiny wanted to be alone with Damon. She sat in his car, and surprisingly felt safe. Despite the chaos of the evening, she felt solaced in Damon's presence.

Damon's mind was reeling. He still couldn't believe that Mr. Cyber was actually Mary's boyfriend, David. Also, Mr. Cyber was the one who told him that Destiny would be there. Why did Mr. Cyber purposely go there, knowing that Damon would be there looking for Destiny? Did Mr. Cyber want Damon to know that he was dating Mary?

He had to push those thoughts aside and focus on the matter at hand. He had found Destiny.

Damon finally found his voice. "I'm so glad to see you. I don't even know what to say. There's so much I want to say, but don't know how. You look great. Pregnancy agrees with you. It's mine, right?"

Destiny got mad for a second. "Of course it's yours! I haven't been with anyone else. I'm almost offended!"

Damon turned on his charm and smiled. "You just left abruptly. I didn't know why you left, or even where you went to. I'm sorry. Come home? We'll work everything out. I promise to give this baby the best life it could possibly imagine."

Destiny agreed. Everything else could be worked out some other time. Right now, all that mattered was that she felt good with Damon. A part of her did love him.

"I'll come home. Under a condition. Be honest with me. Did you kill William?" Destiny had to know the truth.

Damon wanted to be honest with her. He wanted her to accept him for who he truly was. Instead, he answered her question with a question. "Why would you even ask me that? Is that why you left? You think I'm a murderer?"

Destiny didn't respond.

Damon knew now it was best to not be honest. "Just come home. Let me take care of you."

Destiny agreed. She needed someone to take care of her. Maybe she was crazy to think that he murdered William. All that mattered was that she felt safe with him, in this very moment. She just hoped that feeling would last.

AWKWARD

Mary was almost scared to go to work the next day. All she knew was that Destiny must have gone home with Damon, because she sure didn't come home. She was afraid to call Destiny. She couldn't take the chance if Damon was beside her and knew that Mary was calling. All Mary could do was hope that Destiny didn't tell Damon that she had been staying with her.

Mary made sure to arrive extra early. The last thing she needed was Damon mad at her for being late. He had already noticed that she wasn't devoting her full attention to the show. She knew that her position at work was already treading on thin ice.

She slinked to her desk, and got to work in a hurry. She opened her computer, and started working on more reports that the network had requested. Maybe if she was busy, her boss would leave her alone. Not knowing what Destiny had told Damon could be her downfall. After Damon was in the office, she could safely call Destiny and find out everything that she needed to know.

After waiting for what seemed like an eternity, Damon strolled into the office. Mary peeked up from her computer screen, hoping he would walk right past her. Nevermind the fact that he came into work late after he punished her for being late.

"Mary. In my office. Now." Damon demanded Mary's attendance.

Mary quietly followed behind Damon.

Damon pointed to the chair across from his desk. "Have a seat."

Her boss never offered her a chair. Mary sat.

"Tell me more about David." Damon's request seemed simple enough.

Mary didn't know why her boss would want to know more about her boyfriend. He was never the kind of boss to involve himself in his employee's personal life. She had been expecting him to either be mad that she had been harboring Destiny, or a lecture that she had been neglecting her duties. "He's great. What do you wanna know?"

"Are you serious?"

Even though she didn't think it was Damon's business she answered him anyways. "Yes. Honestly, I love him."

"How'd you meet?"

Mary didn't care why Damon was making all the questions. As long as he wasn't getting mad at her, she didn't mind answering him. "I literally bumped into him getting coffee. We've been together ever since."

Now Damon knew that Mr. Cyber purposely had set up meeting Mary. "I don't want you to see him anymore." Damon stated it as if it wasn't open for discussion.

"You can't tell me what to do in my personal life. That's absurd!" Mary was starting to get mad. "Is it my work performance? I won't be late anymore. I'll pay more attention during production. But I won't stop seeing him. You have some nerve telling me how to run my relationship. Especially after everything with Destiny!" Mary knew to stop talking. She had already said too much.

Damon wasn't used to anyone speaking to him like this. Maybe that was why he respected Mary so much.

Damon tried to be more sensitive. "You're right. I'm just your boss. As your friend, I'm just looking out for you."

Friend? Damon was not her friend. "I appreciate that. But he makes me happy. And that's that!" Mary stormed out of Damon's office.

Damon feared for Mary's safety, but he couldn't tell her why. He would have to figure out another way to get Mr. Cyber out of Mary's life.

Mary went to the women's restroom. She needed privacy to call Destiny. After a quick discussion she found out that Destiny didn't disclose to Damon that she had been staying with her. That was a relief. When Mary asked Destiny why Damon didn't want her seeing David, she told her that she didn't know anything about that. They both liked David. He seemed like one of the good guys.

Destiny sounded happy after making up with Damon. The women devised a plan for a double date. Both couples could get to know each other better. Mary and Destiny could make it appear to Damon that they were rekindling their friendship after a period of estrangement. Mary was sure that David would play along.

Damon was sitting at his desk, and his phone rang. His boss was calling. Mr. Styles had kept a close eye on Damon ever since he had put Damon on probation for the death of a contestant.

"You were late today. I'm trying to be nice here Damon, but you need to take this job serious. The network likes the ratings, so they're keeping you and your show. But you have to walk a fine line here. I keep persuading them to keep you around. Just remember, I'm telling you as a friend. I, personally, want to keep you around." Mr. Styles was trying to be friendly, yet he was also stern.

Damon heeded the words of wisdom from his boss. It was rare if another person could make Damon feel inferior. For some reason, Mr. Styles' words had gotten to him. Damon was mad at himself for being late. Destiny was important, but was she more important than his job? Damon had very few loves in his life, now he had F manage juggling 2 of his great loves. Destiny and his show.

Damon needed a quick release. Just something to help him relax. He began to sort through the home viewer's self torture videos that would be discarded soon. The first video that caught his eye was labeled 'Crazy'. Just the single word piqued his interest.

Damon chuckled when he saw a group of young men huddled around each other. There were two boys who took charge of the video, introducing themselves as Tom and Jerry. Even their names were comical.

Tom held a baseball bat into the air. Damon felt Jerry's pain as Tom swung the baseball bat into his groin. Jerry collapsed to the ground, clutching onto his family jewels. The boy's face was beet red. Tom laughed at his downed friend. It took a few moments, but once Jerry regained his footing, he asked for the bat. Tom was not laughing then.

Jerry took a few practice swings, cutting through the air. As Tom tried to use his arms to guard his genitals, Jerry swung the bat upside his head. Damon heard a thunk sound. Tom fell to the ground, with blood oozing out of his ear. Jerry took the opportunity to kick his defeated friend.

Damon laughed so loud, he realized that other people throughout the office might hear him. This was what Damon needed to lift his spirits. All he needed was a good laugh.

DAHMER HOUSEHOLD

Damon now had a reason to rush home from work. He had something to look forward to. He knew that Destiny would be there, waiting to greet him at the door. This time, he was going to be a better man. He would do whatever it took to keep her around. His sanity depended on her. He needed her warmth in his life. His unborn child might be what he needed to change his life.

Destiny was in the kitchen, making dinner. It was the first time in a long time that his house felt like a home. She put down the cooking utensils, and gave him a hug as soon as she saw him. After only a night of being back together, and even though they hadn't discussed any of their problems, they both felt how strong their bond was. They knew that they belonged together.

As he held Destiny in his arms, Damon felt

whole. He wanted to open up to her. He wanted to reveal the fact that he enjoyed life the most when he was hurting people. He wanted her to understand who he really was, but that seemed unimportant right now. Instead of speaking, he held her chin in his hand, with his eyes looking into hers. He made himself vulnerable, and he cried.

Destiny softly wiped away his tears and shushed him. She held her lover tighter, hoping to offer him some peace. She didn't know what was going on in his head, but she felt the love. She felt the security that she longed for. She felt like she belonged.

"I'm here now. That's all that matters. All that other stuff will work itself out." Destiny comforted Damon. She couldn't believe that this sweet man could be a killer. She had to be wrong about him.

"I wanna do something that I should have done a long time ago. Marry me? Please. Without you, I'm just lost." He had no ring. Just a simple question.

How could Destiny refuse him? Despite everything that they had been through, they belonged together, for better or for worse. Marriage would be the ultimate step that would seal them together. Afterall, Damon accepted her despite her past life of drug addiction and prostitution. If he loved her unconditionally, was she capable of returning that kind of love?

All that mattered to Destiny was how Damon treated her now. These were the precious moments of her life. She was going to enjoy them while they lasted.

Destiny smiled and grabbed Damon's extended hand. "Yes! I will marry you!"

They embraced each other, finally feeling that they had both found a place where they belong.

After a comforting evening in bed, the lovers finally found the time to talk.

"Mary called me today. I missed seeing her, too. I was thinking that maybe we could go to dinner with her and her boyfriend sometime?" Destiny hoped that Damon didn't catch on to the lie that she hadn't been living with Mary.

"No. I don't like that guy." Damon jumped out of bed and started to get dressed.

She wondered why Damon didn't like David. As far as she knew, they had never even met until that night at the restaurant. Destiny grabbed her lover's arm and pulled him into bed with her. "Mary was my friend. Why can't we all just get along?"

Even though Damon didn't like the idea, he gave in to what Destiny wanted. Afterall, he had to figure out what Mr. Cyber had been up to. Damon knew to keep what few friends he had close, and his enemies even closer.

HURT BANK (FOURTH EPISODE)

"Welcome to the most exciting show on television! I'm Peter Conway. I'd like to thank our viewers for making us the most talked about show of all time. Don't worry, we have an hour of pain for you tonight! I love hosting this show. Parents, you might want to get the little ones away from the Tv. We have a bloody show in store for you tonight! Who's ready to play 'Hurt Bank'?" Peter hated lying, but he had to read the words on the teleprompter. He didn't love hosting this show. They just paid him to say that. Actually, he hated this show. He just loved the big paychecks.

"Let's meet our player, Tony. Tony, what made you want to be on our show?" Peter shook the large man's hand.

Tony wiped some sweat from his forehead.

"I'm Tony. My wife is currently in the hospital. I can't afford her healthcare. We lost insurance when I lost my job. And boy, let me tell you, hospitals are expensive. We are in so much debt, and our debt just keeps growing. I'm pretty much desperate to win some money. I've watched this show. I know it's gonna hurt, but that's what I gotta do."

Peter being the good host that he was, comforted the contestant. "I'm glad to have you here. Let's go over the ground rules. Each round is worth money. After you complete a round, the money goes in your hurt bank. Then you decide to take your money home, or to keep playing. If you keep playing, but don't complete the task, then you go home with no money. Are we clear?"

Tony shook his head yes. "I understand completely. I'll tell you right now. I need about $100,000 to get out of medical debt. Actually, that's what the hospital needs, or they're gonna kick my wife out and not even treat her. Then, they're gonna charge us more and more. I'm here to play the long game. I need this money."

"Okay then. The first round is worth $10,000. And it's fairly simple." Peter held up a pair of tweezers. "All you have to do is pull some nose hairs. This might be something you've done before, now you're just gonna get paid. I've done it, and it hurts. It actually hurt so bad it made my eyes water. But for 10 grand, I don't think it would be that bad." Peter handed the tweezers to Tony.

"Serious? That's all I have to do? Too easy. I've got this!" Tony was excited. Tony raised the tweezers to his nose. The small tool was shining from the lights. He stuck the object up his nose, and squeezed them shut. He yanked on the tweezers, and his eye squinted as he pulled. He held up the tweezers for the camera to see a couple of unattached nose hairs. Tony's eye was watering.

"Congratulations Tony! You have $10,000 in your hurt bank. Do you want to leave with your money, or do you want to keep playing?" Peter had to ask, even though he knew what the player was gonna do.

"I already told you, Peter. I'm playing a long game here. I can't go home. I need more money!"

"Okay then." Peter tried to disregard the fact that the player had an angry tone towards him. "This next round is worth $30,000. That will be a total of $40,000! All you have to do is pull out your large toe toenail." Peter cringed his face as he thought about this one. "We have wire pliers and forceps available to you."

Tony laughed. "I can't believe this is so easy. I was awake all night worrying how bad this would be. This ain't bad at all." Tony sat down on a chair and pulled off his sock. "I wish I had known. My feet are so ugly. I would've gotten a manicure or something if I knew my foot would be on television."

Tony chose the wire pliers as his weapon. He grabbed on to his large toenail with the tool, and wiggled and grunted until he was holding his detached toenail above his head. The camera zoomed in on the bloody fleshy area of his toe.

"This is too easy! I could do this all day." Tony laughed as he displayed his toenail.

Damon, watching production from side stage, took that as a personal insult. This wasn't easy. Not to normal people. Damon couldn't wait for the next rounds that started to get progressively harder. That would put Tony in his place.

"Congratulations Tony. You now have $40,000 in your hurt bank. I have to ask. Do you want to keep playing? Or do you want to leave with your money?" Peter hated it that he sounded like a broken record.

"Duh. I'm gonna play."

"Okay. This next round is worth $60,000." Peter held up a staple gun. "This is a staple gun. For this challenge, you have to shoot yourself with this staple gun. The only stipulation is to shoot it in your navel. Whew. I can't imagine what this would feel like. I don't know about you, but my belly button sure is sensitive." Peter laughed into the camera.

Tony raised his shirt and started using his

finger to poke around in his belly button. "When I poke it, it's kinda tingly. Yeah, this one's gonna hurt. But that's a lot of money. I can't say no."

Tony didn't even hesitate as he raised the staple gun to his belly button. It only took a few seconds for him to get it lined up and aim directly into the center of his navel. He looked up to Peter, and took a deep breath. Sphew! The staple ejecting made a slight noise. Tony cried out a loud visceral moan. He almost sounded like a large wounded, whining animal.

The camera zoomed in as close as it could. Due to Tony's large belly, his navel was exposed in an outward direction. The staple sparkled within his red skin. A small line of blood leaked out of his body. It was flowing in a downward direction towards his pubic region.

"That got me Peter! I'm not gonna lie. That hurts!" Tony tried to maintain his manhood and not appear to be weak. He was on television. He didn't want to show his pain. He feared that viewers would see him as a wimp, and he was no wimp.

Peter turned on his movie star smile. "Congratulations Tony! You have a total of $100,000 in your hurt bank! Do you want to keep that amount, or keep playing?"

"That's a lot of money. I need just a little bit more. What's the next round worth?" Tony was pulling the staple out from his belly.

"$150,000!"

"I'll play. I have another round in me." Tony was sure that he could do whatever it took to earn more money. His wife's life depended on it.

Peter shook his head sympathetically. He knew what was next. He held up a spoon. "Let me start off by saying, we have consulted a doctor for this next task. You have to pop your eyeball out from your head. That sounds extreme right? We were told, that if done correctly, a doctor can safely put the eye back in place, and as long as you're careful and don't damage any nerves, then you won't go blind."

Tony got mad. "No way! That's crazy! I can't do that. Give me another." Tony was demanding.

Peter wiped the smile from his face real quick. "Are you quitting? That means that you leave with zero dollars. You lose all the money in your hurt bank."

"I want my money. I earned it. This ain't right." Tony was on the verge of tears.

Peter handed the spoon to Tony.

"Just wedge that spoon beneath your eye. From what we were told, it's not hard. The eye can pop out easily. You will bleed. A Lot. It's your decision."

Tony thought about it. His wife depended on him. He needed that cash. He figured that the sooner he got it over with, then the better off he would be.

Tony took the edge of the spoon and placed it convexly under his eye ball. He pressed it firmly into the skin of his lower eyelid. Tears filled the spoon and ran along the glistening handle.

Tony jerked his wrist, forcing the spoon deeper into his eye cavity. Sure enough, the small white ball squeezed out. Along with blood. The eye dangled from his exposed nerves. He started screaming hysterically. Medical came out and tried to calm the man. Peter was informed that Tony wanted to go home.

"That's all folks. Tony takes home the $250,000 from his hurt bank. Thanks for watching. See ya next show." Peter waved goodbye to the cameras.

Damon was thrilled. That player, Tony, thought that he could downplay the challenges. Sure, they do start out easy, but if you play long enough, they get very painful. Damon's only regret was using a staple gun for the navel. He should have stuck to his original script of using the nail gun instead.

Mary was the voice of reason that explained to Damon that the player would quit after using the nail gun. Maybe she had been right. Perhaps he wouldn't have made it to the spoon challenge. In Damon's eyes, seeing the man's popped out eyeball was the highlight of the show.

TABLE FOR 4

Mary prepped David for the big double date night. She didn't have to tell him too much, just to pretend that he didn't know Destiny. That shouldn't be too hard. The hardest part of it was explaining to David that they feared Damon, and what he might do if he knew Destiny had secretly lived with Mary when she left him. He couldn't understand why Destiny would be with a man that she feared. Mary couldn't wrap her mind around it either.

Damon was a perfect gentleman, even though he detested the fact that he would be breaking bread with David. He did not like that guy. He knew too much about Damon. Damon couldn't risk David telling both of his girls about his extracurricular activities. David even had photos and video as proof.

Damon opened the door for his glowing fiance. Destiny was excited to share the news with Mary that they were now engaged. Destiny was walking on air knowing that soon she would be Mrs. Damon Dahmer. She hadn't been this happy in a long time. Even though they didn't have a definite wedding date, Destiny knew it would be soon. She loved her unborn baby and fiance more than she thought possible.

Destiny was grinning from ear to ear as she ran to Mary and David's table. She held out her hand with the large sparkling diamond that Damon had just bought her.

Mary jumped up, and tried to act like she was happy for her friend. "What? Are you for real? Engaged? I'm so happy for you!"

The women hugged like the long, lost friends that they were pretending to be. Then Mary introduced Destiny and David as if they had never met before.

Damon got the privilege of sitting next to David. He shook the man's hand, pretending to be happy to see him. Damon stifled his emotions of hatred. Just because he hated David didn't mean that he wasn't capable of making small talk with him. He had to keep up the charade that David was a total stranger to him.

Mary and Destiny did most of the talking over dinner. Which was a relief to Damon. At least he wasn't forced to interact with David too much. Damon kept envisioning in his head jumping across the table and stabbing David with his steak knife.

When the women excused themselves to go

to the ladies' room together, Damon had his perfect opportunity to get some answers from David. It was a mystery to him as to why women always went to the restroom together. What did they do in there, anyways? Oh well, at least he was finally alone with Mr. Cyber.

"So Mr. Cyber, why don't you tell me what you're doing with Mary?" Damon's friendly face quickly turned into a vicious snarl.

"I don't know what you mean." David played coy. He was calm and collected.

"I know you didn't meet Mary by chance. What's your game?"

David thought for a moment. "I like you Damon. So I'll be honest. My boss wanted a way to leverage you to be on our show. Just in case you needed more motivation. I accidentally 'bumped' into Mary." He used his fingers to make quotation symbols. "Turns out, I didn't need her to get to you. And I genuinely like her. Maybe she's the one for me. Maybe I'll marry her someday."

Damon laughed. "Leverage? The pictures of me in the desert wasn't enough? I don't believe you. Who's your boss?"

David looked very innocent with his large green eyes. "I'm telling you the truth. I was just following orders. I already told you about the donor that wanted you on the show."

Damon was losing his patience. "Who. Is. He?" Damon refrained himself from wrapping his fingers around the man's neck and strangling the life out of him.

"I'm sworn to secrecy. Boy scout's honor." David crossed his heart. "Anyways, he wants you to make an encore performance. What do you say?"

This was the first time in a long time that someone had the upper hand on Damon. He had no other options. He had to play along, then he would come up with a plan. "Sure."

"Whew! That's a relief." David softly landed a fist on Damon's shoulder, like they were buddies. They were not buddies. "My boss will be happy. Be there, two weeks from tonight."

Damon heard Destiny's giggle from across the room, and put that smile back on his face. He wanted tonight to be special for her.

"Mary says she will help plan the wedding! Isn't that great?" Destiny was bubbling with happiness as she kissed Damon on the cheek.

Her joy instantly shifted his gears from anger to happiness. "It sure is, darling."

For the past few years, Damon thought maybe his heart had been made of stone, completely without feeling. As he looked around the dinner table, he realized he was full of love. His soon to be wife was going to have his child. Mary was the best assistant he could hope for. She loved his television show just as much as he did. As he turned his head towards David, he realized that he would do anything in his power to protect these ladies.

MUSHY STUFF

Damon opened Destiny's car door as he led her into their home. He tried to push any ill thoughts of David from his mind. He was very aware that he had to keep his fiance happy. He didn't want her to leave him again. The last time that she had left with no warning had left Damon devastated.

After she removed her coat, he placed his hands on her stomach.

"This baby is our tiny miracle." Damon kissed his seed inside of her. "I'm gonna be a better man, I promise you." Damon was at peace. He almost felt the need to confess his sins. He wanted Destiny to accept him for the person he truly was. He wanted her love to be unconditional. In time, maybe he could reveal his truths to her.

"I'm so sorry that I left before. Ya know, I was already pregnant. I was hormonal. That's no excuse, but that's the worst thing I've ever done in my life." She got down on her knees next to him. "I was lost without you. Almost as if I was just floating through life with no reason."

Damon knew exactly what that felt like. Destiny pressed her body as close as she could to Damon, with the baby being the only thing between them. She wrapped her tender fingers on both sides of his face, and stared into his eyes.

"Promise me. Make me a promise. That you'll never hurt me again." Damon was full of passion as he pressed his lips to his lover's mouth. He pushed his monster from his mind. In this moment he was tender, and soft. His only urge was to please Destiny. He had no desire to see people in pain. When he was with her, he felt like a different person

Damon had struggled so long with suppressing his true self. Destiny made that so easy. He would try to be a better man for her. His child depended on him, too. This was the only motivation that he needed to live a better, non violent life.

The next morning, Damon hated leaving Destiny all alone. He wanted to spend all of his time with her. Today, another thing he loved required his attention. His television show. He had been asked to attend a very important business meeting.

She looked so beautiful spread out across

their bed, her pregnancy was on display. He very sweetly bent down to give her a kiss on her forehead.

Destiny tried to open her eyes. She smiled when she saw Damon over her. She raised her hand in the air.

"It's still there. I'm not dreaming!" Destiny rubbed her engagement ring with her other hand.

Damon sat on the bed next to her. "No, darling. You aren't dreaming. This is real."

"When do you wanna get married? Do you want a big wedding?" Destiny was eager to plan the big day.

Damon was easy when it came to her. "I want whatever you want. All I know is the sooner the better. I can't wait to make it official." If Damon knew anything about women, he knew that planning the wedding was their dream.

She grabbed his hand, and pulled him down into a lying position next to her.

Damon knew that he couldn't be late for his meeting. But how could he refuse her? He stroked her hair. "Let's pick this up after work. I'm gonna miss you today."

Destiny kissed him bye. She laid in the bed, thanking her lucky stars. Damon was the best thing that had ever happened to her. He took her from a drug addicted prostitute, and turned her into a housewife. Her life couldn't get any better. She pinched herself, just to make sure that she wasn't dreaming. But it was real. All of it.

BUSINESS REVAMP

Damon straightened his tie before entering the meeting room. He checked his watch. Right on time. He walked into the room, full of confidence.

Mr. Styles was ready to start the meeting. "Thank you for joining us Mr. Dahmer. Have a seat."

Damon saw Mr. Styles sitting with a few of the network board members. He unbuttoned his suit jacket, and sat. He didn't know that there would be other board members here. He sat up straight. He wanted his professionalism to impress his bosses.

Mary opened the door. "Sorry. I'm just a tad late. But I'm here."

Damon was relieved to see Mary here. She was an important part of the show. He relied on her assistance. When the network renewed their employment contracts, they had placed both of them on temporary probation. The network put conditions in the contracts that their new show 'Hurt Bank' had to maintain a certain ratings status to stay on air.

Damon wasn't worried. He knew that his show was a hit. The network needed his show. Mary did not share Damon's confidence. She tended to worry about everything. It was just in her nature.

"As you know, the board isn't fond of pain shows." Mr. Styles cleared his throat. "However, with the ratings that you're getting, you're obviously doing something right. Good job."

The board members shook their heads in agreement.

"Then why call a meeting today?" Damon didn't understand. Why would they call a meeting just to tell him that he was doing a good job?

Mr. Styles sat up straight in his chair. "I can't believe that I'm gonna say this." He shook his head in disbelief. "After reading fan mail, the network wants more pain. They want it to be more extreme." Mr. Styles looked like he was disgusted by the thought of extreme pain.

Damon laughed. "This is wonderful! We can do that!" A more extreme show was in his blood. He was already flooded with excruciating pain ideas.

Mary looked at Damon. She wondered how they could make the show more extreme.

She thought that their players were already experiencing enough pain.

"The board called this meeting as a reminder." Mr. Styles focused his full attention on Damon. "No more deaths on television. We can't go through that again. There's still the clause in your contract, stating that you will be terminated if a contestant dies from injuries sustained on the show." Mr. Styles raised his finger to point to Damon. "I don't get it. I don't know why people watch the show. But they are watching this garbage. And I'm watching you."

Damon took Mr. Styles' pointing finger as a direct threat. What did that mean he was watching him? He was fully aware of the terms of his employment. He didn't appreciate being treated like a child with this reminder. Damon was not a child.

Knowing that you get more flies with sugar, Damon smiled. "More extreme. No deaths. Got it. Anything else?"

Mr. Styles hung his head and took a deep breath. "Yes. One last thing. Next season, your show will be live. Viewers like an unedited show. They think it's more believable. But you're walking a fine line here. I mean it. Nobody dies."

Damon was ecstatic. The network was allowing him to pursue the original vision he had for his show. A live show. A live audience. And more intense pain. Damon could work with this.

Mary wasn't as enthusiastic as Damon. She didn't know how much more extreme the show could be. They just had a man pop his eyeball out of socket. She had seen a lot of pain since they started making pain shows, but that was still horrific. If the people hadn't been so appreciative of the money, Mary wouldn't be able to live with her conscience that haunted her.

"This is great Mary. A live show. Once again. Isn't this the best news ever?" Damon could not contain himself.

Mary still hadn't forgotten that Damon planned a death of a player on live tv. She knew that she would have to babysit Damon on this venture. She hoped he wasn't tempted to try and kill anyone else on live tv.

"I'm so full of ideas! It's like they gave me a license for full creativity." Damon stopped when he noticed that Mary didn't look happy.

"Mary, I need you on this. I can't have you distracted. Yes, I know, live shows are harder. It will require more of our time. But Destiny and David will understand." Damon hoped that was what Mary was unhappy about.

Mary didn't want to tell her boss everything that she was thinking. She tried to push her worry aside. She only hoped that Damon wouldn't let his creativity spiral out of control on this live show.

"You're right. David will understand. Isn't he great? Last night, it was wonderful seeing how happy Destiny is. After meeting him, tell me what you think of David." Changing the subject was the only thing Mary knew to do.

Damon was thinking of the multiple ways he hated David, but couldn't tell Mary. "He seems like a good guy. I'm happy for you. I think Destiny liked him, too. But you girls were in your own little bubble last night. I don't even know why you girls brought us along."

"Because we're excited. I have to start planning a baby shower, and a wedding!" She nudged Damon with her elbow. "I just hope my boss gives me a little free time to do everything."

Damon realized she was referring to him. "I don't know about that. I heard your boss was a jerk!" Damon wasn't lying.

Damon felt human. He was actually behaving like a normal human being. He hadn't joked around at work in quite some time. It felt good. Having Destiny back in his life was already changing him.

FINAL HURT BANK (SEASON FINALE EXTREME EPISODE)

"Welcome to the season finale of 'Hurt Bank'. I'm your host, Peter Conway, thanking you for keeping this show as the top rated show on television! I can't believe it! This is the most watched show! As a special thank you, we have an explosive show in store for you! Tonight's show is going to be a little different. We have 3 players tonight. You, the viewers asked, and we're answering. We're skipping the easy challenges. We're jumping straight to the high dollar challenges! This will be the best, most painful 'Hurt Bank' ever!"

A large video screen played behind Peter, highlighting the best challenges of the season. First there was a tribute to Howard. The screen flashed as he shoved the fish hook through his cheek. The next scene showed his mangled, bloody hand from holding the firecracker. Quickly, there was a video of Emily flinching as the mouse trap gripped onto her tongue. Then there was a glimpse of her stepping into the bear trap. Next, there was Mark, with a line of blood mixed with saliva, holding up his pulled teeth. The screen changed to Mark shooting his knee with the nail gun in slow motion. The slow motion really displayed the look of pain in his face.

Then there was Damon's favorite player of the season, Tony. Damon watched the monitor as he stared at Tony's large belly with the large staple in his navel. But Damon's favorite part was Tony's eye. The monitor was a full view of his eye dangling from blood and nerves. It reminded Damon of a button hanging by a thread. Except this was bloodier, and way more interesting.

"Let me explain tonight's rules. We're starting with the round worth $150,000! If the players complete that task, they have the option to leave with their money. Or they can advance to the round worth $250,000. They could possibly leave with $400,000! But the viewers who have watched us all season know that no player has made it to the last round. Let's hope we have someone bold enough to play both rounds!" Peter was doing his best acting tonight. He wanted the network to renew his contract for next season. He had grown accustomed to his large paychecks. "Let's meet our players."

Damon tuned out the part of meeting the players. He knew that they all had a sob story. He just wasn't in the mood to hear what those stories were. Ever since Destiny had moved in with him, he put playtime out of his mind. For now, this was the closest thing he had to playing. He loved having Destiny around. But inside, he was at the point of needing to hurt someone. He felt like he might physically burst if he didn't get to hurt someone soon. It was a constant nagging feeling.

"Janice, you get to go first. Are you ready?" Peter shook Janice's hand.

"No, not really." The contestant looked timid.

"For $150,000, you have to stick your foot into the blade of that lawnmower." Peter pointed across the stage.

"No way. Nuh uh. Won't do it."

Never had a player told Peter no before. "You don't want to win the $150,000?"

Janice started crying. "I guess I have to. I need that money. I have no choice." Janice looked at the camera. "Can't someone just send me money? Is there anyone out there willing to help me?" Janice pleaded with the camera.

Damon laughed. They weren't live. This would easily be edited out. He couldn't blame her for trying. They would have to implement stricter casting for the live show. He couldn't risk an outburst like that on live tv. What would his viewers think? He didn't need his viewers to feel sympathy for his players.

Peter got the player's attention. "Janice, this isn't live. You either do the challenge or you don't. Your choice."

Janice was frustrated. In her mind, she had no choice but to complete the task. She needed money. Money was a fact of life. Money made the world go round. There was no other way she would get such a nice lump sum of cash, ever again.

Janice approached the lawn mower. Now it was just a quiet hunk of machinery.

Peter offered her instructions. "We've got it set up for you. All you have to do is turn that key. That engages the engine. There's a large green switch. That activates the blade. Then slide your foot under that guard. It will be over in seconds."

Janice just looked at the large machine. She stood frozen and unmoving. She was deep in thought, weighing the pros and cons of doing this task.

"We have medical staff here. I have to admit,

I don't know what this will do to your foot. I imagine you could lose the whole foot. This is your own decision." Peter kinda hoped that Janice wouldn't do it. He was tired of seeing blood. But this show paid nearly double of other shows.

Janice turned the key, just like she was starting a car. The engine sprang to life. She felt like the mower was violating her sense of sound, making this task even harder. She fiddled with the green switch, and the noise got louder. The whirling of the blade sounded ferocious.

She thought about not going through with it. She didn't want to do it. But she knew she would never run into a leprechaun offering her a pot of gold at the end of a rainbow. She didn't even take off her shoe. She thought maybe it would offer her foot some protection.

Janice placed her foot flat onto the stage, and started to slide her foot under the blade.

"I can't do it. I won't do it!" Janice stormed offstage.

Damon laughed at the weak contestant. Perhaps they could get another player and edit that into the show.

"Well that's a first." Peter looked at the 2 remaining players.

A prop crew came on stage to quiet the loud machine. Then they returned with a chainsaw and handed it to Peter.

"You're next Jase." Peter motioned towards the muscular man. "This is heavy. Do you wanna take this?"

As Peter handed the chainsaw to the man, a frightful expression flooded Jase's face.

"What am I supposed to do with this?" Jase held the chainsaw away from him.

"For $150,000, cut off your foot." Peter was matter of fact about the situation.

Jase weighed the pros and cons. He had used a chainsaw before, to cut down a tree. He had to apply pressure into the chainsaw, and it took time to cut into the tree. He didn't like this option. It wouldn't be over immediately. Plus, what if he lost control of the tool, and accidently cut into another part of his body? "Can I do the lawn mower instead?"

Peter looked at Damon. Damon gave him a thumbs up.

The way Jase figured was that this would be easier. The aftermath wouldn't be great, but at least it would be over quickly. Where else could he get $150,000?

Like a champion, Jase approached the mower and turned the key. He pulled up on the green switch. He heard the blade kick into motion. He decided to remove his shoe, because he didn't want it getting stuck in the blade.

Jase just acted. He didn't even think about it. He slid his foot under the blade. Damon stood to see what was happening, but there was a safety guard blocking his view. The legal department of the network would not let them remove the safety guard of the mower. This way there would be no lawsuit against the machine's manufacturer.

Jase fell sideways to the floor, gripping his leg. As the blade kept spinning, blood splattered onto his face. The camera zoomed in real close to show his exposed bone. Not only had his foot been cut up into tiny pieces, but it appeared that his ankle was also mangled. Peter's heart broke for this player.

Damon laughed. He knew none of the players would advance to the last round. He made these challenges too tough. The network asked for extreme challenges. Damon was more than happy to oblige.

Even though this was great, he couldn't wait until next season for the live version of a pain show. No editing. Real pain in real time. He hated it that viewers thought this show was possibly being faked. This show couldn't get anymore real than what it was. It was true reality.

HURT BANK (SEASON FINALE) DAMON'S FAVE

After Peter congratulated Jase on winning some money, and also losing his foot, it was finally time for Damon to watch what he had waited for all season. He had to lower how much the challenge paid. But at least he would finally see someone use the blowtorch on themselves.

"Welcome Evelyn. Tell me what's going on." Peter welcomed the player to the show.

Evelyn was an older woman. A much older woman. She was almost 70 years old. Old people have financial hardships, too.

"My Barry was put in a nursing home." The old woman spoke slowly. "I guess they cost more than I realized. The nursing home took everything out of our bank account. They left me penniless. And they still want more money. I miss my Barry being at home but I can't take care of him. Now I have to pay those vultures money that I don't even have."

Peter waited patiently for this slow talking woman to finish speaking. Each word she spoke was slower than the word that preceded it. "Today is your lucky day. Are you ready to earn $150,000?"

"I don't. I don't know. I watched the other players. I don't know." The old woman seemed confused, but she had passed her psychological evaluation with flying colors. Just because she was old and slow, didn't mean that she was not mentally sane.

Peter walked to a corner of the stage to retrieve the blowtorch from the prop guy. "Evelyn, how do you feel about heat?"

"I love warm weather, but something tells me that you aren't sending me on a vacation to Cancun." The old woman still had some spunk in her.

Peter laughed. "You're right about that. But what I do have is a blowtorch. You have to hold the flame of this blowtorch on your bare skin for 5 seconds. Do you understand?"

The elderly woman shook her head yes, and very slowly responded. "For $150,000, I have to burn my skin for 5 seconds."

"Very good." Peter was impressed. At least

she could retain information.

"Well give it here then. Do you have a chair?"

The woman impressed Peter even more. She was a trooper. Evelyn took what seemed to be baby steps towards the chair, inching along very slowly. The old lady sat in a chair, and rolled up her long skirt, revealing bare leg up to her knees. The whole process actually took minutes.

"I can do this for my Barry." Evelyn was trying to convince herself that this was a good idea.

Damon hoped that someday he and Destiny would be like Barry and Evelyn, still pledging their love for each other in their old age. Even though he was divorced, he knew that this time it was different with Destiny. Their love could stand the tests that time would give them.

Evelyn pulled her glasses closer to her face. "Peter? How's this thing work?" It wasn't like she had ever worked with a blowtorch before.

"Just turn that end there, then squeeze there." Peter pointed at the object as he told her what to do, then stepped away very quickly. He didn't want to be nearby when she fired it up.

"Okay then." She fumbled with it until it was spewing an angry flame. She was pointing it away from her, and made a catholic cross symbol across her chest. Maybe she was saying a prayer.

The old lady slumped down in her chair to reach her calf. She held the flame to her bare skin.

Peter began counting. "1,2,3,4,5"

She held the flame to her body the entire time, and barely even flinched. Evelyn threw the blowtorch down. "Pay me. I need my money!"

Damon couldn't believe his eyes. This old lady made everyone on their show look like babies. She knew how to handle pain. When Damon asked her after the show what her secret was, she revealed to him that she hadn't had feeling in that leg for many years. She called it the curse of old age. Damon couldn't help but laugh. Evelyn might be his favorite player ever.

BABY BUMP

Being the perfect fiance, Damon took off work for every doctor visit with Destiny. Today, they would be finding out the sex of the baby. Damon was excited. He could feel it in his bones, she was gonna give him a baby boy. Of course, this boy would never replace his son that died, but he would love it all the same.

Damon helped his lover into the stupid paper gown that the doctor gave her, opened to the front just like the nurse had stipulated. She waddled onto the table, and placed her feet in the stirrups. Damon was tracing hearts onto her exposed baby bump with his finger. Her heart instantly melted.

Destiny had seen a change in him lately. He gave her every minute of his free time. When he was home he waited on her hand and foot. He even nicely requested that she quit her job. He said that her job now was to care for this baby. They didn't need the money from her working, so she didn't mind one bit quitting her job.

Damon held Destiny's hand as the doctor rubbed some sort of goo onto her belly. The doctor ran a wand in circles through the goo, then stopped.

"Look there. It's your baby!" The doctor seemed just as happy as they did.

Damon didn't see a baby. He saw a black and white picture that resembled some abstract piece of art. He didn't see a baby.

"Look Damon. We did that. Me and you. A baby made out of love." Destiny was ecstatic.

Damon was still scratching his head trying to figure it out, but agreed just for argument's sake. "It's lovely. Almost as lovely as you."

The doctor got serious all of a sudden. "Do you want to know the sex? Or do you want to be surprised?"

"Just go ahead and tell us. It's a boy, right?" Damon didn't even bother to check whether or not Destiny wanted to know. Anyways, he was sure his seed would be a boy.

Destiny lightly smacked at Damon. "We haven't discussed that yet. Maybe I want a girl." Destiny turned her lips into a pouty gnarl.

"I'm sorry. But I know it's a boy. We can name him Damon junior." Damon laughed. "So, what is it?"

The doctor turned to Destiny. "If you wanted a girl, then you got your way!"

Destiny's face lit up. That was exactly what she wanted.

Damon froze. He was stuck in time and space. A girl? He knew what men liked to do to his girls. He couldn't raise a girl. He would have to spend all his time protecting her from men. First it would be teenage boys, then men. Possibly men like him. He couldn't stand the thought of it.

"This is great. We can name her something new age. Like Zodiac. Or Stream. What do ya think?" Destiny wanted to get Damon's reactions to her suggestions.

Damon's head was still spinning. Little girls were precious. And innocent. He wanted a boy.

Once again the doctor congratulated the couple, and sent them on their way.

FROM DAMON
TO DEMON

Destiny wanted a night out on the town to celebrate, so that's what Destiny got. Damon made sure to go to a seafood place. She had been craving shrimp and lobster. Damon's unborn little girl was already spoiled! Damon vowed that it would be nothing but the best for his baby.

Destiny got lost in Damon's charm. His smile melted her heart. She felt like she was living in a movie. When they got home, Damon hand fed her grapes. When she was obese, she had plans to blame it on Damon.

While he was rubbing her feet, Damon got bored. He knew that he should be treating her like a princess. Obviously, she was a princess. To cure his boredom, Damon started unbuttoning his shirt. He turned on the radio. A little jazz was always a good thing.

Damon slowly unzipped his pants, swaying

his hips to the rhythm. Throwing his pants across the room, he turned and gave his best look of seduction to Destiny.

"I'm so tired. Can we just go to sleep?" Destiny had a hard day.

Damon nuzzled up to her warm body. He took her hand and placed it onto his stiffened member. He put his mouth close to her ear and started whispering. "Are you sure you wanna sleep?"

Destiny turned over. "I'm sure."

Damon didn't want to take no for an answer. He had given her the world on a silver platter. He had even stopped spending time with his playtimes. He hadn't been with a hooker in what felt like forever.

"C'mon. Let's play. Like we used to." Damon was not too proud to beg.

Destiny bolted straight up. "Play? Like we used to?" She over pronounced each word to make her questions clear.

Damon thought fast. He was already ashamed of himself. "It's just that I've been rubbing on your gorgeous body. You've got me so turned on right now." Now, Damon was proud of himself. Great cover up.

"That is not what you meant. I know what you meant!" Destiny did not think she was being irrational. Destiny pulled the blanket from her bosom, and pointed at her absent nipple. "You meant this."

That was exactly what Damon meant. That was a glorious day when he sliced off her nipple. But he couldn't tell her that. "That's not what I meant at all. What do you really think of me?" Damon couldn't stop staring at her chest. His handiwork really made him horny. "You must think I'm some monster!"

"No. I'm sorry. That's not what I meant. I'm just tired. And moody." Destiny started being sweet. "I'm sorry. It's this baby. Hormones are making me crazy. I really just wanna go to sleep."

Damon saw an invitation to shut her up. He tenderly raised a single finger to her breast. "I'm so sorry that I did that to you." Lie. But since he was there anyways, he softly licked her blemished nipple. He looked at her to get her permission.

Destiny leaned her head back and started enjoying the warmth of his mouth. Damon couldn't control his inner beast. He had a primal need to ravish her. He wasn't getting his urges filled with violence. Sex was the only option he could resort to.

Damon tried to be sweet. He tried so hard. His mouth went from her breast, to all along her baby bump. He kept going lower, but since he was trying to be sweet, he bypassed her v-zone. When he got to her thigh, and his mouth found the large D he had branded into her flesh, his inner beast took over. He had been reminded of all the times that he hurt her. He was mad with passion.

Damon grabbed both of her frail wrists and pinned her arms over her head. He lowered his full body weight onto her, and wiggled his hips until he found entry inside of her. He began to pump himself into her as hard as he could. He was lost in the moment.

"Damon you're hurting me. STOP!" Destiny cried out.

Damon couldn't hear anything. He was in the moment. His inner self was on a mission of self pleasure. Destiny spat on him, which only made him wilder.

"Stop! Get off me! Now!" Destiny tried to throw his body off of her, but he was too strong. No matter how hard she tried to wiggle away from him, she couldn't. He was holding her wrists too tight. He was too forceful. She was helpless. She couldn't do anything except cry.

Damon was determined to get his pleasure. He tuned out Destiny's words. He couldn't hear anything, except his inner voices urging him to satisfy himself. It wasn't until Destiny bit his ear, really hard, that he realized what he was doing. Damon released his grip from her arms, and Destiny pushed him off from her.

"Get off me! Now!"

All of a sudden, Damon was back in reality. He looked around the room, trying to remember where he was, what he was doing.

As soon as he saw the tears that had streaked her face, he couldn't believe what he had just done. He wasn't sure what had just happened. He had blacked out.

"Destiny, I'm so sorry. You have to understand. I don't know what came over me." Damon also cried.

Destiny threw his pants at him. "Get out of here!" She was clutching her belly.

Damon got off the bed, to give her some room. He got down on his knees. "Darling. I'm so sorry. I don't know what happened! Is the baby okay? I'm so sorry. I would never hurt you."

Destiny just cried.

"I need your help Destiny. I don't know what's wrong with me." He gazed into her eyes, with a sincere look. "Please. Please help me." He wished that he could tell her what was going on in his head. Would she understand? How could she understand if he couldn't even make sense of it?

He had lost control of himself. He wasn't sure why. At this point, Damon was almost scared of himself. He was mad at himself for hurting Destiny. He was a bigger monster than he had realized.

Destiny took his hand, and they cried together.

LADIES' NIGHT

Finally, Destiny and Mary got some alone time. Just a girls' night out. They told Damon and David that they were going to be discussing wedding plans. There was no place for a man in that discussion.

Secretly, they just wanted time alone to bond. Damon had always been around them, and they didn't have a chance to do any serious talking. Mary was worried about Destiny. She wanted to make sure that Damon was treating her right.

"He's perfect." Destiny hesitated. "Most of the time. Sometimes, he's scary. I love him. I know he's trying real hard, but I'm in a tough spot here."

Mary was really worried about her friend. After hearing about Damon pretty much raping her friend was enough for her to give her friend some advice. Especially after seeing Destiny's bruised wrists. She had really dark spots on both of her arms.

"I'm saying this because I love you. You

have to leave him." Mary was being serious. She wanted her friend to be happy, but not if it meant being abused.

Destiny shook her head no. "I can't. I love him. I can't explain it. When I was away from him, I felt like a piece of me was missing."

Mary tried to be logical and explain that Destiny had to also think of the welfare of the baby. Was Damon the kind of man that she wanted to raise a baby girl with? For some reason, Mary just couldn't get through to her.

"Maybe we should go to a counselor or something. There has to be another way. Underneath it all, he's a good man." Destiny tried to rationalize her poor decisions.

"A counselor? Serious? How about the police?" Mary wanted to grab her friend by the arms and shake some sense into her. Why couldn't Destiny realize the danger that she was in?

"He didn't exactly rape me. Maybe I explained it wrong. He was just different. Then he was sweet. He even apologized. He asked me for help. I only wish I knew how to help him." Destiny tried to clarify her statement.

Mary didn't like this. "Look at your bruises! Did you tell him that you didn't want sex?"

"Well, I told him that I was tired."

"Then did he get sex?" Mary was trying to find a way to explain. Maybe if she simplified it, then Destiny would understand.

Destiny shook her head yes.

"That's called rape. Plain and simple." At least it was simple to Mary.

Mary knew that Damon was capable of evil deeds, but she had no clue his evilness had evolved to rape. She wasn't sure how she was gonna handle this. She owed it to her friend, at the very least, to try and help. But Damon was still her boss. Plus, if he raped Destiny, what could he do to her? Mary needed to come up with ideas. There had to be a way to resolve this.

Since Destiny had gone out for the evening, Damon saw an opportunity to sneak in some playtime. Having spent his whole life being proud of being in control of himself, he couldn't believe what he had done to Destiny. Damon wasn't the kind of man to lose control of anything. He had control at work being the boss. He had control over his whole life.

It only made sense that he had lost control because he wasn't feeding his inner beast. The evil beast was never satisfied and always desired to see more blood. His inner self was always wanting to hurt people. If Damon was hurting people, then he wasn't the one being hurt. It made sense to him.

It was time to regain control. What better way than to please his needs? He was sure that

Destiny would approve of what he was doing, if only she knew. He was doing this for Destiny. If he pleased his inner demons, he would be nicer to Destiny. He had to keep her from harm's way of his own demons.

Damon drove to the usual spots, trying to find a woman to play with. He needed a woman that would be around. He didn't want to kill this one. He needed a long term set up.

As soon as Damon saw her, he knew that she was the one. She was standing, literally, on a street corner. Her skirt was so short that he could almost see her business. Her legs were so skinny. When he looked at her sunken face, he couldn't help but notice how bad her eyes were. Her arms even had marks, from where she had obviously used a needle. A drug addict was exactly what he was looking for.

Drug addicts made the best toys. They always needed money. They didn't mind a little pain. Plus, they loved Damon's generosity. If she were to play with him willingly, and oblige to his every whim, he would never have to kill her. She was perfect!

Even though his car was rented, it was still a flashy car that got the hooker's attention. Damon's twinkling eyes and charming smile were all the women needed to climb inside. After a brief negotiation, and Damon's promises of paying her well, they drove to a motel.

Damon wanted to ensure that he did everything right with this one. He needed a perfect approach. He didn't want to scare her off too soon. He was sure that he could mold her into what he needed her to be. First he knew that he had to get her attention. Money always got a hooker's attention.

"Guys don't usually get a room. Are you some wierdo or something? Scared of getting caught in a car?" The woman chewed on her gum, loudly. Smacking her lips.

Damon laughed. Normally, being accused of being weird would make him mad. However, he couldn't afford to be mad. He had to be nice to her. "I just wanted this to be special. What's your name?"

"I'm Candy. Nice to meet ya." She smacked her lips more. "I charge $50. You still have to pay that, even though you paid for the room."

"No problem." Damon saw the opportunity to expose his money. He pulled out a wad, and set it on the table.

Candy's eyes looked at the money. "You can get this room for longer, and I'll work extra hard for ya. Days if you want."

Now Damon knew she did like money. Now to find out if she was willing to do what it took to earn it. "I'm like no client you have ever had. I have unusual requests." Honesty was always the best policy.

"Unusual requests? For that kinda cash you

could bring in a donkey. I don't care." Candy was not shy.

Damon tried to ignore the gross donkey remark. But he couldn't stop thinking about it. Maybe that would hurt her. He had never seen a male donkey's anatomy, but it had to be large. It would have to be painful. Damon tried to refocus on Candy. "I like to watch people in pain."

"Ya know, everyone is talking bout that tv show. I don't watch it. But sure. I get ya." More chomping of gum.

Damon was glad that she didn't watch the show. But maybe this was too easy. She agreed too fast. He wanted to test her limitations.

Candy started digging around her small purse. She pulled out a smaller bag and excused herself to the restroom.

"Wait. What is that?" Damon pointed at the object in her hand.

She hid it behind her back, and pretended to not know what he was referring to. Damon wasn't stupid. He recognized a drug kit when he saw one.

Damon grabbed her wrist and made her expose it.

Candy was testy. "What are you? Police?"

Damon reassured her that he wasn't police. Just that he didn't want her to be high during their time together. He learned that heroin was her drug of choice. After another brief negotiation, Damon agreed to let her inject the drugs in her arm, and then he could do anything he wanted to her. For the wad of cash, of course.

As Damon watched her prep her arm for the needle, he was thinking about his best approach. He wanted to hurt her, but he didn't want to injure her so badly that she wouldn't see him again. He needed a side woman, for Destiny's sake. If he had an outlet for his anger, he would not have to take his aggression out on Destiny.

The woman penetrated her flesh with the small needle, and pressed down on the plunger. Her face instantly displayed an expression of euphoria. She fell backwards onto the bed, with the needle still in her arm.

Damon lightly smacked her face, but she didn't respond. Her eyes seemed to open slightly, but it was obvious that she wasn't alert. She made a faint cooing sound.

Damon ran his fingers through her thick hair, and gripped tightly. He pulled her to a sitting position, but she still didn't wake. As soon as he released her hair, she collapsed onto the bed. Damon began to undress her. Her skirt was so short, he just rolled it up around her hips. He pulled her shirt over her head. Even though she was thin, she still had perky breasts.

Damon admired the nude anatomy of the

hooker, wishing she would wake up. It was more fun when they screamed. He wanted to see terror in her eyes. Damon raised his hand in the air, and came down with a firm backhand to her jaw. The sound of her teeth clanking together turned him on. Damon rubbed his growing crotch.

Quickly, he flipped the limp woman's body over. Since she was now face down on the bed, he had a great view of her backside. He scratched her back with his fingernails until he saw blood. The fluid leaking out of her was what he wanted to see. He pulled out his car key. He firmly jabbed the jagged edge into her tender skin. He had always loved marking his toys.

Even though he was disappointed that she wasn't awake, he enjoyed carving the large D into her back. The bloody D excited him so bad he felt like he was going to explode. He made use of her woman parts in a sexual way. He released more than just his anger on her.

Pieces of her flesh were hanging from the edges of the car key. He couldn't return a bloody key to the car rental place. He licked the blood to clean the key. He felt a small chunk of her flesh in his mouth, and chewed on it. He savored the raunchy flavor before he swallowed.

He examined the large D on her back. It wasn't perfect. Lines weren't straight. But since he had used a car key, he thought he had done pretty good work. The short imperfect lines were what made it authentic. Perhaps this was his greatest masterpiece ever.

Being the honest kind of man that he was, he made sure to leave the cash laying on the table before he left. She would see it when she woke up. He saw potential in this toy. Next time, he wouldn't let her shoot up first. He wanted interaction. But he knew next time, he could injure her badly, since she had her own pain medication on hand.

For now, he was satisfied. He reminded himself that he loved Destiny so much that he had to do this. Destiny was his whole world. He loved her more than anything, even his show. Releasing his urges on other women would make him a better man for his soon to be wife.

DEEPER INTO THE DARK WEB

Damon just wasn't thinking straight lately. He hated David. He hated that David originally planned to use Mary as leverage. He hated that David had pictures to blackmail him into being on his internet show. He hated everything about David.

Usually, Damon was good at coming up with plans so that he would regain control over whatever situation he was in. Not this time. His mind was mush and not in planning mode. Even though work was going great, it occupied too much of his mind. Then there was Destiny. Her and the baby were the best things in his life. He had to devote a lot of his attention to her.

When would he take some time for himself to figure out how to deal with David? There just wasn't enough time in his life. For now, Damon shrugged it off. In time, a plan would come to him. For now, Damon packed his black ski mask and a bag of toys. It was time to perform.

The drive to the large warehouse was easier this time. Damon knew where he was going, so the buildings didn't appear as angry this time. Even though he hated the fact that he was being recorded, he loved having an outlet for his anger and hatred.

Damon secured his mask over his face before entering, and gave David a startle. Damon thought about killing David right then in that moment. But he needed information. He needed to know who else knew about this dark venture. Hopefully in time, David would reveal his secrets.

David was flipping switches and looking at multiple screens. "I sure am glad to see you. Her sedation should be wearing off soon."

"Why'd you have me come back? You know I don't like this." Damon was blunt.

David stopped what he was doing. "They loved you! We've seen a lot of twisted stuff here. But never a blowtorch used in a sexual way! It was a shame it killed her so quickly. Take it slow this time, okay?"

"Who's they?" That's what Damon really needed to know.

"They are not important. What's important is keeping you happy. Speaking of that, I have something for you." David handed Damon a bag.

Damon peeked inside the bag. There was a ton of cash. "Do me a favor."

David looked up.

"I want you to stop seeing Mary." Damon was sure of what he wanted.

David started to get angry. "I love her. She's so innocent, and pure. I can't do that. Why do you care anyways?"

Damon set his bag of cash aside. "You admitted to meeting her to get to me. Now you have me. Leave her out of this."

David flared out his chest. "She's separate from this. Don't worry about me telling her. I don't want her to know about the dark web, either."

For now, that would have to be enough to soothe Damon's worries.

This time, the woman was tied to a bed, and blindfolded. Her nude body was on display in front of him. Damon counted the cameras in the room. There were a few of them. Apparently they wanted to see every view and angle of the torture.

She was waking. "Who's there? Why are you doing this?"

Damon tried to distract his mind from wondering who this girl was. He didn't want to know where they got her from. He didn't want to know anything about her. She made him think of his unborn baby girl. He would kill someone if they did this to his little princess.

Damon shook off the negative thoughts. He kept telling himself that there were no cameras. This woman was just a person, not his daughter. He had to focus on why he was there.

"Please. You don't have to do this."

Damon felt the woman's cries seep into his bones. His inner beast was awakening. Now, his mind was only focused on one thing, hurting her. He smiled as he laid his toys out on the table. The only thing that was better than him playing with his toys was showing his toys to his victim.

Damon untied the tear dampened blindfold from her eyes.

"Please. I'm begging you! I have a child! Don't do this to me."

Damon ignored the comment of her having a child. He wondered if all the women always begged like this. He tied the blindfold around her mouth, to shut her up.

"MMM. mmmm."

That was better, she could only scream now. He looked forward to hearing her shrill sounds of pain.

Damon held his boxcutter into the air for her to see. That was when she really started struggling. Damon inspected her bindings.

There was no way she could squirm loose.

First, he ran the boxcutter along her face. She was screaming, even though he hadn't exposed the blade yet. He felt how cold the tool was, even through his glove. As he ran it further down her neck, then her chest, he noticed that her nipple became erect.

He started thinking of Destiny. He had to force her out of his mind. He continued to run the old tool along her body. He clicked the button, and the small blade exposed itself. While she was screaming, her eyes begged and pleaded with him to release her.

He let her sounds resonate in his body. He placed the tip of the blade in her navel. On television it was a staple, here he could use a blade. Damon made sure the blade was firmly buried into the notch, and spun it around. Her body started jolting and shaking violently. Damon paused for a moment to enjoy the sight of her blood. He stuck out his tongue to lick the sticky substance. She tasted like a dirty coin. Damon dipped his gloved finger into her fluid, to smear some blood in with the tears on her face.

Her cries became louder. Damon was in his element. This was his opportunity to see lots of blood. He had to quench his inner desire to see blood. He wanted to see all of her red fluid outside of her body.

Damon went back to his bag of toys. He held

up a hand saw, with prickly teeth. Damon sat on her leg, on top of her knee. He grasped her ankle. She was trying to kick him, but she was tied too tight. He pierced her soft skin with the saw, and began to move it in a back and forth fashion. He didn't know if it was possible to saw through a human leg, but he wanted to find out. He knew there would be lots of pain if he could at least get to her bones.

As he was cutting her leg open, he noticed that she had stopped squirming. Damon looked at her face. She was unconscious! Damon wanted her alert and awake for this. He hadn't seen enough blood yet. Damon was not happy.

Damon resorted back to his boxcutter. He buried the tip into the folds of her cheek and slashed her open. Her eyes opened up. Finally, she was awake. He fiercely yanked her eyelid. He wanted her to watch. He wanted her to be aware of what he was doing. As he shoved the blade under her eyelid, he punctured her eye. He was being reckless.

Damon stopped to compose himself. He needed more self control. While Damon was lost in his head, the woman passed out from the pain. Damon was bored. He took the blade to both of her wrists and watched the blood drain from her body.

Her warm fluids were a beautiful sight. He sat and watched the blood flow down her arms. The mattress absorbed the sticky substance, until puddles formed. Damon took his gloved finger and ran it into the puddle. He drew a bloody smile around the woman's mouth. That just didn't look right. He wanted her to be sad. He dipped his finger back into the blood, and drew a line of bloody tears down each side of her cheeks.

Now, she looked better. She wore a smile, and she was crying at the same time. That was how Damon was feeling most of the time, nowadays.

HUMDRUM
WORK STUFF

Fearful that he was on the edge of a nervous breakdown, Damon stopped by the liquor store on his way to work. Something was happening inside of him. He couldn't figure out anything. He couldn't think clearly. He needed his head on properly to work. Hopefully, alcohol would calm his nerves.

It was time to plan next season's show. Work was important. Running a live show would require a lot of time and dedication. Plus, he had to think about a wedding and a baby. Damon's world felt like it was closing in around him. Where did he belong? What was wrong with him?

He chewed gum to cover the smell of alcohol on his breath, and the excessive chewing made him think of Candy. Maybe he needed time alone with her. Maybe that internet show didn't do it for him because he was aware that he was being watched. Now he was paranoid all the time.

There were too many scattered thoughts. Damon couldn't keep track of anything. Work. If he threw himself into work, then he would get better. Damon went through some old emails that were marked for the discard pile.

The first email he clicked open was marked 'Cutter', which had a video attached.

"I'm Patrice! I am the biggest fan ever! 'Easy Money' was my favorite, but I like 'Hurt Bank' too! I really, really, really wanna be on the show. Oh yeah, did I mention that I really wanna be on the show!"

Damon was glad that the viewer's didn't heed Peter's warning of not submitting their homemade videos.

The video continued to play.

"Look at my leg!" Patrice raised the leg of her short pants, revealing multiple scars. "I love to cut myself! I thrive on pain. Pain is my distraction from reality."

Damon was fascinated by this woman's marred flesh. He could relate to her. He also needed distractions from reality. However, he preferred to hurt other people, not himself.

"I could play until the last round. I know I could. Let me give you a little demonstration." Patrice raised a butcher knife to the camera. She ran the sharp object along the full length of her thigh. Her skin opened up, just like she was cutting a steak. Thick, dark blood poured from the wound.

Even though Damon was aware that this woman could not pass a psychological evaluation, he wanted badly to cast her on his show. He needed players like her, especially if he was planning more extreme pain.

Watching these videos offered Damon some reprieve from the chaos in his mind. This was exactly what he needed to clear his head. It was just another tough day at work.

Mary was ready to pounce when she saw Damon. She would not allow him to treat her friend that way. She didn't care if he was her boss or not. This was personal. Mary marched right into his office.

Damon did not appreciate Mary distracting him from watching viewer submitted videos.

"You have some nerve. You do know Destiny is my friend, right?"

Damon was shocked. Mary never spoke to him like this. "I am aware."

"Then why? How could you treat her like that? She is carrying your baby?"

Damon had to contain himself. He couldn't believe that Destiny told Mary. "I don't know what you're talking about." Damon ignored his assistant, and looked at the computer on his desk, ready to get some work done.

Mary got closer, and stood between him and the screen. "You know what I'm talking about. Did you rape her?" There was no other way. Mary had to say what was on her mind. She braced herself for the wrath of Damon. There was a time that he cursed her because his coffee wasn't hot enough. She knew that this would surely push him over the edge.

Instead Damon said nothing.

Mary realized this wasn't the normal Damon. Something wasn't right.

"Well, say something! Remember, I'm the one you exposed your truths to. I know how you planned Marty Blevin's death. I will not stand by while you do this to Destiny!"

Damon lowered his head in shame. He couldn't even look in Mary's face. "I'm sorry."

Mary thought that she had imagined it. Damon had never apologized for anything, ever, in his life. Damon was actually being sincere. She didn't know what to make of it.

She left Damon's office, knowing that she had said what she wanted to say. Now, if she could only make sense of his response. Damon seemed like a broken man. Mary was speechless. There was nothing left to say.

Working with a few writers, Damon and Mary were busy planning the next season. They were brainstorming ways to produce shock value. Usually, Damon would be overflowing with ideas. But not today. He never came up shy in the creativity department.

Mary stepped up and took charge of the situation. "I don't think it's possible to top anything that we've already done. Let's go back to the original. Back when there was initial shock value. Let's brainstorm on that. What was so great about 'Easy Money?'."

Just the mention of the name 'Easy Money' was what Damon needed. His first pain show was his baby. It was that show that he put his heart and soul into.

Instantly, Damon sprang to life. "Yes. 'Easy Money'. The mother of all pain shows. She was the alpha. The beginning. She was the greatest shock of all. We've neglected her. Let's go back to the beginning."

Damon was back to his usual self, speaking but not really saying anything. Mary was glad that she had seen a glimpse of the old Damon. Maybe there was still hope for him.

"Maybe new isn't better. Sometimes old is the best. 'Easy Money' was the best. You can't get any better than best. There's no reason to transform something that already works. Perfection. Perhaps maybe we could just modify it a bit. Maybe an update. Or a new look. Not a complete redo." Damon spoke in riddles.

Mary scratched her head. This was the way that Damon worked the best. When he spoke his own language, that only he could decipher. Mary hoped that he wasn't having a nervous breakdown, and that his words made sense to him.

THE HAIRY SPIDER

Damon worked extra late to nurture his next show. He saw each and every one of his shows as his own children. Not only did he create them, but he would also mold them into greatness. He was the person responsible for their well being. Of course, he did have Mary's help, but ultimately, all responsibility fell on him.

Working made Damon feel good. It was what he did. Working was his thing. Even though he had been mad at himself for what he had done to Destiny, he didn't think about that while at work. Work was the distraction his mind needed.

Damon realized that Destiny was his weakness. He couldn't afford to have a weakness in his life. He was Damon Dahmer. A superior man. He couldn't let her go either. He needed her in his life. He was danged if he did, danged if he didn't.

Sitting in his car, very much looking forward to going home to her, he remembered Mary's words. He was humiliated. Not only had he hurt Destiny, but Mary also knew about it. Mary was his assistant. He didn't need her thinking any less of him. Damon tried not to cry. Instead, he transferred his sadness to anger.

Anger was an easier emotion. Anger could be released. Sadness, on the other hand, was complicated. Sadness was not productive. Sadness had no reason, no meaning.

Damon felt his anger bubble within him. His anger was what made him powerful. His anger ensured that he was always in control. It was time to regain control of everything. His life. Work. Destiny. His future child.

He looked into the moon. That was when he realized what he must do. There was something that he had to take care of.

Damon walked straight into the dark warehouse. He didn't care who would be there. He hoped to find David alone. David was always alone whenever he was there. Hopefully, there would be no one there filming right now.

Even though David was surprised, he wasn't alarmed. "Hey Damon! Did we have something planned tonight? Because I was just here to set up for tomorrow."

Damon looked around. There was nobody else. It was just David. "I must have my nights mixed up. Anyways, just curious. How's this place work?" Damon looked down at the controls. There were so many knobs and buttons.

"It's pretty easy. At least for me." David smiled. "I've worked with computers my whole life. This is a little different from television, but it's kinda the same. That switch right there activates the live stream to our members. Kinda like your show being broadcast to television sets around the world."

Damon thought that he would try and be nice. "Who are these members? Don't you think I have a right to know who's watching me."

David threw his hands in the air. "Trust me. I can't tell you some stuff for your own safety. Some of them are normal people. Some are well known. They are each hand selected. You just have to trust me."

Damon would never trust David. Knowing that he wasn't getting anywhere, Damon knew that the kind approach wasn't gonna work. Damon really needed to know who he had been working for. Luckily there were other ways to get answers.

When David wasn't paying attention, Damon raised his expensive leather shoe, and kicked David square in his man parts. Men were so much easier than women. They were vulnerable. David dropped down to his knees, guarding his crotch.

Damon mustered all of his anger. He grabbed David by the throat with both hands. He slammed David's head into the concrete floor multiple times.

When David woke up, he was the person tied to the bed. Many times before, he had been the person doing the tying up. Now the roles were reversed. He pulled on his chains with no luck. He was at Damon's mercy.

Damon's shadowy figure was in the corner. Waiting for David to wake up. Damon poked his lips through his ski mask when he saw David's eyes open.

"Boo." Damon pointed up. "Wave to the camera. I work in TV. I know how to work a camera. I didn't need your stupid tutorial."

"What are you doing?" David began to panic.

"I need names. People who pay for this. People who watch this. People who wanted to use Mary against me. Names. Tell me, then I untie you. Simple." Damon felt like his old self again. This was what he needed. He needed to be in control. He needed to be powerful.

David was shaking his head. "I can't. I'm not

supposed to. They'd kill me!"

"So you would rather me kill you?" Damon laughed.

David knew he was in deep danger. He had to try to reason logically with Damon. "I don't want anyone to kill me. We can talk this out. Just untie me."

Damon was very bored with the same pleas and cries. All victims wanted the same thing. They wanna be untied. They didn't want him to hurt them. Damon hoped that someday there would be a creative victim.

Damon started with David's toes. He had his trusty boxcutter in his car. He spread David's toes and sliced the webbing between his small digits. David was screaming.

"Right now, you aren't bleeding so bad. You could start talking. You could still live." Damon offered the man an opportunity.

David knew that Damon would not let him live, no matter what he told him. "I'm not stupid. You're gonna kill me! You're sick. We could be friends. It would be perfect. Our girls are best friends. I bet you didn't know that, did you!"

"Us? Friends? You were gonna use Mary to get to me. Friends don't do that!" Damon slapped David across his face with his fist.

David spit some blood from his mouth. "I was gonna use Mary. But why would I use Mary when Destiny was there?" David started laughing.

Damon was really getting mad. He didn't want this man to even speak Destiny's name, nevertheless threaten her. "Just tell me who you work for!"

Damon started unzipping David's pants. "I can make you talk!" Damon was now threatening David's man parts.

"You didn't know, did you? Yeah. She was under your nose the whole time! Destiny was living with Mary. They didn't tell you. They hate you! Both of em!" David made it a point to get under Damon's skin.

Damon didn't want to hear David speak anymore. Could it be true? Did Destiny run to Mary when she left him. It didn't make sense. They wouldn't do that to him. Mary was always loyal to him. But it did make sense. Destiny and Mary were so close now. They wouldn't be this close if they hadn't seen each other in months.

Damon grabbed David, square around his jaw, and tried to squeeze his mouth open. David struggled against his grip. Nearby, there was a pipe in the corner of the room. Damon thrust the pipe against David's jaw.

As David was spitting out pieces of teeth, Damon saw the opportunity to insert the pipe into his mouth. He wedged his jaw open, and grabbed David's tongue. It was moist and slippery, but that did not deter Damon from slicing off the end of his tongue with the boxcutter.

"You can't talk now! I'll tell you what! I'll give you a pen. Write down who you work for!"

David was choking on his own blood. Making bubbling sounds, he grasped onto the air, trying to breath.

Damon stood and watched David die.

CLARITY

Nothing made sense anymore. Damon's head was scrambled. He had always relied on Mary. Did Mary betray him? She knew his secrets. He trusted her. Even though they were complete opposites, their balance had always worked. They complimented each other.

Could he be mad at Destiny for getting close to Mary? He knew they were friends, but not best friends. He loved Destiny so much that it hurt. She was giving him the greatest gift in the world. A baby girl.

Was it too late to fix this? Had Mary told Destiny all of his secrets? Was that why Destiny suspected him of killing William? He couldn't blame Mary for thinking he killed William, but he didn't want Destiny to think he did.

Destiny was good and pure. She was the goodness that he needed in his life. He was going to be a changed man when his baby arrived. He was gonna try to be a better person.

Now, he was so full of doubts that he didn't know what to do. For now, all he could do was try to find out who David was working for. Damon searched boxes of papers, only to find receipts for the electronic equipment. There had to be files or something somewhere in this warehouse.

Damon found a closed laptop computer on a desk in a dark corner. He opened the laptop, only to find that it was protected by a password. Maybe the information he needed would be there. Damon grabbed the laptop, and he was going to leave, but then he had a thought.

He was thinking about Mary. Mary claimed to love this man. Then, he remembered that Mary was always texting David at work. Surely, David's phone would have information on it. David had to be communicating with this dark web boss. Afterall, it wasn't fair that the dark web man knew who he was. It only seemed right that Damon should know who he was in return.

With David's laptop and phone, Damon left into the night, not sure how he was going to handle the situation with Destiny and Mary.

Turn the page for Deadly Reality TV Series Book #4: Roll Credits..

DEADLY REALITY TV SERIES BOOK #4 ROLL CREDITS

By Sea Caummisar

THE RETURN OF EASY MONEY LIVE

"Hello folks! I'm Peter Conway. It is with great pleasure that I welcome you to the return of 'Easy Money'! We have a great audience here tonight! The show is being filmed live, straight to your living room. The events you will witness tonight are happening in real time. There are no stunts on this show. I cannot stress this enough, what you see is very real. Do not try this at home. Grab some popcorn, sit back and relax. Viewer discretion is advised. Now let's get on with the game!"

Damon Dahmer, executive producer, looked around at all of the audience members as they cheered and clapped. Being in charge of a live show was such a thrill. These people came to see his creation, a live television pain show.

Peter read the teleprompter like the trained monkey he had proven himself to be. "Let's go over some ground rules. This version is played a bit different than the original 'Easy Money'. We have several contestants waiting backstage. There will be a random draw. The lucky winner is given a task, and a prize amount. They either complete the task, or they don't. If they don't, the task is given to the next randomly selected contestant."

Damon's bosses had asked for a more extreme show. They wanted more blood, more pain. It was Damon's choice to have extra players on standby, just in case a contestant decided to opt out of doing a task.

Peter continued to read the screen. "Our first randomly selected contestant is Julia! Come on out Julia."

A woman walked out on the stage, blinded by all the lights. As she approached Peter, she nearly tripped over her own feet, and the audience laughed.

"That's okay, Julia. Don't be nervous. You're here to make money, right?"

Julia replied. "That's right Peter. I just wanna make some easy money."

"Tell us why you're here tonight. There's a bunch of viewers at home watching right now. They wanna know why you need to do this."

Julia looked into the camera as she squinted her eyes into the lights. "I need cash. Lotsa people need cash. I really need cash. I'm going through a really bad divorce, and I'm losing everything. My home, my car. Everything. I have no job, no education. I figured why not make some easy money until I figure things out."

Peter tried to comfort the player. He really did try his best to be a comforting host. "We understand Julia. I'm glad you're here. Are you ready to play?"

Julia almost got happy as she relaxed a bit and stopped focusing on the cameras and the lights. "I'm ready to play!"

"As you know, if you've ever watched the show, tasks start out kinda easy. Then they get harder. Since you're the first player, your task is the easiest. But also worth less money. Your task is worth $100,000."

Julia did get happy this time. "I can use that kind of money. Just tell me what to do."

Peter held up the legendary staple gun that had been used many times on the previous shows. "All you have to do is staple your eye. Not your eyelid. Your eye. The actual eyeball. You think you can do it?"

Julia lost all enthusiasm. "Won't I go blind?"

Peter shook his head no. "Actually, we've researched this and found out it has happened accidentally before. And after surgery, which we will provide, there's a chance that you won't lose your sight. But nothing is guaranteed."

Julia thought for a moment before speaking. "I do need that money. But I don't wanna be blind. I suppose maybe if I just staple the white part of my eye. This is gonna hurt though. I don't know."

"Julia, we're live. You have to decide whether or not you wanna do this challenge."

Julia shook her head. "I guess I'll do it, Peter. I've had babies before. That's real pain. I can handle this. Give me that staple gun."

The camera zoomed in on Julia as she began to tear up looking at the staple gun. The audience sat in silence and watched as she used her hand to open her eye. A large screen above the stage showed the camera zoom in on her eye. Her eyelids were spread wide, exposing her vulnerable eyeball. The lights glared off the staple gun as she slowly raised it to her eye.

Julia's hands were in an awkward position, but she somehow managed to aim the staple gun into the white of her eye. Her cheeks swelled up as she loudly exhaled. Julia squeezed the staple gun, and the audience could hear the faint click through her microphone. As she dropped the staple gun, she shrieked in pain.

The audience members that weren't covering their eyes erupted into an applause.

Peter watched as a staff member of the medical team came to escort Julia off the stage. "Congratulations, Julia. You just won $100,000 of easy money!"

Even as Julia walked away, the camera stayed zoomed in close to her eye. The metal was embedded deep, and her eye was twitching.

"Next we have Jeremy. Come on out Jeremy. Are you ready to play 'Easy Money'?"

A tall college student walked onto the stage, waving at the crowd.

"Welcome, Jeremy. Let's get down to business. Your task is worth $150,000. What would you do with that money?"

Jeremy was brave as he answered the question. "I'd get out of debt, put a down payment on a house. I've got a baby to think about. Maybe I could start a college fund for her."

Peter tried not to frown as he explained the next challenge. "For $150,000 all you have to do is grind your hand."

Jeremy looked puzzled. "What? Come again?"

Peter walked over to a bench grinder. "This is what's called a bench grinder. Mostly used to sharpen metal objects. When you turn it on, this circular part spins, really fast. Grinding anything that it comes into contact with. All you have to do, is spread your fingers, and let the circular part grind between your knuckles. Can you do that?" Peter was secretly hoping that he wouldn't do it. He didn't want to see all that blood.

"I don't know. It can't do that much damage can it? I go to the hospital afterwards, right?"

Peter shook his head yes. "We have medical here. Plus, we cover medical expenses. We need to know. What are you gonna do?"

"That's too much money. I'm not gonna say no. I'm gonna play." Jeremy walked over to the grinder. He laid his hand flat on the table and spread his pointer finger from his middle finger. He slid his hand to where the circular grinder intersected with the vee of his hand.

"How bad can this be? It can't be that bad. So what do I do next, Peter?"

Peter stepped away knowing that this can be that bad. He didn't want any blood splatter on his new suit. "There's a red switch right there. All you have to do is turn it on. Then you win $150,000."

Jeremy smiled into the camera, not knowing that it was only focused on his hand. He hit the red switch, and the machine came to life with a high pitched whine. The grinding wheel ate through Jeremy's flesh, throwing his blood all over the stage. As Jeremy tried to pull his hand back, a knuckle at the base of his hand got caught up in the grinder wheel. The camera zoomed in on the open wound, exposing bone and tendons and sinew. As the wheel kept spinning, Jeremy's blood was speckling his own face.

Medical came out and powered down the machine. Jeremy's guttural scream pierced the audience's ears. Soon enough, a crew member turned off Jeremy's microphone as he was escorted away.

Peter tried to act excited, but he was dying inside trying to forget what he just saw. "Congratulations Jeremy! You just won $150,000 of easy money! On with the game! Next we have Abbie. C'mon out Abbie."

Abbie looked frightened as she walked out on stage. Maybe she was traumatized by the man versus machine task.

"Welcome Abbie. You're our last contestant tonight. Do you want to win $250,000?"

Abbie's eyes got large as she dreamed of all the dollar signs. She was ecstatic, until she realized that she had to do something to earn the money. "I want to. But what do I have to do?"

Peter held up a pair of pruning shears. "All you have to do is cut off your ear."

"No way." Abbie stepped back and shook her head no. "I need my ear."

Peter turned on his television smile to calm the woman. "We have medical, ready with ice. I'm told that the ear is mostly cartilage. And easily reattachable. But can you stand the pain?"

Abbie was hesitant. "That's not fair. I really need that money."

"Is that a yes or a no, Abbie?"

Abbie started to cry. "My parents are depending on me. I'll do it. But are you sure they can put it back on?"

Peter couldn't believe how stupid some of these contestants really were. "As you know, I'm not a doctor, but there's a chance they can."

Reluctantly, Abbie took the handheld tool from Peter. She opened and closed the sharp blades and watched as they glistened in the studio lights.

"Those are really sharp, Abbie. Be careful." Peter knew how stupid that remark was when he said it. Being on live television, he had to recover. "I mean, just watch your fingers. But we've made them very sharp so that they will cut through your ear easier."

The audience started laughing. Despite all the blood that they had seen tonight, they still had a sense of humor.

Abbie stood by the mirror that the studio had provided for her. She opened the mouth of the tool and placed it around her ear lobe. She closed her eyes, not wanting to see what she was about to do to herself. As she squeezed the tool shut, the blades easily carved her ear lobe from her head. Blood began to run down her neck. She froze and just screamed.

"Abbie, you're not done. It'll take another

snip or two to cut off the whole ear. Remember, this is for $250,000." Peter tried to encourage her to keep going. It would be a shame if she quit after already doing so much damage.

Somehow, Abbie mustered the strength and ignored her pain as she kept cutting up into her ear. Peter was right, it only took a couple snips. By the time Abbie's ear fell off her head, the whole side of her head was covered in blood. The hair on her neck was matted into a crimson red mess.

"Congratulations! You just won $250,000 of easy money. Thank you for joining us tonight! Remember, do not try this at home. Please, don't send us videos of you hurting yourself. Just click the link on our website to apply to be a contestant. Until next time. I'm Peter Conway. Goodnight viewers."

Damon was proud of himself. He created this show. Now 'Easy Money' was live once again. The network had given him a license to free his creativity.

This was his chance to show the world what he was really capable of. His viewers could see how warped his mind really was.

AFTER THE SHOW

Damon was walking on air. He knew in his gut that the show was an instant hit. People, including himself, loved to see people in pain. They loved to see blood. It was him that made this show possible. He was the one responsible for making all of his viewers happy. The thrill that came with a live show was instant gratification. Watching the audience flinch and squirm in their seats was an added bonus.

As Damon was watching his beloved fans talking about the show, he was called back to reality.

Mary, Damon's assistant producer needed his attention. "Damon. Wait up. Can I talk to you?"

Even though Damon did not like the interruption, he looked to his assistant. Ever since he found out that Mary had kept a very big secret from him, she was not his favorite person. However, his fiance, Destiny was her best friend. He already murdered Mary's boyfriend. She just didn't know it. All she knew was that David had disappeared. He also had plans for Mary. He didn't like people that he couldn't trust. He could not trust Mary.

Damon very rudely finally responded. "What is it, Mary?"

Mary ignored Damon's harsh tone. He was always short with her, anymore. "Well, I won't see you until the big day. I just wanted to touch base. Are you sure you're okay with Destiny having a bachelorette party tomorrow night? She told me that you refused a bachelor party. I just wanted to make sure you wouldn't be mad about it." Mary looked as innocent as ever.

Damon was thinking to himself that Mary didn't care what he thought when she let Destiny live with her, in secret, for several months when she left him.

"No. It's okay. She's so pregnant and moody anyways. She needs a night out before the wedding. I'll have her all to myself for the honeymoon." Even though Damon was mad at his assistant, he couldn't help but smile as he thought about Destiny. They would be wed in a couple of days. Then the baby would come shortly after the honeymoon.

"Okay. Good. I promise we'll be on our best behavior. Anyways, Mr. Styles called. He said he needs to see you. He didn't say what about."

Damon checked his suit pocket. "I guess I left my phone in the office. Okay. I've gotta go then." Damon wanted any excuse to not make small talk with Mary. Soon, she would have what was coming to her.

Damon knocked on his boss' door as he walked in. "I was told that you wanted to see me."

"You were told right." Mr. Styles barely looked up from his computer screen to pay any mind to Damon. "What do you call that?"

Mr. Styles' question was very vague, and Damon didn't understand what his boss was asking him. "Excuse me. Call what?"

My. Styles turned the computer screen around for Damon to see. It was a replay of Julia stapling her eyeball. Damon enjoyed seeing the small piece of metal wedged into the sight organ.

"That was crazy, right? She actually did it. I couldn't believe that she actually did it." Damon's heart pounded through his chest as he watched the video replay of the contestant playing the game. A live show really got his adrenaline pumping.

"I can't believe I'm saying this." Mr. Styles paused for a moment, and raised his eyes to meet Damon. "Especially to you. The network hated it. They asked for blood. Violence. This is not bloody. Barely. Unacceptable."

Damon was insulted. He thought his idea was great. "Well, that's not bloody, per se. But it's painful. I was thinking outside of the box."

"They reminded me, to tell you, viewers want blood." Mr. Styles used his finger to point at Damon. "No deaths. Just blood. Are we clear?"

Damon shook his head in disbelief. He thought the eyeball challenge was genius. He couldn't believe that the network hated it.

Mr. Styles just looked at him. "Anything else? Do you have anything you'd like to say to me?"

Damon had a ton of things to say to Mr. Styles, but instead he bit his tongue. Mr. Styles hated this show since the very beginning. Instead of telling his boss off, he chose to be kind instead.

"More blood. I can do that."

Damon had been insulted by being told that his show wasn't bloody enough. He was proud of his show and hated the fact that the network was breathing down his neck, criticizing his challenges.

Damon left Mr. Styles' office, thinking about ways to make the show bloodier. He was happy just seeing people in pain. He was sure that his viewers were happy with that, too.

But the network wasn't happy. Pain wasn't enough. They wanted blood. If blood was what they wanted, then Damon would give them so much blood that their heads would spin.

BACHELORETTE / BACHELOR PARTY

Destiny was glowing in her pregnancy. She was the kind of woman that pregnancy agreed with. Even though her mood swings had gotten the best of her most days, she was chipper for her last girl's night out as a single woman.

Mary, being the maid of honor, wanted to send Destiny into marriage with a spectacular party. Destiny, being eight months pregnant couldn't drink alcohol, but that didn't mean that she couldn't have any fun. Mary made special plans, despite Destiny's protests of not wanting a male stripper at the party. So Mary agreed to not have a male stripper, instead there would be many male strippers at an all male revue.

Mary had to practically drag Destiny into the male strip club, in a very playful way. Destiny said that she didn't want to go inside, but her laughs suggested otherwise.

The ladies cheered with wine glasses full of water as they watched the men strip down to practically nothing.

"Thanks for bringing me here tonight. I feel so pregnant that I haven't been out of the house much lately." Destiny started to loosen up and enjoy herself. "I can't help but feel a bit guilty. Damon's sitting home all by himself, while I'm out having a good time. Maybe he's enjoying the peace and quiet. He's not having to help me off the couch tonight." Destiny's laugh resonated with pure happiness.

"Damon's been acting pretty strange at work lately." Mary shrugged her shoulders as she eyed a muscular man in a soldier uniform wiggle his hips on the stage. "If I didn't know any better, I'd think he's been mad at me. Maybe it's the stress of the live show. Maybe it's the baby. I don't know."

Destiny tried not to pay attention to the half naked man on the stage and focus on what her friend was saying. "He's been perfect at home. He's been so great. I just know he's gonna be a great daddy to our little girl. I haven't noticed anything odd about him."

Mary really was happy for her friend. "I'm so glad you guys have worked through everything. Cheers to you and Damon." Mary raised her water filled wine glass in the air.

As Destiny clinked her non alcoholic beverage to Mary's glass, she noticed that Mary didn't look as happy as she sounded. "One day, you'll find the man that's right for you. David didn't deserve you."

Mary's boyfriend David had just disappeared one night. Everything about their relationship had been perfect, then it was just like he fell off the face of the earth. She didn't know that Damon murdered him.

"I know. But tonight isn't about me. It's all about you. I've got plenty of single dollar bills. Now let's go stuff that soldier's g-string!"

Destiny couldn't help but think about Damon as she watched the nearly naked men parade around the stage. He was at home, all alone.

She might have had her doubts about Damon in the past, but he had really proved himself to be a good man. He was definitely above the average man, who would want a bachelor party with naked strippers dancing around.

Destiny pushed her guilt out of her mind long enough to place the dollar bill next to the soldier's sex package. She would make it up to Damon by being the best wife that she knew how to be.

Damon did sit home all alone, enjoying the peace and quiet. For just a few minutes. He saw a perfect opportunity to get out of the house and feed his inner demon. He had a special part inside of him that desired control over people who were weaker than him. While Destiny was gone, he had plans to go and play with Candy.

Damon didn't cheat on Destiny in a sexual way. Of course, she didn't know that he visited prostitutes. This was the only way he knew to control himself. He needed power over people. He needed to see people in pain. Even though he saw plenty of people hurt themselves on his show, it just wasn't the same as his own personal private viewings.

Damon arrived at Candy's small apartment without the worry that Destiny would wonder where he was. Sure, he lied to her when he told her that he was staying in for the night, but it was best that she didn't know. Afterall, she was carrying his baby. She was giving him the gift of his legacy living on after he died. His seed, his baby, would be his gift to the world. Even though Destiny had lied to him before, he couldn't possibly be mad at her. The lies were all Mary's fault. Mary was the one to blame.

Candy was happy as usual to see Damon.

Since she had started seeing Damon, her financial situation had greatly improved. Not meaning that she had any savings. Instead, she spent all of the money on drugs. Heroin was her preference, but she would do any kind of dope that she could get her hands on. Now she never had to worry where she would get the cash for her next high.

She gave her sugar daddy a slight peck on his cheek, and he pulled away. Damon didn't want affection, especially not from this prostitute. He wanted to see pain. More specifically, he desired to see her in pain.

Damon sat in his usual chair across from the bed, and laid a spread of cash on the table. "Do you wanna play?"

Even though Candy was a drug addict, and still kinda high from her last hit, she was still good at pleasing her clients. "Of course I do." She playfully flipped her hair over her shoulder. "I've been thinking of things you might like, unless you have any ideas."

Damon thought for a moment. He had brought a pocket full of safety pins with him, but was curious as to what she had in mind. "Try me. You go first."

Candy placed her hands out in front of her. "I thought you might like to tie me up. And then do whatever you want to me."

Damon's eyebrows raised. He was very interested. "Anything I want?"

"Well… Maybe we could have a safe word?" Candy shrugged her shoulders.

"A safe word?" Damon didn't like the idea, but if she was tied up, what could she do if he ignored her safe word?

Candy shook her head yes. "If I say banana, then you stop. That means I don't like what you're doing."

Damon just laughed at the idea. He was getting married tomorrow. This was essentially his bachelor party, and he wanted it to be memorable. "I have $3000 here. Do you think we could do this without the safe word?"

"The only way you tie me up is with a safe word."

Damon agreed, even though he knew he wouldn't care whether or not she said her safe word. After instructing Candy to undress and bare her back to him, he admired the jagged 'D' he had carved into her delicate flesh with a car key. He traced the 'D' with his finger, the scar raised slightly from her skin.

Candy supplied the nylon stockings for Damon to tie her arms and legs to the bedposts. He made sure that they were tight around her wrists and ankles. Her bare body laid beneath him, and she looked into his eyes, awaiting what he had in mind for her. She was hoping that it would be sexual, not painful. Luckily, the heroin helped her to not feel too much of the pain he might inflict.

Damon climbed on top of her, straddling her around the waist. He pulled out a handful of safety pins, and Candy felt a sense of relief. He couldn't possibly hurt her too badly with safety pins.

Damon pinched her eyelashes that were caked full of mascara, and the gritty makeup stained his fingers black.

"What are you doing?" Candy's eye twitched as her eyelid was pulled away from her eyeball.

Damon just laughed and held the sharp and pointed safety pin in the air.

"Banana! Banana!"

Damon ignored Candy's cries. He didn't hear her words anyways. He just heard screams that sounded like a symphony of his kind of happiness.

He gently led the tip of the safety pin into the underneath of Candy's eyelid. Candy squirmed, but she couldn't get loose. She tried shutting her eye, but the grip on her eyelashes was too tight. When she eventually managed to close her eye, Damon was left holding a few detached eyelashes in his fingertips.

It was fairly easy to pierce completely through her eyelid. He expected it to be tough, and form some sort of resistance, but it didn't. Damon admired the puncture wound. Candy repeatedly blinked, each time feeling the small piece of metal rubbing on her actual eye.

She kept squirming, and when she shifted her weight enough for her waist to make contact with his male genitalia, Damon was called back into reality. He realized now that her lips had been moving, and soon his ears could hear her words.

"Banana! Get off me. Take that out of my eye! Stop!"

Damon laughed and Candy got scared. She was merciless to his control. He had full power over her. She was stupid enough to agree to being tied up. Tied up by him, of all people!

Damon found another safety pin laying on the blanket of the bed, and opened the point from the latch. He used one hand to spread her eyelid open, and jabbed the sharp tip into her eyeball.

If Candy had said banana once, she had said it hundreds of times. Damon watched as her eyeball squirmed in her socket. Water ran from her eye, her body's only defense to eject the foreign object. But he had forced the safety pin so deep in her eyeball, that it wasn't coming out.

Pleased with his work, Damon decided to play nice.

"Where's your kit?" He was referring to her drugs. If he knew anything about drug addicted prostitutes, he knew they always had their drugs nearby.

"In my purse! Are you gonna rob me too?"

Candy was still squirming, and her eyeball was still twitching.

Damon shook his head no. "I'm gonna help you."

Damon rummaged through her purse, until he found her kit, all the while ignoring her cries for help. He found that her syringe was already full of the poison.

Damon searched her arm for a vein that wasn't already damaged by her abuse. "Be still. This will help."

Damon inserted the needle into her delicate skin, and pushed down on the plunger. Candy's eyes slowly rolled into the back of her head. It didn't take long, and she was pain free, and unconscious.

He checked to make sure that she was still breathing. He didn't want to overdose his playtoy. Her chest was slightly rising with each breath.

Damon admired the silver metal safety pins in her eye and eyelid before removing them. He noticed her naked body, but decided it was best to not cheat on his bride to be. He had to get married tomorrow and wanted to save his sexuality for Destiny. He untied Candy before leaving, and left the cash on the table for when she woke up. With any luck, she wouldn't remember any of this, and agree to see him again.

He knew that it wouldn't matter whether

or not she remembered. Even if she did, she would still want his money. That's all these hookers cared about. Drugs and money.

Damon laughed at the thought of a safe word. Candy must be dumber than he suspected, thinking that a word would protect her from him.

Damon would never look at a banana again and not remember his special bachelor party.

WEDDING/
HONEYMOON

The wedding was a grand event. Destiny looked beautiful, despite the fact that she was super pregnant. Her belly bulged through her white dress, making her look like an odd shaped egg.

Damon tried not to laugh as she waddled down the aisle. Mary stood in the front with Damon since she was the maid of honor, and softly cried a sweet tear of joy for her best friend.

Damon couldn't help but sneer at Mary. He had a hard time controlling his strong dislike for her. She had been his assistant for so long. That's what made the whole situation worse. He had trusted her. She broke that.

Destiny slowly approached the altar. Damon and Destiny vowed their love for each other in front of very few friends. Damon was happy that Destiny was giving him a child, but he didn't see the wedding as that big of a deal.

Damon tried to fake his happiness. When Destiny shed a tear of happiness, he couldn't muster up a fake tear. He just smiled into his bride's eyes and tried to look like he was enjoying himself.

He kissed the bride, and the lovers were off for a short honeymoon. He couldn't take too much time off work. He had another live episode to produce very soon.

Damon was relieved that all the formalities of the wedding were over. Sure, he had given in to all of Destiny's whims and wants, but he didn't understand the actual marriage ceremony. What was the purpose?

Was it not enough that he vowed to be by her side until death do them part? Why did she have to invite everyone she knew?

Damon shrugged it off. It was finally over.

A few days on the beach was a perfect getaway for the newlyweds. However, Destiny was so pregnant she didn't feel like spending time on the beach. There was no way she was gonna let people see her pregnant belly in a bathing suit. When they were in the hotel room, Damon could only make love to her so many times.

The lovers soon became bored.

By the second evening of their wedded

bliss, Destiny turned to the television for entertainment. A bored Damon took the opportunity to check his email.

After Damon tried many times to get information out of Mr. Cyber's password protected phone and laptop, he had no luck. All he wanted to know was who else was involved in the dark web show. Damon needed to know who had watched him murder those women, and blackmailed him with video footage of him killing Bambi in the desert. Even though he had been wearing a mask, he feared who else was involved might know his true identity.

Damon trusted his highly paid private detective with the electronics, hoping he knew some computer geek that could get past the passwords. Damon had been checking his email obsessively for any information from his P.I., and when the email finally arrived, he couldn't wait to click it open and see what it said.

Mr. Dahmer,

My guy had little luck so far with the computer. He got past the password, but everything is encrypted. He says it will take some time to get any information. The only thing he told me is that he found the computer had been communicating with your office. I asked him what he meant by communication, and he said videos.

He spoke way too much technical jargon. All I know is that the laptop was sending and receiving video with your office? Is this the information you needed?

Damon already knew that Mr. Cyber had been spying on him through his home computer. He wasn't shocked that Mr. Cyber had also spied on him through his computer camera in the office. That was definitely not the information Damon was looking for. He quickly sent a reply email.

No. That is not the information I needed. I need to know who else he communicated with. Remember, I am paying you well for this job. Do not disappoint me.

Damon was pleased with his response. At least they were past the password. Soon, he would know who else was involved with the dark web show.

Damon closed his laptop and snuggled up with his wife. It sounded weird to him that he now had a wife. He'd been divorced for many years, and never thought he would ever remarry.

Damon thought of his bachelor party a couple of nights before, and remembered how the prostitute had repeatedly screamed banana. Such nonsense. But he remembered puncturing her eyelids, and his pants began to get that tickle. He felt his member get hard remembering his private bachelor party.

Instead of letting it go to waste, he decided to consummate the marriage, once again.

As Damon made love to Destiny, thoughts of a helpless Candy tied up to the bed flooded his mind. Each memory of him puncturing her eyelid turned him on, making it easy to ignore Destiny's large pregnant body.

After he was finished pleasing his wife, Damon turned off the lights. Now it was time to sleep.

In the quietness of the night, Damon processed a well thought out plan in his head. Soon, he would have his revenge, and Mary would regret that she betrayed him.

EASY MONEY
LIVE EPISODE 2

"Welcome back for another exciting episode of 'Easy Money'. I'm Peter Conway. Buckle up your seat belts people! When I say viewer discretion is advised, I especially mean it for this episode. Do not try this at home. This show is live and real. If you've never seen the show before, you are in for a shock! 'Easy Money', the only show on television that pays you to hurt yourself!"

The audience stood and hollered and clapped their hands, hoping that Peter wasn't misleading them. They wanted to see people bleed.

Peter began to explain the rules, just in case any of the viewers had never seen the show. Damon salivated from his seat, watching from side stage, anticipating tonight's display of gore. Mr. Styles asked for more blood, and Damon aimed to please. Damon grinned from ear to ear, knowing what was in store for tonight's players. He almost expected some of the players to not complete a task, so he made sure to have plenty of extra players on standby.

"First we have Eva. Let's give Eva a warm welcome!" Peter watched as Eva walked out onto the stage.

Eva was a thin, older woman. She walked onto the stage, sure of herself. She firmly shook Peter's hand.

"So Eva, what brings you here tonight?" Peter put his arm around the contestant and pointed her towards the cameras.

"I love this show. I've been watching since the first episode, and I haven't missed an episode since. Amy was my all time favorite player of all time. She was so brave when she shot herself!" Eva could not contain her excitement as she looked at all the audience members that would soon be cheering her on.

Peter didn't understand. Most players weren't on the show due to fandom. They were on the show because they were desperate for money. "What about money? What do you need money for?"

Eva smiled even wider into the camera. "Sure, I could use money, but it's not like I'm in dire straights. I want the fame. I want to be all over the internet. I want to do interviews. I want all the viewers at home to think of me when they think of the show."

The audience laughed, and talked amongst themselves in disbelief.

Peter chuckled. "Okay then Eva. Are you ready to play?"

Eva jumped up and down. "I'm ready! What do I have to do? How much money will I win?" She could not contain her excitement.

Peter dug into his pocket and pulled out a vegetable peeler.

Eva laughed. "That thing? That's not so bad. What do I have to do to peel my skin? That's too easy." Eva was confident she could complete this task.

Peter wished that Eva had waited to hear what he had to say. "This challenge is a little bit different. It's kind of a double step process. First you have to use this vegetable peeler and peel a strip of skin from your elbow to your wrist. Then comes the hard part."

Eva was still laughing thinking this was way too easy.

Peter continued. "Then you have to pour sulphuric acid into the open wound."

Eva stopped laughing. "Sulphuric acid? What's that? How much money?" She was full of questions.

"This challenge is worth $200,000! That's a lot of cash! Sulphuric acid is abrasive on the skin. I'm not sure, but I think it can almost melt skin. Do you accept this challenge?"

Eva wasn't sure. She had dreamed for so

long what it would be like being on the show. She knew it wouldn't be pleasant, but she didn't have a degree in chemistry. She wished she knew exactly what kind of injury she would sustain.

It didn't matter. She was on live television, and had to make a decision.

"I'll do it." Eva only hoped that she was doing the right thing.

The audience was quiet as Peter led the player over to the staged area for this task. He handed her the vegetable peeler and opened the door to the glassed cube. Eva walked inside, and saw a bottle of the acid.

Peter gave the player instruction. "The first thing is to peel off a strip of skin. Just start near your elbow, and make sure to skin yourself all the way down to your wrist."

Damon knew the network wanted more blood, and even though the peeler itself wouldn't be too bloody, the acid would make the blood drip as it dissolved her skin. Applying the acid to an open wound would just make it hurt worse. He wanted to watch the player's face grimace in pain.

Eva was shaking as she held the peeler close to her skin. She laid the tool flush on her skin, and slowly began to glide the peeler down her arm. It easily peeled through her skin, and parts of her skin curled up around the tool. The camera zoomed in on the open wound. The small instrument left a path of blood behind it.

Her skin opened up, and there was more blood than Damon had anticipated. As Eva kept peeling, blood started rolling down her arm. There were murmurs from the audience. Most of the audience had already turned their heads so that they couldn't see what was happening.

When Eva got to her wrist, she let out a growl of accomplishment. She dropped the vegetable peeler, and raised her arms over her head like she was a champion. Blood dripped into her hair.

Even though Peter wasn't looking directly at her wound, he knew that she was done peeling by the way the audience cheered. "Okay Eva. Now all you have to do is pour the contents of that bottle on your arm. You have to empty the bottle entirely. Are we clear?"

Eva shook her head yes. She understood.

Eva was still shaking as she raised the bottle in the air. She stuck her arm with the open wound as far from her body as she could. She turned her head away, but yet she still brought the bottle above the gaping bloody wound. She turned her wrist to pour the acid on her skin. A stream of the liquid ran from the bottle. As soon as it made contact, her skin began to shrivel up. The blood from the open wound bubbled, and red was dripping heavily to the floor. She started shaking her arm up and down, and blowing on her arm, as if it was hot.

She was screaming uncontrollably and they had to turn off her microphone.

Damon studied her face to see the pain, but was fascinated by the way her skin had been dissolved. He was looking at a wrinkled bloody mess of an arm. The skin was not even recognizable. Her flesh looked more like a failed science experiment as it dissolved into a foamy mess.

Peter ignored the player as she was escorted away. "Congratulations! Eva just won $200,000 of easy money! I'm sure all the fans will remember her for some time to come!"

The audience agreed with Peter by their cheers of appreciation.

"Okay, we have randomly selected our next contestant. Come on out Oscar! Are you ready to play easy money?"

A middle aged man stepped out onto the stage, with small, non confident steps. His face was horrified. He had just witnessed the player before him melt her arm practically down to the bone.

"Hi. Peter." Oscar didn't have much to say.

"You okay? Do you need some water or something?" Peter was worried that this player might pass out.

Oscar was looking kind of pale, but shook his head no. "I'm fine."

Peter needed something to work with. He had strict guidelines to follow. He needed to introduce the player properly. "Tell us why you're here Oscar."

Oscar started stammering. "A wild fire. I lost everything."

Peter put on his sympathetic facial expression. "That's so sad. Would $250,000 help?"

Finally, Oscar was alert. "It sure would. But what do I have to do?"

A curtain raised behind Peter, and Peter walked over to the table. There was a small contraption. "This is our version of a miniature guillotine. It's kinda small. But don't let the size fool you. It has a razor sharp blade on it. All you have to do, Oscar, is stick your tongue in the contraption and let it slice off part of your tongue."

Oscar looked even paler. Then he almost turned a shade of green.

"We have medical staff here. It will hurt. And there will be plenty of blood. But I assure you, our medical team says that a tongue can be reattached. Especially after such a clean cut. So there'd probably be no permanent damage. But I can't say for certain. And it would be done really fast. What do you say, Oscar?"

Oscar swallowed so hard the audience could see his adam's apple swell in size. The man didn't speak, but he sure started to cry.

Peter got impatient. The live show only had a certain amount of time to air. If the show exceeded the given time, he would be at fault. "We're live. I hate to pressure you, but we need a decision. Now."

Oscar whined like a small child. "I guess. I guess I have to. I need that money."

Oscar dragged his feet over to the small contraption that would be the demise of his tongue.

"All you have to do is lay your tongue on that little flat part. Then push the red button. The blade will automatically fall, slicing off the tip of your tongue. It will be over in no time." Peter made sure that he wasn't looking at the contraption. He did not want to see this.

Oscar strained his neck to position his tongue into the weapon. He stuck his tongue out as far as it would go. The camera zoomed in, and Oscar's face appeared to be rather large, with even larger tears flowing down his cheeks. As he positioned his finger over the button, he closed his eyes tight, forcing out more tears.

His trembling finger found the button, and as he pushed it, instantaneously the shiny blade fell into his tongue. About an inch of his tongue fell into a trough. So much blood flowed from his mouth that the trough filled with blood, and the inch length part of his tongue was floating in a crimson red pool. Medical came out to collect the specimen so they could ice it and preserve it for reattachment.

Oscar tried to scream, but it sounded more

like a gagging sound from him choking on his own blood. As he released air from his mouth, blood floated in the cloud of his exhale.

"Congratulations Oscar. You just won $250,000 of easy money!"

EASY MONEY OVERTIME

Peter cleared his head of what he just saw so he could read from the screen in front of him. He was at work, and he still had to perform, despite what he had just seen. "We still have another challenge tonight! Let's meet our next player, Daisy."

Daisy was a college student in debt. She came out on stage wearing a pair of short shorts and the male audience members gave her an extra loud greeting. She strutted her stuff across the stage like she didn't just see a man just cut off his own tongue.

Her young, toned, tanned legs even caught Peter's attention. "Welcome Daisy. What brings you here tonight?"

Daisy flipped her long hair behind her shoulder. "I gotta get out of debt. As long as it won't hurt too bad." She giggled like a young girl.

Peter smiled his most charming smile towards the girl. "Well, I don't know about that. But this challenge is worth $350,000." Peter cleared his throat, and tried to stop himself from eyeing the contestant up and down. "How would that do you?"

Daisy jumped up and down, and her young firm breasts flopped with the grace of gravity. "I want that money. What do I have to do?"

Peter looked into the camera so he wouldn't be caught staring at her chest.

A curtain raised behind Peter, and he motioned towards a large machine.

Innocently, Daisy furled her lips. "What's that?"

Peter didn't want to tell this young student what this challenge was. He was hoping he wouldn't have to watch her deface her beautiful body. "It's a meat grinder."

Daisy shook her head no.

Peter knew it was his job to try and get her to perform the task. "It's not that bad. It would be a quick challenge. All you have to do is put your hand in their, and turn it on. You'll probably only lose your fingers. Maybe your whole hand. Unfortunately, they probably won't be able to reattach them."

"Are you crazy? That's all I have to do? You say it like it's nothing. This is my hand we're talking about!" Daisy was full of spunk, and didn't hesitate as she turned her back to Peter and stomped off the stage.

Peter watched every step she took as her backside jiggled ever so slightly in her shorts. For a moment, he forgot that he was on live television and had a job to do.

Peter snapped out of his trance to read the teleprompter. "How unfortunate. Luckily, we have more players backstage."

The audience cheered.

"Let's welcome Wilma. Come on out Wilma."

Wilma walked out onto the stage. Being the aging woman that she was, the audience did not greet her with the same enthusiastic cheers Daisy got.

"Hi Peter. I'm so glad to be here."

"So Wilma, tell me about yourself." Peter was not distracted by this player.

Wilma spoke bluntly. "I'm terminal. Lung cancer. Diagnosed, a few months ago. I'm dying anyways. Why not go out with a bang? Maybe I could finally go see the tropics before I die with that kind of money. Then leave some inheritance behind for my kids."

Peter was shocked and didn't know what to say. Instead, he just went forward with the show.

"I'm sure you heard. Your challenge is to stick your hand in that meat grinder, and turn it on. It has a safety on it, and it will automatically shut down after three seconds. But, I warn you, three seconds is a long time when you're in pain. You're gonna lose your fingers." Peter wanted the player to know what she was getting into.

"Fine by me. I won't need them for too much longer, anyways. Let's get this over with." Wilma walked over to the machine.

Peter was shocked by how brazen this character was. "All you have to do is stick your hand down that green chute, and press the red button with your other hand. Anytime that you're ready."

Damon got a text on his phone from Mr. Styles.

The show is running too long. You only have one minute of airtime left.

Damon spoke into his earpiece so Peter would hear him. "Hurry up Peter. We only have one minute left."

Peter looked like a deer in headlights. "Okay, Wilma. Go ahead."

Wilma scratched her head. "Do you really think I'll lose my fingers?"

Peter began to sweat, under pressure from the time limit. "I don't know. There's only one way to find out." He was trying to rush her. His orders came directly from Damon, and he knew Damon was not the kind of man that you wanted to make mad.

Damon texted Mr. Styles back.

Just give us one more minute. That's all we need.

Wilma hesitated as she slowly stuck her hand into the machine that shredded beef. She looked like she was still thinking about it as she went to press the button. The machine hummed to life with an intrusive sound, and Wilma began to scream. From the ejection chute on the other side of the machine, meat that somewhat resembled fingers slowly grinded out of the machine. Skin was tangled with bone and blood. The machine shut itself down, and Wilma fainted.

Damon got another text from Mr. Styles.

Time's up.

Damon watched as the monitor shut off. The network quit airing the show. Damon watched as Wilma fell from fainting, and her bloody nub of an arm squirted the stage with strong spurts of blood. Damon was so mad, thinking to himself how the viewers at home were missing all this blood.

Damon's phone vibrated again, and he almost threw it across the room, wanting to break it rather than to read Mr. Styles angry words. Instead, Damon glanced at his phone. It was Destiny.

The baby. She's coming. Meet me at the hospital. NOW!

CHANGES

Damon ran across the parking lot to his car in a frantic rush. Mary must have gotten the same text because she chased behind Damon, but Damon ignored her. He did not want her to ride to the hospital with him. He already hated the fact that he had to work with her. He reminded himself that soon he would not have to worry too much about her being around.

Damon sped to the hospital, all the while Mr. Styles had been trying to call. Damon didn't answer. He knew what his boss was going to say. He would be upset that the live show ran too long. Damon planned to speak to Peter. He would blame it on Peter, and the fact that he flirted too long with the young college student contestant.

None of this mattered right now. All that mattered was that soon his precious angel would be in this world. His daughter. His legacy, his name, would live on well beyond his own years.

He made it to the hospital in time, before Destiny had actually given birth. He refused when Mary requested to also be in the delivery room. He did not want her in the room. He hated the thought of spending time with Mary, nevertheless such a precious moment.

Damon heard Destiny's cries of pain. When they had previously discussed the birthing process, he was adamant about her giving birth naturally, without any pain medication.

Destiny screamed at the doctor, demanding an epidural or some other form of pain killer. Damon reminded her that they had discussed how drugs were bad for the baby. He honestly didn't care if the drugs affected the baby, he just wanted to see Destiny in pain. What worse pain was there than the birthing process?

Damon extended his hand for Destiny to squeeze it, but he stood the closest he could to the foot of the bed.

Damon watched, loving every minute of the baby squeezing its way into the world. Destiny's vagina began to spread, and Damon could see a hint of a fuzzy head of hair.

It almost looked like her pubic hair was growing inside of her, not the head of a baby. Destiny hollered and squeezed Damon's hand as she pushed the baby out of her body. A bloody /mucus fluid mixture drained from her woman parts, providing lubrication for the baby to slither out.

Damon swore that he could hear her bones crackle as her vagina expanded even more.

What was once a beautiful tiny entrance to Destiny's body, was now a large gaping hole, bleeding and stretched out like an entrance to a cave.

The doctor fit his hand into the enlarged hole, grabbing a hold of the tiny baby, pulling out a mess of fluid. The baby's entire body was covered in slime and looked like something from a science fiction movie.

Damon tried to pay attention to Destiny and calm her once the whole process was over, but he was trying to watch the doctor as he stitched up the damaged vagina. The doctor kept inserting the needle into soft tissue, and pulling the string around in circles.

The doctor inserted many stitches into Destiny's vagina before he was satisfied with the size of her entrance. Damon watched every moment, wishing he was the one sewing his wife closed. He wanted to be the person hurting her.

Damon watched as Destiny held the precious child for the first time. Something inside of Damon changed. He was now a father, to a perfect baby girl. He remembered all the bad things he had done to women, women who were someone else's daughter. He wasn't capable of feeling shame, but he definitely felt something different inside of himself.

He couldn't stop Mary from coming into the room after the baby was born, and he hated it when Destiny announced that Mary would be the baby's godmother. Damon hated the idea that Mary would be a major influence on his child's life. Why didn't he see this coming? He hadn't dealt with Mary soon enough.

Once again, none of that mattered when he looked at his darling daughter. Since the death of his son many years ago, this baby was now his prized accomplishment. He had almost even forgotten that Mary was standing a mere few feet from him cooing over the baby.

Destiny kissed the baby on her egg shaped head. "She needs a name. I vote for Phoenix."

Damon despised that name. His daughter wasn't a bird. "She's too sweet for that. I like Miranda. She looks like a Miranda to me."

"But Phoenix has a meaning. Recovering from burnt ash for another youthful life cycle." Destiny wanted to get her way. She wanted the name she picked out. "What do you think Mary? What name do you like for your goddaughter?"

Mary shrugged her shoulders and bit her lip. "Honestly, I think she looks like a Miranda."

Damon thought to himself that at least Mary was still good for something. However, her agreeing with him wouldn't stop him from planning her demise.

Damon hated it, but he had to leave his daughter and wife in the hospital overnight. He was told that it was routine. Damon wanted to celebrate.

He picked up his phone, and called Candy, with hopes that she would answer and agree to see him. He hoped that she didn't remember how many times he ignored her screams and cries of repeatedly saying banana. Luckily, she sounded excited that he was coming to see her.

As usual, Candy greeted him at the door wearing a sexy short skirt, and a low cut shirt. Damon's eyes traced the full length of her body from her toes to her head. When his eyes finally found her face, he noticed that she was wearing an eye patch.

Damon's heart sunk deep into his gut. What he had done to this girl. Now, she had to cover her eye. What if she had been his daughter? Would he approve of her line of work in prostitution. Of course not! Then, what if his daughter got mixed up with a crazy man like him! Paying her to torture her!

Damon calmed his thoughts, and focused on his play toy.

"Your eye. Are you okay?" Damon wasn't actually concerned for Candy, but he was concerned thinking about the what ifs and his daughter.

Candy just shrugged her shoulders. "I dunno. I didn't go to the doctor. I'm not blind or anything. It's just ugly right now."

The ugly part caught Damon's attention. He immediately forgot about his daughter. He wanted to see what pain he had caused her, but he didn't want her to know that he wanted to see it due to his own selfishness.

Damon dialed his charm to the top notch that charm could be. "You. Ugly? Never. Take that thing off. It's me. You can show me."

Candy slightly raised the eye patch, and then quickly put it back on.

Damon put his arms on the prostitute's shoulders. "No. Take it off. All the way. Keep it off."

Candy did as she was told. Candy's eyelid was swollen and red. Perhaps even infected. There had been some clear fluid running out of the small, pin sized hole.

Damon did this to her. At first his mind had been on his daughter and how he should protect her. Now, after seeing Candy's eye, instead he got horny. Damon grabbed his crotch to tame the devil in his pants and tried to push it to the side where it would be unnoticeable.

Damon spoke before he had a chance to think about his words. "It's not that bad. I tell you what though, how about I pay for your trip to the doctor. It might be infected." Damon was shocked by his own words. He had never paid for any of his hookers to see a doctor. Well, he did with Destiny, but she was different.

Candy laughed at him. "Yeah. Sure. I'll tell him how it happened, too."

Damon was a quick thinker. "Tell him you got drunk and lost a bet. Drunk people do stupid things."

Damon pulled Candy closer to him. He didn't know where this compassionate part of him was coming from, but he didn't like it. He concentrated on what his inner demon wanted.

"Let's play. How about something a little tamer today." Damon's mouth was getting the best of him. He didn't want to be tame. He wanted to be wild and rough.

Candy finally smiled and plopped down on the bed. She kinda bounced as the bed adjusted to her bodyweight. "I like tame. So what's tame?"

Damon was trying to think to himself. What was tame? He didn't know what tame was. But he had charm. Maybe he could convince her that something wild was tame.

Damon softly placed his hand on the hooker's chin. "I'll tell you what. Let's forget about playtime. Let's work on this eye. Maybe I can squeeze some of that infection out of your eye. Then I can pour some of that vodka in it. That should help with the infection. Let's focus on making you feel better."

Damon was proud of himself. He knew that wouldn't cure an infection, but it sure would cause her some pain.

First, Candy reached for her drug kit. Damon wanted her awake and alert, so he took the small package from her hand and set it aside.

Damon patted a pillow at the head of the bed. "Just lay back and relax, there will be plenty of time for that."

Candy laid back, and braced herself for what was to come.

Damon looked at the wound of oozing puss on her eyelid. He was gentle as he shushed her to calm her down. Then he took two fingers, and placed them around her eyelid. As soon as he squeezed, Candy shrieked in pain and gritted her teeth. Damon kept squeezing until the small scab broke loose and blood flowed in the puss mixture.

Candy kicked her legs. "I need my medicine."

Damon scoffed at the idea, claiming that heroin was medicine.

Damon was calm as he shushed her. "Shhh. It's almost over."

He truly enjoyed watching her face as she squirmed in pain. The fluid flowed into her eye, and she tried to wipe it away with her hand.

Damon got up to grab her a towel from the bathroom, and also grabbed the bottle of vodka. He handed Candy the towel, who now had both eyes closed. As she raised the fabric to her face, Damon quickly, heavy handedly poured the alcohol into her eye.

"Stop! It's getting in my eye! It burns!" Candy bolted straight up in the bed like she had been struck with lightning.

Damon placed his hand gently on her cheek, smearing her blood on her own face. "It's okay, the alcohol will clean it out."

Candy kept wiping her eye, shaking her head in pain.

Damon looked on the table and saw her cigarettes and lighter. Even though he wasn't a smoker, he lit up the cancer stick.

Candy was still busy trying to clean her eye and get the burning vodka out of her eye with the towel.

Damon gently placed his hand around her chin to hold her face still. "Hold still. Just a second. I'm doing this to help you."

He took the cigarette and quickly snubbed it out on her eyelid. Hot ash fell on her eyeball and she cried out like a wounded animal.

Damon shrugged his shoulders, and tried to muffle his laughter. "I had to cauterize it. It helps with infection."

Candy ran to the restroom to run cold water over her eye. When she came out, Damon looked at her eye. The cigarette had left behind a large hole exposing the inner layers of her eyelid.

"On second thought, here's some extra cash. You might wanna have a doctor look at that." Damon left the cash, and went home for his night of solitude.

INTRUSION

Even though Damon missed Destiny, and wanted to spend time with Miranda, he knew this would be his last night of peace and quiet at home for a long time. Once the baby came home, there would be constant crying and sleepless nights.

Taking his last opportunity for some free time, Damon fired up his computer. Maybe he could watch some bdsm porn, maybe he could get some work done.

As his computer slowly booted up, a small screen popped up on his screen.

Mr. Dahmer CLICK HERE

Damon tried to close out the small box. He clicked the 'x' repeatedly, but it wouldn't go away. Had he gotten a computer virus? Maybe he should stay away from some of that internet porn.

The small box turned into a video. Damon watched as a man dressed in black stood before a naked woman hanging from chains. His speakers were muted, but as he raised the volume he could hear that the woman was screaming.

No matter where Damon clicked, the box remained, forcing him to watch the video.

Damon watched as the mysterious man in the video pulled a large hunting knife from a sheath, and waved it in front of the woman's eyes. She spat on her attacker, only making him angry

Damon didn't want to watch this. Yes, he loved watching it. Torture porn really got his juices flowing, but he didn't want any part of that kind of life. There was no privacy on the internet. He couldn't have this kind of video linked to his computer in any way.

Still, his eyes were glued to the screen as the man firmly grasped the woman's breast. The man struck the long blade into her fatty breast tissue, and started sawing into her chest.

Damon heard the man laughing as he hacked away at the woman's bosom, but the woman's screams were even louder. Soon, the man was holding the woman's boob in his hand as it fell from her chest. The man shoved the woman's own nipple in her mouth to quiet her, and her screams were muffled.

Damon stared at the blood pouring out of the woman's chest. The sweet liquid flowed down her flat belly, forming a line to her shaven crotch. His prick hardened against the zipper of his pants.

The video cut out, and a new video started to play.

Damon watched as another masked man stood in front of a naked woman hanging from chains. The woman pleaded with the man as he slapped her rump. The man went for a bag, and pulled out a blowtorch.

The woman in the video looked vaguely familiar. Damon's face froze in terror as he realized he was watching a video of himself shoving a blowtorch into the woman's delicate sexual parts.

He quickly closed his computer. He hated it that there were videos of him doing this to an innocent victim. Who was sending him this video? Was this blackmail?

Damon searched his brain for answers, but came up empty.

All he knew for certain was that he could have his own computer looked at by his private investigator's computer geek. Maybe he was one step closer to finding out who was running the deep web twisted torture show.

BOSSY BOSSY

When Damon arrived at work the next day, he was greeted by Mr. Styles. Mr. Styles was standing outside of Damon's office, with a briefcase in his hand. It was unusual for his boss to make the journey across the parking lot from the corporate office to Damon's office.

"It's so nice of you to decide to come in and do your job today." Mr. Styles face turned red. "We need to talk."

Damon slid his key into the door, until he heard the click of the lock. He pushed the door open, and didn't bother offering his boss a chair.

Mr. Styles laid his briefcase on Damon's desk, and started shuffling through some papers. "Here's what I'm looking for. Can you read this for me?"

Reluctantly, Damon took the papers from his boss, and silently skimmed his own employment contract with his eyes.

"You signed that. You acknowledged that

the live show would not run any longer than the time allotted. You seem to have forgotten about that. Then, you didn't call me back last night."

Damon pulled out his cellular phone, and pulled up a picture of his daughter. "This is Miranda. She arrived last night. Right after the show."

Mr. Styles smiled. "She's cute. Congratulations. That's still no excuse for the show running an extra minute long."

Damon wasn't at fault. "Blame Peter."

"It's your show. You blame Peter. This is on you. One more time, and I'm pulling the show from you." Mr. Styles collected his stuff, and left.

Damon was fuming. The network was threatening to take his own show from him. He could not allow that to happen.

The show was his creation. His love, his life. He wouldn't let anyone take that away from him.

Since Peter only showed up for rehearsal and taping, Damon had to call him into the office. Peter didn't act too happy about having to come into the office on his off day.

"One minute. What's the big deal?" Peter asked innocently.

Damon had to be firm. "The big deal? The

big deal is that not only did the network have to shave some time off of a sponsor's commercial, but the viewers missed Wilma passing out and bleeding all over the stage."

"It's not my fault!" Peter was being difficult. "I can't control how long the players take to decide!"

This started a full blown screaming match between the two men.

Damon could scream louder. "It's your job! You've been doing this long enough to know how to lead the contestants. Plus, you made a fool of yourself on television, flirting with that girl."

Hearing all the screaming, Mary ventured into Damon's office. "What is going on in here?"

Peter knew that Mary was the nice producer, even though she was just an assistant producer. "Damon is being mean about the show running long, one measly minute!"

Mary stood back and watched. She knew that Damon was not a man to be argued with. She knew better than to choose a side and anger Damon.

Damon's face turned red as he puffed up his cheeks and screamed even louder. "I'm being mean! You have the easiest job ever and you messed it up! This is your only warning. One more mess up, and I'll replace you!"

Peter was smug. "Replace me? I'm

contracted. Two years."

Damon opened the door for Peter to leave. "Get out of my sight! One more time, I'm warning you!"

Damon slammed the door behind Peter.

Mary was stuck in Damon's office, alone with him. "Calm down, Damon. Peter's not a bad guy. He will not do it again."

Damon was still fuming mad. "Do you know Mr. Styles made it a point to show me my contract this morning? To remind me of the show's time slot. He threatened to take me off the show. We both remember what happened to William when he tried to take my show from me!"

Mary knew that William died in a house fire, but now it sounded like Damon just admitted to killing him. She had suspected foul play, but she never had any proof. At the time of William's death, Damon looked super guilty, but he had an alibi.

Mary's lip quivered. "You... You killed William?"

Damon bit his tongue. He could never admit that he murdered William. Especially not to Mary. She would tell Destiny. Then Destiny would probably leave him again, taking Miranda with her.

Damon tried to calm himself. He took deep breaths. "No. He died in that explosion. It was karma. Not me. I need to be alone."

Mary knew what that meant. When Damon was in this kind of a mood, it was best to not be around him. Now she knew that Damon killed William. He practically admitted it to her. Now, she just had to decide if she should tell Destiny.

Destiny had Miranda to think about now. Mary felt the need to protect her best friend and her goddaughter from Damon. But was it the best time to tell Destiny? A new baby was a lot of work.

Mary knew now that she had to keep a close eye on Damon. She wasn't sure how she could protect them, but she vowed to herself that she would die trying.

PLANNING THE BEST SHOW EVER

After having plenty of time to cool down, Damon called a meeting with Mary and a few writers. Mary sat in the conference room, writhing her hands, fearful of why Damon would want an impromptu meeting.

Damon opened the door, and entered the room, full of confidence. He loved being the boss. When he spoke, his employees listened. And if they didn't, he could figure out a way to punish them.

Damon began the meeting with a smile. "Let me start off by saying, this has been the best season ever for the reality pain shows, and I'd like to thank each and every one of you for your hard work on the show."

A rush of relief flooded Mary as her

blood pressure dropped to an acceptable level. She thought Damon was still angry from his argument with Peter. He had obviously cooled off.

"BUT. With that being said, there is always room for improvement. Does anyone have any ideas on what we can do better?" Damon looked around the room at the blank faces.

Mary bit her tongue. Was this a trap? She already knew that Damon was in a bad mood. Did he actually want suggestions? Or did he just want an excuse to show off his own creativity to the room full of writers?

As a writer began to speak, Damon raised his hand in the air, prompting the writer to stop talking.

Damon raised a finger over his lips, like he was in deep thought. "Let me tell you what we can improve. Let's go over the top. Hardcore challenges that will bring the players to the edge, almost on the brink of death."

Mary did not like this idea. She felt like it was her duty to remind Damon of their employment contracts. They both signed legally enforced agreements that no contestant would die on the show. Mary was trembling on the inside, but found the strength to use her voice anyways. "We agreed no deaths on the show, remember?"

Damon glared in Mary's direction, his face full of contempt.

"Mary." Damon over pronounced her name to get her attention. "I said near death. NOT death. Stay with me here."

Damon shook his head at her ignorance, and continued with the meeting. "For extreme challenges, we need extreme players. That's the problem. That's why I need you." Damon pointed at each writer sitting at the conference table.

The writer who tried to speak previously knew this was now his opportunity to be heard. "We just need desperate contestants. Players who need money so bad that they'll risk death."

Damon gave a thumbs down. "We do that already. We've even had a player refuse a challenge this year. That attractive college type girl. She had to be cast by a man, and it wasn't me. Any other ideas?"

Mary had a great idea, and sat up straight as she cleared her throat. "All stars."

Damon raised an eyebrow, and looked to Mary. Even though he hated her, he was very interested in her idea. "C'mon Mary, spit it out. We can't read your mind."

"Oh yeah. Okay." Mary paused to gather her thoughts, so she could present her idea to her boss in the best possible manor. "Well, do you remember Amy? We've stayed in touch. And she wants to be on the show again."

Damon did remember Amy. She was on

the very first episode of the very first 'Easy Money'. "Brilliant. She loves pain. She shot off her pinky with that gun. I bet she would do any challenge we gave her. We can find the best players from previous seasons. We already know that they'll do any task." Damon choked back his words before complimenting Mary for her idea. He didn't want to give her any praise, even if she did actually deserve it.

It was almost like everyone else in the room disappeared as Damon ran ideas through his head. He could make a show so great that it would be remembered for some time to come. Mr. Styles would regret threatening to take him off the show.

Damon could show the network how much they needed him. He would get even better ratings than he was already getting. He would prove himself valuable to the network.

Also, another plan he had been brewing was finally coming to fruition. And of all people, Mary was the one to help him.

It was perfect! Mary would be the one to carry out the plan that would be her own downfall.

FATHERHOOD

Damon picked up his wife and baby from the hospital for their first night together as a perfect little family. He held Miranda in his arms and rocked her gently. She was the most perfect baby ever with her head full of dark fuzzy hair and brown eyes.

Destiny daunted over the baby, refusing to leave the child's side. Damon could already tell that she was going to be a wonderful mother, tending to the baby's every want and need.

Damon admired his small bundle of joy as Destiny put her breasts in the baby's mouth to feed. He watched as his daughter made little fistballs with her hand as it sucked from his wife's nipple.

It was probably the cutest thing that Damon had ever witnessed. Then, the feeding was done. Destiny handed Miranda to Damon, and told him to pat the baby on it's tiny back. It stopped being cute as the child vomited a juicy liquid all over his nice button down shirt.

Destiny laughed as Damon handed the baby back to its mother. Damon didn't remember doing any of this kind of stuff when his son had been a baby. He realized that he didn't have much to do with his son in the nurturing kind of way. Damon didn't have a nurturing bone in his body.

Destiny was exhausted and fell asleep with Miranda coddled to her chest. Damon took the child and laid her in a cradle in their bedroom, and led Destiny to bed.

He watched as mother and child slept peacefully. For only a few minutes. Then Miranda started crying.

Destiny was so tired that she slept through the child's screams.

Damon checked the diaper, and of course it was dirty. He was wiping poop off his daughter's bottom, when she urinated all over his hand.

After cleaning himself and the baby, he finally rocked Miranda back to sleep. He laid in bed watching the vile creature softly breathe. He couldn't figure out how such a cute creature could be so disgusting. Miranda had only been home for an evening, and she had already threw up and peed on him. Damon knew that he wasn't cut out to be a father.

He was envious of his wife who had slept peacefully through this horrible evening. The baby refused to sleep, waking Damon every hour.

Damon closed his eyes, taking the opportunity to sleep while the vicious child allowed him a few moments of peace.

Destiny woke, feeling completely refreshed from her long night of sleep. She found a disheveled Damon in the kitchen, trying to get the baby to take a bottle.

Damon's eyes were red, his hair was messy all over his head, and the bags under his eyes showed how tired he really was.

"Good morning Daddy! Isn't she just lovely?" Destiny kissed Miranda on her little head.

Damon did not think it was a good morning. He had gotten very little sleep, due to the baby crying every couple of hours.

Damon's tired eyes looked at his wife. "I thought the baby crying would wake you last night, but you proved me wrong. How did you sleep all night last night?"

Destiny laughed. "The hospital gave me something for the pain. I guess it knocked me out." She kissed Damon on his cheek, and swept his hair from his eyes.

"Aha! That's why I couldn't wake you. I don't know what to do. I haven't slept at all. I don't know if I can do this." Damon was so mad at life right now.

Destiny was taken back. "What do you mean can't do this? Marriage? The baby? Fatherhood? What?" She was now frantic.

Damon was thinking in his head *yes, yes, and yes*. But knew not to tell Destiny that. "I'm sorry dear. I meant I don't know if I can work without much sleep." Whew. He covered himself well.

Destiny chuckled. "Oh? That? No big deal. I'll call Mary. I'm sure she'll help you out today."

That's the last person Damon wanted any help from, but in this position he had no other choice. However, Mary would be helping him in more ways than she knew.

CASTING ALL STARS

Damon showed up at work looking like crud, and walked straight past Mary's desk, and into his own office. She followed him inside, and he laid down on his couch, and instantly fell asleep.

Destiny had already called and warned Mary that Damon was tired. Mary didn't mind. She wanted to take charge of the all stars show. She almost feared what would happen if Damon was in charge of everything.

Mary did not want another Marty Blevins blunder. She shuddered at the memory of the woodchipper eating Marty Blevins alive, spitting out chunks of blood and flesh.

Mary already had a cast outlined. Naturally, she had kept in touch with many of the past players over the years.

She had the strongest bond with Amy. Amy was where the show started. She was the original contestant that Mary had especially hand picked for the first episode.

Amy just loved pain. Plus, she loved all the publicity that came with being on the show.

Mary had also asked Jasmine if she wanted to reappear on the show. Jasmine was from an episode of 'Pain for Gain'. At the time, she had a sick baby, and let her husband hurt her on live television for the baby's sake. Mary learned that even after the show, viewers had also sent donations to help the baby.

Jasmine agreed to come back on the show to show appreciation for the viewers that cared about her baby.

From 'Hurt Bank', Mary wanted Tony to be on the show. Just because he was a trooper. To pay his sick wife's medical bills he had plucked his own eyeball out of his face. If he could do that, he could do anything.

Mary shuffled through the papers on Damon's desk, seeing if he had any notes of what he planned for this special episode. Damon was snoring so loud, he didn't even budge as she made noise and turned on the light.

After finding the papers that she needed, she tiptoed out of his office, and quietly closed his office door behind her.

She had to decipher his handwritten

notes, but she saw a few of his jotted down ideas.

She started putting the prop list together. She needed a chainsaw, a snow blower, and a blowtorch.

Mary was relieved that she was the one putting this show together. With her being in charge, she didn't have to worry about Damon staging anymore deadly accidents.

ERRANDS

Damon woke up after a full day of sleeping on the couch in his office. He felt good. He dreaded going home to the house with the crying baby. He didn't know if he could survive another night with Miranda.

As he walked past Mary's desk, he had an idea. "Mary, I'm gonna surprise Destiny with something special for her and the baby, so I'm gonna run to the store before I go home. Do me a favor? Don't tell Destiny what time I left work, okay?"

Mary agreed. She knew that Destiny loved surprises. Mary was impressed that Damon was taking his role as a father seriously.

Mary entertained the idea that maybe the baby would persuade Damon to change his ways. She decided it would be best to not tell Destiny that Damon practically admitted to killing William.

Damon planned a quiet evening all to himself. First, he had to make a quick stop to see his private investigator. He needed to drop his own computer off , and have his computer looked at. Surely, they could find out who had sent him those videos.

Then, he wanted to go back to Candy's place. After the horrible night he had lived through, he thought he deserved a little bit of playtime. Spending more time with Candy would be Damon's way of rewarding himself for taking such good care of the baby the night before.

When he arrived, he had no plans, no motive. Other than to see her in pain. Luckily, with the heroin in her system he could do practically anything to her.

Once again, Candy had the eye patch covering her eye.

Damon scoffed at his toy. "You must like looking like a pirate. Did you go to the doctor?"

Candy shook her head no. "I spent the money. But I did get my hands on some antibiotics. I figured that's all I need anyways."

Damon felt his blood boil. "I was just here a few nights ago. I left you thousands of dollars. What could you have possibly spent that kind of money on?"

Candy shrugged her shoulders. "I needed

some stuff."

Damon flicked his angry eyes towards her. "By stuff, you mean dope."

Candy got defensive. "What are you? My father now?"

The word father resonated in Damon's head. He was a father. Certainly not Candy's father, but still he was Miranda's father. Then the thoughts hit him again that Candy was somebody's daughter.

Having struggled with his inner demons for some time now, he realized it was a losing battle. No matter how hard he tried to be good, he just wasn't.

Even the gift of creating a precious life wasn't enough to change him into a better man.

Damon just sighed. "Okay then. Let me see it. Maybe I need to do some work to it."

Candy, being high, wasn't thinking straight and agreed. She removed the eye patch, revealing a festering mess of puss and blood. Where he had put the cigarette out left behind a large blister on her eyelid. Her eyelid was like an open sore, swollen with red lines tracing into her forehead and cheeks.

Damon was thinking that he could do the right thing and take her to the hospital. It looked like the infection was spreading.

Or he could use this to advantage. She already had a weak spot. He could easily hurt her.

It only took a couple of seconds for Damon to realize that it just wasn't in him to get this poor girl medical attention.

"I tell you what. I think it needs more vodka poured in it. A whole lot of vodka. Plus, maybe I could stitch it closed. That might make it heal faster. Do you have a needle and thread?" Damon knew that stitching it wouldn't help her. It would just cause her immense pain.

Candy reached for her needle of poisonous drugs, and Damon didn't stop her. He wanted her passed out for this. He could sew her eye closed, and she wouldn't know it until after he was long gone. Damon laughed.

This was the best kind of errand ever.

DOCTOR DAHMER

Candy passed out with a needle still hanging in her arm. Damon knew it would only be a matter of time until she overdosed anyways. In the larger scheme of things, an infected eyelid was a minor problem.

Damon examined the needle as he plucked it from her flesh. He wished he could use something like this to make Miranda sleep at night.

Damon pushed that thought from his mind. His job was to protect Miranda, not harm her. He would just have to make sure Destiny started doing her job as a mother. He would just have to make his wife wake up to feed and change the baby.

He couldn't stop thinking about home. Here he was, with a small knife in hand, and an unconscious woman beneath him, yet his mind drifted to his child.

The infected wound grabbed his attention once again, and Damon used the sharp side of the blade to slice into Candy's delicate eyelid. As he sliced into the blister, an inner layer of skin exposed itself. Fresh blood flowed down, caking up in her eyelashes. Candy didn't even flinch.

Damon positioned both his thumbs around her eyelid, and squeezed. Fresher blood, mixed with the thick puss escaped from the incision.

Just for good measure, he poured the entire contents of the bottle of vodka on her eyelid. The alcohol cleansed away the bodily fluids, exposing a gaping wound in her eyelid.

Damon had never even sewed a button onto a shirt, nevertheless had he stitched human flesh before. He figured that it couldn't be too hard. He had watched the doctor do it after Miranda had been born.

Damon could have chosen just to sew the wound together. But what fun would that be?

Instead he inserted the point of the needle all the way through Candy's upper eyelid, then led it to her lower eyelid. He pulled tight on the thread to ensure that it was tight. There would be no way she would be able to open her eye tomorrow. Hopefully, she wouldn't cut the stitches.

Maybe, instead of tending to her eye, she would just get high and pass out again.

Damon circled the needle back around to the wound on her upper eyelid. He forced the needle to hard, and the tip of the needle stabbed her eyeball. A small speck of blood surfaced into the white part of her eye.

That didn't stop Damon. He continued on with his work, and shoved the tiny point into her lower eyelid, once again pulling the thread tight to close her eye.

He circled the needle around her eyelids many times, until her lids were entirely covered with thread. At one point when he jabbed her actual eyeball, she almost woke up.

Candy's head jerked. Her other eye almost opened, and Damon remained still, until she fell back to her state of unconsciousness.

When Damon was pleased that her eye was sufficiently sewed closed, he put the needle away.

He looked at her eye. The thread had already absorbed so much blood that the stitches were now red. Her eyelids were bunched together, where he made the stitches too close and too tight.

He left without leaving her any cash. He didn't want her to buy too many drugs. He didn't want her to overdose. At least not yet.

HERE AGAIN

As soon as Damon walked in his front door, he was greeted by a screaming baby.

Destiny rushed towards him. "She won't stop crying! I don't know what to do! You take her."

Damon backed away, crossing his arms refusing to hold Miranda. "You're her mother. You need to learn." He was firm with his words, using a tone that meant business.

Destiny turned into a nagging wife. "It's late. Where have you been?"

Damon turned on his charm, smiling the largest grin that he could muster. Luckily, he had time to do some shopping before he got home.

He pulled a small box out of his suit jacket pocket, and held it in the palm of his hand.

His wife was happy. She threw her arms around his neck as she snatched the box from his hand.

Destiny used her petite fingers to open the

gift. It was a sparkling gold necklace, with a large stone pendant.

"It's Miranda's birthstone." Damon kissed her on her cheek. "I thought it was appropriate for you to have it."

Miranda continued to cry as Damon helped Destiny put the necklace on.

Destiny looked into her husband's eyes and saw a sincere man. A man who was dedicated to their family.

She pulled Damon in close to her, ignoring the crying child. She pressed her lips to his.

Damon explained how tired he was from a rough day at the office, and hoped that Mary hadn't called her best friend to tell her how he had slept all day at work.

He asked very nicely that Destiny tend to the baby that night. He needed his energy for work. He was on a tight deadline. He was working on a live show.

Destiny was still ecstatic from her expensive gift, and told Damon that she'd let him rest that night. Her husband had been so thoughtful, and he worked so hard to provide for their family. The least she could do was be a good mother to their daughter.

Destiny didn't know much about being a mother. But she was willing to learn. Even if it meant never sleeping again, she would do everything in her power to keep Miranda and Damon happy.

BEFORE THE SHOW (SET UP)

Damon was still in his office, running just a few minutes late. The all stars live show would be starting soon, but he still had some last minute details to cover.

He couldn't find Amy's contract. Without her contract, she couldn't be on the show, and she was the most popular player ever. Amy had to be on the show.

Damon buzzed Mary on her earpiece. "Mary, I messed up. I guess it's lack of sleep with the baby. I lost Amy's contract. I'm gonna get you a new one. Can you get her to sign it before she goes on?"

Mary scurried to Damon's office to retrieve the papers. It was very important that Amy be on the show. Her fans were waiting to see her encore performance.

Once Damon finally made it to the studio, he had one last thing to do. He stopped by the prop room. The crew didn't even notice him as he admired the blow torch, chainsaw, and the snow blower.

Mary stopped by the contestant waiting room/ dressing area. She finally made it to Amy's room with just a few minutes to spare.

Amy was applying some thick make up to her cheeks to give her a punky look.

"Whew! I just ran all the way over here from the offices. We lost your contract." Mary stopped to catch her breath. "Do you mind signing it again?"

Amy signed the paper, no questions asked.

"Thanks so much for bringing me back! I'm so excited!" Amy hugged her friend.

It was moments like this when Mary loved her job. Even though tonight was gonna hurt, Amy loved every minute of it.

EASY MONEY
ALL STARS LIVE

"Welcome to a very special episode of 'Easy Money'! I'm Peter Conway, and I wanna take a moment to thank each and every one of the viewers for making 'Easy Money' the most watched show on television. We have two full hours of show tonight! And we have brought back some of the favorite players of all time! It is with great pleasure that I present to you the all star version of 'Easy Money'! Tonight's stunts will be extreme! Bloodier, gorier, more disgusting! Do not try this at home. Viewer discretion is advised. Now on with the show!" Peter was relieved that he had two hours of show tonight. He was told to spend plenty of time talking to each player.

Damon sat in a producer's chair, and got comfortable. He was excited to see this show.

"First tonight, we have Jasmine. Come on out Jasmine." Peter welcomed the first player of the night.

Damon didn't really remember this contestant. When she appeared on 'Pain for Gain', he hadn't even bother to learn her name.

Jasmine limped out onto the stage.

"I see you still have a limp. Let's remind the viewers how you earned that limp." Peter pointed towards a large movie screen that hung above the stage.

A video started to play, and there was a husband and wife, trying to decide who would do which portion of the challenge. Jasmine was adamant when she said she would be on the pain receiving end of the task. The video played in slow motion as her husband raised a pair of bolt cutters to her achilles tendon. The playback slowed down even slower as the sharp blades of the tool snipped into the back of her foot.

A puddle of blood instantly appeared beneath her foot.

Jasmine turned her head, not wanting to watch the video.

Peter put his arm around the player. "That's rough to watch, huh? Tell us what was happening there."

Jasmine looked into the camera. "At that time, my baby, she was sick. I vowed that I would do anything to save her life, and I did. We couldn't afford her treatment. If I have to live with a limp, I don't mind. Also, I wanna say thanks to all the viewers that showed us their support even after the show. So I'm back tonight. Hoping to give y'all an even better performance tonight!" The contestant was full of vigor and energy.

Peter used his loudest television voice to keep up with the player's enthusiasm. "Are you ready to earn $500,000?"

Jasmine jumped for joy. "Are you serious?"

"I'm serious. This is the all star show, it comes with all star prizes!" Peter smiled into the camera.

Jasmine stopped jumping, fearful of her next question. "What do I have to do?"

A curtain raised behind Peter, and he turned around to look at it. "I know this looks complicated, but it really isn't."

The curtain revealed a chair backed up against a wall, with some sort of a tall arm stemming from the back of the chair.

"Sit down, and I'll show you."

Jasmine sat down. A prop guy brought something out to Peter.

Peter held up the object. "This is a blow torch. It clamps into the piece of the chair right here. Then I adjust it. Right next to your ear. When you pull this string, this blow torch will breathe fire into your ear for three full seconds."

Jasmine stood up. "Fire? In my ear? Are you serious?"

Peter shook his head yes. "Unfortunately, I'm very serious. But remember, this challenge is for $500,000!"

The audience cheered with enthusiasm, encouraging Jasmine to play.

Damon sat up straight in his chair, with his face close to the monitor. He had been looking forward to a decent blow torch challenge since last season of 'Hurt Bank'.

Jasmine looked into the crowd and saw the hundreds of people cheering her on. These were the same people who had sent her money when she needed it. The least she could do was put on a good show for them.

Jasmine was sweating under the bright lights, beads of the moisture popping out of the wrinkles on her forehead. She sat down in the chair, and looked at the blowtorch attached next to her head.

"And you say it's only three seconds?" Jasmine questioned the host.

Peter shook his head yes. "It's only three seconds. It will be over before you know it." Peter tried his best to get her to complete the challenge. He needed to do something to get back on Damon's good side.

Jasmine hesitated as she thought about the damage the blow torch could do to her head. She wondered if she would go deaf from this challenge. She pulled her hair onto the other side of her head.

She tried to think about what she could do with half a million dollars. That was a lot of money.

The more she thought about the task given to her, the harder she cried. She looked at her foot, and remembered the pain from a clipped achilles tendon. She lived through that, and she would live through this, too.

Thinking made it worse. She shut off her mind, and raised her fingers to the chain string dangling from the blow torch.

The audience went silent. Peter turned his head to look away. Damon scooted his nose even closer to his monitor, which was a camera view zoomed in close to the side of Jasmine's head.

Jasmine pulled the string. *Whoooosh.* Three seconds felt like an eternity, even though it was rather quick. She didn't even have time to pull her head away from the flame's path of destruction.

Damon watched as the flames devoured Jasmine's porcelain skin. Her cheek and the side of her forehead turned red, then blister like wounds bubbled up on the side of her head. The cartilage of her ear melted into the bone of her skull.

A clear mucus like fluid surfaced, and oozed down her cheek. Jasmine's face was frozen with pain. Her first instinct was to touch her wounds. But as her hand brushed up against the melting skin, all of her nerves reminded her that it was too painful to touch.

Even though Peter hadn't been watching, he saw the aftermath. He knew that he had to congratulate her on winning the money, but he couldn't produce any words. It took a few moments before he could speak.

Medical was already on stage, ushering Jasmine backstage.

Peter finally produced a voice, barely louder than a whisper. "Congratulations, Jasmine! You just won a half million dollars of easy money!"

EASY MONEY
ALL STARS
TONY

Peter welcomed the next player onto the stage. "Welcome Tony. You're looking a lot better than the last time I saw you."

Tony shook his head in agreement.

"Just curious, what brings you back tonight?" Peter asked the player.

"My wife. She's still sick. Hospital bills are breaking us." Tony appeared to be strong, despite his last appearance on 'Hurt Bank'.

"I'm sorry to hear that. Let's remind the players of your last performance." Peter turned towards the large movie screen once again.

The first scene was Tony injecting a staple from a staple gun into his navel. Then the video played in slow motion, as Tony inserted a spoon around his eye. He shoved the spoon into his eye socket, and twisted the spoon until his eyeball plopped out his orbital bones.

Peter cringed. "How's the eye doing?"

Tony was doing surprisingly well. "The doctors fixed me right up. Would you believe that didn't hurt as bad as it looks? The doc put my eye back in, and I haven't had any problems with it since."

Damon remembered this player well. Tony thought that he was tougher than Damon's challenges. Tonight, Damon would remind this man that he wasn't as tough as he looked.

Tony continued talking. "Pain is temporary. I need money. I can do this. No matter what task you give me."

That was exactly what Damon was counting on.

The crowd went crazy, anticipating what Tony would have to do to himself.

Peter laughed. "I'm so glad you said that. Because this next task is intended for a tough player."

Tony beat himself on his chest in a barbaric fashion. "Well then it's a good thing that I'm a tough guy."

"Are you ready to earn $500,000?" Peter kept the high energy flowing through the studio.

Tony beat himself on his chest even harder. "I sure am. Just tell me what to do!"

A prop crew member came out from

backstage, and laid a chainsaw on a table.

Tony's eyes enlarged, and he finally started to show some fear. "What do I have to do with that?"

Peter simply stated the facts. "Cut off your own leg."

Tony sounded like a small child arguing with their parents. "That's not fair! It's not like I will grow another leg!"

Peter shook his head. "Maybe if the cut isn't too jagged maybe a doctor could reattach your leg." Peter shrugged his shoulders and stressed his next word. "MAAYYBBEEE"

"I need the cash. You really think they might be able to sew it back on?" Tony questioned the television host, as if he had a medical degree or something.

Peter didn't respond.

It was so silent in the studio that you could've heard a pin drop.

Peter broke the silence. "What are you gonna do?"

Damon was pleased. This tough player wasn't so brave now. He was no longer pounding on his chest like some alpha male.

Tony's lip quivered. "I guess I'm gonna chainsaw my leg off."

The audience jumped to their feet and cheered. Their energy was contagious because Tony started cheering with them.

Peter picked up the saw, and it was heavier

than he expected. He quickly handed it off to Tony. Like the macho man he was pretending to be, Tony raised the chainsaw above his head.

After giving the crowd adequate time to cheer, Peter began to speak again.

"We've supplied two chairs, over here for you. Perhaps the best method would be sitting. However, that's completely up to you."

Tony walked over to both of the chairs, thinking about his strategy. After a few brief moments, Tony plopped his butt into one of the chairs. He practiced the best angle to hold the chainsaw.

Without the tool powered on, he practiced swiping it right above his ankle.

Tony then raised his other leg into the chair opposite of him, with his foot flat on the seat. He felt comfortable in this position. He had to overextend his reach to get to the lower half of his leg, but it worked for him.

After being patient for long enough, Peter decided to interject. "Anytime you're ready Tony."

Tony's beady eyes looked into the camera. "Here goes nothing!"

Tony pulled on the pull string. The chainsaw purred very loud, rumbling like thunder. Tony's hands vibrated with the machinery. Maybe it was forced by the tool, maybe he trembled with fear.

Tony brought the moving blade down on

the top of his shin, and blood splattered in his eyes. The machine started smoking as it hit resistance.

Tony dropped the chainsaw, and it slowly powered down, a safety feature.

The camera zoomed in on Tony's leg. His flesh had been ripped open, the bone protruding through the skin. Blood dripped off his calf, forming a red pool below him.

"I can't do it! I just can't do it!" Tony screamed in pain.

Peter reminded the player of the rules. "You have to cut your leg off. You've only sawed half way through it. Do you want to earn easy money or not?"

Tony hollered like a wounded animal. "I quit! I can't do it!"

Medical came out with a bed on wheels, and wheeled Tony off the stage.

Peter looked into the camera. "How unfortunate for Tony. He did not win any easy money! Still, let's give him a hand!"

The crowd cheered even though he didn't complete the task. They got to see blood anyways.

Damon was proud of himself. Tony didn't prove himself to be too tough. Damon had outplayed the player.

EASY MONEY
AMY

"Now, for the player we have been waiting for all night! Come on out Amy!" Peter clapped along with the audience.

Amy walked out, donning her normal facial piercings and arms full of tattoos. The camera zoomed in her nub of a pinky finger.

Peter shook her hand. "Amy! One of our very first contestants ever! How are you feeling tonight?"

Amy grinned from ear to ear, unable to contain her happiness. "I'm so glad to be back. I'm glad I have the opportunity to win big money. When I played, the cash prizes were low. And I'll tell you what's even better than the money. After the show, my social media blew up. I was an internet celebrity. Everybody wanted to be my friend."

"For our new viewers, let's remind them of your performance on the very first 'Easy

Money' ever!" Peter directed his attention to a video on the screen.

At first the video was Amy piercing her ears with the staple gun, then shooting staples in her shoulder. Then the video slowed down, as Amy raised a hand gun. She held her other hand out in front of her. The video played so slow, you could see the bullet strike her pinky, and splattering it all over the glass cube.

Peter just shook his head. "Wow!"

"I know right?" Amy was proud of herself. "I became a household name after that. I did so many publicity interviews. And I have the scars to remember it by!" Amy held her missing pinky up for the cameras to see.

"If I remember right, you just love pain?" Peter questioned the player.

Amy shook her head to agree. "That's right. I feel alive when I'm hurtin'."

"Do you wanna feel alive and earn $500,000?" Peter emphasized the money amount.

"What do I gotta do? I'll do it!"

Damon got extra comfy in his chair. At last, this was what he had waited for all night.

A curtain raised behind Peter, revealing a large machine.

Amy pointed at the contraption. "What's that thing?"

Peter looked at Amy as he answered her. "That's a snowblower. It removes snow. It has razor sharp blades to break up ice and snow. It suctions it up, then spits it out."

Amy tried to be playful. "I guess we don't see too many of those around here, with this warm weather here."

Peter laughed along with the contestant, trying to make her feel more comfortable.

Amy stopped laughing suddenly. "Okay. Now I know what it is. What do I have to do?'

Peter held his hand in the air. "Stick one of your hands in the rotating blades."

Amy looked at her crippled hand already missing the smallest finger. She took a deep breath, then shrugged her shoulders.

"Okay. Let's get this over with."

The crowd jumped to their feet, the loudest roar of the night. They were gonna see the machine devour her hand and spit blood all across the stage, along with chunks of flesh.

Amy gulped, but didn't hesitate as she walked over to the snowblower. She wanted her fans to recognize her bravery. Afterall, she was Amy, the contestant that just loved pain.

Peter told her how to turn the machine on, and she did it. The machine sprang to life, it's sounds offending Amy's sense of sound.

Amy bent down and felt the air swooshing into the machine, and that was when she was struck with fear. She looked at the audience. They were watching her. She didn't want to let her fans down.

Amy watched as the metal blades rotated. She looked at her already damaged hand, and decided to just get it over with.

The camera zoomed in on her hand with only four digits as she fed the angry machine.

The first moment that her human flesh collided with the metal, she knew that she had messed up. The pain started in her hand, then her wrist, running up to her elbow.

People watched as the machine spit chunks of Amy's arm onto the stage, spraying blood everywhere.

When the pain reached Amy's elbow, she tried with all of her might to pull away from the machine. The suction was too great. She couldn't get out of the machine's path of destruction.

By the time the pain was in her shoulder, her entire arm had gone numb, obviously because it was no longer attached to her body.

The machine continued to suck Amy into it. Everyone watched as the force of the suction forced Amy to lie flat on the stage.

The snowblower eventually vacuumed Amy's entire body into its rotating blades. By the time it was all over with, chunks of Amy littered the stage, lying in puddles of blood.

The screen went black for the home viewers. The network had cut the live feed.

People in the audience sat frozen and quiet, shocked by what they had just seen.

Damon smiled. His plan was now in play.

Mary cried for her friend. She had been helpless as she watched Amy die on live television.

"I quit! I can't do this anymore!" Peter yanked his microphone off his shirt, and stomped his way offstage.

AFTER THE SHOW (REST OF PLAN)

Damon's phone went crazy with texts and phone calls. Naturally, his boss, Mr. Styles had been calling. A death of a contestant was obviously stated in his contract as grounds of dismissal.

Damon almost answered the phone call from his boss, but a text caught his attention instead. It was from his private investigator.

That video sent to your computer came from within your own office.

Damon searched his mind for answers. Who in his office had been involved with the dark web?

It didn't matter right now, Damon had to go see his boss, and go forward with his plan.

Mr. Styles was strumming his fingers on his desk, waiting for Mary and Damon's arrival.

Damon had to pull Mary out of her grief long enough to drag her to Mr. Styles' office.

Damon led his assistant producer to a chair directly across from Mr. Styles.

Mr. Styles began screaming as soon as they walked through the threshold of the door. "You're fired! Both of you! How are we gonna clean this up?"

Damon hid a smile as he looked to Mary and her tear streaked face.

Mary said nothing. She couldn't because she was crying too hard.

Damon finally spoke. "I had nothing to do with this show. In all honesty, I've been at work, but sleeping on the couch in my office ever since the birth of Miranda. Mary planned all of this."

Mary had a hard time comprehending Damon's words, but it sounded like he had just blamed her. She was the good producer, not capable of hurting anyone.

Mary lashed out at Damon. "Me! Amy was my friend!"

Mr. Styles watched as both of the producers had their own screaming match.

Damon lashed back at Mary. "Did you, or did you not get the props?" Of course, Damon omitted the part that he visited the prop room prior to the show and made a few adjustments to the snowblower making it too powerful.

Mary tried to speak. "Yes, but.."

Damon cut her off. "I have Amy's contract right here. It has a death clause. In case of death the network isn't liable. Did you or did you not get Amy to sign this right before the show?" Once again, Damon didn't admit to being the person that added the death clause to the newly revised contract.

Now Mr. Styles was really mad. "A death clause? We don't have a death clause. We took that out after season one! We ensured the network that no more players would die! Is this true Mary?"

Mary was shocked. "Well, I took it to her to sign it. But I didn't add the death clause!"

Mr. Styles directed all his attention to Mary. "You mean to tell me you had her sign something you didn't read? I don't believe it!"

"Damon lost the original contract. At least that's what he said. He gave it to me at the last minute. The show was getting ready to go on. We needed a signed contract from Amy!" It all started making sense to Mary. Damon had somehow set her up, and she didn't even have a clue that it was happening. She finally realized how evil Damon really was.

Mr. Styles shifted his focus to Damon. "Damon! Is that true?"

"I've had lack of sleep. I haven't even been working. Mary did it all!" Damon was ecstatic. He was going to teach Mary a lesson about what happens to people who lie to him.

"Mary. Leave us. I need to speak with Damon."

Mary left the office, but stopped outside the door. She had to know how Mr. Styles was going to handle this situation. She stood and pressed her ear to the door to hear her bosses.

Mr. Styles slammed his hand on his desk. "That's low. Pinning this on Mary. After everything I've done for you!"

Damon got defensive. "After everything you've done for me? What have you done for me? After Marty Blevin's death, you suspended me. Ever since you've been on my back about work. Reminding me of my employment contract. You haven't done anything for me!"

Suddenly, it hit Damon. The videos had come from his own office. Mr. Styles was behind the dark web show.

"You! You're the one blackmailing me! You wanted to use Destiny to get to me!"

Mr. Styles shook his head. "You better watch what you say in here. This isn't the time or the place."

Damon refused. "I will not watch what I say! You're running the web show. Murdering defenseless women!"

Mr. Styles calmed his voice, afraid of

someone hearing his words. "And you fit right into that world. I have videos of what you're capable of. I was giving you an outlet for your anger. Plus, it was very profitable. Then what about David?"

Mary pressed her ear to the door harder. David? Her boyfriend who had disappeared. How did Mr. Styles know David?

Mr. Styles smiled. "Does Mary know you killed him? I could show her the video. It's all on tape."

Damon saw red. He could no longer control himself. He lunged across the desk, grabbing Mr. Styles around his throat. He found every ounce of strength within him. He finally figured out who had been blackmailing him. He finally had a hold of the man that forced him to kill on camera. Mr. Styles had used Destiny as a pawn to force Damon onto his dark web show.

Mary barged back into the room, startled by Mr. Styles gargles for help.

Damon stared Mr. Styles right into his eyes as he strangled the life out of him. Mr. Styles tried to struggle, but he was no match for Damon.

"Damon! Stop! You're killing him." Mary tried to pry Damon's hands from the man's throat, but Damon was not deterred.

"This man! He put me through hell! He threatened Destiny! I cannot let him live!"

A minute or so later, Mr. Styles body

had gone limp and lifeless. Mary backed away, fearful of Damon. She did the only thing that she knew to do. She pulled out her cell phone.

Damon thought for a moment, debating whether or not he had to kill Mary now.

Mary raised her phone in the air. Damon saw on the screen that it read *Destiny*. It was on speakerphone.

BACK TO REALITY

A tired voice, Destiny's voice, filled the room. "Hello."

Mary in a panic, started talking. "Damon. He killed David. And Amy. I just watched him strangle Mr. Styles!"

Destiny screamed into the phone. "Mary, you're not making any sense. What are you saying!"

Mary was still frantic. "He's a murderer. He's cold hearted. You have to leave now! He's gonna kill me next!"

A single tear fell down Damon's cheek. He had tried to hide his true self from Destiny, but now he was exposed. Damon approached Mary, and hatefully plucked the phone from her hand.

Damon didn't know what to say. "Destiny. I'm sorry. I need you. You can help me."

"What? It's true? No Damon! No. It can't

be! No!" Destiny's words were hard to make out through her tears.

Damon realized that his wife was not going to ever accept him for who he was.

"Kiss the baby for me. Remind her that I love her." Damon dropped the phone, and ran out of the office.

CANDY CRUSHED

Damon raced across town. He knew what he had to do. He just needed a pen and a piece of paper. Destiny and Miranda deserved better than him.

This night had gone terribly wrong. Mary was supposed to have been the bad guy tonight. Mary should be the one ate up with guilt.

Instead, it was Damon wondering how he could now live with himself with all of his secrets exposed.

Damon arrived at Candy's in a rage. He banged on her door, until she answered, thankful that she hadn't passed out.

Damon grabbed Candy by her arms and threw her down on the bed.

"What's into you? You like it rough?" Candy tried to flirt. She was unaware of the danger in Damon's eyes.

Damon climbed on top of Candy's frail

body and pulled off her eye patch. Her eye was an oozing mess that made Damon gag. The stench coming from her face was the worst smell Damon had ever had to suffer through. He tried to refrain himself from vomiting all over her face, but he couldn't.

Everything he had eaten that day came spewing out of his mouth, all over her face.

Candy tried to squirm loose from Damon's grip, but he held her wrists too tight.

"That's sick! Get off of me!" Candy tried to kick Damon off of her, but he was too strong.

This was what Damon wanted. He wanted his playtoy to be alive, not unconscious from the dope. All it took was spraying her face with vomit.

Damon pinned Candy's arms to the bed with his knees, and placed his hands on her face.

He used one hand on the upper part of her eye, and another hand on the lower part of her eye. He pried her eye open, the stitches giving to his strength.

Pieces of her eye lid tore off with the thread, and blood ran down her face.

Damon enjoyed her screams, and wanted to hear more.

Damon smeared his thumb into her bleeding wounds of her eye.

Then, Damon got paranoid. He could've sworn he heard a neighbor. He got off Candy.

"I'm sorry. I was just trying to help you." Damon pulled some cash out of his pocket.

Candy cried, the tears mixing with blood, staining her face with red trails. She reached for her drug kit, exactly what Damon wanted her to do.

She found a vein and inserted the needle into her pale flesh. She pressed down on the plunger, and instantly passed out.

Quickly, Damon filled the syringe with more of the poison. He tapped the end of the needle, and examined her eyeball. He stuck the needle into her pupil, and released the heroin straight into her eyeball.

He hoped it was enough to cause her overdose. Damon searched the room for a pen and paper, and scribbled a note. His last words to his wife and daughter.

He collected the cash from the table, and left.

HEARTBREAK/ GRIEF

Destiny was still trying to make sense of everything that happened. Mary showed up at her house, wanting to protect her best friend and goddaughter from the monster that Damon revealed himself to be.

Mary calmed down long enough to explain everything. She told Destiny everything. How Damon had practically admitted to killing William. How he tried to blame Mary for Amy's death. Also, how Mr. Styles said he had video of Damon killing David.

Mary had loved David, and David had also proved himself to be a great friend to Destiny.

Destiny was hearing Mary's words, but she just couldn't comprehend the seriousness of the situation.

When Mary went into detail, explaining how she had watched with her own eyes as

Damon strangled Mr. Styles to death, Destiny couldn't do anything but cry.

Destiny knew that Damon had a dark side, but she had no clue that it was this dark.

Mary reached for her phone. She had completely forgotten to call the police, due to her worry for Destiny.

Destiny's phone rang and they both froze, thinking it would be Damon calling. But it wasn't. It was a phone number that Destiny didn't recognize.

Mary drove Destiny to the police station, just liked the police had requested. They wouldn't tell her anything over the phone, but Destiny knew it would be bad news. She feared that her husband had been arrested.

Mary rocked Miranda in her arms, trying to calm the fussy baby. It was almost like Miranda could sense that something was terribly wrong.

A police officer took Destiny into a room, and Mary watched through the glass window. The officer said something, and Destiny clutched her newly adorned necklace and collapsed to the floor, crying on her knees.

Damon's car had been found on a bridge. It was abandoned and a note was attached to the steering wheel.

Destiny,

I'm so sorry. I have a demon in me. You deserve better.

Tell Miranda how much I love her. Tell her that my legacy will live on through her. I have always loved you in my own way, and that's why you're better off with me dead.

The police said that they were searching the river for any traces of Damon's body, but they hadn't found anything yet.

AFTERWARDS (CUBA, MAYBE?)

A hungover man stumbled into another bar. The wind was blowing up the dirt outside. The man closed the door behind him, and made his way to a barstool. He chose the stool closest to the bartender.

The mirror behind all of the alcohol bottles revealed the man's reflection, and he hardly recognized himself. His hair had grown long, his face was scruffy. He hadn't shaved in days.

He was far from the man that he used to be. The man he used to be wouldn't leave the house with any stubble on his face. Now he was just another unkempt man, dressed in clothes stained with dirt.

The man snapped his fingers to get the bartender's attention. "Bourbon. On the rocks. Now!" He was a very demanding customer.

The bartender looked at the man and just

shook his head no.

The man angrily pounded his fist on the bar. "What? No bourbon? What's wrong with this country?"

The bartender spat on the floor. "Gringo. Go back to where you came from."

A woman's laugh caught the man's attention. He turned around to see an attractive woman wearing a short skirt sitting with another woman.

"Fine. Beer. That'll do." The man took his drink, and stumbled over to where the women with the dark skin were sitting.

The man patted his pocket. "Hello, ladies. Who here wants to make a little money?"

KEEP READING FOR BONUS CONTENT

Note from the author.... Then some bonus content...

Well, I guess that's the end of the Deadly Reality TV Series (maybe), but it's not the end of Damon Dahmer. Now available "Damon Dahmer and Sly Verdict", a 2 book series where Damon is teamed up with Sly Verdict (from Verdict Realty, a 3 book series of extreme horror).

Follow or like my Facebook page (Sea Caummisar) or Twitter (@Seacaummisar) to stay up to date on whatever books I'm writing. I'm working on a couple of ideas, but I must warn you, they're kinda dark. (Viewer discretion is advised!!!)

Let me know what you thought about the series. Thanks bunches for reading. See ya next read.

Bonus content next

An unaired 'Pain For Gain' episode….. And a real life experience

PAIN FOR GAIN BANNED EPISODE

'Pain For Gain' (deleted footage… banned by an animal activist group)

First of all, no animals were harmed in the filming of this episode, but an animal activist group didn't like that it made the animals appear angry.

"Welcome to another exciting episode of 'Pain For Gain'! The only show on television that pays you to hurt your partner! I'm Peter Conway. We have a very special show for you tonight. We have live animals, vicious and ready to attack. Viewer discretion is advised. Parents, get the little ones away from the television. Snuggle up on the couch, get comfortable. Now let's play 'Pain for Gain'!"

The camera panned across the stage.

There was a glass cube full of snakes.

"With this being a special episode, we have three lovely teams here tonight. Each team will complete different stunts, before being rushed to the hospital!" Peter laughed, but then realized that his joke had made the players uncomfortable.

"First, let's meet the red team! Hello Marcus and Antonio. Welcome. Tell us a little bit about yourself."

Marcus spoke for the team, as he held Antonio's hand. "We've been married for three years, well not legally... Unfortunately, gay marriage isn't legal where we're from, but we have lived together as a married couple. Anyways, Antonio is the light of my life."

Antonio smiled at his partner. "He's just too sweet. Anyways, I'm very involved in an AIDS Foundation, that is trying to find a cure for aids. That's how I met Marcus. For our own personal reasons, we wanted to be on the show and donate all of our winnings to the foundation!"

The men bounced like cheerleaders, happy and enthusiastic.

Peter tried not to laugh. "Okay then. Are you ready to win some money?"

The men got even happier and shook their heads yes.

Peter turned towards the cube full of snakes. "In this glass cube, we have 100 live snakes, all different types. Some are poisonous, some aren't. Your challenge is for one of you to enter the cube. The other player will be at the door, and decide when to let you out. We will pay you $5,000 per minute that you keep your partner locked in the cube with the snakes."

Marcus and Antonio stopped jumping.

"I hate snakes. You go in." Antonio had always feared snakes.

Marcus didn't look very happy, but he loved his partner. "This is important to you, isn't it?"

Antonio shook his head yes and grabbed his lover by the hand.

Marcus just sighed and looked Antonio in his eyes. "Okay. I'll do it for you."

Peter watched as the loving couple gave each other a quick smooch.

Peter looked at his watch, bored with how long this was taking. He knew that most of this would be edited out. "Okay guys. Are we ready?"

Marcus approached the glass cube and realized how small it was. If he was guessing, it wasn't more than six feet wide and six foot deep. He then realized that if he were to die, six feet would be the depth that they would bury his dead body.

He watched as snakes tried to climb the sides of the glass cube. There were so many snakes that they were piled on top of each other.

Marcus wasn't sure about going in there. "You said poisonous? There's a doctor here, right?"

Peter shook his head yes. "There is a doctor, with some anti-venom, but I'm told that you can still get very sick."

Marcus looked at his lover and gave him one last peck on his cheek. "If I say let me out, you better let me out."

Antonio agreed.

Marcus tried to push his fear from his mind as he opened the door to the glass cube. He shoved a slithering snake out of the doorway (with his foot) that tried to escape.

Peter watched as the door closed. "The time starts now. Antonio, it's up to you as to when you let him out."

Marcus tried to step so that he didn't step on any of the reptiles, he didn't want to make them angrier than they already were. A snake tried to climb up his leg, and he wiggled his leg to shake it off of him.

Antonio was paralyzed from his phobia even though he wasn't the one in the cube.

As Marcus shook a snake off his leg, another snake climbed up his other leg, and buried his fangs in his kneecap. Two seperate wounds opened, and even though they were small, they still bled.

"Let me out! I can't do this!" Marcus

pleaded with his partner.

Antonio looked at the clock. "You haven't even been in there a full minute!"

Marcus continued to scream. "I don't care. Let me out." He started banging on the door, and the vibrations woke up all the snakes.

Marcus' legs were covered with snakes and he tried to use his arms to get the creatures off of him, but then they started biting his arms.

"I will divorce you if you don't let me out now!"

Antonio checked the clock. He wanted at least $10,000. It would take another twenty seconds before they earned that much money.

Antonio tried to calm Marcus before opening the door on the two minute mark. "Okay, are you sure? I'll let you out."

Marcus yelled profanities as Antonio bided his time and very slowly opened the door. Marcus rushed out of the box with a few snakes still hanging from him. An animal keeper came out on the stage to remove the vicious animals off of him.

Marcus was looking kinda pale, and felt nauseous.

"You should've let me out sooner!"

As the men argued with themselves, Peter listened to direction from his earpiece. He was told that Marcus had been bit by a copperhead and needed an antivenom shot.

Peter directed Marcus to a chair to sit

down. "We have medical staff coming out with some medicine for you."

The camera zoomed in on the various bites on Marcus' arms and legs. The small incisions were swollen and red. Some of the wounds even appeared to be blistering up.

After Marcus was sufficiently tended to, Peter approached them.

"This is a two part challenge, if you choose to play. You can either go home with $10,000, or play for a chance at $100,000."

Antonio got giddy again. His mind dreamed of how good it would feel donating that much money to his favorite AIDs charity. Marcus did not share in his partner's enthusiasm.

Before even listening to the rules, Antonio spoke up. "We'll do it."

Marcus didn't look too happy, but Antonio didn't care.

"Okay. All you have to do is spend a full five minutes in the cube." Peter tried to make it sound simple.

It didn't sound simple to Marcus. Two minutes was too long for him.

"So Antonio, are you ready?'

Antonio looked like his dreams were just crushed. "I have to do it? I have a phobia. I hate snakes."

Marcus smiled. "Oh honey, you can do it. It's only five minutes. That's a lot of money.

They'd be $100,000 closer to finding a cure for us."

Antonio stood outside the glass door, unmoving. He watched as the snakes appeared even angrier after the intrusion from Marcus.

Marcus put his arm around his lover's waist. "It's not that bad."

Marcus slowly scooted his lover from the doorway, and quickly opened the door, pushing Antonio in the cube with all the snakes.

Marcus closed the door, and locked it, laughing at his partner.

Antonio was truly frozen with fear as the snakes climbed up on him.

Marcus watched the timer, determined to not open the door until the five minutes were over. This would serve Antonio right, not opening the door when Marcus had asked him to.

Antonio started looking pale as he was paralyzed with fear. He couldn't even bring himself to swat the snakes off of him.

Marcus started to get worried when Antonio didn't even bother to scream at him. He realized that Antonio really did have a phobia, and that phobia was now getting the best of him.

Marcus watched as the sharp teeth tore into his lover's delicate flesh, peeling back layers of skin and blood oozing from his wounds.

Marcus thought about letting his lover out of the cube, but he wanted to win that cash. Eventually, Antonio passed out, falling into the mess of snakes, and they climbed on top of his face.

Marcus watched as fangs bit his lover's face. The tiny wounds dripped blood, attracting more snakes.

Time was almost over, they just had to wait a few more seconds.

As soon as the clock had run through the full five minutes, Marcus opened the door, and started pulling the snakes off his unconscious lover. The animal trainer came out and started helping them.

Peter looked away. "Congratulations red team, you just won $100,000!"

"Hello blue team. Are we ready to play 'Pain For Gain'?"

The husband started speaking. "We're so happy to be here. This is gonna get us out of some legal trouble. Lawyers sure are expensive."

Peter agreed with the player before describing the next task.

"Well, you're lucky that there's two of you for this next challenge."

A curtain raised and all the way in the back of the studio was a large fenced in area.

Peter directed his attention towards the fenced in area. "That is Major." Referring to the large bull in the fence. "You have to spend five minutes in the pen, with the angry bull. Luckily, since there's two of you, you can try to help each other and get the bull's attention from different sides of the pen."

The married couple looked at the bull from a distance, noticing the large horns protruding from the sides of the bull's head. The bull was just wandering aimlessly around the cage, snarling his nose every time the bright lights struck him in the face.

The married couple talked strategy as they walked back to the fence.

An animal trainer opened a gate for them, to allow entry. At first, it wasn't so bad. The first minute that they were in the pen the bull didn't pay them any attention. Both players stood completely still.

Then a noise from backstage startled the bull, and he looked at the contestants that had wandered in on his territory.

The bull stomped his front hoof on the ground, and grinded it into the floor before charging towards the couple. The wife ran one direction, and the husband ran in another direction. The bull had so much speed and momentum that he couldn't slow down, and charged his head into the fence, his horn caving in the upper section of the fence.

The bull looked mad, and found his targets once again. This time, he chose to run towards the wife, and she was terrified by the thought of an animal that weighed a ton coming for her. Right before the bull approached her, she managed to roll out of the bull's path, but the animal still managed to strike her down with a kick from his hind leg.

While the wife tried to get up, but found it difficult due to the possibility that her back was broken, the bull zoned in on the husband. The husband was scrambling towards his wife, determined to save his wife from the beast, but the bull was too fast. The bull rammed his head into the husband, his horn tearing through his flesh. The bull bucked the man from his horn and threw him across the bullpen.

Peter started counting down. "Five, four, three, two, one! Congratulations blue team! You lasted five minutes with the bull and won $100,000!"

Animal trainers quickly ran into the bullpen and lassoed the animal before he could do anymore damage to the players. Once they got the beast under control, medical came out and put the couple on gurneys and wheeled them away.

"Hello pink team! You look like a young, energetic couple." Peter meant that as a compliment.

"I'm Josh. This is my sister, Jennifer. We're playing for our folks tonight."

Peter, being the inquisitive host that he was, questioned the boy. "What's going on with your parents, Josh?"

Josh kinda hung his head. "Well, my dad died. My mom can't even afford to bury him. Then she's gotta sell our house. It was Jennifer's idea to come on the show."

Jennifer shook her head and gave her best half-hearted smile.

"Do you wanna win $100,000?"

Both of the young adults shook their heads yes, awaiting what their fate may be.

A curtain behind Peter raised, revealing a large glass sided swimming pool. "Do you see that alligator? Do you think you can spend three minutes in that water tank with a gator?"

Jennifer got scared. "What if we drown?'

"If you're underwater for more than sixty seconds, the animal trainer will come rescue you. But then you forfeit the money. So you have to work as a team, and figure it out."

Josh examined the shallow pool. It wasn't but maybe three foot deep. But it was really large and round. The alligator had to be at least ten feet in length.

"We don't have swimsuits." Josh spurted out.

"That's okay. Your clothes will do just

fine." Peter reassured the players.

The brother/sister combo talked amongst themselves, trying to figure out the best way to do this.

Peter watched through the glass. The alligator appeared to be very calm, with his eyes just barely poking through the surface of the water. He hated thinking about what kind of damage this animal could do the players.

The pink team climbed the short ladder looking down at the aquarium. They moved very quietly and very slowly, hoping that the gator wouldn't notice them.

Peter checked his watch. "As soon as the both of you get in the water, the timer will start the three minute countdown."

The brother and sister tried to lower themselves gently into the water, but as soon as the water moved, the alligator became alert.

"Three minutes. Starting now."

At first the gator stayed very still, and studied his prey. The brother gently walked away from his sister, hoping that if the animal chose to attack, that it would attack him.

All of a sudden the gator swiftly swam towards Josh. Josh tried to run in the waist deep water, but realized that it's impossible to move fast against the resistance of water.

The alligator opened his mouth, exposing many sharp teeth. The beast wrapped his mouth around Josh's skinny shin, and started swimming, pulling Josh behind him.

Blood leaked from his wounded leg, staining the water a red color. Josh had never felt so much pain in his life, yet he tried not to think about it as he flapped his arms, trying to keep his head above the water where the precious oxygen his lungs needed was.

Out of nowhere, very bravely, Jennifer approached the large animal, and jabbed the gator's eye. The gator spit Josh out, and continued towards her.

When the beast opened its mouth, Jennifer tried to move out of the way. But she was too slow. The animal clamped down on her shoulder, piercing into her skin with its razor sharp teeth. The animal took Jennifer's body to the bottom of the pool, as red blood floated throughout the whole pool.

Josh tried to walk to his sister and save her, but his leg was too busted, and the bone was sticking through his skin. Instead he swam to her and latched his arms around the gator's head, forcing it to the surface. Finally, Jennifer felt the air on her face and inhaled the sweet oxygen.

"Five, four, three, two, one! Time's up!"

A few animal trainers invaded the pool and unclenched the gator's jaw to release Jennifer. The meat on her shoulder had been ripped to shreds.

"Congratulations pink team! You just won

SEA CAUMMISAR

$100,000!"

TRUE STORY (AROUND A CAMPFIRE)

Jesse pinched a worm in half, watching the two separate halves squirm. He had always been amazed at how the worm could still live, despite the fact it had just been severed. He picked up half of the worm, and squeezed it between two of his fingers.

The worm left a trail of slimy goo on his fingertips. He began threading the worm onto the sharp tip of his fishing hook. Even though it was only his imagination, he swore that he could hear the worm cry out each time he punctured it. Jesse cast his victim into the water, hoping to catch a fish.

"I'm telling you! This book is crazy!" Sara said spilling her beer all over herself as she jumped up.

"Well, I don't read much. So just tell me

bout it." Jesse said as he laughed at her spilling the beer on herself.

Sara got excited as she remembered the story she had just read. "It's about paying people to hurt themselves."

"That's stupid." Jesse belched. "Nobody would do that." Jesse was tired of hearing Sara run her silly mouth all night long. He just wanted to get drunk and relax. Maybe catch a fish.

"It's not stupid!" Sara wanted to play a game with Jesse. "People like money. People like stuff."

Sara settled herself down to have a moment to think. Jesse was just glad to be getting a moment's peace of not having to listen to Sara.

"You like my car right? You wanna drive it?" Sara was referring to her car. She had a brand new sports car that her father had given her as a present, and all the boys envied it. They always wanted to drive it, but her father had strictly told her to never let anyone drive it.

Jesse knew that Sara was playing with him. Of course, he wanted to drive the car. He wanted to see how fast it could go. He wanted to drive to an empty parking lot and see how fast it could make donuts. "You don't let anyone drive your car. But I'll bite. Sure, I wanna drive it."

Sara got a sinister look in her eyes. "Okay.

Just stick your hand on that grate in the campfire."

Jesse didn't understand. "What does that have to do with me driving your car?"

"It's like that book I read. Instead of paying you to hurt yourself, I'll let you do something that you wanna do." It made sense to Sara.

Jesse thought about it for a minute before answering her. "Well if you wanna give me something that I really want, why not tempt me with anal? You never let me do that."

Sara was not a fan of anal, but it was really important to her to prove to Jesse that the book wasn't stupid. She wanted to show him how easy it was to make people hurt themselves.

Sara shrugged her shoulders. "Okay. But first, you have to stick your hand in the campfire. All the way down to that grate we cook on, and press your hand on it. If you want anal, you just can't do it really quick."

Jesse, like any other red blooded guy enjoyed sex. Sex seemed to motivate him. But this wasn't just any sex. It was anal sex. He had never stuck his junk in a girl's butt before, but all his friends told him how good it felt. And Sara did have a nice rump.

Jesse turned his beer up, emptying it, and grabbed another cold one. "Okay. If I touch that hot grate, under that fire, when we mess around tonight I can take the back door?"

Sara shook her head yes. Her boyfriend

was considering actually doing it. She started to feel kinda powerful.

Jesse killed his beer drinking it in one long gulp. He exhaled a loud belch,the kind you can smell. Sara turned her head in disgust, but didn't say a word.

Jesse threw the empty aluminum can on the fire, and watched as the flames engulfed it, turning it an ember color.

He stood close to the fire pit, enjoying the warmth on his body.

Sara watched, contemplating which hurts worse... a hot fire, or a hard object being rammed into her bum, stretching out her tight sphincter.

Jesse put his hand close to the fire, but quickly yanked it back.

"Nah. Not even your arse is worth it." He began to step away, as his foot twisted between two large rocks.

Jesse stumbled, almost regaining his balance as he tried to steady himself by adjusting the position of his arms, but he was too drunk.

Sara watched and tried to jump up and help her boyfriend, but it all happened way too fast.

Jesse's weight shifted to one side, and his body toppled over sideways. With his arm extended, his hand fell down onto the fire. Then his arm, up to his elbow, was covered in the flames.

"Godangit!!!"

Sara rushed to his side, grabbing his other unburned arm, and pulled his body out of the fire pit. Jesse was still screaming when Sara could see his damaged flesh, the only light coming from the flames.

She left Jesse, crying on the gravel as she quickly got the flashlight and a cup of ice from the cooler.

"Shhh. This'll make it feel better." Sara put the cold ice on his blistering arm, and turned on the flashlight to get a better look at the injury.

In the spots where his arm wasn't red, were spots of black (almost charcoal color) skin deposits.

There were several blisters, some already had a clear fluid seeping from them.

Sara tried to calm Jesse, wondering if she should take him to a hospital, but she had been drinking, and didn't want to drink and drive.

Jesse requested a beer and she obliged.

After he stopped screaming, Sara sat, just stroking his head.

"Screw your damn book." Jesse finally spoke. "But I think I deserve anal every night for the rest of my life."

Printed in Great Britain
by Amazon